songs EIGHT six

Lisabeth Posthuma

JASPER LIGHT
BOOKS

To my granny,
Joyce

And the secret garden bloomed and bloomed and every morning revealed new miracles.
—Frances Hodgson Burnett

PROLOGUE

A teacher once told me, "Good authors do things on purpose. They create characters and set them in motion. And then, they let them go, guiding only their circumstances, not what they become."

The writer of this story is a good author.

But I am not he.

I am Cosette, his character, the storyteller.

And I believe he chose me on purpose.

CHAPTER 1

As the movie ended, I peeked at Westley, hoping—though I knew better—he'd been moved even an ounce as much by it as I was pretending not to be.

But at that moment, he was punching at his calculator with the eraser end of his pencil, oblivious to how George Bailey became "the richest man in Bedford Falls."

The screen faded to black.

"Could you get the lights, Cosette?"

I obeyed my teacher's request and swiveled around in my seat to reach the switch. This time, when I stole a glance at Westley, he met my eyes.

"I finished," he mouthed, holding up our packet of trigonometry worksheets. Though I wished he'd been as captivated watching the movie as I had instead of jump-starting our weekend homework, I reflexively returned his smile.

"*It's a Wonderful Life* is an iconic American film. What is it about this story, do you think, that makes it so engaging?" As she posed her question, Mrs. Holloway sauntered over to her desk to retrieve a stack of papers and then counted them out, one for each member of the first row.

I never volunteered to speak in class, but if I were going to, I knew how I would answer this: the love story. Without it, the movie is a bleak tale of a man repeatedly forced to choose between his own happiness and the well-being of others. It's a no-win. Minus Mary, I was pretty sure that no guardian angel could have convinced George he had a wonderful life. Without the love story, George Bailey jumps off the bridge.

I related to him in this way. I had decided long ago that without Westley, my existence would have been intolerable. Like George, my life *sans* love story, was meaningless.

Mrs. Holloway paused just long enough for a few hands to raise to half-mast before indicating that her question was merely a rhetorical segue into what would become a five-page essay assignment.

"You didn't think I was gifting you three days of class time with a movie and not expecting something in return, did you?" My teacher—whose charm and beauty made her easily forgivable—flashed an electric smile, and all grumbling ceased. "Let's talk about what from this film pulled at your heart strings. And Westley Greene, before you argue the scientific validity of my metaphor, let me say that I believe that even you can find some sort of relational point of connection in this movie...That is, if you were able to catch a few scenes in between solving your functions of x." She arched an eyebrow and pointed at Westley's trig sheets.

This wasn't the first time he'd been busted moonlighting with math homework in English class. Lucky for him though, Westley was equally as charming and beautiful as his accuser.

"I think I caught the gist of the movie, Mrs. H. It was about a department store and a high-profile lawsuit against Santa Claus, right?" Westley flashed a dimpled grin and sheepishly ran a hand through his blond hair.

Mrs. Holloway, too easily won over, stifled a smile. "Just remember that a letter of recommendation from a teacher who can vouch for your wonderful communication skills would look very nice in your college applications, *Dr.* Greene. Even MDs need to know how to read and write." He nodded with apology, and Mrs. Holloway moved on. "So, let's do some brainstorming." The screen behind her lit up as she typed the headline for our notes from her wireless keyboard.

I had made it through the first three periods of the day with no homework. But now, with the trigonometry assignments and a five-page essay due on Monday, I was sure to be dividing my weekend between my graphing calculator, a blinking cursor, and audible groans.

2

After a page and a half of notes and a round of Q&A about the assignment, class ended.

Moments after the bell, Westley stood next to me at my desk. "I really wish teachers would let us know ahead of time if we're even going to use our books in class. It would sure save a lot of useless hauling," he commented as he set his pointlessly heavy literature book on top of mine. He slid them both to the edge of my desk before folding them under his arm.

"You really don't have to carry my books for me, West," I responded quickly, attempting unsuccessfully to take it back.

"C'mon, you're gonna start this again?" He laughed, now palming what had to have been ten pounds of classic world literature in one hand, just above my reach.

I smiled and shrugged. I hadn't won this argument in six years, and I knew today would be no different.

"And besides, if your arms are full, how are you going to hold my hand?" he asked.

With my fingers laced in his, Westley led me to the hallway, squeezing his grip as he bulldozed us through the end-of-the-day crowds. Over the course of our high school years, maneuvering through the halls of Camden High had become increasingly easy, thanks to Westley's incessant growth spurts. The same swarm of students we plowed through on that Friday had taken twice as long when we were only fifteen years old, and Westley was fifty pounds lighter and six inches shorter.

When we finally reached my locker, I rolled the dial through the digits in the combination and opened it.

Westley stacked our books on the shelf, pulled out his letterman jacket—the one he earned *before* he became a giant—and held it out for me. "So, I've got baseball conditioning until five thirty. I'll grab dinner at home and head over afterward. We'll breeze through those trig problems in no time."

I made a face. "You already breezed through them," I reminded him, slipping an arm into the sleeve he offered me.

3

"I, on the other hand, will—what's the opposite of breeze through?"

"Hmm...suffocate in stagnancy?"

"That sounds about right." I imagined myself drowning in a festering swamp of complex numbers. It was the most accurate illustration of my feelings toward math I'd ever entertained.

He offered me the other sleeve. "OK, then I'll just show you how to get the answers I got, and you can fill me in on *It's a Boring and Pointless Life* so I can decide how to write five pages on a movie I paid five minutes of attention to."

I frowned. "You missed out, Westley. It was a good movie. The love story, especially."

He scoffed. "You're just a sucker for a happy ending."

"What's wrong with that?" I couldn't deny Westley's observation, nor did I feel a need to defend it. Most people enjoyed happy endings. That was why they were called *happy* endings.

"Absolutely nothing. You're an idealist. It's one of the things I love most about you." He kissed my nose in loving condescension. "But I'm realistic. Most people don't get a feel-good resolution in life."

"All the more reason to appreciate one when you see it," I countered, taking his hand in mine.

"Fair enough." Westley let the subject drop, not because I had defeated him, but because he knew no matter what he said, I was still going to love the movie.

The hallway had cleared enough by this point that Westley and I could walk down it side by side as a couple, instead of with him as my bodyguard.

"Have I ever told you that green looks good on you?" Westley offered after a few minutes of silent walking.

"No." I considered for a moment what had prompted the compliment, noting I was wearing a blue sweater under his jacket. "Why?"

"Because it does." As we walked, Westley smoothed all of my hair over to one shoulder. He traced a line under the

4

surname sewn onto the back of his jacket. "'Greene' looks *really* good on you."

"Ha-ha." I groaned, but secretly thought he was clever. "How have we been dating since we were eleven, and you just now come up with that?"

"I don't know, but I'm going to say it all the time now."

I laughed. I was sure he would.

"Seriously though. 'Cosette Greene' has a nice ring to it, right?"

I blushed. I probably had a dozen notebooks with that very name doodled in the margins, along with "Mrs. Westley Greene" and all of the names I'd chosen for our children. "Sure. But what if I want to keep my own name when we get married? I'm kinda attached to Miller." I was lying. Miller was the most common name in my town, and I'd wanted a different one since kindergarten when there were six other kids in my class who had it.

"Miller's an Amish name."

This was true. Four of those kindergarteners had been Amish, as well as about 30 percent of our hometown population.

"So?"

"Then it's settled; you're taking Greene."

I rolled my eyes, but I was enjoying our banter. "Isn't it customary to propose to a girl before demanding she give up her last name?"

"Fine." Westley stopped in his tracks and looked at me, his brown eyes sober. "Marry me."

My heart stopped.

"Marry me, Cosette. And take my name." He dug his free hand into his pocket.

I remained frozen. We were in a stare down. I was calling his bluff; I couldn't let him know that my body had gone completely numb from the inside out, paralyzed by the hope that his proposal might be serious.

He began to fiddle with my left hand, and I felt him slide something onto my finger, past the knuckle.

My poker face cracked. "Westley..."

5

Swarms of butterflies hatched in my stomach before dropping instantly dead when I looked down at my hand to see a Camden baseball key chain dangling from my finger.

"Oh, you suck, Westley!" I slipped off the key ring and threw it at him, embarrassed by my disappointment.

"Aw, c'mon, babe. You know I'm kidding." He tried to flirt his way through an apology, but he couldn't form the words through his obnoxious laughter.

I shook my head. "That's it. I'm keeping Miller. And becoming Amish. And a nun."

Before I could deliver any more empty threats, the alarm on his phone buzzed. Westley wrapped his giant arm around me to restrain my wrath before checking its screen. "Well, while you're doing all that, I need to get to practice."

I pouted. I didn't want West to leave me alone so soon after hurting my feelings, but at least with him away at baseball conditioning, I could lick my wounds without him seeing how ridiculous I was being.

Westley sensed my sadness and slid both arms around my waist. "I'm sorry for teasing you, Cosi. Forgive me?"

I melted into him; his familiar comfort was medicine for my mood. Of course I forgave him. "Maybe."

"Well, I hope you can. All joking aside, I am going to marry you."

My fragile hopes were reluctant to rise again. "Really?"

"Of course. And when I finally do ask you to marry me, you won't have to wonder if I'm kidding."

I found healing in his reassurance and allowed myself to smile.

"I meant what I said about happy endings. Not everyone gets one. But you're going to. I promise you that." Then, Westley pressed his lips against mine and kissed me for so long that I was sure he would be late for practice.

CHAPTER 2

With Westley gone, I headed home. As I walked through the cold air to my car, I squinted against the wind. The sky was dark and threatening, but I assumed it was bluffing as it had been for all of December thus far. Up until now, this month had been extremely disappointing, winter-weather-wise. Usually by the week before Christmas, snow had interrupted the school calendar more than once. I saw this as one of the few benefits of living so close to Lake Michigan this time of year; snow days were the geography gods' compensation to the residents of Northern Indiana for its endless cornfields and boredom.

Middlebury, Indiana, like many towns in our surrounding latitude, was mostly farmland. During the warmer months, when the fields were alive with activity—planting, blossoming, growing, and harvesting—it was beautiful...almost beautiful enough to make me forget that there wasn't actually anything to do there. But then came late fall when the last of its life and color were reaped away, leaving the decaying, leftover shards of cornstalks to freeze solid in the ground like someone had stabbed the fields to their empty, naked deaths.

I could usually stomach the barrenness of my surroundings through about Christmas, but once the distraction of the holidays had passed, I hated it. In some backward, claustrophobic way, I found the openness of the stripped land suffocating. I couldn't wait for spring, when new green life would sprout up from the ground and somehow make me feel a little less insignificant.

But as much as I hated a Middlebury winter, there were aspects of my hometown I loved—one in particular made all the dismal parts bearable. No matter where on the planet I lived, I was at home as long as Westley was nearby. My address in life was merely the setting for what was really all that mattered to me—my love story.

I hopped into the cab of my Honda Element and started it up, dialing the heat setting to defrost. Though no snow had fallen, my windows had iced over, and since I definitely wasn't going to reenter the cold to scrape them clean manually, I would have to wait for them to thaw on their own. Westley would have certainly commented how lazy this made me, but then again, had he been there, he'd have cleared them for me.

I hardly noticed my cell buzzing in my purse over the noise of the heater, and when I saw the name of the caller, I wished I hadn't heard it at all.

I turned down the vent. "Hey, Bronwyn, I didn't forget," was my greeting to my sister. I then moved the phone back from my ear, bracing for her reply.

"Where the hell are you?" she demanded. "Because evidently you aren't where you said you'd be; otherwise, Grandma wouldn't be calling me to find out who is going to watch Ginger."

"I'm on my way," I assured her. Or I was almost on my way, at least. I hadn't forgotten my promise to baby-sit my niece that afternoon, and I still had plenty of time to get home to relieve my grandma for her doctor's appointment.

"Liar," Bronwyn challenged, and I glanced at my rear-view mirror to see if she was somehow spying on me. She always knew when I wasn't telling the whole truth, but I had no idea how. "You're probably out somewhere stuck up Westley's ass, like you always are."

"I'll be home in five minutes," I promised, though I knew it would more likely be ten. "Did you need anything else?"

There was an audible scoff on her end of the line. "Yes, actually. If you're taking orders, I'll have a more responsible little sister with a side of consideration for others, hold the loser boyfriend."

I rolled my eyes at the phone. "Is that all?"

"Just get home. And wash the skank off yourself before touching my daughter, all right?" She ended our conversation without salutation.

Tossing my phone in the passenger's seat, I cranked the heat back up and decided my windows were clear enough to drive home.

Our house was exactly four miles from the high school. The commute on the country roads, even at idle the entire trip, was fifteen minutes. But because I could feel Bronwyn breathing down my neck all the way from the reception desk at my dad's realty office downtown, I punched the accelerator hard until the speedometer read ten miles per hour over the limit.

Our exchange on the phone was a fairly accurate illustration of the overall nature of our relationship—she hated me, and I dealt with it. Her detesting of Westley, I assumed, also wasn't unique to him but rather a by-product of her general distaste for anyone who brought me happiness.

I would like to be able to justify my sister's unrelenting callousness toward me by her life of hard knocks. But I doubted that growing up the daughter of Will Miller, a successful realtor in a suburb with the lowest crime rate in the state counted—by any stretch of the imagination—as thug life. Perhaps it would have been easier to cut my sister some slack had I not been dealt the same hand in life as she had. Our childhoods weren't perfect; we'd lost our mother to cancer when we were very young. Dad worked a lot, which didn't leave him much time to chaperone school field trips or run a car pool, but that was what Grandma was for. My father's mother had lived with us since my earliest memories, packing our lunches, braiding our hair, and filling in all the areas that kept most people from knowing we were motherless. We'd basically grown up in a two-parent household, which was more than I could say for most people my age. It didn't make sense that I could be so well adjusted while

9

Bronwyn was the Queen of the Harpies, when we were raised under the same circumstances.

I reached the intersection to turn into our subdivision, still ten minutes ahead of the time I'd promised to be home. As I eased onto the brake, I exhaled with relief. While I couldn't predict what Bronwyn would want to fight about when I saw her later, it wouldn't be because I'd been late.

"Hey, Cosi!" Grandma greeted me with a kiss on the cheek. "Sorry for poking the bear—I just wasn't sure if I was expecting you or her to be here. Was Bronwyn too hard on you?"

"No, it was about the usual amount of palpable hatred," I answered, dropping my backpack onto the kitchen table.

"Oh, that child..." Grandma trailed off. "Well, thanks for watching Gigi. She's been asleep for about ten minutes, so you've got some time." Grandma glanced at her wristwatch. "I should be back to make dinner. Westley eating with us?"

"No, he'll be over after though." I grinned. Unlike Bronwyn, Grandma appreciated Westley.

"Well then, I have something to look forward to tonight." She squeezed my arm, grabbed her car keys, and exited through the kitchen to the garage, calling good-bye over her shoulder.

The familiar silence of Ginger's naptime comforted me. This quiet was conducive to studying, and as I unzipped my backpack, I remembered just how much of it I had. The baby monitor screen featured my niece balled up in a sideways fetal position, one arm flung over her face to cover her eyes. Grandma was right; she'd sleep for a while.

With the monitor under one arm and my laptop under the other, I headed up to my room. I wasn't about to attempt trig without Westley, but I could get a jump-start on my essay before the baby woke up.

English had always been one of my better subjects, though this year I'd found it more challenging than in previous grades—probably because I, like everyone else, thought Mrs. Holloway was beautiful and sweet. People who were as beautiful and sweet as she was deserved to have people work hard to impress them.

At my desk, I thumbed through my English folder, perusing a stack of assignments covered in old-school red pen. Almost every one of them had been judged B worthy. I struggled to reach the bar Mrs. Holloway set, despite my best efforts to please her. Her assignments always insisted that we "dig" or "reveal" or "discover" things about ourselves that I was pretty sure I didn't have inside me. Maybe my peers benefited from the soul-searching she assigned, but I was much better at analyzing the psyche of the fictional characters in our literature book than I was at any sort of self-reflection.

What I wanted to say to my teacher in response to suggesting that my writing needed to be more "personal" or "bolder" was that, apart from Westley, my life was boring. I wasn't the kind of person who grappled with the meaning of life. Sister and trigonometry aside, life was good, comfortable. And anyway, it seemed the really good writers we studied in class had all had to suffer deeply to achieve a great story. Despite her beauty and sweetness, I had my limits in what I would do to win Mrs. Holloway's affection. If the only way to get an A in her class was through intense inner turmoil, I would settle for a silver-spoon-fed C.

I pulled out the assignment specifications and my notes from *It's a Wonderful Life*.

> *Consider how George Bailey's life affected so many others. Do you think that this is realistic? Can one person in one small town have such an impact on the world around him or her that the absence of that person would alter existence so dramatically? And also, how do you think the world we live in would be different had you never existed?*

I took a deep breath. Considering my nonexistence a week before Christmas? This felt a bit existential for the holidays. I was pretty sure that the essay I'd written the previous Christmastime was about my favorite seasonal foods. My paper on peppermint cocoa had earned me high marks in junior English; writing it had made me a little thirsty but inflicted no other pains.

My cursor blinked in time with the second hand of the hallway clock. I had found the movie, even the impossibilities that Westley would have hated, intriguing. Guardian angels aside though, I didn't see what made the rest of the plot so farfetched. Didn't everyone love a good soul mate love story?

I decided to approach my paper from this angle:

> *What impressed me most about George Bailey's character was not that his web of influence affected so many people, but how intertwined it was throughout his entire life with one person in particular—Mary Hatch. Devoted to him since their childhoods, Mary's life story was incomplete without George, her soul mate, in it. This is illustrated in the encounter between the two of them when George is given a glimpse of what the people in his life would be like had he never been born to influence them otherwise. In a world without George, Mary is alone, an outsider. Her appearance is less inviting, her expressions are joyless. She lacks everything George brought out of her, a fulfillment that only specifically he could sustain within her. Apart from him, she is deficient.*

I continued to support my claims for about a page more before arriving at the second part of the assignment.

My fingers lingered upon home row. Five minutes passed. Then ten.

How was I supposed to know what life would be like without me? Hypotheticals were not my specialty, no matter how long I dwelled on the what-ifs.

Fortunately for me, from down the hall, I heard the stirrings of the cutest reason for procrastination known to humankind. I slammed my screen closed and practically leaped down the hallway to greet my niece.

When I reached Ginger's bedroom door, I opened it slowly to allow her eyes time to adjust to the light.

Through a scrunched-up squint at my silhouette, I detected happy surprise in her face. "Coco!" she squealed, holding herself upright with a tight grip on her crib rail.

"Gigi!" I responded, and we reached for one another as I hurried to her crib.

She wrapped her tiny arms around my neck and rested her head on my shoulder, and I became putty. Even though we lived in the same house, such moments were rare. Ginger was Bronwyn's after all, and Bronwyn didn't share.

I pressed my face into Ginger's hair and inhaled deeply. She felt bigger than she had the last time I'd held her, and I switched on her light for a better look.

She was angelic in the soft lamplight, a chubby cherub with wild curls, and I completely loved her. It was hard to believe someone so wonderful had been born of someone so not. But then again, Bronwyn had never revealed who Ginger's father was, so it was possible all her lovability had been inherited from him.

But whoever the guy was who knocked up my sister, his chromosomes were full of genes less dominant than Bronwyn's. With dark hair and coffee-colored eyes, curvy features and full lips, my niece and sister could be physically described with all the same nouns and adjectives. I supposed the same was also true for me, too. Strangers who saw my sister and me together when we were younger always inquired whether we were twins, but people who knew us were able to tell us apart by the differences in our noses, voices, and hairstyles. And because Bronwyn was evil and I wasn't.

After a quick diaper change, Ginger and I made our way to the kitchen for her dinner. I'd just finished warming some leftover mashed potatoes and canned peas for her when I heard the garage door rising.

"Eh, Momster's home." Ginger smiled, and I pretended she got my joke. I bent down beside her. "I love you, Gigi!" I whispered, and she grabbed my nose with a handful of potatoes. I kissed her on the forehead and then stepped away just as soon as the door to the garage opened and my dad and Bronwyn stepped in.

"Hi, guys," I greeted casually as I wiped the food from my nose. "How was work?"

Dad shrugged with a monosyllabic grunt, which I interpreted to mean he mustn't have sold any houses today.

Bronwyn's reply was a much more straightforward indicator of her mood. "You are just now feeding her dinner?"

"Yeah. So?" Ginger blew raspberries with a mouthful of peas, and I held up a paper towel to protect myself from the green spray.

My sister reached for something on the counter without breaking her glare and held up a scrawled-on half sheet of notebook paper. "Five o'clock," she seethed and pointed. "Dinner, *five o'clock.*"

I had been entirely unaware of any written instructions for Ginger, but I didn't want to throw my grandmother under the bus for forgetting to tell me. "She didn't even wake up until after five, so I couldn't have fed her then anyway."

"*What?*" Bronwyn screamed so loudly that Ginger jumped in her seat. Evidently, she had not had time in her short little life to anticipate her mother's overreactions the way the rest of us in the house did. My father—who'd had the fullness of Bronwyn's twenty years to learn to tune out her tantrums—meandered about the kitchen looking for a bottle opener for his Guinness, unfazed by the yelling. "It says *right here...*" She gestured to the note and continued, "that her nap should have ended no later than four thirty. Do you know what this means, Cosette?"

I heaved a sigh. Yes, I did. It meant a verbal pistol-whipping. "I'm going to guess it means you are pissed."

Ginger stirred uneasily in her high chair. "Mama?" she asked hesitantly, trying to diffuse her mother's wrath with the one word in her small vocabulary she thought could work. "Mama?"

Bronwyn took slow but intimidating steps toward me as she spoke. "This means that Ginger is off her schedule. Which means she's not going to sleep tonight. Which means that I am not going to sleep tonight. And if I'm not going to sleep tonight, then *you're* not going to sleep tonight."

I attempted to placate her. "I would be happy to stay up with Ginger if she won't sleep." I knew Bronwyn wouldn't want me anywhere near her daughter when she could help prevent it, even if it truly meant that she'd be up all night.

She ignored my offer and switched to her old standby for getting under my skin. "I suppose it is partly my fault, assuming you could read the instructions I wrote. I mean, your boyfriend isn't here to read it for you."

I rolled my eyes and went to the refrigerator to fill a sippy cup with milk for my niece. It was always no-win with my sister; she would goad me to fight with her. If I tried to ignore her insults, she'd keep poking at me until she found a chink in my armor.

Bronwyn turned her attention to Ginger, changing her tone to a sugary sarcasm. "Well, Ginger, I guess Auntie Coco doesn't love you enough to take care of you the right way. Maybe we'll just have to not let her watch you anymore. How does that sound?"

Unable to translate her mother's vitriol against me, Ginger felt herself victorious in diverting her anger and responded with giggles. "Oh! Cosette? Did you see that? She is so happy to not have to spend any more time with you."

This wasn't the first time she'd threatened to cut me off from my niece, but the thought hurt nonetheless. I glanced at my dad out of the corner of my eye, praying that for once I'd find an ally in him.

He'd sat at the breakfast counter and spread out the day's mail to sort through. Currently, he was thumbing through a home improvement magazine, and Bronwyn's unpleasantness was nothing more than familiar white noise.

I handed Ginger her cup just before Bronwyn unhooked her high-chair tray, pulled her onto her hip, and set off upstairs. "Say good-bye to your bitch aunt, Ginger!"

Her words stung, though I knew they shouldn't. She just wanted the last word, and I should have just let her have it and been done, as usual.

But for some reason, this time, I didn't.

"So I guess next time you need a sitter, you'll just ask Ginger's dad to help you instead," I said.

My sister's glare softened briefly, pained by my words, and I instantly regretted them.

I couldn't understand how Bronwyn could get such pleasure from torturing me; seeing the hurt my comment had caused her brought me no satisfaction. In fact, knowing I'd stooped to her level, that I'd purposely picked at a scab that covered a serious sore, made me feel the opposite. I was ashamed.

I took a breath and started to apologize. "I'm sorry. I take it ba—"

Before the words were out of my mouth, Bronwyn's hand met my cheek with a slap that echoed against the kitchen tile. My sister stood poised in front of me as though she'd just fouled a ball off her bat and was ready for a second crack at a home run.

"I dare you to say that again."

My cheek began to pulse. The throbbing made me angry. Bronwyn had always been mouthy but never physical in her abuse. I instinctively wanted to her hit back, but one look at Ginger and my urge to retaliate faded.

"That's what I thought," was Bronwyn's declaration of victory, and she swept my niece away up to her room.

I remained motionless with my hand over my cheek until an almost-familiar voice spoke to me and snapped me out of my daze.

"Cosette." My name sounded strange coming from my father, as I'd rarely heard him use it. I gave him my attention dutifully, part of me hoping for a scolding for what I'd said to my sister.

But of course, that would have meant he was my parent and not just my dad.

"You knew better," he said, and then chased the words with a long drink from his bottle.

I stared my father in the eyes until he looked away, returning his interest back to his magazine.

For the second time that day, I felt foolish for the hope I'd felt.

He was right. I did know better.

◆◆◆

"When are you going to let me say something to her?" Westley asked. He had put down his graphing calculator a half page into explaining the trig assignment to listen to me recount the latest Bronwyn drama, minus the slap in the face. If he'd known she had hit me, nothing that I could have said after would have stopped him from killing her. But it wasn't as much my interest in protecting my sister as it was keeping Westley out of jail for murder that compelled me to remain silent about it.

"What good would it do?" I asked the question I'd considered many times myself. "She already hates us both."

"Exactly. So what do we have to lose?" Westley reached for my face, and I willed myself not to cringe as he brushed the back of his hand against my cheek. Some extra foundation and intentional mood lighting had hidden the lingering pink outline of Bronwyn's handprint.

"Nothing, I guess, except for Ginger," I considered, with full understanding that I likely wouldn't be seeing my niece anytime soon the way we'd left things. "But it also doesn't make her and my relationship any better."

"Why in the world would you want a relationship with someone like that?" West's words were purposely loud, and I automatically reached behind me to push my bedroom door the rest of the way shut. "See? You are even afraid in your own bedroom. We can't even talk about how she's treated you without you having to be afraid of what she's going to do if she hears it." Westley put his arm around my shoulders. "C'mon, Cosette. Just let me talk to her."

"I shouldn't have told you," I replied. "Because there is no possible scenario of you talking to her that ends well. There are many scenarios that end in bloodbaths. I know that it just makes you mad. I'm sorry."

17

"I'm not scared of your sister, Cosi." Westley laughed. "You have a victim mentality. Your sister just ripped you a new one for doing her a favor, and you are apologizing for that upsetting me." He grabbed my hand and held onto it, interlacing our fingers. "Seriously though, you know you deserve better than how she treats you, right?"

I paused for a moment. Part of me felt silly for needing to vent about a fight I'd had with my sister. Siblings were supposed to outgrow that by the time they were our ages. Still, it was nice to have Westley in my corner, as he always was.

"I know," I began with the same old, tired defense I used every time we had this conversation. "She's just such a miserable person. Sometimes I feel sorry for her."

"She doesn't deserve your pity," Westley whispered. "Or your excuses."

"Reasons," I whispered back. "And maybe she won't always be this way. Maybe she'll change." When I was being honest with myself, and not just knee-jerk reacting to her perpetual unfairness toward me, this was my hope for my sister—a reason to change.

"People don't change, Cosette."

I didn't know if I agreed with Westley, but I knew I didn't want him to be right. "Is it wrong to still want a happy ending for Bronwyn?"

"Wrong? No." Westley realized he was not going to get my blessing to confront my sister, so he was preparing to drop the subject. "But probably a complete waste of your time."

Trig took much longer to complete than it should have, and when I finished the final problem in the packet, it was after eleven o'clock. Westley looked up from the laptop where he was researching *It's a Wonderful Life* long enough to grade my homework.

"Not bad, kiddo. Gold star." He kissed me on the lips. Then, finding it more appealing than his essay, he kissed me again. Soon, the computer was shut, and Westley and I were wrapped up together, the unpleasantness of Bronwyn fading away.

"Can I stay the night?" he whispered to me.

I smiled. It wasn't the first time, but it had been awhile. I was happy he'd asked, happy he wanted to.

"Yes," I whispered back. "Stay forever."

CHAPTER 3

Morning came too soon.

"I can't believe you have baseball practice on a Saturday." I pouted, still wrapped up in the warm sheets Westley had left behind on the bed. "Exactly how many muscles does Coach Bowen expect you to build anyway?" He unfolded a clean T-shirt from the drawer in my dresser he'd long ago claimed for himself and pulled it over his head. Its snug fit around the contours of his upper body perfectly affirmed my point.

Westley flashed me his dimples in appreciation of my compliment. "It's not weight training today. The team's getting certified in first aid and CPR. New Camden athlete requirements."

"But you're already certified," I protested. Westley had lifeguarded at the Middlebury Community Pool the past two summers, and the same training had been required for that job. "Can't you skip it?"

"Sorry, babe." He sat back on the bed and ran his hand through my hair. "Wouldn't look good for the team captain to bail on this." I frowned. "But trust me—you're a lot more fun to make out with than a mannequin."

I offered Westley a reluctant smile as he handed me my robe.

We quietly descended the stairs together in hopes he could leave the house undetected. Our overnights were not a secret to anyone, but it wasn't like my father welcomed Westley to the breakfast table the next morning. This was why I mostly slept over at his house. The Greenes understood our relationship better.

He pulled on his shoes and jacket before kissing me good-bye. We cracked the front door, and a gust of cold air swept through the house, kicking on the furnace. "Close the door." My father growled from the kitchen, and I knew we'd been busted.

My cheeks burned, immune to the cold air.

"I'll call you," Westley whispered before slipping outside, unfazed by my father. I watched him through the window until his Mustang disappeared down the road.

Just then, Bronwyn appeared in a towel at the top of the stairs, running a comb through her wet hair. My eyes met hers for a moment before she turned away, muttering, "Slut," under her breath.

◆◆◆

After wasting half the morning in front of the computer, I was no closer to figuring out what the world would have been like had I never been born than I was before attempting to finish my English essay.

I'd grown weary of contemplating not existing. It wasn't like I'd accomplished anything so great in my eighteen years that life as the world knew it would be worse off without me. In fact, aside from my absence obviously affecting Westley's life, I couldn't really imagine the world being much different had I never breathed its air.

I had a feeling that this was supposed to bother me...but it didn't.

What it did instead was make what Westley and I had to-gether feel even more special. To me, this meant that he was the sole owner of all that I had to offer the world; I'd reserved everything good in me for him alone—like Mary had for George. For some reason though, that answer did not seem like the "right" answer.

I just couldn't pinpoint what was "wrong" about it.

I decided to consider this assignment from another per-spective. I ran through my mental address book, wondering who would leave the biggest gap in existence if removed from it.

Westley's parents came to mind. Of course, they'd created my boyfriend, so in that way, they had had a huge impact on *my* world. But aside from me personally, their lives influenced many others.

The Greenes were a pillar in the Middlebury community. West's dad had built a successful financial planning firm from the ground up, and countless people had prospered by taking his money advice. Mr. Greene's savvy had afforded his own family a very comfortable life too. Westley's mother had the luxury of staying home to raise her children since the eldest Greene child, Eastlyn, was born eighteen months before Westley. Almost three years after him, his brother Southeby came along, and the Greene family as I knew it was complete.

The good looks and charm Westley enjoyed were traits shared by each member in his household, as were his intelligence, confidence, and athleticism. They were the perfect family, the one featured in the photograph that comes with the picture frame—all with varying degrees of blonde hair and dimples and eyes that rare shade of brown that almost looks gold. Surely, the absence of any one of them would leave a bigger mark on the world than I ever could. They were pedigreed, destined for greatness. I was just lucky enough to associate with them.

My life had always been fairly ordinary. I didn't excel at any one thing, or at least I'd never really explored what I might be good at if I tried. My dad and grandma weren't the cheerleaders for Bronwyn and me the way the Greenes were for their kids—but I didn't mind. It wasn't as though I felt neglected because I'd never auditioned for a school play or made the volleyball team. I'd just filled my time with another hobby I found enjoyment in—Westley.

Having exhausted all other possible avenues for my essay, I finally settled back where I'd begun:

22

I would like to say that the world would be worse off without me in it, but I don't think that is true. My universe centers on only one person, and if I had never been born, his life would be drastically altered—but no one else's. However, I am content with my life, my comfort, my routine, my boyfriend. I don't believe that this is the answer you were searching for with this assignment, but it is my honest one.

If I were to say that all this troubles me, that I have discovered a giant void in myself and am having an epiphany of what I need to change to be a more-fulfilled person, I feel that it would get me a better grade on this assignment. But, staying on the theme of honesty here—I haven't. Where I am now, I want nothing. I lack nothing. Unlike George Bailey, I don't need to be reminded how good I actually have it.

I already have love. What more is there?

After double-spacing and setting the font format, my essay was still just under a page short of the requirement.

It may not have been spoon-fed to me, but I was fully expecting that C.

CHAPTER 4

I e-mailed my essay to Mrs. H. early that afternoon, and as the adage went, out of sight, out of mind.

The afternoon was spent cleaning, a chore I detested much less now that Bronwyn and I no longer shared adjoined rooms. Before Ginger, I'd occupied the room connected to my sister's through a bathroom, and the years I'd spent brushing my teeth and showering in that war zone were not soon forgotten. My new room was the master suite that had been relinquished by Grandma, who'd had enough of climbing the stairs to the second floor and settled in the guest room. It came with its own bathroom, twice the square footage of my previous room, and—much to my happiness—a lock on the door.

After scrubbing my sink and shower, I ran a dust rag over the picture frames that lined my bedroom wall. Each photo featured a posed snapshot of one of the dozen formal dances Westley and I had gone to over the years, a time line of our relationship from the fifth grade forward. Lots of people had dedicated wall space to showcase their accomplishments. The Greene children's bedrooms were decorated with plaques and trophies, certificates and awards—tangible proof of their superiority to others, verification they were winners at life. No one had ever given me a prize for anything I'd ever done, but I still considered this my own wall of fame.

I'd just finished hanging up our latest portrait from the winter formal we attended two weeks prior when Westley called to invite me out to dinner with his family. Eastlyn was home from college for the holidays, and to the Greenes, this was a reason for celebration.

"What am I supposed to wear?" I asked, both excited and nervous to be seeing Westley's sister.

"I dunno. Normal clothes. We're just going to Rulli's."

"Right, but your whole family will be there," I pointed out. "I don't want to be the sole ugly duckling in a flock of swans."

Westley scoffed. "*Seriously*, Cosi. You could wear nothing but garbage bags for the rest of your life and still be the hottest girl on the planet."

I fought the reflex to argue with him and accepted his compliment, though I knew it wasn't true. I then spent the next two hours trying on clothes and fussing with my hair to make myself presentable enough to eat pizza with the Greenes.

◆◆◆

When we arrived at the restaurant, the rest of Westley's family had already occupied their usual table. Eastlyn saw us from across the dining room, and she was on her feet to greet me before we could get to them.

She hugged me, and then her lips parted into a smile that drew the attention of every man in the restaurant in a single, coordinated head turn. "Cosette, you look beautiful!"

In addition to being gorgeous, she was also gracious.

Eastlyn spent Thanksgiving break with her sorority sisters in the Bahamas, so I hadn't seen her since she left Middlebury in August for her second year at Purdue. She'd cut her hair since then, and her soft blonde waves now stopped at her shoulders. Even in her "normal clothes" of a mod-print dress and leggings, she looked runway ready, en vogue from head to toe.

"I want to hear everything that's been going on with you two!" Eastlyn declared as our waiter brought the additional place settings for Westley and me. "What's new?"

Westley spent the next ten minutes filling his sister in on baseball, a conversation that Southeby was able to join in on now that he was a freshman and had made the junior varsity team.

When the boys had finished, Eastlyn turned her attention back to me. "What about you, Cosi? What are you up to these days?"

"Oh...you know," I stammered, searching for something interesting to share. But aside from the backhand from my sister the day before, my life was uneventful.

It wasn't a big deal that I had nothing to contribute to the conversation, however, because Eastlyn had plenty to talk about: making the dean's list, winning a gold medal at her latest gymnastics competition, getting an internship at a marketing firm, and so on.

Westley's sister had grown up while away at school. She'd always been mature, but the independence of college life had been just what she needed to blossom into everything her parents cultivated her to become. More than once during our conversation, I was grateful that she shared so much DNA with Westley, lest she be my competition rather than his sister.

When the waiter came with our orders, I heard Mrs. Greene whisper to her daughter, "So, are you still seeing Justin?"

Eastlyn pursed her lips and shook her head. "No, it didn't work out. I mean, he was great, and maybe something could happen for us down the road. But right now, I've just got too much going on."

"Good for you, honey," Mrs. Greene replied, squeezing her daughter's shoulder. At first, I wondered if she was encouraging her in her hope for a reunion with this Justin guy or congratulating her independence from dating. But as I watched Eastlyn through dinner—so poised, confident, and detailing the fullness of her future to her adoring family—I realized that I probably could figure out which was the answer.

◆◆◆

Upon my insistence, I stayed the night at home alone so that Westley could spend some time with his sister. I didn't want to be away from him, but something about the way that the Greenes all worshipped Eastlyn throughout our meal had clouded my mood. I'd never found myself so blatantly jealous of her before, but hearing all about her endless accolades and accomplishments immediately after writing an entire essay about how I had none stirred up a hollowness within me that left me in a funk.

Westley could sense my mood was off, and I tried to describe my feelings to him.

He quickly brushed them off. "Eastlyn has nothing that you couldn't have if you wanted it. But you have something she wants and doesn't have. So just think about that."

I smiled at his vote of confidence, but having never wanted anything for my life other than to have him in it, I doubted the truth of his statement. Absent complete physical reconstruction, I could definitely never have her beauty. And her confidence and likeability had been partly good genes and partly thanks to a lifetime of encouraging parents. Neither of which I had.

There wasn't a guy in the whole northern hemisphere who wouldn't have given his right arm to be with Eastlyn, but I understood what Westley meant when he said I had something she wanted. Despite the endless stream of good luck in Eastlyn's life, she'd never had a real boyfriend—not one she'd connected with in the way Westley and I had.

Even knowing this, though, it was hard for me to feel sympathy for her. I didn't doubt that Eastlyn would find the man of her dreams. She was the kind of girl who actually had the potential and pedigree to take her pick between a movie star and a prince of some wealthy country. She would not end up a lonely old maid, never to have loved or been loved.

I, however, would always have a really awesome boyfriend and likely nothing more.

We pulled into my driveway, and Westley ran around the car to open my door for me. As he helped me out, he pointed up toward a rare, cloudless winter's sky.

27

"You want the moon, Cosette?" Westley said in a butchered Jimmy Stewart impression, and I felt my heaviness lighten. "Just say the word, and I'll throw a lasso around it and pull it down."

"I thought you didn't pay attention to the movie?" I joked, staring up at the three-quarter moon and its hazy, golden halo.

"I can't help it if George Bailey had some amazing pickup lines." Westley fell back into character. "That's a pretty good idea. I'll give you the moon, Cosette."

And I knew that he would.

I smiled.

"I'll take it."

◆ ◆ ◆

I got home around eight, which was past the bedtimes of everyone in my house but Bronwyn. She'd marked the living room as her territory that night and sprawled herself out on the sofa with an open package of red licorice and—because my father didn't enforce a legal drinking age at home—a glass of wine.

My entrance had gone unacknowledged, for which I was grateful since I didn't feel like sparring with her two nights in a row. I slipped off my shoes and flung my coat onto the rack before starting up the stairs.

"You know what I hate about these shows," Bronwyn said, her back to me. I stopped midstep and lifted onto my tiptoes to see if someone else was in the room with her.

"Are you talking to me?" I asked blankly.

"Yeah, get in here and watch this with me." She bit off a piece of licorice as if she were trying to kill it.

Without thinking, I obeyed Bronwyn's wishes. I would have probably turned on the television in my room anyway, and the one in the living room was much bigger.

"Anyway, this show is pissing me off," she continued, pointing at the screen with her candy. I glanced at the television and recognized some new teen drama I'd heard advertised. "It's so formulaic. I mean, this is the first episode, and I already know who I'm supposed to want to hook up, who I'm supposed to hate, and who I'm supposed to feel sorry for."

"Hmm," I responded neutrally so that she'd know I was paying attention but not agreeing or disagreeing with her since I knew what it would mean to do either. I watched the show in silence for a few minutes, searching for something to add to her commentary. "Oh, yeah..." I made a face when the show went to commercial. "I see what you mean. They're definitely going to take the love-triangle approach with this series."

"Exactly." She held out a strand of licorice to reward me for seeing her point. "It's so overdone."

"Thanks," I mumbled, playing down how happy the gesture had really made me. I accepted the candy and chewed off a piece. "So who do you want the homecoming queen to choose?"

"I don't really care. And it doesn't matter anyway, because at some point, she'll end up with both of them, and whoever she's with first will be who she ends up with at the end. These stupid shows are all the same."

"But you're still going to watch it, aren't you?" I half-smiled, enjoying our near-normal discussion. She may not have been the sister I always wanted, but she was who she was without apology. And after spending the evening counting the ways I didn't measure up to Eastlyn Greene, I found myself appreciating that about Bronwyn.

"Of course I am," she scoffed. "Now shut up. The commercial's over, and if you talk through my show, I'll punch you in the eye."

CHAPTER 5

I didn't see Westley at all on Sunday. He and his family had gone to South Bend to Christmas shop, and the invitation wasn't extended to me. This told me that I was the one being shopped for, and that Westley had probably been waiting for Eastlyn's opinion on whatever he was buying. West's sister never disappointed in her dispensing of gift-giving advice, which meant I was going to love whatever he had chosen.

Had Westley not reminded me, I might have forgotten that my own Christmas shopping was unfinished. My family didn't really do holidays like everyone else. When we were younger, my grandma made sure that Bronwyn and I had Halloween costumes, baskets at Easter, and presents on birthdays and Christmases. We did the big meal thing on Thanksgiving for a while, but when I started celebrating with the Greenes, her efforts stopped. I wondered if anyone in the family considered restarting some Miller family traditions now that Ginger was with us, but if they had, I was likely not to be invited anyway since I had a permanent place setting at Westley's.

In West's absence, I decided to seize the day alone for my own holiday errands. If I finished everything now, I wouldn't have to miss time with him later to do it.

I'd planned to drive in the opposite direction of the Greenes, to Goshen, so there would be no chance of running into them and potentially ruining the surprise of my present.

I checked my bank account online to set my spending limits, grabbed West's letterman jacket and my shoes, and bounded down the stairs. My hand was turning the doorknob to head outside when a voice from the kitchen called to me, "Where are you going?"

It was Bronwyn. I paused, alarmed by the almost cheerful tone of her question. We spent almost two hours watching television together the night before without a catfight, but I had learned that Bronwyn's favor changed with the wind, so I had no expectation we'd still be friends this morning.

"Shopping," I replied over my shoulder. Then I waited for her permission to leave.

It didn't come. "Westley going?"

"No."

"Then hold on. I'm coming with you."

Grandma was as confused as I was when Bronwyn asked her to watch Ginger so we could go out together, but she immediately agreed. I hadn't hung out with Bronwyn on purpose outside of home since I drove her to the hospital to deliver Ginger, and even then she insisted on walking in alone so people wouldn't think we were together.

Upon entering my car, she immediately threw a pair of Westley's baseball cleats to the backseat and made a face. I expected the reminder of him to launch Bronwyn into her typical tirade about how much she hated my boyfriend. Instead, she played with the radio dial from the passenger's seat while I maneuvered my way over the unsalted roads that led from Middlebury to the real world.

As she scanned the channels, my mind raced, searching for something to fill our time with that would be neutral enough not to set her off in any way, but also not appear as though I was trying too hard to make small talk. I decided on, "So, what are you getting Ginger for Christmas?"

"Pshh," she responded, still punching the radio buttons. "She has enough shit as it is."

Her answer hadn't given me much fodder for furthering the topic. "Oh, so does that mean you aren't getting her anything this year?"

"No," Bronwyn scoffed. "Of course I'm still getting her stuff. What kind of mother doesn't give her kid gifts on Christmas?"

The conversation dead-ended.

My sister settled on a station and sang along with the music until we pulled into the Village Shoppes in downtown Goshen. As I fed the parking meter, I looked to Bronwyn for the decision of where we'd go first. I mostly needed to buy for Westley, but I wasn't about to choose a store that would make it obvious I'd come there for him, lest she spend the rest of our trip in loud disgust.

I followed my sister into toy, book, and houseware stores. Among these places, we both found gifts for Grandma and Ginger. I even purchased a photo album on the sly that I contemplated filling with secret pictures I had of Ginger and giving it to Bronwyn, assuming we were still on good terms the following weekend. I wanted to be sure my efforts wouldn't be set afire.

We returned to my car and filled my backseat with our purchases. I fed another few quarters into the meter.

"We're not leaving?" Bronwyn accused rather than asked. "What's left?"

"Oh...oh," I stammered. "Uh, I wanted to run into the sporting goods store."

She answered with a dramatic eye roll. "Really? You are going to waste your money on him?"

I could have lied and said I needed to shop for Dad, but I would have had no idea what to even say I was buying for him. I remembered that when I was about six, he'd bowled on a local league for realtors, but that was the extent I knew about my father in the area of sports. On the other hand, I could have recited the RBIs, batting averages, and on-base percentages for just about every player on the Chicago Cubs because of how passionate Westley was about them. I only needed about ten minutes in the store to choose the jersey I wanted, and then we could leave. Bronwyn countered with an offer of five minutes and followed me inside.

I had Westley's gift in my hand in less than two and took my place in line. Bronwyn stood behind me, too annoyed for chitchat. The store swarmed with people all doing what we were with seven shopping days left before Christmas, and I

32

hoped that my sister wouldn't count the time we had to wait in line against me and cause a scene.

"Excuse me," a male voice from behind us said.

Bronwyn and I both turned around at the same time. There before us stood a boy around our age, halfway smiling, his blondish bangs covering one eye.

I didn't recognize him, so I assumed he was talking to my sister. Her expression was as expectant toward me.

"Um, hi," I offered as a greeting.

"Cosette, right?" the stranger continued. "It's Micah, from your English class."

I furrowed my eyebrows searching for something familiar, but I didn't know him from Adam. "I'm sorry, I'm having a hard time placing you..." My cheeks flushed.

"Mrs. Holloway's class, fifth period. You sit in the front by the door? I'm a few rows over in the back."

I again failed to make the connection, but he obviously knew me. I didn't want to be rude, so I said, "Oh, OK. Yeah, how are you?" I fumbled my speech.

Bronwyn offered her own apology for me. "I'm sorry—what did you say it was? Micah? My sister has this problem with names and faces. If you aren't Westley Greene, she can't remember you. It has something to do with the fact that her head is shoved so far up his ass. Don't take it personally."

My cheeks burned brighter.

"It's not a problem, really," Micah fixed his eyes on mine, ignoring my sister's impoliteness. "I'm new to the school, so that's probably why you don't recognize me. I'll make sure to say hello again tomorrow." He smiled a lazy smile at me.

"Yeah, I'll look for you," I replied, feeling incredibly awkward at both my sister's comment and because I almost never talked to boys other than Westley.

"See you tomorrow." Micah turned away and disappeared into the crowd of shoppers.

Bronwyn checked him out as he left. "Your friend's hot."

"He's not my friend," I clarified automatically, even though I didn't know why it mattered. "Just a guy in my English class." I wasn't even sure that was true, but I took him at his word. I knew I generally wasn't observant, as Bronwyn had so eloquently pointed out, but I was pretty sure I'd never seen that boy before in my life.

"Anyway," my sister said dryly, "I don't really care who he is; he's better looking than Westley. You two should hook up."

"What in the world are you talking about?" I whisper-yelled at her. I was next in line to pay, and the cashier was someone I did happen to recognize from school—a junior named Allison who had dated one of Southeby's friends—and I didn't need her spreading rumors about me "hooking up" with anyone. "I don't just randomly sleep with people I hardly know, Bronwyn." I knew it was risky to argue with my sister in public, but I only needed to keep her quiet another sixty seconds and we'd be out the door. Once we were alone, she could wax hatred for Westley all she wanted.

"That's right, you don't sleep around." Bronwyn grinned snidely. "You just go at it with Westley like animals every night while I'm trying to get my daughter to sleep in the next room."

I hushed my sister. "Bronwyn!" My face burned as both of Allison's eyebrows darted up her forehead.

"What? I'm sure this isn't a news flash to anyone. Everyone knows you guys are doing it. Why else would Westley have stayed with you for so long?" I locked eyes with my sister, silently pleading with her to stop embarrassing me, but I found nothing relenting in her cold stare. "All I'm saying is that if you are going to whore around, you might as well have some variety. You can't think *Westley* isn't sleeping around. I mean, why wouldn't he?" She looked me up and down with disgust.

I couldn't speak. I couldn't move. I had lost my ability to react.

How could I have been so stupid? Sitting in the same room with my sister nonviolently for two episodes of a teen soap did not make us best friends. I should have expected this—or at least some type of hurt—because it always happened. Without exception.

I knew better.

"Hurry up. I'll be in the car." Bored with how easy it'd been to humiliate me, Bronwyn pushed her way through the crowd and exited the store.

Hot tears burned my eyes as I slid my debit card across the counter to Allison.

Westley and I were private about our sex life, in part for this very reason—we didn't want what was between us to be cheapened. Because we'd been together so long, I was sure people assumed lots of things about us, but I certainly wasn't open about the subject. I knew that Westley loved me more and would never objectify me in the locker room.

My sister, on the other hand, did not love me. In fact, she thrived on inflicting pain upon me. And it was this, the pleasure she took in my embarrassment, her intentions more than her words, that cut me the deepest.

This was just the beginning of the damage she'd set into motion. I wasn't naive. I knew the reality of what would happen next. I could see the satisfaction on Allison's face. She had firsthand gossip, and she would get the pleasure of sharing it with all of Camden High School.

I felt sick. Violated. Ashamed.

I signed the purchase slip handed to me by a glib Allison and left the store.

In my car, I drove slowly and silently while Bronwyn sang with the radio all the way home.

CHAPTER 6

I avoided Westley Sunday evening by hiding behind a text message that said I wasn't feeling well and was going to bed early. Both excuses were true.

I didn't go to bed to sleep, however. I went there to figure out a way to tell him what had happened without it resulting in him violently murdering Bronwyn.

From experience, I knew that if I just ignored her, she'd lose interest in torturing me for a while. I just had to play dead, and she'd move on to more interesting prey. Over the years, though, Westley had grown tired of watching me be hunted for sport by my sister. I knew this would be the final straw for him; I just was not sure exactly what that would mean.

Westley drove me to school on Mondays, and I couldn't come up with any believable reason to drive myself that morning, even though it would have bought some extra time to plan how to tell him why our sex life was headlining the gossip column.

After skipping breakfast to rehearse in the mirror, I was hopeful I could downplay how upset I'd been about the incident. That would have been the part that infuriated Westley the most anyway. He wouldn't care so much about people talking about us as long as I didn't show him how badly it bothered me.

And realistically, if Allison ran her mouth too much, Southeby would shut her up. The Greenes stuck together. He'd seen me stay the night with his brother dozens of times and never breathed a word about it at school. Why would he?

He respected his brother's privacy. He was a normal, human sibling, unlike Bronwyn.

I didn't waste any time in bringing up the subject after kissing Westley good morning. Our commute was short, and I needed him to be informed before we got to school, just in case someone had emblazoned the word "slut" upon my locker.

I breathed deeply to calm myself. In order to avoid arousing suspicions, my delivery needed to show annoyance but not anger at Bronwyn, and concern but not panic regarding Allison. "So I need to talk to you about something that happened yesterday during my shopping trip," I began with feigned nonchalance.

Westley stiffened. "OK," he kept his eyes on the road but gave me his attention. "I'm listening."

I took another breath. "Bronwyn and I were having a private discussion and the cashier—Allison Myers, actually—overheard us. The more I thought about it, I got worried that she was going to start gossiping about it to people. I just wanted to give you a heads up in case you heard something."

I felt a twinge of guilt pain my stomach, knowing I was withholding an abundance of details he would probably want to know, but I beat it into submission with thoughts of Westley and Bronwyn fighting gladiator style to the death.

"What kind of private discussion?" he asked, more curious than accusatory.

"About our sleepovers?" My statement came out as a question. I was no actress, and I knew it would be a tough sell to make him believe that Bronwyn and I were having a consensual conversation about anything—let alone something as intimate as sex.

Westley looked as unconvinced as I sounded. "Um...why?"

"It just came up," I answered, trying to brush past his question. "And Allison was definitely eavesdropping." I felt another twinge for painting the cashier as the only villain in the situation, but better her take the fall than begin World War III.

"All right then." His answer was shorter than I expected, but it felt like an end to the conversation. I leaned back into my seat and soaked in my own relief. I'd been prepared for explosions, but instead the situation had fizzled like a wet firecracker. "It's not like I care what people think about us. So if it doesn't bother you, then I'm cool with it."

"No, I don't care what anyone thinks either."

◆◆◆

Aside from a few snarky looks from the table of sophomore girls at lunchtime, I made it to fifth period without anything making my ears burn. Westley hadn't let on he'd noticed anything out of the ordinary, so I allowed myself to breathe easier that my legacy at Camden High was safe from sex scandal.

When the bell rang, Mrs. Holloway was already positioned at her podium at the front of the classroom, ready to go.

"So," she began excitedly. "Thanks to the wonders of technology and the fact that my husband was out of town and I had nothing better to do, I graded all of the *It's a Wonderful Life* essays that were e-mailed to me over the weekend. And props to you guys, because for this class in particular, well over half of you got them to me by Saturday night. So, thanks for that."

I'd forgotten to ask Westley about his essay. Despite his not having paid attention during the movie, I was sure he'd still end up with an A.

"And I must say, you all inspired me..." She paused for dramatic effect, placing her hand over her heart. "To give you another assignment."

The class groaned in unison.

"Now, hold on. I just spent my weekend reading essays about how you all think your lives are meaningless." I blushed, and at the same time was relieved that I had not been the only one to struggle with that part of the assignment. "So I'm going to give you a chance to change that." Mrs. Holloway's eyes sparkled. Her enthusiasm was conta-

38

gious, and I could tell by how many of them leaned in to listen that most of my classmates were already on board with whatever she was about to suggest.

"We are going to write our eulogies!" she announced with grandiose faux excitement. A confused murmur rumbled through the class, and she put up her hand to shush it. "OK, I get that this may sound a little morbid for the holidays, but listen to this. I simply cannot have my students living their lives as if they don't matter." She pointed to all of us. "As if *you* don't have the power to impact the world. Because you most certainly do."

I knew that Mrs. H. believed what she was saying much more than we believed it, and for that reason, I jumped on the bandwagon with the rest of my classmates.

"The common theme in the essays that I read this weekend was that you all believe you are too young to have influenced the world around you." She looked at us with sincerity. "That is simply untrue. In fact, if we were to remove any one of you from this class, we'd all be impacted."

Mrs. Holloway's optimism made me smile. I wanted to know who taught her to be so hopeful, and then go to that person for a crash course.

"This will be partner work," she continued as she distributed the assignment. Westley and I shot promising glances at one another. "You will each be assigned to write the eulogy of one of your classmates seventy years in the future." Then as an aside, she added, "I'm putting it far out there since I gathered by your essays that most of you aren't yet comfortable with your own mortality."

I smiled. This would be a great excuse for Westley and me to seriously outline our future together. I loved this assignment already.

"Fortunately, in this class, we have an equal number of ladies and gentleman, so this is the easiest way to leave your partnerships to 'chance.'" Mrs. H. instructed the girls to write their names on squares of paper she distributed. She then collected them and dropped them into a basket. My face fell as I calculated the odds of ending up with Westley as a partner. His look reflected my disappointment.

One by one, she announced a guy's name from her attendance list and drew a partner for him.

"Andreas Williams and Alexa Kite...Eric Freshour and Brynne Leamon...Westley Greene and Julia Davis."

I inadvertently released a sigh that caught Mrs. Holloway's attention, and then sank into my seat.

I knew Julia pretty well. She dated Westley's best friend, Patrick Wellman. She was bubbly, fun, and on the cheer squad. As far as ballplayers' girlfriends were concerned, she was probably my favorite. If someone else had to be partners with my boyfriend, then I didn't mind that it was Julia. I just wished it was me.

"Collin James and Betsy Yoder...Nehemiah Hochstetler and Tracey Black...Micah Quinn and Cosette Miller."

I scoured the faces for one searching for mine and locked eyes with an almost-familiar face—the boy I'd met the day before in line at the sporting goods store. He smiled that same, lazy smile, and I returned it halfheartedly with a wave. I guessed that if the only thing I knew about Micah was that he was friendly, things could have been worse.

Mrs. Holloway finished announcing the pairings, and then allowed us the rest of the class to get to know our partners. She handed out a questionnaire to get us started.

Micah brought his books up to the desk behind mine, and I turned around backward to face him at it.

"So, we meet again," he greeted me. "Get all your shopping done yesterday?"

I paled remembering the incident at the check-out counter and silently prayed that Micah had not heard my sister's suggestion that we sleep together. "I think so. You?"

"I found what I was looking for." Micah held up the list of questions on the paper. "So, you ready to die?"

I surprised myself with a laugh. "As ready as one can ever be, I suppose."

Micah was a natural icebreaker. He picked up his copy of the assignment and started reading. "All right, it says here:

40

'Obituaries always include the deceased's address. Where will your partner be residing at the time of his or her death?'" Micah poised his pencil to record my response.

I was blank. I glanced at Westley. I wondered if I should consult him before answering these questions so that our futures aligned.

Micah followed my eye line. "Want me to wait here so you can go ask your boyfriend?" he joked.

I apologized. "No, it's just that it's hard for me to imagine where we'll be going to college next fall. I have no idea where to even begin thinking about seventy years from now."

"Oh, so planning college together? You guys must be serious."

"Well, we've been together since fifth grade," I answered with a smile, remembering Westley as an adorable eleven-year-old.

"That's *forever* in teen years," he teased, and then paused for a moment before redirecting himself back to the worksheet. "All right." Micah nodded. "We'll just skip that question for now." He scanned his paper for an easier topic. "OK, what sort of jobs did you work during your lifetime?"

I found myself chewing on my thumbnail, unable to answer this question either. I shrugged.

"No problem, moving on," Micah reassured me. "How did you die?"

This was one I thought I could handle. "Isn't everyone just going to put 'in their sleep' or 'of old age' for this question? I suppose either one of those would work for me." I imagined Westley and me, wrinkly and frail, having just celebrated sixty-five years together, crawling into our bed and taking our last breaths in one another's arms. It sounded cheesy, but I couldn't imagine a better way to go.

"Oh, absolutely not!" Micah responded quickly. "I want to give my life for a purpose, not just have it slip away from me." He glanced up at me from his paper and read my expression. "That's not to say your answer is wrong, I mean. It's just...I..." He stumbled over his words. "I just made this decision a long time ago that I was going to do something

41

meaningful with my life, up to the point I die. It was a pretty big decision, actually. A long story. But right now, we are talking about you. Sorry for the tangent."

"Yeah, sure, no problem," I answered, my curiosity piqued. This was the first real conversation I'd had with someone other than Westley in a long time. I didn't really know how to navigate it well, but it was refreshing.

"Since I'm the new guy," Micah said and smiled, "and probably the only one in the whole school who hasn't heard you tell the story—how long have you and Westley been together now? Almost seven years? Why don't you fill me in? Unless you need time to prepare for this line of questioning too."

Micah was a charmer. He reminded me of Westley in that way, which was probably why I was so eager to share our story with him. He was easy to talk to. And he had just asked to hear about my most favorite subject.

"Well, I do happen to know this story really well." It wasn't like we were celebrities or anything, but most people at Camden knew about us. And without any real girlfriends to speak of and a sister who would rather have a root canal than ask about my relationship, I didn't often get the chance to tell someone how Westley and I came to be.

"We met the first year in middle school. He was in my language arts class. We were reading *Charlotte's Web*, and I was having a really hard time with it."

"Too many big words?" Micah asked sarcastically.

I laughed. "Hardly. I couldn't stand the suspense of whether or not Wilbur the pig was going to die. Then, at the end, when Charlotte died instead, I had to be sent home by the school nurse because I cried so hard I threw up." I felt my cheeks redden at this admission. It wasn't normal for me to be sharing such intimate details about my life with anyone but Westley—especially details about bodily fluids.

"And so for Westley, pigs, dead spiders, and vomit equal love at first sight?" Micah's wit was quick, and I appreciated it.

"Actually, I think it was because I cried so hard for Charlotte." I smiled, remembering Westley approaching me in the school cafeteria with a box of tissues in hand. He told me he didn't want me to cry anymore, and if I'd let him be my boyfriend, he'd make sure I was always happy. Such a sweet and simple promise—and one that he'd kept.

"Cute story. Think you'll be telling it to your grandkids one day?"

"Definitely. I'm sure we'll get married. Westley's my soul mate."

Micah's expression changed to one of disgust. "Aw, it was a great story up until that last part."

His strong reaction took me off guard, and I glanced at Westley. He was eyeing Micah.

"It's just the term, *soul mate*. I think when people say that, they are really meaning something else." Micah sat forward. "*Soul mate* has this sort of...predestined connotation to it, like two people can only be with one another or they'll never be happy."

So far, I didn't see how my intended definition differed from Micah's.

"But that would be a horrible thing, if you think about it, right? Because then there is no free will. Then, there's just some puppeteer pulling strings and planning your life without you having any say about it." Micah spoke quickly, excited to drive his point home. "I think what people really mean when they use that term is that the other person is their *choice*. They mean that out of all the people on the planet, they are *choosing* that one person to give all of their love to. No one's making them do it; it's not left up to the fates. And how much more would it mean to know that you and Westley chose one another than were just some crappy, forced-to-be-together-by-nature-or-whatever soul mates?"

I opened my mouth to argue, but I couldn't think of a single point for rebuttal. I had never thought of Westley and me in those terms—as one another's "choices." But that's what we were, after all. Nothing and no one had forced us together the way the term I had used implied. I found myself liking how Micah explained this to me. Suddenly, what Westley and I had together felt even more special.

"You're awfully wise for a high schooler."

"It's true," he agreed, deadpan.

We chitchatted a bit more before returning our attention to our assignment. By the time Mrs. Holloway retook her position at the podium to signal class would be ending, I'd managed to decide that Westley and I had retired to Arizona since that was where the Cubs held their spring training. I hoped this would please him.

"All right, there are about two minutes until dismissal, so make sure to exchange contact info with your partner. We won't be doing the entire assignment in class, so you'll probably have to meet up once or twice outside of here to get it done." She flashed her "forgive me" smile at us, and we did.

I pulled out my phone to enter in Micah's digits.

"Oh, so I don't do the whole cell thing," Micah said slowly. "But I can call you."

Aside from the Amish kids, I knew of no one who didn't carry a cell phone, but I didn't say that to him. Instead, I gave him my number as the bell rang. Before I could stand up, Westley was at my desk stacking my books onto his.

"Hey, sorry, man. I don't think we've met." He extended a smile and a hand to Micah. "Westley."

"Micah," he replied with equal pleasantry as he stood up. As they were standing next to one another, I could see Westley had at least four inches on Micah. Between the two of them, I felt miniature. "Weird having another guy writing about your girlfriend's death?"

"A little bit, yeah. I'm not gonna lie." I could read a slight edge in Westley's voice, but I doubted that Micah would detect it. "But no, it's cool."

"Play ball?" Micah pointed to Westley's warm-ups. They were Camden green and yellow with "Varsity Baseball" written across the shirt and down both legs.

"Yup, shortstop." The firmness in his tone lessened. "You?"

"Used to play. It's been awhile. Love the game, though." Micah filled his backpack with his books and politely excused himself. "Nice seein' ya, man. Gotta run." Then he turned to me on the way out and said, "I'll call you about the assignment."

The hallway was its usual chaos, so Westley and I didn't speak again until we'd reached our locker.

"So, how does Julia knock off?" I asked him as I switched my literature book for my trig.

"It's funny you should ask that, because she was way more concerned about you being knocked *up* than discussing the assignment." Westley broke his silence with an obvious bone to pick.

I stopped. "What are you talking about?"

"Yeah, so what exactly did Bronwyn say? 'Cause I get the impression I don't know the whole story about yesterday." The edge in his voice returned, now even sharper. It was rare for him to be upset with me, but I could tell that was where we were headed. I instantly regretted not handling that morning's conversation any better.

I sighed heavily. "I told you all the important stuff. I just spared you the details of her typical meanness because it would just make you mad."

"Well, I'm mad anyway," West retorted hotly. "Did she tell you I was sleeping around?"

I nodded in an effort to come clean. Stupid Bronwyn. Why had I been trying so hard to protect her?

"Did you believe her?"

"Of course not!" I was offended that Westley had even asked. "She wasn't serious; she was just trying to get a rise out of me—which she didn't. And you shouldn't let her get one out of you either."

"Why the hell not?" He was on the edge of losing his composure. "You know what, Cosette? I'm a little disappointed in you. There isn't a person on this earth I would let accuse you of sleeping around on me and not do something about it. Apparently though, your sister can say whatever she wants about me, and you do nothing in my defense."

His words made me flinch. "What she said had, West. I didn't want to dignify it with a response." Tears spilled onto my cheeks. I felt on trial.

Westley and I stood there silently at our locker for so long that the hallway was beginning to empty. He wouldn't have time to drive me home before practice if we didn't wrap up our argument soon, and my stomach knotted fearing our fight wouldn't be settled in time.

"I am so sorry, Westley." I broke the silence, the tears still running down my face.

"You should be," Westley replied, now with more sadness than anger. "You are a coward."

The insult knocked the wind out of me. It was the harshest thing he'd ever said.

"I gotta go lift. You can take my car home if you want. I'll get a ride from Trick." His words were flat.

Westley grabbed his backpack and slung it over his shoulder. He wiped my tears away with the back of his hand but offered me no additional comfort before taking off toward the gym.

I stared after him, motionless.

Minutes passed before I regained my senses enough to pack up. My eyes wandered down the hallway, chasing after Westley. But he was gone.

Eventually, I shut the door to my locker and set off for the parking lot. It was the first time I'd walked that hallway alone.

CHAPTER 7

Before I left the school, I stopped off at the ladies' room. I'd hoped to put myself back together before driving home—and to give Westley time to regret sending me away and text me an apology.

I'd washed my face completely, removing all evidence of my tears, and had begun reapplying my makeup when I heard female voices approaching. Not in the mood for company, I pushed past three cheerleaders as they came through the door.

"Hey, Cosette, are you OK?"

I glanced back to see Julia Davis looking at me with concern.

"I'm fine," I retorted and kept walking. Fair or not, I was upset that Julia had confronted Westley with the gossip she'd heard about us.

"Hey, wait up, Cosi!" Julia addressed me on more familiar terms than I felt she was allowed after the trouble she'd help to stir up.

I ignored her and kept walking.

She caught up to me and pulled my arm like a parking brake.

"Hey!" She spun me around to face her. "Are you all right?"

I hadn't the energy to pretend to Julia that I didn't know about her and West's conversation. "Yeah, just one of those days, you know?"

"So I heard." Julia's voice was less snarky than I expected. "And I'm sorry if I got in the middle of something with you two. I only brought it up to tell him how awful I think your sister is for what she said to you. I was kinda surprised that he didn't seem to know much of the story. I thought you guys told each other everything." Her apology seemed sincere, but I wasn't ready to be won over. "Looking back, I know I shouldn't have said anything. I'm trying to work on taming my tongue."

I found Julia's word choice odd. "We do tell each other everything. It's just complicated." I was unwilling to get any more detailed with her than that.

"I get it," she responded with a smile. "If it makes you feel better, I'm pretty sure Southeby threatened Allison Myers's life today. Of course he did it in such a way that I think made her fall in love with him while he was chewing her out." Julia held a ponytail holder between her teeth as she explained this, and then piled her red hair atop her head and fixed it into a bun with the rubber band. "I'm guessing it was the famous Greene dimples. Women can't resist them. But you already know that, don't you?" She winked at me.

I laughed in spite of myself, grateful for West's little brother. Julia's friendliness made it difficult to hold onto a grudge against her. My mood brightened against my will. "They're charmers."

"And not that you need me to tell you this, but there is no way Westley's cheating on you. That boy is in love with you."

I didn't need her to tell me that, but it felt good to hear it anyway. "I know."

Julia walked with me toward the parking lot. "So..." A hint of mischief laced the syllable. "Patrick told me what Westley got you for Christmas."

As much as I wanted to assess all the blame to Allison for spreading the gossip about me and West, Julia's segue into my Christmas gift made it hard to see her as completely innocent in the rumor department. She just loved to be in the know. "What was it you just said about 'taming your tongue'?" I couldn't help but take the bait, though I tried not to let on to Julia. It was out of character for Westley to share details like that with the guys. Whatever he was getting me, it

48

must have been a big deal. "I don't want to know, Jules," I warned her in case she planned on dangling the information out there like a carrot.

"Bummer." She shrugged. "I thought maybe I could trade you for what Trick got for me."

"Sorry." I didn't know, and even if Westley did, he wouldn't have found it interesting enough to share with me. "Guess we'll both have to be surprised."

"Oh, sweetie." She winked at me. "I don't think your gift will surprise anyone." She glanced at the wall clock. "Gotta go be cheery." Julia turned and bounced back toward the bathroom where she'd left her fellow cheerleaders.

Julia's encouragement convinced me that I was blowing West's and my fight out of proportion. She was right—that boy was in love with me. And after almost seven years together, if him calling me a coward—which he arguably had every right to do—was the worst fight we'd ever had, then we must be a pretty solid couple.

My load was lightened, and I hardly noticed the chilliness that met me as I pushed through the double doors into the parking lot.

Cars were scarce by this time of day, especially during the winter when students moved their loitering indoors. Westley's Mustang was parked in the fourth row, and I shuffled quickly over the frozen pavement toward it. It wasn't until I was inside adjusting the driver's seat so I could reach the pedals that I noticed something flapping between the wipers and the windshield.

At first glance, I assumed it was a flier, an advertisement about car repair or some community event. But before I switched the wipers on to blow it off, I noticed its thickness. Whatever it was, I would have to manually remove it.

I rolled down the window in time with the wipers so that I could snatch the papers without leaving the seat. As the window closed, I found the front page of the packet.

The title read in bold, red letters, "Why Wait?"

I folded back the now windblown cover. There were photographs of teenage guys and girls dressed in out-of-date clothing and hairstyles, depicted in various scenes—a couple in the backseat of a car, a guy and a girl in a doctor's office, a girl holding up a pregnancy test. Each face in every picture delivered the same message—*something terrible has happened.*

There were statistics with percent signs on every page, and the word *abstinence* appeared several times per paragraph. It was basically a summary of the human sexuality unit from sophomore health class, with one difference.

Highlighted in between paragraphs in the literature were verses from the Bible.

"Proverbs 6:25: Do not desire her beauty in your heart,and do not let her capture you with her eyelashes."

"Song of Songs 8:4: I adjure you...that you not stir up or awaken love until it pleases."

"Proverbs 31:30: Charm is deceitful, and beauty is vain,but a woman who fears the Lord is to be praised."

Churches were a dime a dozen in Middlebury, and pamphlets like this weren't exactly a rarity, although I'd never found one on my windshield before. I shrugged it off and began rolling up the booklet like a newspaper to chuck in the recycling bin at home when something caught my attention.

On the backside was a picture of a blond-haired, blue-eyed Jesus, halo aglow, hands outstretched. Beside him in the margin, written in black Sharpie, was a message.

W&C—

Repent from your sin before it's too late. Stop having sex, or your souls will burn in hell for eternity.

God loves you, and so do we.

I shivered but not from the cold.

So this was the tangible evidence I'd been waiting for—my private life had become public discourse. And furthermore, people were damning me for it. People. *We.* An anonymous group of judges who had chosen Jesus as their mascot, the face to represent their message of condemnation.

A churning now replaced the relief Julia had given me about Westley. Had someone said these words to me, I'd have blown them off. But there was something powerful in the intention of Anonymous, of the permanence of the ink on paper. And it wasn't love. No love I had known threatened me with an eternity in hell.

I was irritated and exhausted by the emotional ups and downs of the day. I tossed the paper into the passenger seat.

Westley had called me a coward because I wouldn't defend him to my sister, and maybe he was right.

But I'd rather be a coward afraid to stand against a tyrant, than become a tyrant because I was a coward.

CHAPTER 8

"Cosi? Cosette?" a voice whispered. My eyes opened in response, and I realized I was lying facedown in my trigonometry book. I slowly turned my head to the side so that I wouldn't rip the page that had adhered to my cheek.

"What time is it?" I asked, forgetting that I should be surprised to find Westley in my room. "What are you doing here?" I rubbed the blur out of my eyes.

West was sullen. "It's seven thirty, and I came to apologize." He was kneeling beside my bed so that our eyes were level. From behind his back, he revealed a large bouquet of white and red roses arranged with baby's breath. It appeared there were at least three dozen of the flowers, which made for an overindulgent bouquet. But they were beautiful, and I understood the gesture. Westley often brought me flowers for special occasions and as surprises. He had never given them to me as an apology. He had no protocol for how many were appropriate. "I shouldn't have said what I said to you, and I'm sorry."

"I am sorry too, Westley. I will try to talk to Bron—"

Westley interrupted me. "Absolutely not. I was out of line. I was frustrated because I have seen her hurt you so many times, and I feel like I can do nothing about it. That is going to change."

A wave of relief washed over me, followed by another of panic.

"I am your protector, not the other way around." Westley was resolved. "The next time she needs to be put back in her place, I will do it."

I exhaled as my response, unsure of how to argue with him. The complication of my relationship with Bronwyn couldn't be solved in this conversation, but the problem between West and me could.

"OK."

◆◆◆

Westley stayed just long enough to help put the roses into vases—they required four—and to check my trig homework. Patrick had dropped him off, but he was expected to pick up his car and be home before nine.

That night, the lake-effect snow that the weatherman had been promising for the past week finally came. Camden issued a snow day that Tuesday, which would have been much more exciting had Christmas break not been right around the corner. The automated message sent to my phone with this news woke me up at six o'clock in the morning, and I couldn't fall back to sleep.

Westley's mother was sure to intercept the call for her sons so that they could sleep in. I was excited at the prospect of a school-less day with him. The thought of snuggling with Westley under a warm blanket, drinking cocoa and watching Christmas movies, yesterday's spat a fading memory, made me smile.

My fantasy had put me in the holiday spirit, and with nothing better to do until West woke up, I decided to wrap the gifts I'd purchased over the weekend.

In the hasty end to my shopping trip with Bronwyn, I'd failed to pick up wrapping paper. So, I threw on my robe and headed downstairs to the laundry room storage closet where Grandma kept such things.

The kitchen light was on, so I tiptoed through the hallway in hopes that I would not be noticed by whoever occupied it. Halfway to my destination, I heard my father's throat clear. Assured that there was no imminent threat of a tussle with Bronwyn, I detoured through the kitchen.

"Morning, Dad," I greeted him, realizing it was the first time I'd spoken to him in several days.

"School's closed," he said in slightly more of a statement than a question.

"Uh-huh."

"Well," he said without looking up from the computer screen. "Stay out of trouble today."

"OK."

I lingered a few minutes longer. I poured myself half a cup of coffee and took the seat across from my dad at the table, just in case there was anything more he might want to talk about. I knew there probably wasn't since the transcript of our last ten years of conversations was as generic as this morning's "talk," but I still felt that I should give him the chance to ask me about my life, even though I knew he never would.

When my cup was empty, I left my dad as I'd found him and exited to the laundry room.

Grandma kept the house organized on her own terms, which weren't always obvious to everyone else. In fifteen minutes, I had not found any wrapping paper, but I had located my birth certificate, Bronwyn's baby shower decorations, and a few shirts I thought I had lost. I'd just about given up and decided to wrap the gifts in pages from an old *Soap Opera Digest* I found, when I came upon a box in the back of the closet that was actually labeled.

Corryne.

Corryne, my mother.

I slid the box off the shelf and into the light streaming in from the laundry room. It was heavy and covered in thick dust, which told me that no one had looked inside it in years. Grabbing a dirty rag from a laundry pile, I wiped the box down. If someone did come looking for it, I didn't want my fingerprints left behind as evidence of my snooping.

We didn't talk about Mom. Ever. It had never occurred to me that remnants of who she was still existed, that she—as a person—was accessible to me.

I drummed my fingers on the cardboard lid of the box, debating the possibilities before me. I should have been excited. Whether or not I'd ever considered it before, my mother was truly a mystery to me. I didn't know what I didn't know about her. She'd given me life. Half of me, presumably the half that communicated in more than grunts, came from her. I should want to know who she was.

But I didn't.

And I knew that was the wrong answer—just like being satisfied with Westley as the epicenter of my life was not the right answer for Mrs. Holloway's essay.

I'd never felt incomplete without knowing her. I was well adjusted and stable despite losing her at such a young age. Was I ready to gamble all that away for snippets of her life? An inevitable jigsaw puzzle whose picture I'd never be able to fully complete?

I returned the box to its home, not willing at this time to unleash its powers—good or bad.

I shut the door to the closet, empty-handed. It was best to leave well enough alone.

After shuffling through a few more drawers, I hit the gift-wrap jackpot. With Scotch tape and scissors in one hand, gift boxes and wrapping paper in the other, and curiosity stuffed back into the recesses of my mind, I retreated to my room.

However, though I refused to indulge in wondering about the box, my holiday spirits had been doused by my discovery. I shoved my purchases and the means to wrap them underneath my bed before falling back on top of my covers, where I lay in silence and counted the minutes until Westley called.

CHAPTER 9

As it turned out, the snow day was just what we needed to wash away the aftertaste left by the previous day's unpleasantness. Westley picked me up midmorning after the plows had come through, and we spent long, lazy hours indulging in our unexpected day off at his house.

There was only one small hiccup to our perfect day together, and it didn't happen until Westley was driving me home late that night.

"What's that?" he asked, pointing to some rolled-up papers wedged under his floor mat.

I immediately identified it as the religious tract that had angered me the day before.

"Oh, it's some brochure on abstinence." I brushed it off flippantly. "With a note attached about how we're going to burn in hell." Westley would take my cue, and if I wasn't bothered by it, he wouldn't be either.

"Are you serious?" He pulled the papers from where they were lodged and flipped on his dome light. After skimming the pages, he turned to the back where the message in Sharpie had been written. He read the words and laughed. "Nice," he muttered sarcastically. "Well, if there is a hell, I can't imagine it's that bad if I get to be there with you forever." He rerolled the pamphlet and chucked it into his backseat. "And if whoever wrote that is the kind of person who gets into heaven, I don't want to go there anyway."

I smiled, grateful that Westley had put the problem into a new perspective.

What did it matter what some closed-minded people thought about my relationship?

I didn't need their savior. I had my own.

◆◆◆

School resumed the next day, but the glances and whispers about West and I did not. Allison's fifteen minutes were up, and we'd been replaced as front-page news by rumors that a senior girl and her twenty-one-year-old boyfriend had stolen a car.

My morning was uneventful. I was completely unimpressed that my trig teacher gave us a pop quiz, and likewise, he was unimpressed that I left half of it blank. I reminded myself to schedule an appointment with my guidance counselor to discuss career possibilities that did not involve Pythagorean identities.

I was still cursing math when I arrived at Mrs. Holloway's class and suddenly realized I had more to fear—death. My death, precisely, and the fact that I'd not thought about my English assignment at all in the last two days.

"I'm really sorry, Micah," I confessed as the class reconvened into our partnerships. "I don't think I'm any closer to figuring out how I'm going to die than I was two days ago."

He chuckled. "Well, you may not have thought much about your death on your day off, but you are two days closer to finding out how it's really going to happen, so look at the bright side." He smiled. "Maybe we can drag this assignment out for the next seventy or so years, and you'll never have to decide."

"If that were the case, then I already know how I'm going to die—suicide!" I grimaced. Evidently, Micah only laughed at his own jokes, because his response to mine was silence.

Just then, from across the room, I heard Westley's voice. "Hey, are you all right?"

He was addressing his partner, Julia, who'd gotten up from her seat and dashed across the room toward the door where Micah and I were sitting. She was moving clumsily, as if her feet were too heavy for her body.

"Jules?" I automatically scooted my desk backward so that she didn't run into it. We locked eyes for a moment, but I got the impression that she couldn't see me. "Julia?"

Directly in front of me now, she fell to her knees at my desk and vomited onto the carpet. Then, she tipped onto her side and continued to wretch.

I instinctively covered my eyes. Ginger's were the only bodily fluids apart from my own that I could handle up close and personal.

There was unison of gasps followed by waves of disgusted groans. I removed my hands from my eyes to seek out my boyfriend. Westley, not the least affected by the bodily fluids of others, had quickly made his way to Julia's side and scooped her up into his arms. "I'm taking her to the nurse, Mrs. H.!" he called behind him as he ran out of the room and down the hallway.

The whole event happened so quickly that it didn't register if I should be more concerned than disgusted or the other way around.

There were awkward murmurs around the classroom for the next several minutes until the janitor arrived with the red sawdust that traditionally remedied the age-old problem of neutralizing throw-up from commercial-grade carpeting.

I sat facing away from Julia's lunch, hand over nose, willing my own to stay put.

"Are you praying?" Micah asked, and I realized I was so focused on not getting sick that I'd closed my eyes.

"Oh, no!" I laughed because I thought he was joking.

He wasn't. "Do you want to?"

I blinked at him several times. "Why?"

"Well, obviously, Julia is sick. I thought maybe you'd like to pray for her."

Even though Micah wasn't being the least bit pushy, I felt cornered. What I wanted to say was, "No, thank you, I don't want to pray because I don't do that sort of thing and I think you are a weirdo for asking me," without sounding insensitive. Was there a way to tell someone that you didn't want to pray for someone in need without appearing coldhearted?

I decided on, "I'm sure there's nothing to worry about," because it gave the outward impression that I was confident that Micah was concerning himself about Julia for no reason. "She probably just has the stomach flu."

But he volleyed back at me. "I didn't say I was worried. I asked if you'd pray with me." Micah looked intently into my eyes as if he were trying to read my thoughts.

Having no other excuse, I nodded. I could feel all the blood in my body rushing to my face. In all my life, I'd probably prayed fewer than five times. Three of those times were at Greene family Thanksgiving dinners when Westley's grandfather blessed the food. The other two went something like, "If you are up there, please don't let Bronwyn find out I borrowed her sweater and ruined it."

Before I could determine what my part of praying for Julia was supposed to sound like, Micah took my hand in his and bowed his head. "Lord, we ask for healing for our friend Julia. If it be your will, we pray that you would touch her body and cure her sickness. Be with Westley and the nurse as they determine Julia's needs. Grant comfort to Julia and wisdom to those who will help her..."

My eyes were closed, my hands were sweaty, and all I could think about was that I was holding the hand of someone who wasn't Westley.

I was trying to concentrate on Micah's words because I thought that it must count more to whomever received the message if I was paying attention too, but I didn't understand a lot of what he was saying.

If it be your will...what did that even mean?

If I'd been edgy up to that point, I was completely freaked out by what happened next. In the middle of his prayer, Micah started speaking words I'd never heard before. His voice had lowered, and I guessed he was talking in a different language. I was sure it wasn't Spanish or the fake German the Amish kids used when they didn't want the regular kids to know what they were saying, but beyond ruling out those two, I wasn't cultured enough to define it.

When he finished, he raised his head and looked at me. "Thank you," he said in normal English.

"Sure." I couldn't tell if it was standard practice to express gratitude to someone in this situation, or if Micah was treating me specially because he knew I was uncomfortable. I shifted in my seat and stared down at my assignment paper, pretending to give it my undivided attention.

I could feel Mrs. Holloway's eyes on us, and I suddenly wondered if we'd broken some sort of "no prayer in school law" that could land me in detention. I connected my eyes with hers and saw she was smiling warmly. I figured that even if I'd committed a crime, she'd give me a pass.

The noise level of the class was average of what would be expected for collaborative assignments, so we couldn't hear the sirens until the ambulance was practically outside our classroom window.

Everyone ran to the glass to see an emergency medical team race into the school, two paramedics pulling a gurney on wheels from the back of the vehicle. The scene unfolded so quickly that it took me longer than it should have to remember that Westley still hadn't come back to class.

At that moment, an alarm bell sounded in the hallway, followed by an announcement over the public address system: "Teachers, we are in lockdown. Please follow procedure and keep all students in your classrooms until further notice."

I felt my stomach sink into my shoes. Why hadn't Westley returned to class? Was Julia the one who required the ambulance? Were we on lockdown because of the ambulance, or was the ambulance here because of the reason we were on lockdown?

Where was Westley?

Mrs. Holloway shooed us under our desks and pulled the blinds. She then went to the door to the hallway and locked the bolt while turning out the lights.

I sat on the floor beneath my desk and tried to rationalize the confusion that had so quickly surrounded me.

The ambulance was not for Julia. Of course not. That was ridiculous. Julia threw up; that was it. Bad cafeteria food—it wasn't that uncommon. Or maybe she was pregnant? Or having an allergic reaction? Or maybe talking about her eulogy had made her nauseated? I could relate to that. Or maybe she got sick for one of the million other reasons people throw up that don't result in them needing an ambulance...

And Westley. Obviously, he had stayed in the nurse's office with Julia to answer questions for her since she was ill. He'd been the last person with her before she got sick, and he was probably just dispensing the details of what happened...

So then the ambulance wasn't for Julia, and of course it wasn't for Westley. It had to have been called for some completely unrelated situation.

The sound of doors slamming, followed by the wail of the siren, told us that whoever it was the ambulance had been called for had been loaded into it and taken away. As the noise faded, it left behind a stark silence in our classroom.

In the quiet, all that I'd been trying to justify before the ambulance sped off seemed impossibly optimistic.

As much as I tried, I couldn't fight off the sinking reality that something horrible had happened, something life changing. And the further off in the distance the sirens drove, the more irreversible that change felt.

I looked over at Micah sitting under his chair, eyes closed, lips moving furiously. I repositioned myself so that I could reach his clasped hands, closed my eyes, and listened to him pray.

CHAPTER 10

The waiting room was packed.

The emergency room of Goshen General Hospital was crawling with Camden High School letterman jackets. The entire cheerleading squad and dozens of our classmates were sandwiched in a room meant for no more than twenty people. I'd been one of the first to arrive. After being locked down for a total of twenty-five minutes, the second Mrs. Holloway opened the door to our room, I ran out of it in search of Westley.

When I reached the office, I'd found a group of administrators gathered in a clump. School counselors, receptionists, and our dean of students were standing in a cluster too close to be engaging in professional conversation. There were tears on their solemn faces. I didn't wait for anyone to notice me.

"Where's Westley?" I demanded of whoever had the answer.

Mr. Culp, the freshman guidance counselor, raised his head. He glanced at the rest of the adults to see if anyone else was willing to field my question, and when no one did, he spoke.

"Cosette, Westley's fine. The paramedics just thought that it would be a good idea for him to head along to the hospital too. The ambulance took Julia to Goshen General. We've already phoned his parents to let them know to pick him up there."

"Why?" I insisted on more information. "Was there a reason he needed to go too?"

"Cosette, why don't you just wait here, and we'll find someone to drive you there?" Mr. Culp spoke cautiously, which instantly alarmed me. Before he could get within arm's reach to stop me, I bolted from the office and ran toward the parking lot.

He said Westley was fine, I repeated in my mind, reminding myself it would help no one for me to die in a car accident trying to get to him. Still, I determined my own speed limits and arrived at the hospital in record time.

The ER receptionist informed me that because I was not a family member of Julia or Westley, I was not entitled to any information. Mr. and Mrs. Greene had already been admitted back into their son's room, and she would let them know I was there.

That was an hour ago.

I looked around at my fellow students. Of the nearly fifty in the room with me, I knew the names of five. Patrick had been there earlier, but a nurse had taken him back about twenty minutes before—presumably to see Julia. I was annoyed that he'd been allowed beyond the waiting room while I continued to sit in it.

The others I knew were Westley's teammates and a couple of the cheerleaders. I thought that I had seen Micah there too. If I had, I either lost him in the crowd or he'd left because I could no longer see him from where I sat.

Strangely, I wished he was there. He'd remained so calm during our lockdown, and in the absence of Westley, I had leaned into his strength.

We'd been under our desks for a full ten minutes before he stopped praying.

"Are you OK?" he'd asked me with genuine concern.

"I just want to know what's going on," I'd responded, frustrated. "I tried texting Westley, but he's not responding."

"I'm really sorry," Micah had emphasized. "If there is anything you need that I can do, I'm here."

My replay of the afternoon came to a halt when I heard my name being spoken loudly by a hospital worker. "Cosette Miller? Are you here?"

"Yes!" I jumped from my seat and pushed my way through the crowd. I was consumed with both relief to be getting answers and fear of what they would be.

When I reached the woman in blue scrubs, she instantly eased some of my anxiety. "Westley Greene is asking for you. Would you like to see him?"

"Yes! Yes, where is he?" My arms and legs tingled with new blood flow. I'd been on edge and in that chair for so long that I hadn't noticed my appendages falling asleep. I seized control of my body and forced my legs to follow the woman to Westley.

We pushed through two sets of swinging doors that required a scan of the woman's badge for access. The second room we entered was partitioned off into many tiny rooms with curtained walls. She walked in front of me and poked her head into one of the rooms to announce my arrival. Then she moved out of my way.

In the small space stood the Greenes—all of them. West's dad had his arm around his wife, her face stained with tears. In the chairs on the opposite side of Westley's bed, Southeby had his arm around his sister in a similar manner. And on the bed, sitting in a hospital gown and the jeans he'd worn to school, looking ashen and sad, was my Westley.

I threw myself at him without considering that he could have been injured. But when he didn't wince, I squeezed him tighter. "Are you OK?" I asked, surveying faces around the room for some sort of hint. It still didn't make sense to me why Westley was there if Julia was the one who had gotten sick.

"Yeah, babe. I'm not hurt or anything." Westley answering for himself encouraged me, though he sounded as if he'd just woken up. "I guess I just went into shock."

I stroked his face as he talked, so grateful to be holding him. "What do you mean *shock*?" I'd only ever heard of that happening to people who had low blood sugar or had lost large quantities of blood. I'd never known it to happen from witnessing someone vomit.

64

Mr. Greene took over speaking for his son. "He means that he went into emotional shock. His body shut down, and he blacked out."

"Oh." I was almost overjoyed with relief. "Is that all? I was so worried, West. You're going to be just fine!" When my smiles were not returned by anyone else in the room, my happiness plunged.

"I am going to be just fine, Cosi..." Westley paused for a long moment. "But Julia is not."

I heard Eastlyn sniffle loudly, and then sob quietly.

Mr. Greene continued for his son. "Sweetie, Julia suffered a brain aneurysm. It caused her to have what appears to have been a massive stroke."

"The doctors don't have all the information yet," Mrs. Greene interjected, sounding nasally and tired. "But—" Her voice broke.

"She's brain dead," Westley said, finishing the sentence no one else could.

The switch in my head that received and decoded sound shut off. I couldn't even tell if anyone else was talking. I only heard static.

Julia was not brain dead. She was a high school senior, just like me. She was a cheerleader and loved her boyfriend. She was a friendly girl who was working on taming her tongue. She just had the stomach flu. This was a terrible misdiagnosis.

"Cosette?" Westley squared my shoulders to his and looked into my eyes. "Do you understand what I'm telling you?"

I just shook my head that I did not. How could I? No one was making any sense.

"In Mrs. Holloway's class, Julia was complaining about a headache. The next thing I knew, she was headed for the door and got sick. She was sick all the way to the nurse. I had just put her down on the cot in the office when she started seizing."

Mrs. Greene put a hand on Westley to let him know he didn't have to finish the story.

"I'm OK, Mom; I need to tell her." Westley swallowed hard. I didn't know what he was building to that could be worse than Julia being brain dead.

Brain dead? What did that even mean?

"Mrs. Evans called 911, and we waited for Julia to stop seizing. But when she did..." Westley paused. "She wasn't moving at all. And she stopped breathing." I could feel Westley's heart beating faster, and his feet began to shake.

"Cosette, I tried." He looked into my eyes, pleading with me. "I did everything I was supposed to do!"

Mrs. Greene put her arms around her son from behind him. "Westley, it's OK. This isn't your fault." Tears streamed down her face.

"I performed CPR, Cosette! And she died! Right there in the nurse's office. Right there, with me pumping her heart! That is not what's supposed to happen!" Westley paled and shook.

My heart was breaking—first for Julia, but also for Westley. He'd watched her die. He couldn't save her. He felt responsible.

"Westley, you are not to blame for this," I began gently, though my own emotion was too much to manage. I burst into tears, coughing, hiccupping, and sobbing without restraint. Why was this happening?

"What was I supposed to do, Cosi? Huh?" Westley's eyes were wild. I'd never seen him so out of control before. "I'm so sorry!" He ran his hands through his hair, repeatedly grabbing and pulling handfuls. His jaw was so tightly clenched I was afraid his teeth would break.

Eastlyn's hand pulled me away from Westley, and she enveloped me into her and Southeby's huddle.

"I'm getting you another sedative," Mr. Greene addressed Westley, and exited the curtain while West's mother rubbed his back.

I buried my face into Southeby's chest, wishing he were Westley and that life was normal. But there were only traces of Westley in his brother's younger frame, not enough to pretend even for a moment of solace. "Shh. It's OK, Sis," he whispered to me.

But it wasn't OK. Nothing was OK. Nothing would ever be OK again.

CHAPTER 11

Julia was kept on life support until Thursday morning. Her brother Joe flew in from California early to say good-bye, and her parents delayed removing her from the machines until doctors could harvest her organs for donation.

Julia's parents arranged her funeral for Friday, the day before Christmas Eve.

Wednesday night, after Westley's release, I went home with the Greenes. Eastlyn drove my car, and I rode in the back of their Yukon with West's head on my lap. He was calmer, thanks to medication, but he wouldn't let me out of his sight. This was perfect for me, as I didn't want him out of mine either.

He slept all of Thursday, aided by a prescription. I lay beside him for most of the day, watching him, worrying about the days to come as he processed everything.

Westley was the only person I knew who had ever watched someone physically die. I could only imagine how vivid those images would forever be in his mind. I couldn't even watch someone die in a movie without having nightmares.

Thursday evening, I had to return home to gather some clothes for the funeral the next day. Westley begged to come with me, but knowing his fragile state, I didn't want to risk him running into Bronwyn. I promised to return quickly, and he reluctantly agreed to let me go.

I came into the house through the garage and was greeted by my grandmother. She held me for a long time, but neither of us spoke. The rest of the family was also in the kitchen. Dad shifted uncomfortably in his seat at the table. "We sent some flowers from the agency," he said to me, thin-lipped. I didn't know if he meant to Julia's family or Westley's, but since it didn't matter, I didn't ask.

Bronwyn said nothing, which was its own precious gift. She even restrained herself long enough to allow me to kiss Ginger on the cheek.

How much I wanted to pick up my niece and hold her forever—to tell her I loved her. To give her the world. To watch her breathe and smile and live for the next seventy years the way we were all supposed to get to.

All of a sudden, life was made of glass. So delicate in a way I'd never known it to be before.

On my way up the stairs, I noticed that Julia's obituary had been cut out of the newspaper and left on the lampstand. Assuming it was for me and wanting to read it privately, I folded it under my thumb and ran up to my room.

Having been shut up for the previous two days, the scent of Westley's roses was strong, almost too sweet when I opened my door. My inattention to their needs for water and sunlight had led to early decay. I frowned, upset that they died before I'd had a chance to enjoy them. Then, I looked down at the paper in my hand and regained perspective.

I sprawled across my bed. While I was anxious to get back to Westley, I needed a quiet moment for myself. He was sure to be in a medicated sleep by the time I got back anyway, no matter if I hurried.

I unfolded Julia's obituary and stared at her picture.

It was black and white, and I couldn't tell that her curly hair was red. However, even in gray scale, she was a pretty girl.

Julia Mariella Davis, 17, died Thursday, December 22, at Goshen General Hospital after complications arising from a sudden illness. Ms. Davis is survived by her parents, Marsha and Charles Sweisburger of Middlebury and Rick and Estella Davis of Plymouth; and a brother, Joseph, of Huntington Beach, California. Her high school sweetheart, Patrick Wellman of Middlebury, also survives.

My eyes filled with tears thinking of Patrick. *Her high school sweetheart...also survives.* Did he? Was he surviving this? We would see him at the funeral the next day, and I had no idea what we would say to one another.

I felt a rock in my stomach. Julia and Patrick had been dating for over a year, and while I knew little about their relationship, a year was a long time for high schoolers to date one another, generally speaking. I couldn't fathom what he must be going through. I didn't want to try.

Ms. Davis attended Camden High School where she was a cheerleader and competed on the tennis team. She had a longtime love for horses, and she spent many summers riding near her home in Middlebury. She is remembered for her wonderful sense of humor and her warm, bubbly nature. Ms. Davis had plans to graduate in the spring and had recently committed to a long-term missions trip to Latin America. A funeral service will be held for her on Friday, December 23, at Northridge Community Church in South Bend at 3:00 p.m.

I flipped the clipping over to see if there was any more written, and was surprised that there wasn't. Was there nothing more to be said of Julia after seventeen years of living, day in and day out, other than she was a cheerleader who liked horses?

I wondered if my own obituary would look any different. I had been trying to figure that out for days with this stupid English assignment, and now I felt even more urgency to reconcile it.

I set Julia's obituary on my desk and picked up my laptop. In my inbox was an e-mail from Mrs. Holloway to our fifth-period class. School had been in session in spite of the tragedy, but permission was granted to those who needed it to stay at home until after Christmas break. I couldn't imagine that there were many students left in the halls with that sort of invitation handed down. In reading Mrs. H.'s note, it was obvious attendance in her class had been sparse.

My Dear Students,

Like you all, I am heavyhearted with the loss of our dear Julia. My prayer for you all during this time is one of comfort, of peace, and of renewed appreciation for your own lives and loved ones. I hope you all use this season as a time of reflection and growth.

I do not believe that it is mere chance that we have been covering the topic of death in our class lately. Our futures and legacies, in as much as they are up to us, should never be far from the forefront of our minds. But, given our sad circumstances, our eulogy assignment is hereby cancelled.

That isn't to say that I don't want you to be thoughtful about the things we've talked about.

But rather than dwelling on death, let us focus on life.

Your new assignment is this—spend an afternoon with your partners. Talking with them, learning about them, encouraging them. Three hours—that's all I'm asking. A conversation.

We have but a mere few months left before you all graduate and will be scattered from one another, some of us forever. Let us seize our time together.

In love,

Mrs. H.

The relief I felt at the cancellation of our assignment was paired with an equal amount of guilt. I would write a hundred of my own eulogies if it meant Julia could come back. But those were pointless thoughts.

I welcomed the replacement assignment in theory. It would definitely be easier to complete than the previous had been. However, in Westley's state, I couldn't exactly see leaving him for an afternoon to hang out with another guy.

I opened my closet in search of an appropriate outfit for mourning, unsure of what criteria to use in making my selection. The last funeral I'd attended was Mom's, and I doubted I could still fit into a toddler's size three.

I grew angry, staring at my wardrobe. What a waste of time it was, trying to coordinate an outfit. What did it matter what I wore? Julia Davis was dead, and this was meaningless. All of it.

A few miles away, Julia's parents were no doubt staring at her closet, choosing what she would wear for her own funeral—attempting to decide for her what she would want to be remembered in that last time anyone ever laid eyes on her.

It was unfair. No parent should have to go through that.

Without looking, I threw as many clothes as would fit into my overnight bag, taking no time to change the water in my rose vases. They were just going to die anyway.

I needed to get back to Westley.

CHAPTER 12

"Are you sure you're up for this? The doctor said you shouldn't be pushing yourself," Mrs. Greene asked Westley for the fifth time on the way to Julia's funeral the next day. The Greene family and I were all riding together in the Yukon. Westley's mother was in the front passenger seat, watching her son in the rearview mirror and frowning.

Westley and I held hands in the first row of backseats. I too admitted that he didn't look as though he felt up for going to a funeral. He had yet to recover his coloring since he had rushed out of English class with a dying Julia in his arms. I wondered if he was ever going to.

"Mom, I have to do this, so please don't ask me again." Westley was firm but kind to his mother, and I could tell he was trying not to let himself be talked out of going.

Dressed in the same suit he'd worn for winter formal, West didn't look seventeen. I debated whether it was his clothing or the stress of the last two days that had aged him. Since the incident, he'd barely eaten and slept only with the help of pills. I couldn't blame him for not looking his best.

Not that I looked any better. I'd given up on recognizing my reflection in the mirror. Without a prescription of my own, sleep had eluded me the past two nights. Makeup did little to reduce the bags under my eyes, and I couldn't muster the energy to care.

Mr. Greene slowed his speed as we took our place at the end of a line in the right turn lane that was backed up a mile away from the church. We inched along with other cars full of mourners. The parking lot to the church was packed, so police officers were redirecting cars to a nearby RV plant that was on shutdown for the holidays. We were supposed to park there and be shuttled back to the church by a bus borrowed from the high school.

Did all funerals have this many attendants? Or was Julia the George Bailey of our time and I just hadn't cared enough to get to know her better?

We parked only a quarter mile away from the church, and Westley told his parents he wanted to walk rather than take the shuttle. Eastlyn and Southeby offered to stay back with us, but Westley insisted they catch a ride too.

We walked in silence until we saw the Greenes pass by in the school bus.

"All right, Cosette, I wanted to do this in front of you so that you didn't wonder what I was doing behind your back." Westley's tone alarmed me immediately. He pulled out his bottle of prescription Valium. "I haven't taken any of these since last night, but if I don't do something now, I'm going to lose my mind." He poured four pills into his hand and within the same motion, swallowed them.

"West! That's way more than you're supposed to take!" I gasped, reaching for his bottle.

"I know. That's why I wanted you to see me do it. From what I read, someone my size can handle it, but just in case...I wanted you to know." Westley looked disappointed in himself. "I am so sorry, Cosi. I just need to get through this day. I haven't seen Trick since it all happened and..." Westley trailed off. "I don't know what's going to happen when I see *her.*"

I reluctantly held my tongue and nodded.

We passed a trash bin on the sidewalk, and I watched Westley throw his half-full bottle of pills inside. "Don't worry; I'm done." He reassured me with a long kiss, and I was grateful he initiated getting rid of the pills instead of me. Not that West was inclined to abuse drugs—I just didn't know how easily he could become dependent on them. I had enough to worry about with him that I didn't want to add potential addiction to the list.

Westley's kiss was the first real affection he'd shown me since our snow day, which suddenly felt like a lifetime ago. "We'd better get in the church, West." I pulled away grudgingly. While it was not the most appropriate time for a make-out session, I couldn't remember a time when I wanted to kiss Westley more. I wanted to do anything I could to take away, or at least delay, the inevitable sadness of the day.

The building we walked toward didn't look like a church to me. It was gigantic, and outward appearances suggested more of an indoor soccer arena than a place of worship. But what did I know about churches?

Despite its size, we had to wait in a line to get inside. Both outside and in, we were surrounded by familiar faces, but all of them with puffier eyes and more sober countenances than we were used to. Camden High School had a total of eleven hundred students spread over the four grade levels, and the community was relatively close. Everyone in our small town was separated by no more than two degrees, so it made sense that the death of a young person would bring together such large numbers of mourners—but still, this was a lot of people.

From the vestibule windows, I peered into the room marked "sanctuary," and I could see the seats were filling up. There were classier versions of folding chairs instead of pews lined in rows on the main floor, which made me wonder if they actually did hold indoor soccer games there. A second floor provided additional seating, most of which was also folding chairs.

We entered the main floor and spotted Patrick Wellman and his family a few rows from the front. I realized that we had business to take care of before taking our seats. Westley squeezed my hand.

"I love you, Westley," were the only words of encouragement I could think to whisper to him, and he took steps toward his friend.

Patrick Wellman was a ballplayer of entirely different build than West. He was the shortest guy on the baseball team, but Julia had been the most petite of all the cheerleaders, so while Patrick may have looked odd in the starting lineup, he and Julia had been perfect together.

Apart from me and his siblings, Westley was closest with Patrick. So while West was dealing with his own grief in watching Julia die, he was additionally suffering that he hadn't been able to save her for his friend.

Patrick was also dressed in his winter formal suit, complete with a pink tie. I recognized it from that night when before the dance a few of the players and their girlfriends met at the Greenes' for photos in front of the fireplace. I remembered now that in those photos, I'd been standing next to Julia.

Much more than I would have imagined, Patrick was holding himself together. While his dark hair was disheveled, his blue eyes bloodshot, and his nose red and chapped, he smiled when he saw Westley.

"Greene," Patrick addressed Westley with an authentic embrace. I stepped to the side for the guys to have their moment.

His body shook, and I knew he was crying. Westley stared ahead blankly.

Finally, Patrick pulled away. "Thank you for everything you tried to do, man," he said through tearful hiccups. "Seriously, you're the only kid I know who would have thought to do anything like that. Everyone has been telling me how amazing you were, trying to help her." Patrick's eyes turned to look toward the front of the church.

I shifted my eyes downward. I knew he was looking at Julia's casket. I couldn't follow his eyes there yet. I needed to stay focused on Westley.

"I'm so sorry, Trick." Westley's voice was even. "I did everything I could."

"There was nothing you could do," Patrick said, and I hoped his words released Westley from some of the guilt he carried. "You're going to make a great doctor."

I found it odd that he was so calm, and I wondered if the hospital had just doled out anti-anxiety medication like candy to all those affected by Julia's death. Had I been in Patrick's shoes, I wouldn't have had to spend so much time choosing my outfit for the funeral because I would have been issued a straitjacket, if the mere experience of losing Westley did not instantly kill me.

"How are you holding it together?" Westley asked the question I also wanted the answer to.

Patrick's eyes filled with tears again. "I'm not really." He swallowed hard. "But I believe she's in a better place and that good is going to come out of this."

His answer was confusing to me. What sort of good could result from Julia dying so young, so unexpectedly? None that I could see.

A few more players from the team arrived, and Westley excused himself from Patrick with a promise that they'd talk more later.

As soon as we were out of Patrick's earshot, Westley released a huge sigh. That encounter had gone better than anticipated, and my burden, too, felt lighter.

However, his exhalation was followed quickly by another deep breath. "I'm just about stoned enough to be able to do this," he began. His speech had slowed, and I could tell the medicine was taking its effect. "But not out of it enough to keep it from sucking." Westley was leading me toward the front of the church where a line had formed to pay last respects to Julia.

There were so many floral arrangements decorating the stage surrounding Julia's casket that the entire front of the church smelled of spring. I wished so badly that we could truly jump ahead three months and away from this day to a time of year when everything got a fresh start, the place on the calendar furthest away from the bleak, dead winter.

As the line slowly crept forward, Westley slung an arm around my shoulders and used me to steady his balance. I stole a glance into his brown eyes and saw they were distant.

"Westley," I whispered. "I can't carry you, so you are going to have to stand up on your own long enough to do this." I remembered him asking his mother to stop giving him an out, that he had to go through with facing what had hap-

77

pened, so it was up to me to make sure that we reached the casket.

When it was finally our turn, I practically had to drag Westley forward. I didn't want to look. I wanted to bury my face in Westley's chest as I did during scary movies. I wanted him to watch the scene for me, to tell me when the sad part was over, to comfort me. I was not supposed to be the strong one. I didn't know how to do it.

Julia's casket shone, the glossy stain that coated the dark cherry wood reflecting the spotlight that lit her from above. Forcing my eyes downward, I took in the image before me of a still, mannequin figure, hands folded unnaturally across her stomach as though she'd fallen asleep with proper form. She was wearing a pink silk camisole and white cashmere cardigan. Her red hair lay in soft piles of ringlets around her face, which had been done up with excessive amounts of foundation and blush in an attempt to give her skin the color of life. Around her neck on a gold chain was Patrick's class ring and a cross. She appeared to be dressed for a job interview.

Nothing about the figure in this box reminded me of Julia. This was a shell, an inanimate marionette of a real live person. A dead body.

I shivered. Why did she look nothing like Julia? This girl hadn't been in a car accident. She hadn't needed to be reconstructed for viewing. All of her damage had happened inside. So what was missing? Where had her essence gone?

I didn't understand this ritual, why we dressed up the dead and put them on public display. Why all of us lined up in droves to inspect the face and body of once-alive Julia. Was this for proof that she was no longer living? I would have taken the doctor's word on it. I didn't need to see this. And I couldn't imagine that this was helping Westley to heal either.

In front of me, he began to teeter, derailing my train of angry thoughts.

His face had hardened, and I couldn't tell how much of it was from the Valium. I wanted to get him to his seat before he was unable to walk by himself, but I was also afraid to hurry him along. I had no idea of the right way to help someone grieve. I didn't even know how to do it for myself.

From seemingly out of nowhere, a hand steadied Westley's back. Another guided him by his elbow, and West was led away from Julia's body by Micah.

"Did we find our seats yet?" he asked over his shoulder as if we'd all bought tickets together for the event. But feeling more grateful than intruded upon, I didn't comment on his sudden appearance. Instead, I scoured the crowd for Westley's family. I spotted Eastlyn and Southeby in separate groups of friends and Mr. and Mrs. Greene in a cluster of baseball parents. Relieved that I wouldn't have to explain Westley's current state to them, at least during the service, I pointed Micah to an inconspicuous row of chairs next to a large decorative pillar. I hoped that wherever the rest of the Greenes ended up, the column would block their view of us.

"Micah?" Westley was confused. "What happened to Cosette?"

"She's right behind us, bro, no worries," Micah assured Westley.

Westley stumbled along now, leaning onto Micah for support.

"He took four Valium about twenty minutes ago. He said he was big enough for it not to hurt him." I offered this information to Micah as an explanation, but I also hoped he would confirm it as truth.

Having reached our destination, Micah lowered Westley into a seat. I quickly sat next to him to allow him a place to lean.

"I'm so sorry, Cosette. I'm sorry I'm not stronger." Westley sounded as if he were talking in his sleep, and I saw that his eyes were closed.

"Shh..." I preferred that he sleep through the funeral than suffer like he had been. I took his sunglasses from his pocket and put them on for him. This way, he would appear to be in deep mourning rather than insensitive, drugged-out unconsciousness.

"Is this normal for him?" Micah interrupted, and I realized he had sat down on the other side of me. "Pills, that is?"

"Oh, gosh no," I replied. "He's just about the cleanest guy at school actually. The hospital prescribed him some sedatives after what happened." I filled Micah in on how Westley had wanted me to witness his plan to self-medicate.

He leaned across my lap and pressed his index and middle fingers into West's wrist.

"His pulse is slow. We'll have to just keep an eye on him, but try not to worry. Westley's a smart kid. I doubt he would have done anything like this without knowing for sure he'd be all right."

"Thank you, Micah." I looked at him with gratitude. Now that someone else was aware of Westley's condition, I felt better.

"Looks like they are getting started." He pointed to the podium next to Julia's casket. There was a younger man in a suit approaching the microphone.

"Ladies and gentlemen, if you would, please take your seats; we'll begin the service in about five minutes."

The crowds shuffled into their chairs from all directions. People were still lined up outside to get into the building, and the main floor filled up completely. By the time everyone was seated, there were only a handful of open chairs left in the whole place.

For someone whose obituary reduced her to nothing more than a cheerleader who liked horseback riding, Julia sure had a turnout at her funeral.

When the man approached the microphone again, the room fell silent. "Good afternoon. I'd like to welcome you all to the Northridge Community Church. I'm the youth pastor here, and my name is Brian Holloway."

My eyebrows rose. I had probably known that my teacher's husband was a pastor at some point, but I hadn't ever expected to run into him, especially at his work. I had never seen Mr. Holloway before, and I was disappointed that I was meeting him for the first time in circumstances that didn't allow me to size him up.

80

"We are gathered here today to celebrate the life of Julia Davis." Brian's voice was optimistic, hopeful even. "I had the pleasure of having Julia join our youth group just a few short months ago, and I had the honor of spending some time with Julia's parents, Mr. and Mrs. Davis and Mr. and Mrs. Sweisburger, over the last few days. Together, we shared many stories about Julia—the bouncy girl she was in childhood, the sassy adolescent she became, and the beautiful, confident woman she was growing up to become."

I felt a lump form in my throat. Everything he said was in past tense.

Brian detailed some of the stories he'd been told of Julia's youth. He shared about how, as a toddler, Julia ran up and down the hallways screaming, "Uh-oh, spaghetti-Joe" at her brother to alert her parents when he was sneaking snacks out of the food pantry. He spoke of her commitment to 4-H and the equestrian program, and how she failed her driver's test three times because she kept swerving to avoid birds.

I felt like these stories brought me closer to Julia, as I was sure they were meant to do. But I was learning of them at the wrong time. I should know these things about her, but *she* should have shared them with me. We should have laughed and teased one another about things like this in the hallway at school. Each new detail I learned about Julia only made me realize what a great friend I could have had in her, what I had missed out on.

"In speaking with all of the people who loved Julia the most, I found myself asking a question that many of you are probably asking yourselves today." Brian cleared his throat and paused. "Why? Why was this vivacious girl so abruptly taken from us? How could this be God's plan for Julia?"

Micah leaned forward and placed his elbows onto his knees, listening. Westley's breathing was deep and steady, and I relied on its rhythm to calm me.

"I feel like as a pastor, I'm supposed to be able to answer these questions. But just because I have a degree in studying the Bible, it doesn't mean that I'm not still human. It's my instinct to get angry when tragedy strikes, to look for someone to blame. And when there isn't a tangible culprit to hold responsible, it's easy to want to blame God."

I saw several heads in the audience bob up and down in agreement with Pastor Brian. I wasn't sure if I agreed or not, but perhaps I hadn't had enough tragedy happen to me to have a standard by which I dealt with the pain. In my hurting, there was always a clear villain to whom to attribute credit, namely Bronwyn, so I didn't have to wonder if a higher power contributed to it.

"But, if we really consider what we know about God, then we realize that this—that death—was *not* in Julia's plan. Nor yours. Nor mine." Brian opened up a Bible and thumbed only a few pages in. "The book of Genesis tells us about the life God intended for us. In the first chapter, starting at verse twenty-six, God says, 'Let us make mankind in our image, in our likeness.'" Brian looked up from the book. "You see, starting right there on basically the first page of the Bible, we start to see the shape of God's plan for humankind—to be in his likeness."

I did my best to track with the sermon, but confusion set in immediately. Having never actually opened a Bible myself, all I knew of the book was based on television and hearsay, and most recently a pamphlet about abstinence. From this information, I had deduced that there were lots of lists of rules about what people weren't supposed to do and advice about what they were. But what Pastor Brian was reading sounded more like a story, which, according to people who believed in God, was true.

My stomach started to flutter the same way it did when I was taking a test I hadn't studied for.

"The following verses detail what was permissive to man and woman—which all sounds pretty awesome if you think about it. They are given rule over animals and free range of any produce and surrounded by the most gorgeous natural scenery imaginable. In fact, they only have one rule—one. And it's not until that rule is broken that there is death. It was through their disobedience that death entered the world."

Was Brian trying to say that the reason Julia died was because she was disobedient to God? I looked around the room to see if others shared the same concern. This seemed like a very tactless agenda to be pushing at someone's funeral.

I began to feel very warm under Westley, who was now dead weight on my shoulder. I tried to adjust him upright to sit on his own, surreptitiously taking his pulse again. I fanned myself with my hands to cool down.

Brian continued on: "So, it wasn't the original plan for us to die. Sin, sickness, sadness, death—none of that was in the blueprint for humanity. But it entered into our history and our heredities, and here we are. And if this was where the story ended, we would have a real reason to mourn this day. But the story didn't end there, just like Julia's story didn't end in a hospital bed."

A few people shouted, "Amen!" to Brian's last statement, and I felt out of place for not knowing why.

"Are you doing all right?" Micah had noticed my fidgeting. "Everything OK?"

I nodded unconvincingly.

Brian went on with his sermon. "Because of Christ, we have hope in death. We mourn selfishly, because we will miss Julia's place in our lives. But we take joy in her reunion with Jesus."

More shouts followed this statement, and there was some applause. I searched around the room, hoping to lock eyes with someone as lost as I was by all of this. Could it be that I was the only one unfamiliar with church behavior? And furthermore, since when was it selfish to mourn? What did he mean by a Jesus reunion? Was I going to have one when I died? How could I be reunited with someone I had never met?

I felt like I was hyperventilating.

Pastor Brian continued to talk for several minutes, but all I heard was the same fuzzy static that had deafened me when I first learned about Julia's death.

"What is going on with you?" Micah's voice was filled with unease. "You are drenched!"

I was aware that I was having a hot flash, but I didn't notice until Micah pointed it out that I'd sweat through my clothes.

"Let me get you guys out of here." Micah leaned forward to stand up, but I put my hand on his knee to stop him.

"Please, just help me get through this." I had no idea what I expected Micah to do, but I couldn't rely on an unconscious Westley to be my rock, and I needed help.

Micah's eyes widened when he saw the panic in mine. He quickly put his arm around me and let his hand rest on Westley's back. "Shhh," he soothed me, taking my hand. I felt my body flush again, another wave of heat washing over me—this time from discomfort at Micah's closeness.

As if in response to my guilt-ridden thoughts, Micah whispered in my ear, "It's OK, Cosette; this is why I'm here." There was conviction in his statement, which made me believe him even though I didn't understand what he meant. But Micah's comfort was a much-needed reprieve, so I surrendered to it.

"And now," Brian seemed to be transitioning out of preacher mode, a change I welcomed. "Julia's brother, Joe Davis, would like to share something with us."

I knew nothing about Julia's brother other than he'd moved to California a week after he graduated two years before. He'd been in Eastlyn's class, but they weren't in the same social circle. A thin, ruddy young man from the front row stood and ascended the short staircase to the stage. From behind a few large floral arrangements, he brandished an acoustic-electric guitar, which he plugged into a speaker. He dragged the microphone stand away from the podium and in front of a stool off to the side closest to where his sister's body lay.

Without addressing the audience, he sat down and strummed a few chords, tuning his strings. From the distance between us, it wasn't clear to me how much he resembled his sister, but he appeared to have the male version of her

84

diminutive stature. Dressed more casually than many of the other funeral attendees, he wore what I assumed to be a California hipster equivalent to funeral attire—skinny black jeans with a dress shirt and Chuck Taylors. I guessed that when someone's younger sister died under such tragic circumstances, they were exempt from traditional church dress codes.

Joe cleared his throat into the mic. "This is for you, Jules," he said, and began to play a song for his sister.

Joe's voice was smooth and poetic, and the lyrics he sang pierced my heart. I could swallow past the lump in my throat no longer. Boxes of Kleenex had been scattered around underneath chairs for the occasion, and Micah handed me tissues just as the first of my tears spilled onto my cheeks.

With the beginning of the first verse, the lights dimmed in the church. Upon two projection screens, a picture of a baby appeared—Julia, presumably, propped up by her mother's arms, sitting in the lap of toddler Joe. This image faded into another of a chubby, curly-haired little girl on a tricycle.

I buried my face into my tissue, now sobbing. Micah squeezed my hand and stroked my hair. I realized that I never would have made it through the service being the strong one for Westley. I was glad he had taken the pills and that he was spared from this. And I was equally glad that though I had to endure this sadness, Micah was there to be the strong one for me.

More pictures followed, one fading into the next. Julia's life was on display before us, like the montage on a television show when a character is written off.

When the girl in the pictures reached high school age, I had real-life memory to tie to her photographs. Julia at the freshman formal, Julia and the cheerleaders at football games, Julia sitting on the hood of her yellow Volkswagen, Julia and Patrick sticking their tongues out at the camera.

These snapshots of Julia were parallels of my own life. I had been at the freshman formal and the football games.

Westley and I had countless pictures of ourselves making ridiculous faces at one another.

A familiar photograph appeared on the screen—the couples' shot of the winter formal dance with Julia in her pink silk gown and Westley and me beside her.

My tears were unstoppable.

When the music died, the sounds of muffled crying and sniffling filled its absence. As Pastor Brian reemerged at his podium, it was obvious he was also choked up by Joe's tribute.

"I had ideas of how I wanted to end this service, but as I was listening and watching Joe honor his sister, God laid something new on my heart."

These words were lost on me, and I didn't care. I was still trying to regain composure, and it didn't matter to me if I even heard anything more Brian had to say.

"In this time of grief, I encourage you all to reflect upon your legacies. Julia's death is heartrending, but it is not in vain. We can take solace in Paul's letter to the Romans where he says that all things can work for good when we love and trust God. So many of us here have been changed for the better by Julia's life, and all of us here have the opportunity to change for the better because of her death. This one girl's life has the potential to be a catalyst for a better world for generations to come, if we choose for it to."

Westley shifted and folded his arms across his chest. I was grateful for his movement because so much time had lapsed since I had last taken his pulse, and I'd forgotten I was supposed to be monitoring him.

The pastor dismissed the service, announcing that Julia would be laid to rest in a private ceremony for family only. I emptied the box of Kleenex attempting to mop up the mess on my face. Micah gave my shoulders a squeeze, and then he scooted away from me. He leaned over to Westley and lifted his sunglasses. He was still asleep.

"I'll be right back," Micah announced. "Don't go anywhere."

He disappeared into the throngs of funeral guests slowly exiting the room. I took the opportunity to rouse Westley.

Gently, I shook his shoulders. "Babe, you gotta get up. We're gonna see your parents."

He was out. I searched the crowd for any member of the Greene family, hoping to spy Southeby or Eastlyn first so one of them could help me come up with a way to explain Westley's drug-induced stupor that wouldn't end with his parents checking him into a rehab clinic.

Before I could locate any of West's family members, Micah returned.

"So, I am going to drive you two back to Westley's after he sobers up," he informed me. "I found Eastlyn and explained what was going on, and she's going to cover for him. I thought it might be better if his parents didn't know about this."

"That was incredibly thoughtful of you," I answered, both relieved and further perplexed by Micah's kindness to us, but I decided at this point just to accept all the consideration without questioning it.

We waited until the crowd had thinned significantly before attempting to make our exit. Micah had secured a parking space in the lot at the church before it had filled up, so we didn't have to deal with the shuttle or the walk back to the RV plant.

What we did have was the task of lugging about a hundred and eighty pounds of nearly dead weight through the church ahead of us.

Fortunately, Micah was stronger than he appeared, and he was able to bear the bulk of Westley's weight as we awkwardly lumbered out the back of the sanctuary and through a side door of the building. We'd each slung one of West's arms over our shoulders so that we could drag him between us, but with the height difference among the three of us, it was impossible to smoothly transition the entire distance. Once outside, Micah threw Westley over his shoulder and carried him the rest of the way.

"Wow," I couldn't help but comment. "I haven't seen anyone lift Westley since he was eleven years old, and he and his dad would wrestle."

Micah smiled at the visual. "'He ain't heavy...'"

He handed me a set of keys, and I manually unlocked the door of an older-model pickup truck. I watched as he buckled Westley into the cramped jump seat. He then walked around to the passenger side of the truck and opened the door for me. "After you," he said as he helped me up into the high cab.

I glanced in the backseat and saw Westley attempting to stretch out in the confined space. Micah hopped into the driver's seat and slid our bench seat forward as far as it would go to give Westley more room.

This small gesture added to the debt of gratitude I already felt like I owed Micah. "I don't even know where to start thanking you for everything you've been doing." My voice was still crackly from crying so much at the funeral.

"I told you, Cosette..." Micah smiled again. "That's what I'm here for."

This answer confused me as it had the first time he'd given it, and now that we were alone, I felt that I could ask him about it. "I don't think I get what you mean by that," I started slowly, not wanting to seem ungrateful. "But we don't really know each other well—we just met, actually. And you are being so nice to us. I guess I'm just not used to it."

Micah pulled out of the church parking lot and onto the main road headed toward the highway. "Well that's pretty sad, if you ask me. I mean, people should be nice to you guys. You are both easily likeable people. But especially right now—you deserve a lot of extra 'niceness.'"

Micah made sense, and I was embarrassed for questioning him. Of course it was logical that people, even those we didn't know well, would want to help us in the wake of Julia's death. I was learning that everyone dealt with this tragedy in different ways—maybe Micah's grief was lightened by helping us make it through ours. West's perspective on the situation would definitely be unique, and the more help I had in getting him through this time—however long it would be—the better.

"So, I have to figure that Westley's going to be out for a while," Micah said, changing subjects. "Where should we go?"

I hadn't considered this. "We can go to my house," I offered hesitantly, wondering how Bronwyn would react if I brought Westley home in his current condition.

"You think that would be OK with your da—" Micah was cut off by a loud popping sound from under the truck's hood, followed by some metal-on-metal grinding noises.

Micah gripped the wheel with a steady hand and used his other to pin me back to my seat as he guided the truck to the side of the road.

We lurched forward before I heard the engine die. Micah brought us to a stop under the overpass, where we'd been about to merge onto the highway.

"What happened?" I asked, my heart racing. Convinced we weren't in immediate danger by the read I got from Micah's body language, I tried to calm myself down.

"I don't know," he responded, releasing the latch to the truck hood with a pull lever under the dash. "Lemme take a look. Be right back." He hopped down from the cab and went to lift the hood. He peeked inside for a moment, and then, within seconds, he returned. "All right, so I have no idea. I'm terrible with cars. If I could borrow your phone, I'll make a call, and we'll figure this out."

I heaved a frustrated sigh. Car trouble was not what we needed right now.

I glanced again back at Westley, wondering how much explaining we'd have to do to a tow-truck driver for him not to call the cops. Could this day get any harder?

Micah held my phone in his hand as if he'd never seen one before. After poking it awkwardly a few times, he handed it back to me. "Any chance you could look up a mechanic for me?"

It was then that we heard a knock on the driver's-side window.

We turned in startled unison to see an older man in a brown Carhartt jacket staring in at us from the outside. Micah looked back at me, shrugged, and then manually cranked down the window a few inches.

"OK, I'm not crazy," the man began, which made me instantly assume that he was. I slowly moved my hand into my purse for the pepper spray that Westley insisted I carry. "But did you all just break a belt?"

"Hmm," Micah began, not nearly as surprised by this stranger and his question as I was. "I don't know, but my guess is that if you are here asking me this, then the answer is yes."

"Mind if I take a look?" The man pulled out a red handkerchief from his pocket and wiped his nose.

"Be my guest," Micah offered and started to open his door. I grabbed his jacket sleeve instinctively.

"What are you doing?" I demanded. "Do you know him?"

"Just trust me, OK?" He jumped down from the cab to peer under the hood with the strange man. "And pay attention."

I locked both of our doors, dialed 911 on my phone, and poised my finger over the send button. I *had* trusted Micah until this lapse in judgment. I should have taken my chances with the Greenes—we would have at least had a safer ride home, even if it meant a pit stop for Westley to attend an NA meeting.

The hood of the truck obstructed my view of Micah and the man, and the cars speeding by us in an endless line prevented me from hearing them too.

After several long minutes, Micah returned to the cab, smiling.

"What is happening?" I demanded, unable to hide my frustration.

"Dave is fixing our accessory belt," Micah informed me happily.

"What? How?" I was tired of being confused by Micah and annoyed by his happiness.

"Take a look." He pointed, and I saw that the vehicle behind us was a white delivery van. "We're being rescued by Dave from Ironwood Auto Supply." He handed me a business card Dave had apparently given him, and then removed his suit jacket and used it as a blanket to cover me. "Sit tight." Before I could demand further explanation, he was gone again, no doubt assisting the stranger with the replacement of the accessory belt.

After the longest twenty minutes of my life, the truck hood slammed shut, and I could see Micah and Dave laughing together. Dave wiped his greasy hands on a faded, terry-cloth towel before shaking Micah's. Then he looked through the windshield, meeting my eyes. He gave me a wink and tipped the bill of his baseball cap. I instantly looked away.

Micah knocked on the hood to get my attention back and motioned for me to turn the key in the ignition. When I did, the truck started right up. Dave slapped Micah on the back with a grin, and the two congratulated one another. His arm lingered around Micah's shoulders, and I saw the two make a quick verbal exchange before their heads bowed and eyes closed.

What the heck? Did Micah have to pray with everyone he met? I had never heard of car repair being an occasion for prayer.

Dave and Micah exchanged good-byes, and both returned to their vehicles. Micah grinned at me sheepishly.

"I'm sorry for the unexpected stop," he apologized. "Now, where did we decide we were going?"

"You have got to be kidding me!" My voice was louder than even I had meant it to be, and both Micah and Westley flinched. I continued on in a lower register. "What just happened?"

"Dave saw us on the side of the road and had a feeling he could help us out." He shrugged. "Turns out, he was in the right place at the right time. Or else we were, depending on how you look at it."

This explanation was not as specific as I wanted it to be. In fact, if I really thought about it, that statement was true about Micah in general.

"Seems like more than a coincidence to me," I said, pushing for information I felt was being withheld.

Micah raised an eyebrow at me. "That's because it is, Cosette." He swept his bangs back away from his eyes with a dirty hand. "Pay attention."

I didn't want to pay attention. I wanted answers, easy ones that would require no energy on my part to understand. I'd been through enough in the past few days.

To demonstrate how upset I was to Micah, I shut my eyes to ignore him. This would have been a much more effective illustration of protest had I not fallen asleep halfway home.

◆◆◆

I was too groggy to continue where I'd left off with Micah when he woke me in my driveway. It wasn't even six o'clock, but the night sky had settled, making it seem much later. Together, we were able to rouse Westley enough for him to walk on his own.

"Hey, man," Westley addressed Micah, still not quite himself. "I'm guessing I owe you one after today. I don't know what all you did, but thanks."

"No worries, bro." Micah hugged Westley with both arms, a gesture I was sure would have weirded Westley out had he been sober.

"Yes, thanks again," I offered halfheartedly. My appreciation for Micah had lessened as the number of unanswered questions I had about him grew.

Micah pulled out of the driveway, and I walked Westley up to my room. We arrived there safely under the radar of anyone in the house, and because my car had been left at the Greenes, I hoped we'd get away with going unnoticed until morning.

West stumbled over to my bed and fell face first onto my comforter.

92

"So on a scale of one to ten, how out of it are you still?" I asked him as I pulled my now-blackened roses out of their vases. I shoved them into a garbage bag, tied it up, and shut the rotten smell in the bathroom.

"Out of it enough to sleep until morning, that's for sure," Westley answered me with a yawn.

"Deal." I pulled off my heels and crawled in beside him, not bothering to turn down the covers. I tugged off his coat, sent a text to Eastlyn regarding our change of plans for the night, and switched off the lamp.

"Good night," we said together, and within moments, we were both asleep again.

CHAPTER 13

I awoke to the sound of my shower running. A glance at my darkened window told me it was early, and my wall clock confirmed it—five thirty in the morning.

Considering Westley had been asleep for fifteen hours, I wasn't surprised he was up. Even though I'd had eleven myself, I would have been happy with a few more hours of unconscious, not-thinking-about-Julia-or-Micah time.

But alas, memories from the previous day were too fresh to put aside once they popped into my mind. Even if Westley offered me a few more hours of rest, it would be pointless to attempt them.

I undressed from my rumpled funeral clothes and slid into a warm plush robe, awaiting my turn in the shower. I had avoided mirrors since the funeral, and I wasn't about to look at myself in one again until I cleaned up.

The shower ran for another ten minutes before I decided to check on Westley. Though I doubted the drugs were still in his system, I began to wonder if they had caused him to somehow fall asleep midshower.

I knocked on the door with the back of my hand. "West?" I called, only loud enough to be heard over the water and—I hoped—not by anyone else in the house.

When he didn't answer, I opened the door.

Thick steam clouds escaped the bathroom. I bent down to pick up West's wadded-up suit pants and jacket and hung them on the towel rack. "Westley?" I called again, and this time, I heard a hiccupping from inside the shower.

I pulled the shower curtain back far enough to poke my head through.

What I saw broke my heart.

Westley sat on the floor of the bathtub, hugging his knees and rocking back and forth. His eyes were so bloodshot that I wondered if they were actually bleeding.

I hid my shock as best I could and approached him gently. "Hey, babe. Can I help you up?" I reached around him and turned the water off.

He hiccupped again, and I saw tears spill over onto his cheeks.

In all the time I'd known Westley, I'd only seen him cry once and it was because he had made an error in a baseball game that ended Camden's season. He was a wreck about it for a few days after it happened.

I reached for his hand, but instead of me pulling him up, he drew me into the tub with him. Wrapping both of his arms around my back, he began to sob.

I didn't talk. I just stroked his wet hair and kissed his forehead.

My chest ached inside. I was helpless. More than he ever had, Westley needed me for advice and comfort, and I had nothing to offer him.

He cried for what felt like hours, but it was still dark outside when he settled down and redressed in his suit.

"I'm going to have Southeby come get me," Westley informed me as he texted his brother. "I'll come back for you later. I need to get my shit together." He avoided my eyes.

"But Westley, I'm here for you—" Westley raised his hand to silence me.

"That's not your job." West's brother immediately responded to his text that he was on his way. Neither of us said anything more until his phone vibrated again ten minutes later indicating that Southeby had arrived.

"I will call you before I come back. I love you." He kissed me on the cheek, and I walked him to the front door.

Southeby, still six months shy of his driver's license, hopped out of the Yukon to offer the keys to his brother for the drive back. Westley grabbed them from his hands without looking at him. Southeby turned around to face the house. He made eye contact with me, pointed to his brother, and mouthed, "He OK?"

I pushed out my lower lip and shook my head no.

"I'm sorry," he mouthed back to me, and then disappeared into the passenger's seat.

As I made my way back up to my bedroom, I couldn't shake the image of Westley in the shower. Each time I thought of it, my heart broke into smaller pieces.

It was only eight o'clock by the time I'd showered and straightened up my room, but by then, the rest of the house was starting to come alive. I heard Ginger giggling from down in the kitchen, and it beckoned to me like a siren.

Feeling brave—or maybe too tired to walk on eggshells for Bronwyn—I went down to the kitchen and beelined for her high chair.

"Coco!" she squealed with delight, and I was so happy to see her that I had to blink back tears.

Ginger held her arms out to me, and I unbuckled her and picked her up. I could feel Bronwyn's icy stare on my back, but she bit her tongue.

My niece grabbed my cheeks with both of her hands and squeezed them. I kissed her on the nose and forehead and breathed in her hair. Her affection was medicine to me.

"Please tell me you at least brushed your teeth before you made out with my daughter." Bronwyn's willpower was short-lived. "I don't want Westley germs all up in her."

"Westley's here?" Grandma asked as she came around the corner. "I thought you two usually spent Christmas Eve at his house?"

I paused. I had completely forgotten about Christmas. I suddenly remembered the pile of unwrapped gifts under my bed. A tiny twinge of excitement flickered within me. "I'm going over later."

Perhaps Christmas would help to snap Westley back to his old self. I was sure he was going to love my gift to him. And he was probably excited to give me what—

I stopped, remembering my conversation with Julia about Westley's Christmas present to me. I had been avoiding thinking about that conversation because I didn't want to guess my gift accidentally. Now I had new reason to circumvent those thoughts. That was the last time I would ever talk to Julia.

My flicker extinguished.

"How was the service, dear?" my grandmother asked.

"Lots of people show up?"

I wasn't ready to relive the previous day for the sake of small talk. "Over a thousand, I guess. Are we still exchanging gifts in the morning? I don't want to miss seeing Ginger open her presents."

"A thousand people came? That's ridiculous," Bronwyn commented. "I swear, anytime anyone dies around here, it's front-page news and all of a sudden, the dead person has a million best friends. I'm guessing that a thousand people didn't show up to her last birthday party."

"You go to a funeral to show support for the family, Bronwyn," my grandmother responded in a tone that showed she thought Bronwyn was being ignorant and not purposefully mean.

I knew better. "It was a nice service, I guess. Her brother sang a song. Everyone cried. The end."

"Good, then maybe people can stop talking about her. I'm so sick of hearing about Julia Davis everywhere I go." Bronwyn said Julia's name as if the words weren't worth her breath. "Everyone talks about her like she was some sort of saint. I remember her from when I was in high school. I always thought she was a little bitchy."

"Shut the hell up, Bronwyn!" The words were out of my mouth before I even registered the thought.

My sister stared daggers into me. She stomped over and snatched Ginger from my arms. "Too bad it was Julia who died and not you. I'd take 'a little bitchy' over a worthless pile of shit like you any day," she spat her words at me.

I hadn't realized my dad was in the room until his face appeared from behind his newspaper at the kitchen table. "It's Christmas!" he barked, giving us both a dirty look.

Ginger looked back and forth to everyone in the room, her lower lip quivering. Seconds later, she began to wail, frightened by all the yelling. I felt instantly ashamed for my part in her sadness.

"Thanks a lot, Cosette. Now look what you did," Bronwyn seethed under her breath and out of earshot of my dad. "Merry Christmas, whore."

◆◆◆

Determined to reignite some excitement about the holidays, I spent the next hour in my room wrapping gifts.

But instead of making me feel more festive, I somehow felt emptier. The gifts I'd purchased for my family were so generic that I felt embarrassed to be giving them as presents.

I'd been a member of this family for eighteen years, and what I knew about my own father could be summed up in a paragraph. I'd bought him the absolute most cliché Christmas present imaginable—a tie.

My grandmother had been my primary caregiver since I was three, and I'd bought her a teakettle. I had no idea if she even drank tea.

Bronwyn was going to end up with an empty photo album.

I contrasted this with Westley's gift.

Was this normal? Were most teenage girls this disconnected from their families? I knew what West and I had was unique, but he was really the only person on the planet with whom I had a relationship that was more than skin-deep.

I thought of Joe Davis singing to his sister. The oodles of pictures of their family on vacations and at birthday parties.

I thought of the thousand people at Julia's funeral.

I couldn't bring myself to picture what the attendance of my own might be like. For sure, there would be no tribute from *my* sibling—if she would come at all.

It was these visions—not ones of sugarplums—that were dancing in my head when the doorbell rang.

Westley hadn't used the doorbell since we were thirteen, and no one else ever came over to the house, so I assumed it was the mailman with a package or someone with the wrong address until I heard a knock at my bedroom door.

"Since when do you ring doorbells and knock, West—" I turned to the doorway and jumped in surprise. "Micah? What are you doing here?"

"I'm sorry; should I not have come? I just wanted to check on you guys." Micah looked hurt. He took a step back into the hallway.

"No, it's fine." I hadn't meant to react so strongly. "I mean, that's really nice of you."

I waved him into my room and cleared off a chair for him to sit in. I couldn't remember the last time there'd been someone in my room other than Westley. I did a quick scan to make sure I didn't have a stray bra or tampon lying about.

"I also wanted to apologize," Micah began as he sat. "I didn't offer much of an explanation about yesterday, and I could tell that bothered you."

"Well..." I began, still not feeling like dredging up anything from the day before. "I mean, how much can you explain about something strange like that? It's not like you planned on breaking a belt or that guy showing up. It was just one of those weird things that happen." I waved my hand to dismiss the apology and end the conversation.

Micah paused a moment. "There's a lot I could have explained about it, actually. I just didn't know if you were really willing to hear about it."

I threw the stray scraps of wrapping paper into my bathroom garbage and wondered whether or not I should ask what he meant. But when I turned back around to face him, he wasn't waiting for me to answer. Instead, he was looking at my wall of Westley.

"You guys sure go to a lot of dances," he said with a chuckle. "How old are you two here, like eight?" He pointed to one of our earliest pictures where Westley stood slightly shorter than me in my half-inch heels.

"Sixth grade." I remembered that night well. It had been the first time a boy had brought me flowers. I was pretty sure I still had a few petals from the bouquet pressed in a book somewhere.

Micah went on to ask more questions about our pictures, and after the past few days, it felt nice to be able to reminisce about happier times. He was a good listener, and beyond that he seemed really interested in what I was saying. But after several minutes of rambling about junior prom, it occurred to me that perhaps he was just being polite. "I'm sorry—you probably have better things to be doing on Christmas Eve than listening to me like this."

His eyes widened. "Oh, no, Cosette. I'm sorry if I gave you that impression. I like hearing about you guys. You and Westley have something special; I can tell."

"Yeah, I believe that too." As much as I enjoyed Micah's attention, I was beginning to feel selfish for monopolizing the conversation. "What about you? Have anything special with anyone?" I hoped the answer to this was yes because it would help to eliminate some of the discomfort I had around him if I had proof for Westley that Micah wasn't interested in me.

He half-smiled. "The answer to that is part of a much bigger story. The one about that 'big choice' I told you about. Why don't we save it for when we complete our new English assignment."

It wasn't surprising that Micah had evaded my question. "It's a deal," I said.

He picked his jacket up off the chair and slipped an arm through the sleeve. "And maybe we'll talk about Dave too."

I laughed. "Why? Are strange, roadside mechanics a different kind of 'big choice' you made?"

Micah finished pulling on his coat and gave me a look. "In a lot of ways, yes."

"OK..." I looked at him skeptically. "Do you know if you confuse everyone else as much as you do me, or am I just special in that way?"

His half smile turned whole. "I don't talk to many people, but I do think you're special. Trust me."

"I'm trying."

"That's all I'm asking," Micah replied. "Oh, and one more thing." He pulled back his coat, revealing a package wrapped in green paper and a red bow. "This is for you. Merry Christmas." He held out the gift to me.

I slowly extended my hand to accept it, puzzled. "You didn't have to do that," I started and realized how ungrateful I sounded. "But thank you." My cheeks started to burn. "Um, I don't have anything for—"

"No worries," he interrupted. "I'll let you buy my coffee when we hang out."

I smiled, the thoughtfulness of his gesture sinking in. "OK," I responded as Micah walked toward my bedroom door.

"Merry Christmas, Cosette!" I heard him descend the stairs and let himself out of the house.

I removed the wrapping paper from Micah's gift to find a leather-bound book with a cross on the front and the words *Holy Bible* carved in it. Pulling back the cover, I read the inscription he'd written:

> *Cosette,*
> *I'm pretty sure that no spiders die in this one.*
> *Love,*
> *Micah Quinn*

I laughed out loud. It felt good after I'd spent so much of the last few days crying.

I delicately flipped through the book. The pages were as thin as a dictionary's, and the layout suggested it was more of a reference guide than storybook. There were colored maps, sidebars, graphs, and glossaries, and as I skimmed through, I saw many words I would never figure out how to pronounce.

Had this gift been from anyone else, it might have made me angry. I would have seen it as I did the pamphlet—a backhanded comment about how I'd been living my life. An assumption that I was lacking something that person had the answer to. Condescension. Condemnation. Judgment.

But from Micah, I didn't feel any of those things. Instead, the gesture was sweet.

As was all he'd done for Westley and me yesterday. And the way he had treated me in class the day Julia died.

And that was when I realized I did trust Micah. Though I didn't know a lot about him, from what he *had* showed me, he was proving himself a genuine friend.

And though I doubted I would spend much time reading the book, I felt grateful that he cared enough to share something with me that was very important to him.

I placed his thoughtful gift on my nightstand and gathered my thoughtless ones to put underneath the Christmas tree downstairs.

CHAPTER 14

My text from Westley came through just minutes before Eastlyn pulled up in my driveway.

Eastlyn is coming to get you.

"Barbie's here!" Bronwyn announced her arrival unnecessarily loudly so that both Eastlyn and I would hear her.

I opened the door and was greeted with a long hug.

"How are you doing, Cosi?" Eastlyn held onto my shoulders with both hand but pulled back to look me in the eyes when she asked her question.

Beautiful Eastlyn, so caring, so nurturing. Westley was incredibly lucky to have her as a sister.

Touched by her earnestness, I felt my eyes brim with tears. Noticing right away and wanting to spare me from a potential scene in front of my family, she suggested we go to my room.

For the second time that day, I scanned my bedroom for embarrassing contraband—which in front of Eastlyn would have been more along the lines of empty candy-bar wrappers and acne cream, proof that I wasn't as perfect as she was.

Once behind closed doors, I allowed my tears to flow. But with an ocean of emotion to cry out and half an hour before I was supposed to be at the Greenes', the tears I was able to get out in the five minutes I had before I needed to get ready did little to alleviate my sorrow.

"How's West?" I asked Eastlyn after I'd calmed down.

Eastlyn chose her words carefully. "Quiet...sad...not himself."

I frowned.

"Try not to worry," she encouraged, "because while this is probably going to suck for a long time, you guys will get through this together. Just be as strong as you can for him. Or as strong as he'll let you." She nudged me on the shoulder with a smile. Apart from myself, Eastlyn knew Westley better than anyone, and I tried to take comfort in her optimism.

She made sense, after all. If Westley had experienced what he had and not been devastated, that would have been more worrisome. What he saw would have been traumatic for anyone. He needed to grieve at his own pace, on his own terms. I would just have to be flexible and supportive.

Eastlyn mothered me a little more before helping me choose my outfit for the evening, applying my makeup for me, and fixing my hair in an updo.

When she finished, I timidly faced my reflection. I was gun-shy to look after all the times that week when the girl staring back had been too puffy eyed and tearstained for me to recognize.

But Eastlyn had worked magic. She minimized the circles under my eyes and tinged my cheeks with just enough pink to mask my previously sallow complexion. Then, she forced me to model several outfits for her before she chose what she called, "the one," accessorized me, and stood me in front of the mirror.

I smiled at my reflection.

"You look beautiful." Eastlyn stepped back to admire her work. "Not that you needed my help."

I hugged her again. For the first time in a long while, I felt beautiful. "Thank you."

I put on a coat and grabbed Westley's gift before Eastlyn and I headed down the stairs together.

◆ ◆ ◆

Christmastime with the Greenes was an elaborate but classy affair, and I was counting on another picture-perfect holiday evening to bring Westley out of his despair—if only for a few hours.

But when we pulled into their driveway, I noticed right away a difference that reduced my hopes.

"Where is everyone?" I asked sorrowfully, pointing to the empty driveway that should have been full of the cars belonging to aunts and uncles and cousins. The Greenes always hosted Christmas Eve, and it was always well attended.

"Our meal got moved to Uncle Don and Aunt Kathy's," Eastlyn explained. "Mom dropped off all the food this morning. We've all been trying to play Westley's needs by ear. She didn't want to be distracted all day in case he needed her."

I didn't ask whether or not Westley and I would be attending the meal at his uncle's house, because I guessed that also would depend on his mood.

I followed Eastlyn up the winding sidewalk to the front entrance of the Greene home. A cheerful wreath adorned with red berry clusters greeted us before we pushed opened the door.

Eastlyn stopped in her tracks and turned around to face me. "I feel like I need to say something to you."

I grew instantly concerned. "What's wrong?"

She shook her head. "Nothing's really wrong...I just...How do you do it?"

Had I missed something? "Do...what exactly?"

"You and Westley," she clarified. "How have you guys stayed together so long?" Eastlyn's eyes reflected the same sincere curiosity as was evident in the tone of her question.

"Oh." Both the nature and timing of her asking this struck me as odd. Westley had mentioned that Eastlyn coveted what we had, but she and I had never really discussed my relationship with her brother. I couldn't figure out what had brought it up at this particular minute. "Um, I don't know, really." I had never dissected my relationship with Westley before to know *why* it worked; I just knew that it *did*. "I think we just have a unique compatibility."

"Like soul mates."

I cringed a bit at her phrasing, recalling my conversation with Micah in English class. "Well, kinda. I mean, it's not like the universe is forcing us to be together or anything."

"But would you feel complete without him?"

"Well, no."

"So then, you *need* him."

I felt slightly on the spot. This interrogation had come out of nowhere, and I was so distracted in trying to figure out where it was leading that I couldn't concentrate on answering her fully. "Well, yeah."

"I don't have that," she stated matter-of-factly. "And people keep telling me that it's because I haven't met the right guy. But I don't think that's it. I really just think I don't *need* anyone. I'm complete without a guy."

"Oh." I was listening to Eastlyn and wondering if this was yet another way she was superior to me. I pictured her clearing some space on her trophy wall for a new award—a plaque given out only to women who were fulfilled without men in their lives. "Good...for...you?" My remark was intended to be encouraging to her, though I was feeling completely self-conscious.

"Oh, Cosette!" Eastlyn's tone was apologetic. "I'm not being clear here. What I'm saying is that I am happy for you. I see what you and Westley have, and it makes me thrilled that my little brother has this amazing partner who loves him so much. I don't know what that's like, but I imagine it's wonderful."

My spirits lifted back up. "Thanks. It is."

She hugged me to show she truly had meant no condescension. "I want you guys to be together forever."

I smiled. "Me too."

She ended our embrace, grinning her dazzling smile.

Eastlyn turned away from me again and used her key to unlock the front door. She let me go in first and then, to my surprise, shut the door behind me without entering it herself.

"Hey—" I started and then stopped. My senses immediately heightened that something was going on—something...planned. I surveyed the scene in front of me for clues as to why I'd been abandoned.

Northrop, the Greene family Labrador, was lying at the bottom of the staircase, and he slowly rose and came to greet me. I scratched behind his ear, and he licked my cold knuckles warm again. "Hey, boy," I whispered to him. "Do *you* know what's happening?" I asked, looking around the house.

Softly in the background, I could hear gentle orchestra renditions of Christmas carols. The foyer was dark, absent any sunlight from the window wall now that dusk had arrived, and the only light I could see in the house was flickering from around the corner in the Greenes' great room. Sensing I had realized the presence of something more important than he was, Northrop left me. I followed the lights, butterflies hatching in swarms in my stomach.

"Westley?" I called out. "Hello?" As my steps brought me farther inside the house and closer to the music and candlelight, my knees began to shake.

I remembered Julia teasing that no one was going to be surprised by what West was going to give me for Christmas.

I had guessed it, I realized. Or at least, I had secretly hoped that *this* was what was going to happen. But I wouldn't allow myself to accept it as a rational possibility; after all, I was eighteen, and it didn't make sense. We had graduation and college ahead of us before we could take the next step, didn't we?

The butterflies escaped my stomach, fluttered through each appendage, and then to my fingers and toes—rendering me almost paralyzed by the time I reached the Christmas tree where Westley stood, as handsome as ever.

All around the room, the candescence of dozens of candles cast dancing shadows on the walls, encircling us.

Westley smiled at me and took my hand. Then, he cleared his throat. "First of all, I want to apologize for this morning." He looked away from me, shaking his head. "I'm going to get through this, Cosette. I'm not going to let this affect us." There was a reemergence of familiar strength in Westley's tone.

I smiled and nodded, my vision already blurring through tears.

"I also want you to know these weren't the conditions under which I'd always imagined asking you this," he continued, his voice confident. "But this isn't some sort of impulse decision. In fact, it doesn't even feel like a decision. It feels like a formality. We've been together forever...since the fifth grade. It's time we made it official."

Westley let go of my right hand. He reached with his into his pocket and genuflected down onto one knee in a single motion. He held both of my hands in one of his, and I was unable to tell which of us—or whether it was both of us—trembled.

"Marry me, Cosette."

The flames continued to flicker and jump all around us like frenzied, expectant spectators.

Westley presented me with a black velvet box, and my heart both stopped and started at the same time.

I began to cry for what seemed like the millionth time that week. But these tears that fell were a very different kind than any of the others had been—they were tears of pure joy.

"Yes," I whispered, barely able to utter the word.

Westley opened the box and removed the ring. He slid the band onto my finger. I threw my arms around him—my fiancé. My husband-to-be. We were engaged.

"Well, what do you think?" Westley asked, and lifted my hand into the light so we could admire my ring together.

We'd never talked about engagement rings. We'd never seriously even discussed engagement apart from his fake proposal. Yet, the ring he'd chosen for me was perfect.

He held out my hand, maneuvering the ring so the candlelight could catch the stones—three of them—a round, emerald center stone with oval diamonds on either side.

"I love it," I finally formed the words.

"Green looks good on you, Greene," Westley replied, satisfied.

And I agreed.

CHAPTER 15

The rest of the night was a dream.

We did go to Westley's aunt and uncle's home, where we enjoyed a warm reception. Eastlyn had gone ahead of us to deliver the news to her parents that she'd successfully lured me into their home for the proposal. While no one doubted what my answer would be, Westley's entire family—a larger crowd than usually gathered for Christmas Eve—waited for me to flash the ring before they erupted into cheers.

Twenty-four hours prior to this celebration had been so unrecognizably different from these moments that I wondered if any of it had been real. How easy amid questions about the future it was to ignore the past week.

"Have you set a date?"

"Do you think you'll wait until after college before getting married?"

"Where do you want to honeymoon?"

We didn't know even one answer, but each question asked thrilled me with new possibility about the future.

No one uttered a word about Julia Davis's death and Westley's hospitalization, probably under the advisement of Mr. Greene, who despite his satisfaction about his son's news, seemed uneasy. He kept both Westley and me under careful watch the entire night.

When center stage finally shifted from Westley and me back to the holiday, gifts were exchanged, and I received another surprise from the Greene family: my wedding dress.

Eastlyn handed me a voucher to a local boutique where, as stated in the fine print, I could select any gown of my choice.

I was overwhelmed. "I can't let you guys—" I began, but was interrupted by my own tears. Westley was as surprised as I was. He ran over to hug each member of his family, and I was right behind him.

"You know we are going to start looking this week while I'm home," Eastlyn whispered to me during our embrace. "It doesn't matter if you guys wait until you are forty to get married, we begin the hunt for the perfect dress now."

Mr. and Mrs. Greene each hugged me and kissed my cheeks.

"You've been a part of this family for a long time, Cosette," Mr. Greene said with a smile. "Mom and I are very excited for you and West. We love you two."

As I hugged my future in-laws, my heart soared.

I felt like I was in a fairy tale. That "happily ever after" was mine, and it was just beginning.

We stayed at the party until midnight. It was then that I remembered Westley's gift, which I'd left beside the passenger seat of the Yukon. West used his key to the SUV to unlock and retrieve the gift, and then we sat in his car while he opened it.

"I love it, Cosi," he said, holding it up against his frame. "Thank you." He leaned in for a kiss.

"It seems kind of disappointing after my gift," I said sheepishly, holding my hand up to the dome light. "And sorta cheap." As I said those last words, it occurred to me that I had no idea how Westley had paid for my ring. I couldn't have imagined he would have allowed his parents to pay for it, and being that he was a high school athlete and hadn't worked since summer lifeguarding, he didn't have much of an income. Judging by the size of my ring, he had to have been saving up since we started dating in the fifth grade to have afforded it.

"We aren't discussing the price of your ring," Westley said. "In fact, I wanted bigger. Eastlyn said anything larger than this would have looked tacky on your little fingers."

"Can you at least promise me that you didn't have to sell a kidney?" As much as I loved the ring, I would have felt bad wearing it had Westley gone into debt to buy it, especially with college just around the corner.

"Kidney, no. Ernie Banks rookie card, yes. And a few others, actually, but the Banks was the one that hurt the most."

My eyes widened. I had no idea who Ernie Banks was, but I did know of the particular card he spoke of. His grandfather had bequeathed him a generation of baseball cards when he died a few years before, and the Greene family regarded this particular card as some sort of heirloom. I was instantly flooded with guilt that he had sold it for my ring.

"You can't—"

"I can. I did. And I'd do it again. I'm serious, Cosette. I *would* have sold a kidney for you."

I paused for a long time, understanding the value of my ring by the sacrifice that was made for it.

As Westley drove me home, I laid my head against his shoulder. I was going to be Mrs. Westley Greene. I would take his name proudly.

Outside in the night, a light snow fell from a seemingly cloudless, starlit sky.

This was my favorite Christmas.

◆◆◆

Christmas morning with my family was a nonevent, at least by comparison to the night before.

Grandma liked her teakettle. Dad didn't *not* like his tie. Bronwyn was confused as to why I'd gotten her anything at all. Ginger enjoyed the wrapping paper more than her gifts, which was just as well because Bronwyn asked for the receipts to take them all back.

I was unsure how to break the news to my family about my engagement. I thought it better to tell each of them separately so that I could best handle their individual reactions.

My dad would assume I was pregnant, even after I assured him I wasn't. I would convince him that Westley would take care of me, that he had been for the past six years, and that the only real change to life would be that I wouldn't be living at home anymore. He'd listen to my explanation and eventually agree with me, whether he acknowledged it aloud or not. Then he'd pass me a blank check and say something like, "Weddings should be nice."

My grandma would tear up, and she'd probably rummage around in her room and give me the "something old" I would need for my big day.

Bronwyn would be angry, because Bronwyn was always angry. But I couldn't predict exactly what about my news she would choose to center her resentment on.

We'd all just finished eating breakfast together—something that happened purely by circumstance of us being in the room at the same time and not because we'd planned a meal together—when Grandma provided me with an unexpected opportunity to share my news with everyone at once.

"So, what did Westley get you for Christmas this year?" she asked politely, cleaning Ginger's sticky, cinnamon-roll-frosting fingers with a baby wipe.

"Well..." I cleared my throat to buy myself some time to think of what to say, but Dad and Bronwyn interpreted it to mean that I wanted their attention.

All eyes were on me, and I panicked. Rather than attempt to speak, I held up my left hand to allow my ring finger to make the announcement for me.

Three sets of eyes blinked at me.

"So what is that? An engagement ring?" Bronwyn spat the words out as if it were the most ridiculous notion in the world. "You guys are in high school." She poured some flavored creamer into her coffee mug and took a sip before redirecting her eyes back to the magazine opened in front of her.

My dad raised both eyebrows. "A real man asks for permission before proposing to a girl." His tone was almost condescending.

My heart fell. Had the previous week not been what it had, I was sure that Westley would have asked for my dad's permission, although I also knew that he wouldn't have felt as though he needed it.

Grandma took my hand for a closer examination of my ring. "Very pretty," she said as if I were six years old and showing her a drawing of a rainbow I'd made. "Really nice."

I stared at my family in disbelief while they resumed life, completely unaffected by my announcement.

Of all the ways I'd considered my family reacting, I had never anticipated the possibility that they wouldn't at all.

CHAPTER 16

Westley picked me up from my house at noon. I met him at the door and ushered him back outside before his presence was noticed by anyone.

"What's the hurry? I was hoping to talk to your dad," Westley protested.

I shook my head to indicate this wasn't a good idea.

His face fell. "I should have told you not to say anything until I had a chance to meet with him."

"It doesn't matter." The truth of my own words surprisingly stung.

Westley lifted my overnight bag from my hands and walked me to the car. I was going to sleep over at the Greenes' so that Eastlyn, her mother, and I could begin the search for the perfect wedding dress early the next morning. I was anxious to be in the presence of people who were excited, rather than annoyed, by our new engagement.

We spent a relaxing afternoon eating ham-sandwich leftovers and watching football. While the Greene men cheered on some blue team, Eastlyn and I sat on the floor and marked several styles of dresses in the wedding catalogues she'd sneaked into my Christmas stocking.

"So, I think with your figure, you'll want a sweetheart neckline," Eastlyn suggested, showing me a page filled with mounds of taffeta. "And we just have to make sure that whatever we pick isn't too prom-y, especially if you two decide to get married sooner than later. You'll want something sophisticated. None of this juvenile princess stuff."

I nodded in agreement with Eastlyn; she obviously knew a lot more about this than I did.

I liked getting dressed up as much as the next girl. I'd always had fun picking out my formal dresses—though those shopping trips were always solo affairs since I lacked girlfriends. The furthest I went in researching what I was going to wear to a formal was reading the sales ads to see which store had the best prices. I imagined choosing a wedding dress with Eastlyn and Mrs. Greene in tow would be a very different experience.

"Hey, I was meaning to ask," she began moments after Westley had excused himself to the bathroom—and I assumed her timing was intentional. "Who was that guy with you two at Julia's funeral?"

I felt my face pale when I realized she was asking about Micah. Perhaps the pillar I'd tried to seat us behind hadn't hidden Westley's near overdose or Micah's comforting me as I'd hoped it would.

"Who exactly?" I asked as innocently as my guilty conscience would allow.

"I think he said his name was Micah," Eastlyn went on. "He came right up to us like he knew who we were to say he was driving you home. He did seem familiar, but I couldn't place him."

"Oh," I hid my relief alongside my guilt. "He's just a guy at school. I think he's new. But he's been really nice to Westley and me. He was also in our English class along with Ju—" Westley appeared in the doorway, and I immediately changed subjects back to dresses. "What's your opinion on beading?"

I exchanged a look with Eastlyn, and the subject was dropped.

"So, West?" Eastlyn waited for her brother to peel his eyes off of the current play on the field before continuing. "When are you setting a date for this soirée?"

From above me on the couch, I felt his hand squeeze my shoulder. "As soon as she'll have me," he said. I tipped my head back to meet eyes with Westley, who winked at me. "But she's probably holding out until I've got my MD, so she can tell everyone she's marrying a doctor. And in that case, about ten years, give or take."

I laughed and shook my head.

From the adjacent sofa, Mr. and Mrs. Greene shifted uncomfortably and exchanged a frown.

For a moment, I worried that their looks to one another signified disapproval at our engagement, but then I remembered how they'd championed the previous night's celebration, barely allowing a syllable about anything but our future together to be spoken.

"Well, that gives us a lot of time to find you *the* dress then, Cosette." Eastlyn played into her brother's sarcasm. And she went back to tagging her favorite pages.

♦♦♦

West and I went to bed early, and I was glad because it gave us a chance to talk about the answers to all the questions his family had been asking us about our engagement.

And while there were lots of future plans to make, I also hoped to determine how West was doing in regards to everything that had happened before the proposal.

"I know there's a lot we need to discuss," he preempted my opening remarks, "but is there any way we can wait until tomorrow to talk about things?"

He must have been exhausted. This would be the first night he'd be sleeping without medication since Julia died, and if he was tired, I knew I should encourage him to rest.

"Of course." I smiled and kissed him good night.

I laid my head on his bare chest, and soon, his breathing slowed. I wrapped my arms around him and snuggled in closer, and the rhythm of his breath lulled me to sleep as well.

♦♦♦

"What are you doing, Westley?"

I had opened one eye to see West kneeling next to my side of the bed. He had slipped one arm under my shoulders—which was what had awakened me—and was trying to get his other under my legs.

He didn't answer. I wondered if maybe I'd annoyed him by snoring, and he was trying to turn me over to silence me.

The blankets were disabling him from getting his second arm under me for leverage. But that didn't seem to register with him, so I tugged the comforter off of me to help him to proceed with whatever he was trying to do.

As soon as I'd freed my lower half, Westley scooped me up and beelined for his bedroom door.

"Where are we going?" I asked, confused and suddenly cold without the blankets. "It's like three in the morning."

"Don't worry; you're going to be OK." Westley sounded on edge. "I'm taking you to the nurse."

"What are you talking about?" I was having a difficult time connecting all the dots, having just awoken. Was there something the matter with me I didn't know about? I wiggled all my fingers and toes and shifted my body around in Westley's arms. I felt no pain. Why did I need a nurse? Did Westley know something I didn't?

We exited West's room and started down the hall. There was a stream of soft, blue light coming in through a window at the end of the hallway—a full moon and cloudless sky made the night perfect for stargazing. Maybe Westley couldn't sleep and wanted to take me outside to watch the sky?

I was reaching for answers, I knew, but Westley wasn't offering any coherent explanation for why he was carrying me through the house over-the-threshold style, and I wasn't thinking clearly.

I turned my head away from the direction of the window and toward the stairs where Westley was leading us.

"Careful on the stairs, West," I reminded him, bracing myself for the jostling I expected as we started our descent.

But Westley took the first step harder than I expected, and my stomach dropped.

"Hey, West—" I started to complain but was cut off when West's heel slipped, and he lost his hold on me.

Westley landed with a thump and a groan, but having not been positioned for my reflexes to calculate my own fall, my face absorbed the impact of the stairs.

When I rolled to a stop at the bottom of the staircase, a warm wetness poured from my nose.

Now, I needed a nurse.

CHAPTER 17

Mrs. Greene pulled a bag of frozen vegetables from the freezer and wrapped it in a dish towel, trading me for the melted one I was using to apply pressure to my nose.

"I really wish you'd let us take you to the emergency room," Westley's mom pleaded in between sniffles. "I am so sorry. I knew that I should have said something to you this afternoon. Or at least insisted that you take the guest room."

"No hospital. I'm sure I'm going to be fine," I lied, having no idea whether or not I'd actually broken my face but certain that I didn't want to heap any more guilt from the situation onto Westley. I knew he would have a hard time forgiving himself for this as it was.

There was a skidding of furniture on the tile floor. Because my face was covered with the vegetables, I couldn't see who had pulled a chair up next to me at the kitchen table. "Westley?"

"No, sorry, it's me," Southeby responded. "West is still pretty mad at himself. He's upstairs with Dad." Then he quickly added, "How are you feeling?"

"Probably about as bad as I look," I answered, pulling the bag from my face so that he could see for himself. Gauging by Southeby's reaction, I'd guessed right.

My nose had a heartbeat.

Mrs. Greene took one look at me and started crying again.

I sighed. What a sad mess.

Westley's entire family had been awakened by me falling down the stairs, and everyone came running to us at once.

119

West had snapped out of whatever was going on with him and was trying to stop my bleeding when his parents reached us.

It didn't take them as long as it should have to assess the situation. Through the chaos, I caught them exchanging a solemn look, similar to the one I'd witnessed in the afternoon during the football game.

Once my injury—a bloodied, possibly broken nose—had been addressed and Westley removed from the situation to be calmed by his father and sister, Mrs. Greene filled me in on what I was missing.

The night before, Southeby had found his brother downstairs in the middle of the night, ransacking the den. Westley had turned the house upside down looking for something. Southeby said that he didn't seem to be awake or asleep, just...distant.

It took him about half an hour to bring Westley out of his daze, but when it was over, he told Southeby what he'd been looking for. Or rather *whom*.

Julia.

"At the hospital, they told us that Westley's behavior was going to be unpredictable for a while. He's never experienced death that up close and personal before. So we didn't have any way of feeling out how he'd cope." Mrs. Greene stroked my hand as she spoke, the only comfort she could manage being so distraught herself. "Obviously, now we know the answer to that is 'not well.'"

"But Mom, what he's doing isn't abnormal." Southeby was quick to defend his brother. "He's reenacting what happened that day at school. It's the same kinda thing that soldiers do when they come back from war, after they've seen all that awful stuff."

Mrs. Greene turned her sympathy to her youngest son. "Oh, honey, I'm not trying to begrudge your brother his right to grieve. He absolutely needs the time and space to do that." She paused to craft her next words carefully. "I just don't think he will allow himself to."

Just then, Mr. Greene and Eastlyn entered the kitchen looking worn down.

"Cosette, I'm supposed to tell you that Westley loves you, but that his 'bully' father has forbidden him from seeing you the rest of the night," Westley's father addressed me. He then turned the conversation to his wife. "I had to tell him we would renegotiate our decision to buy Cosette's wedding dress if he didn't take the rest of the night to calm down." Then, back to me again, he said, "Of course, we'd never do that, but that boy is stubborn."

I nodded, understanding Mr. Greene's methods.

"We need to talk about what needs to happen next for Westley, as a family. But not at four in the morning. Cosette, you can have your pick of bunking with Eastlyn for the night or taking the guest room. My preference is that you aren't alone with your injuries. And if you all are still up for dress shopping in the morning, I think it would be good to have some time alone with West. When you get back, we'll figure this out together."

I took his advice and went to bed with Eastlyn after swallowing some over-the-counter pain medicine to stop the pulsing in my face. I didn't bother looking in the mirror before I went to bed because I assumed I'd look worse in the morning, and I only wanted to endure the disappointment once at the peak of disfigurement.

Eastlyn locked her bedroom door and turned on a fan. I wasn't sure if this was her routine or if she was predicting further incidents with her brother that night and wanted to spare me his noise.

We were both quiet for a long time, though I knew Eastlyn wasn't asleep.

I doubted any more sleep was had anywhere in the Greene house that night.

CHAPTER 18

My swelling had gone down slightly by the time the Greene women and I left for what we told the boys was brunch at the Essenhaus—but in reality was a trip to the urgent care. Purple circles had begun forming under my eyes, a telltale sign that my nose was actually broken, and Mr. Greene strongly advised that I be seen by someone to assess the extent of the damage.

A few eyebrows rose when I detailed my story to the doctors and nurses. Falling down the stairs at my boyfriend's house and then having his mother bring me in instead of someone from my own family was suspicious—but I didn't care. I knew Westley would never lay a finger on me to hurt me intentionally, and I didn't need to defend that to anyone.

The doctor set my nose with a metal piece and some white tape, and gave me a referral to a rhinoplasty surgeon for a consultation.

I left the office looking like a hockey player after a bench fight.

When I reentered the waiting room, Eastlyn and Mrs. Greene winced in unison.

"How bad?" my future mother-in-law asked cautiously, gently touching the unbruised portion of my cheek.

"I'll probably need surgery," I confessed. "Or I could just let the cards fall as they may and have a *Phantom of the Opera*-themed wedding." I attempted a smile in hopes of relieving some of the general guilt that the Greenes all shared. If I didn't let the situation bother me, maybe we could all move on and focus on Westley.

"You know, I hear that 60 percent of brides in California get plastic surgery before their weddings." Eastlyn created a statistic to make me feel better. "Maybe this is all just a sign that you're supposed to have a destination wedding on the West Coast?"

The three of us group-hugged, which I hoped signaled an end to the morning's grief. We then piled into the Yukon and took off to find the wedding dress of my dreams.

◆◆◆

"Very Grecian," Eastlyn commented of the tenth dress I'd tried on that morning. "Love the crystal detailing."

We'd been at Stephenson's, an upscale boutique in the neighboring town of Elkhart, for an hour and a half. Eastlyn had taken over fifty pictures on her phone of me—from the chin down—in different wedding gowns.

As I modeled organza, satins, laces, and chiffons, Eastlyn and her mother made notes in a wedding planner that I'd received as a stocking stuffer in addition to the bridal magazines.

The dresses were gorgeous. And they made me feel beautiful—almost.

I loved trying on these gowns and imagining walking down the aisle toward Westley. But that was all it felt like I was doing—imagining. Pretending.

Mrs. Greene must have been able to read my expression despite the bandages. "Do you think the boys have had enough time to talk?"

I nodded, and Eastlyn promptly helped me out of the last dress.

We were all eager to get back to Westley.

Besides, I had the impression that my appearance was making the staff and fellow brides uncomfortable. Everyone there was on the newly engaged high that I had enjoyed until rolling down a flight of stairs knocked me back to reality. My face was a buzzkill; people felt forced to cast counterfeit looks of sympathy my way, and that dampened their money-spending moods. I was sure there was a collective sigh of relief from everyone inside the boutique when my party exited toward the parking lot.

◆◆◆

Mrs. Greene punched the gas pedal to force the Yukon up their driveway. New snow had fallen while we'd been out, and the roads were patchy. Typically, one of the Greene men would have already salted the driveway, but their to-do list that morning had had a more pressing chore that needed attention.

I hadn't given much thought to what Mr. Greene might hope to accomplish in talking to his oldest son. Did he think Westley needed more medication? Counseling?

Mrs. Greene finally cleared the hill, and as I unbuckled my seatbelt, my door opened.

"Get in my car," Westley ordered, not looking at me.

"Westley, come back in the house," I heard Mr. Greene's firm voice from an invisible place somewhere behind his son.

Westley didn't look at his father either. He left the door open and jogged to his Mustang, where he hopped in and revved the engine before my feet hit the pavement.

Mr. Greene and Southeby stood in front of West's car, gesturing for him to go back inside.

Westley rolled down his window. "Let's go, Cosi!"

I froze in place, unsure to whom my allegiance belonged. Obviously, Westley was upset, but was he mad enough to leave without me if I tried to get him to stay? If he did, I would spend the entire time he was away worried about him.

Unwilling to risk more time apart from him, I started toward the car.

Mr. Greene accepted my choice. "Keep him safe, Cosette."

I nodded, and West had the car in reverse before I shut the door.

By the way he peeled out of the driveway, I assumed he wasn't in the mood for conversation, so I let him drive us wherever we were going in silence. I didn't have to wonder long where we might be headed. After being on the road for only a few miles, we turned into Riverbend, a park that in nicer weather, we could have walked to.

The parking lot hadn't been plowed since park attendance was low this time of year. Westley assumed a parking space and killed the engine, staring forward. The playground before him, covered in untouched snow, had been the setting for many fond memories for us over the years. His blank, icy expression told me he was oblivious to them all at that moment.

I gave him a minute before placing my hand over his on the steering wheel. He immediately pulled away.

"I don't deserve your sympathy," he stated. "I can't even bear to look at you, knowing that I'm the one responsible for what happened." Westley's voice was shame-laden.

Although he was attempting to punish himself, his rejection stung me. "It was an accident, Westley," I tried to comfort him. "And I'm going to be fine, I promise."

More silence.

"What is happening to me?" Westley's question was rhetorical, I guessed, but I wanted to have the answer to it nonetheless. "We should be celebrating—planning our wedding." His tone changed to one full of self-loathing. "But I'm ruining that for us."

"Please stop beating yourself up," I begged, tortured by his visible pain.

"How, Cosette? What am I supposed to do to get over this? Every time I close my eyes, I see that girl—Julia. I see her body jerking around like something was trying to break out of it. I see her getting sick all over me. I hear her gasping for air. And then I see it all stop. I see her die every time I blink. Over and over again." Westley's disgust for himself changed to anger. "She only had to die once, Cosette, but I have to watch it happen a million times. Why? Why can't I get it out of my head?" Westley hit the steering wheel with his fist and elbowed his car door with such force that I thought I heard the interior paneling crack.

His outburst was unsettling. Westley was not ever a violent person. He was not acting like himself.

I pulled my body back from him toward my own door, wanting to give him the room he might need if his fit continued, but not wanting to accidentally be injured by him once more. He didn't need the compiled guilt of hurting me twice in one day.

Westley regained control and rested his chin on the steering wheel. "My dad wants to put me in therapy."

This news brightened my thoughts. "Do you think that would help?" I had been beginning to doubt the possibility of a silver lining in this situation, but any step was better than doing nothing.

"I think it would help get me rejected from any solid premed program," Westley answered flatly.

I found this response odd. "What does you talking to a counselor have to do with what you study in college?"

"Well, nothing, on the surface," he began. I could tell Westley had already explored this avenue without me. "Until they diagnose me as crazy."

I sighed. Westley was never this dramatic, and it was impeding us getting anywhere in our discussion. "You aren't crazy, West. You experienced something very traumatic. If you had the ability to watch someone die and not feel the way you are feeling, then you'd be crazy."

"That's where you are wrong, Cosette," Westley said confidently. "Because watching someone die and logically knowing it's not my fault and being able to separate myself from the guilt—that wouldn't make me crazy." He stopped struggling to finish his thought. "It would make me a good doctor."

"What are you talking about, Westley? You are going to be a fantastic doctor. Julia's death has nothing to do with that."

Westley shook his head. "Cosi, if I can't handle what happened—what I saw—and I rationally understand that I didn't cause it...what's going to happen to me when something happens and it is my fault?"

As the weight of what Westley was telling me fell on me, I slowly sank back into my seat. There was a bigger picture here than what I had seen before.

Westley had told me the story dozens of times. He had been seven years old, and Southeby was barely four. The two of them were playing superheroes in their backyard when Southeby jumped off a low tree branch in an attempt to fly. He absorbed the impact safely, landing on his feet, knees bent in a way that allowed him to drop and roll. However, as he was recovering the fall, a jagged piece of a fallen branch gashed his calf deeply.

Westley immediately took off his shirt and tied it around his brother's leg before carrying him over their acres of yard back to the porch. He called for his mother, all the while locating the first-aid kit in the garage and addressing his brother's wounds. By the time Mrs. Greene heard the cries for help, Westley had cleaned and bandaged Southeby's leg.

At the emergency room, the doctor formally stitched Southeby's wound, and he praised Westley for helping his little brother. "You are going to make a fine doctor someday," he told West. And from that day on, that was all he wanted to be.

So this wasn't only about Julia. Of course, Westley needed to grieve for her—she was his friend, and he'd had a front-row seat to her tragic death. But additionally, he was preparing himself to mourn the death of his dream.

"OK," I started. I wanted to present a commonsense argument in West's own defense. "But I would guess that even medical professionals react like this sometimes. I'll bet lots of them have gone to counseling for things they've seen."

"But I'll bet none of the medical professionals threw their fiancé down the stairs reliving the loss of a patient."

I didn't know how to argue back on this point.

"I can get through this. Please just believe in me, Cosette." For the first time since we left his house, Westley mustered the courage to look at me. His eyes were serious, determined. "I just have to do it on my own terms, in my own way. And if I talk to someone who ends up telling me I'm crazy or wanting to put me on psych meds, then I might actually lose it."

My gut told me to push forward, to beg him to see a counselor, to offer to go with him. But I couldn't. I wanted to give him what he wanted from me.

"OK."

Westley took my hands and kissed them. "Thank you, Cosette." Then he took another breath. "Oh, there's one more thing."

My anxiety doubled. "What?"

"Until this gets better..." Westley's generic use of the word *this* left me slightly confused. "No more sleepovers."

I felt my face fall. As much as I understood Westley's proposal was for my own safety, it felt like another rejection. An unjust punishment for a crime of circumstance.

"You are the crazy one if you think that I want this any more than you do." Westley gently smoothed my hair, careful always to avoid my facial injuries by a wide radius. "But Dad didn't really give me much of a choice, and I didn't really argue. I never, ever want to be the cause of even so much as a hangnail's worth of pain to you again."

I knew that Westley was right, and that I should be thanking him for putting my safety before his own desires—but the thought of sleeping alone for the unforeseeable future brought me little comfort.

Westley ended our conversation by gently kissing me on the lips.

Though we'd stopped talking, our minds were still processing all we'd discussed.

I tried to think of something to say to lift our moods, but all I could think about was the web of sad and unfortunate events we were caught in the middle of.

I stared out the window at the parting clouds and got an idea.

"Wanna push me on the swings?" I asked.

And for the first time in what seemed like forever, Westley smiled at me.

"Yes, I do."

CHAPTER 19

Life returned to as normal as I could expect it to be over the next few days.

With school out, the reminders of Julia's death, at least for me, were few. Westley and I didn't talk about the subject anymore, so I couldn't determine whether or not he was coping any better. Instead of dwelling on what had happened, we passed the days helping to take down Christmas decorations and hanging out with Eastlyn and Southeby.

We played family board games and had movie marathons—all comedies. I tried to look like I was having a good time, no matter what we were doing, in hopes that Westley would forget about our fall down the stairs—or so that he would think *I* had forgotten it.

By day three, my bruising was deep purple. That was the day when recovering from injury shifted from it hurting worse than it looked to it looking worse than it felt. So while it wasn't pretty, I was able to make it through the day without over-the-counter pain relievers.

One of the many positives about spending so much time with the Greenes was that I'd managed to avoid my sister for most of break. My goal was to evade her completely until my face healed since it would be impossible for her not to comment on it. Even by day five, my black eyes were still too dark to cover up with makeup, and my bandages were not concealable, so I tried to plan my comings and goings to Westley's house when I knew she'd be out.

Unfortunately, I couldn't predict when she'd barge into my room while I was sleeping to borrow my jeans.

"What are you doing?" I sat up and waited for my eyes to adjust to the light she'd switched on.

"I need some pan—" Bronwyn stopped midword.

Through my squint, I could see a look of horror on my sister's face, which set off my own panic. "What's wrong?"

"What happened to your face?" Her words were loaded with accusation, disgust, and anger all at once.

Groan.

Her question had me trapped. Plan A of avoiding running into her at home had been working so well that I didn't conceive a plan B. And three seconds after waking up, my mind wasn't sharp enough to give her an explanation that would both protect Westley and satisfy her curiosity.

"Uh, I fell," I stammered. I hoped to find a more convincing story by the time I got to the end of the sentence but came up empty-handed. "And broke my nose."

Bronwyn's eyes narrowed at me, and I avoided them by faking a yawn.

"Liar." Bronwyn labeled me accurately. She looked like she wanted to say more but didn't, and I used her silence as an excuse to change the subject.

"You didn't ask me to borrow my pants."

Her stare became more frigid, if that were possible. "I don't have to. You're going to let me wear them so that I don't say anything to Dad about the two black eyes you are most certainly trying to hide."

Evil genius.

I just nodded and returned my head to its pillow. She lingered at my closet a few more minutes, loading up her arms with more spoils of her blackmail, and then left without another word.

◆◆◆

By New Year's Eve, I stopped wearing my metal nose guard. My bruising was still sensitive to the touch, but I bit my lip and smeared on the liquid cover-up anyway. I'd followed up with the urgent care doctor the day before, and while he was pleased with the progress, he still recommended I see a specialist. I told him I'd make an appointment.

I had hoped that I would have the full duration of our break from school to heal before facing my classmates. School was set to resume January 2, and I was confident that by then, my eyes would at least be at the yellow stage of bruising and easier to hide.

But my plan was dashed when Westley called to say we were attending a small get-together that night with some of the ballplayers and their girlfriends.

"Trevor Thomas's parents are in Chicago for New Year's, so I was thinking about coming over now to pick you up and heading over there." I grimaced and stuck my tongue out at the mention of Trevor's name. I tried to like everyone on Westley's team, but Trevor was awful. Almost to the Bronwynth degree.

The Thomases came from money, but not in the classy way that the Greenes did. Mrs. Thomas's parents owned a successful chain of supermarkets throughout Indiana, so he was third-generation rich and too far removed from the hard work it took to earn money to appreciate its privilege. Trevor's parents were constantly leaving him and his three too-old-to-still-be-at-home brothers alone while they vacationed across the country. There had been multiple occasions where parties got busted at his house, and I was sure at least one of the boys had been arrested for drugs at some point.

I wanted to suggest alternative plans, but Westley seemed excited about hanging out with the guys, and I knew it would be good for him to get his mind off things for a while.

West was finishing the details when I heard a beeping on the line. I held my phone away from my ear to see an unfamiliar number attempting to call.

It was rare I would receive a call from anyone other than Westley or my family. I decided to answer it. "I'll call you right back," I told Westley and switched the line over. "Hello?"

"Hey, Cosette! Happy New Year!" It took me a moment to register the male voice on the phone.

"Micah? Hey, yeah, Happy New Year to you too!" I'd forgotten about giving my number out to Micah for our school project. "How are you doing?" I hadn't heard from or thought about him since I last saw him on Christmas Eve.

"So did you make it through the book I gave you for Christmas? I'm sure you haven't been able to put it down. Such a page-turner, that Bible." Micah was clearly joking, but it didn't stop me from feeling guilty as I glanced over to the shelf beside my bed where the book had lain collecting dust since he gave it to me.

"It's in my reading queue," I responded. "So what's up?"

"So, I'm calling because we haven't done our homework yet, and I was hoping you were free this afternoon."

I started to ask what he was talking about when I remembered Mrs. Holloway's e-mail cancelling the obituary assignment. "Oh, yeah. It totally slipped my mind."

"Yeah, almost me too. Been super busy this week," Micah went on. "So what are the chances you and Westley don't have plans for New Year's Eve afternoon?"

"Well—" I started but then stopped. Westley and I *did* have plans, but spending a few hours in the afternoon with Micah wouldn't necessarily ruin them. This could be the perfect time for me to finish this assignment without having to sacrifice an entire day away from Westley, but spare me of too much time at Trevor's. "Actually, that may work out perfectly."

We made our tentative plans to meet at my house, and I called Westley back for permission.

At first he was reluctant, but then I suggested he head over to Trevor's without me for guy time. I told him I'd have Micah drop me off there when we were done. When he finally agreed, I finalized plans with Micah and gave myself a mental high five for working everything out.

Micah was set to come over at noon. We hadn't outlined what we were going to do, but I guessed it would involve the coffees he had told me I owed him.

I finished straightening my room and covering up my injuries as best that makeup could do and sat on my bed to wait for Micah. I stretched out and reached over to my shelf to grab one of my wedding magazines. While I tried to remember which one I'd already read, another book caught my attention.

I picked up my Bible and set it before me. Then, deciding that reading a few pages in it might give me something to talk to Micah about, I opened it.

I turned to where the ribbon bookmark that was sewn into the leather binding had been placed—intentionally or not, I didn't know. The heading at the top next to the page number said "2 Corinthians." I began to read midpage:

> *So we do not lose heart. Though our outer self is wasting away, our inner self is being renewed day by day. For this light momentary affliction is preparing for us an eternal weight of glory beyond all comparison, as we look not to the things that are seen but to the things that are unseen. For the things that are seen are transient, but the things that are unseen are eternal.*

Light affliction? I wondered what the context of this passage was—something I would have probably known had I not just randomly picked the middle as a starting point for reading the book. And what was this about looking to the things that are not seen? How could anyone look to things that are unseen? I wondered if Corinthian Sr. was any less confusing.

It was too bad Mrs. Holloway didn't teach this book in school. I was sure I wouldn't even be able to figure it out on my own, even with CliffsNotes.

It surprised me that this passage didn't fall into either of the categories I assumed the Bible was divided into—rules for what to do and not to do. This passage sounded more optimistic than condemning or instructing. In fact, when I thought about it in regard to what was happening with Westley and his grieving, it gave me a lot of hope. I would love for what he was currently going through to be merely a "light affliction" that was working toward "glory beyond all comparison."

Perhaps this was a feel-good book, if I took it in the same way I would a timely message in a fortune cookie.

"Cosette!" Bronwyn yelled up the stairs. "Your date's here! Don't let him smack you up like Westley did! Oh, and make him wear a condom—you don't want to give him all Westley's STDs."

I closed my eyes and groaned. Not only would Micah now surely notice my face, he would also assume I wanted to sleep with him and was a carrier of sexually transmitted diseases.

I heard Micah enter my room but kept my face down in embarrassment. "Am I interrupting your prayer time?" Evidently, willing myself invisible had not worked as I'd hoped.

I raised my head to apologize for Bronwyn. "I am sorry about my sister; she's—"

"Cosette, what happened to you?" Micah ran over to my bedside and kneeled close to my face, raising his hand to my cheek, and I instinctively backed away from it. There was nothing that felt right about having Micah this close to me on my bed, especially after what Bronwyn had suggested.

"I'm fine. I promise. I just fell down some stairs," I explained, holding my hands up as if I were surrendering. "It looks worse than it is."

Micah examined me with his eyes, taking slow steps backward. "I'm sorry. I didn't expect to see you like this is all," he said, confusedly.

"Yeah, maybe I should have warned you. I guess I thought I was looking better than I am." Micah's reaction made me wonder if I really should wait until school resumed before facing anyone else.

"No, Cosette, you don't look bad! I'm sorry," Micah apologized again. "It's just that all of a sudden, I feel like I might be too late."

"Too late for what?" I asked, not tracking with him. Here we went again. I wasn't in the mood for another conversation

134

that would end with me knowing less about what we were talking about than when we began.

"Never mind...ready for that coffee?"

I suddenly felt anxious. "As long as we go someplace no one I know is going to see me. Now you've got me paranoid that I'm looking like a monster."

"I know just the place." Micah headed for my bedroom door, and I followed him. "Oh, and Cosette, one more thing. I don't know what your sister was talking about when I got here..." I instantly blushed. "But try to keep your hands to yourself, OK? This coffee date is strictly business." Micah winked and smiled again, and I rolled my eyes.

CHAPTER 20

We found a table for two at a small coffee shop in downtown Elkhart and claimed it before placing our order.

"What are you drinking?" Micah asked, staring at the menu.

"Vanilla latte," I stated the name of my caffeinated beverage of choice. "But I should be asking you since I'm buying."

"Well, I was always more of a double shot of espresso kind of guy myself, since you asked," Micah offered. "But you aren't paying."

"This is supposed to be my treat, not yours, remember?" I was no stranger to chivalry, thanks to Westley. But while I knew I couldn't win an argument like this with him, I was pretty sure I could outlast Micah on who would pay the check.

"Actually, I'm not going to pay either." There was a twinkle in Micah's eye.

I frowned. "I hadn't judged you for the dine-and-dash kind, Micah. Besides, that's a hard thing to attempt when you have to pay before they serve you." I pointed to a transaction happening at the cash register.

"Oh, Cosette of little faith."

We waited in a line three customers deep to place our order. I had my debit card in hand to pay for our drinks in case Micah was simply trying to divert me from treating with all his mysterious talk and planned to swoop in with his cash at the last second.

The café was busy. I scoured the patrons scattered among the tables and was glad to see no familiar faces. Micah was also checking out the clientele, though probably not for the same reason that I was. When it was our turn, he repeated our drink selections to the barista, who promptly started to steam the milk and grind the beans to prepare them.

"Can I show you something, Cosette?" Micah asked casually as he glanced around the room.

I followed his eye line. "Sure."

"OK then, pay attention." He instructed me before inconspicuously grabbing my hand.

This was such an unexpected move that I didn't have the time to pull away before what happened next stunned me still.

When my hand connected with Micah's, I felt an instant electricity—not the metaphorical, romantic type but an *actual* electric current. A tingly energy shot through my body from the source of our joined hands; it washed over me like an enduring shiver.

The chaos coursing through my veins was a direct contradiction to the shift in what my eyes observed of my outward surroundings. At Micah's touch, the atmosphere blurred. The world's tempo powered down, and everything began to move in slow motion, as if I were watching it frame by frame on video.

In less time than it took me to blink, which could have been seconds or minutes—I didn't know—my attention was physically drawn by a magnetic force that turned my head to a table in the café occupied by a woman and her cell phone. In the minute-long second that I saw her, I observed her entirely—her wool business suit, her flawless makeup, the glint of light reflecting from the cross on her necklace. She was contemplative, staring straight into me. Her pupils dilated at our eye contact.

Suddenly, the magnetic field drawing my sight to the woman was overpowered by another that turned my head away. On the other side of the room, a middle-aged gentleman was rising from his seat, an empty coffee mug in hand.

He was with someone younger than he was, his son, maybe. One of the father's hands was shoved inside his coat pocket, the index finger on the other lifted in a point toward Micah and me. The son's eyes followed it and met mine.

At this moment, I successfully willed my hand apart from Micah's and finally broke the connection.

The electric energy coursing through me evaporated, and time regained a recognizable speed.

I shook my head and tried to blink away the vertigo I was feeling, my heart pounding so hard against my ribs I was sure everyone in the room could hear it. I widened my eyes in horror at Micah, who appeared perfectly unfazed by whatever had just blown my mind.

"You all right, miss?" the barista asked, her head cocked sideways, as she poured hot milk into a large ceramic cup.

I stared dumbly at her.

"She's fine. Just hasn't had her coffee today," Micah answered for me. Then he flashed her a grin and ran his hand through his hair.

She returned the smile. "I know the feeling."

I was too furious about what had happened to feel condescended to by their exchange.

What had Micah done to me? Slipped me some skin-absorbing psychedelic drug through my palm? That had to have been what happened, though Micah didn't seem to have been on the same trip I had and it had started and stopped so abruptly...

Why hadn't I paid more attention during drug awareness week?

I couldn't decide if I wanted to scream or cry or bludgeon Micah to death with a coffee mug.

I was still struggling to regain my speech when the man I'd seen pointing in our direction stepped between Micah and the counter. He leaned over and began talking to the barista in a hushed voice.

I finally recovered my vocabulary, which was about to consist of a long slew of four-letter words. "Micah, what the—"

He cut me off with a shush. "*Pay* attention."

Micah's command made me see red. *He wants me to be quiet?* I didn't want to be quiet! I wanted an explanation as to what had happened. In detail. Accompanied by a million apologies.

Having no comeback that wouldn't have caused a scene, I bit my tongue and tried to kill Micah with a look.

The man lingered in front of us a few moments longer before turning around and giving Micah a wink.

The barista set our beverages on the counter with a sly smile. She watched out of the corner of her eye until the bells on the front door of the café jingled, and then she addressed us, "Well, kids—it's your lucky day. No charge."

My eyebrows automatically arched.

"Can you say that again?" Micah asked her, looking at me.

"That gentleman who was just here said to tell you both Happy New Year." She was beaming, obviously enjoying the part she was playing in the stranger's gift to us.

"Well, how do you like that?" Micah's tone was a mixture of gratitude and feigned surprise. "Thank you so much. And if you see him again—please tell him that his kindness really meant a lot to us." He peeked at me from the side of his eyes. "More than he could have known it would."

Micah handed me my latte by its saucer; my unsteady hands sloshed it everywhere.

He grinned. "Maybe you should have ordered a decaf."

CHAPTER 21

"What just happened? What just happened?" I repeated broken-record style while Micah basically carried me weak-kneed across the café. I screwed my eyes shut in fear of the sensations returning.

"Calm down, or people are going to think you're weird."

"Me?" I spat out. "*You're* the one with the freaky super-powers!"

Micah scoffed and sat me down in my chair. Our table was far enough removed from the other patrons that I didn't have to stifle my anger too much to be discreet. "Start explaining *now*." My mind was swirling with too many questions chasing after each other to find a natural starting point.

Micah casually stirred his espresso with a spoon. "I'll tell you anything you want to know, Cosette, but it's not going to mean anything if you don't have an open mind and trust me."

"Why in the world would I trust someone who did...whatever it was you just did to me?" I choked out my words at him.

"Why would I bother explaining anything to someone unless I felt they trusted me enough to believe my explanation?"

I screamed internally.

"I want to tell you everything you want to know, Cosette." Micah spoke to my frustration. "But you're going to have to cooperate."

"*Cooperate*?" I demanded in hushed anger. "That's an awful ballsy request from someone who just used mind control on me!" Micah wasn't showing even an ounce of the ton of remorse I felt he owed me after doing whatever he'd done. Everything about him at that moment irritated me—his calmness, especially.

"I'm sorry that you feel violated," he tried to placate me with an insincere apology. "But I think you might be overreacting. I mean, were you hurt?"

I refused to answer with anything but a glare.

"Do you assume, based on what you just experienced, that I *could* have hurt you if I'd chosen to?"

I continued to bore holes through him without blinking.

He assumed his own answers. "So what should that tell you?"

I heaved a defeated sigh. "Fine." I was more interested in figuring out what had happened than winning an argument. "Explain what you mean by *cooperate.*"

"Tell me what happened. From your perspective."

I grudgingly offered Micah the details of my experience with my limited, ninth-grade physics vocabulary. He listened intently without interruption, his smile my only indicator whether or not my explanation was making sense.

"That's amazing," he commented when I finished. "I love it."

I didn't expect him to seem so surprised, having been equally present when time shifted. "What? Is your version that much different?" I was eager to understand the truth beyond what I knew firsthand.

"Yeah, definitely." Micah nodded with excitement. "What happened over there has a bigger picture, and you and I only get to see parts of it."

"Of course, you know that makes no sense to me," I stated flatly.

"Yeah, I know. But it will. I hope. Sooner than later." Micah's clarification did little to satisfy my curiosity.

"So that's it? That's all the answers you've got for me? Just that you agree I should be confused?"

"I can't answer why it happened to you. That is up to you to discern. I can only explore what lesson I'm learning from

141

it." He didn't wait for me to ask the obvious question before answering it. "For me, that lesson was about provision."

"Provision?" I repeated. I hadn't paid much attention in physics, but I was almost positive that in all our talks about time, space, and motion, "provision" hadn't come up one time.

"Yes. An unexpected intervention that provided for a need we had."

"I don't need the dictionary definition, Micah. I need answers as to what you did to me back there!"

"That's what I'm trying to tell you, Cosette. What happened here was the same thing that happened when my truck broke down and Dave showed up. You just got a wider glimpse at all the factors that went into what was provided for us this time."

I remembered our drive home from Julia's funeral. I'd long ago tried let go of how coincidental everything had seemed—the timing of the mechanic driving by, the diagnosis he'd given our problem before even looking under the hood of the truck, the fact that he happened to have the exact part we needed in his van—but Micah kept drawing my attention back to it. "How are these two situations at all alike? In one, someone miraculously rescued us when we were stranded on the side of the road with Westley OD'ed on painkillers in the backseat, and in this one, you bent time and we got a free cup of coffee."

"You're right, and you're wrong, Cosette." Micah was excited now. "It was *miraculous* that so many factors had to fall into place in precise timing for Dave to have helped us like he did."

"OK, so what is he then, your guardian angel?" When I thought about it, Dave did look a little like Clarence from *It's a Wonderful Life*, but *that* probably was just a coincidence.

"No, of course not—he's a man, just like me, who's just trying to be obedient."

"To what?"

"To God."

I should have guessed that somewhere in our conversation, God would show up. After all, on just about every occasion I'd been with Micah, he'd spent some of the time praying. He even gave me a Bible. Obviously, God was his answer to this. "So, God sent Dave to fix our car. And he bought me coffee?" None of this seemed like God's jurisdiction, based upon what I knew of him—though I wasn't an expert, having prayed now six times in my life and read one verse from Corinthians.

"No, God prompted Dave to stop to help us. Just like he prompted that woman you saw on her cell phone to buy us coffee. She just didn't respond to it. So, he tried again—and the man obeyed. That guy probably used the moment to teach his son a lesson about generosity, but his willingness to act out his prompting taught something to more people than just his kid." Micah looked across the coffee shop at the table of the woman I had described staring at me in the moments of frozen time. "What do you think she's thinking about right now?"

I tried to glance at her inconspicuously, but she was staring at me, and I couldn't avoid her eyes. She looked as bewildered as I imagined I did.

"Or what about the barista?"

I shifted my gaze to the cash register where the girl who had served us was wiping down the counter, a small smile spread across her lips as she stole a glance our way.

"OK, well, this is all a lovely idea, Micah, but I still don't understand how you did what you did or why God wanted to buy me a latte."

"Well, that's the part you were wrong about. I'm pretty sure nothing about any of this has to do with coffee." He whipped his hair from his eyes. "God didn't provide you with caffeine. He provided you with the experience."

I impatiently tapped my finger against my coffee cup.

The clinking of my engagement ring against the ceramic attracted Micah's attention, and his expression instantly clouded. "What is that?" He pointed at my ring with his eyes.

I immediately blushed, a wave of guilt washing over me for not yet mentioning my engagement to Micah. "Westley asked me to marry him. He proposed on Christmas Eve." As much as I would have normally loved to gush about my future nuptials, I was leery to share any more details about myself with Micah until I knew more about him and how he'd done what he had to me.

"When? Did you set a date?" His impatience caught me off guard.

"I don't know yet. Now, can we get back to—"

"But you're going to wait awhile, right? Like, you aren't getting married while you are still in high school?"

I didn't understand why this mattered to Micah. "Again, I don't know. We haven't really talked about it much yet, but I'll be happy to let you interrogate me about it just as soon as you are finished explaining what you did to me over there!" My exasperation was getting the better of me, and I fought the urge to storm out and forget anything had ever happened.

He stared off into space, shaking his head. "This makes no sense."

"Hey!" I yelled. Micah was dangerously close to wearing my coffee. "You know, relatively speaking, I'm pretty sure that Westley and I getting engaged is the only part of the conversation you and I have had today that *does* make sense." His strong reaction made me suspicious of him—my own father hadn't been nearly as distraught at my announcement, and he arguably had the right to be.

"C'mon." Micah stood up and hastily tugged on his jacket. "I need to go somewhere."

"*What?*" I was incredulous. "This conversation is not over."

He was quick to respond. "I don't know about that, Cosette. You may have decided otherwise."

Micah headed for the door. I grabbed my coat and chased after him, leaving behind my untouched latte, grateful for the first time that I hadn't paid for it.

144

CHAPTER 22

The growl of Micah's truck faded down the road as I stood waiting on the Thomases' front porch for my knock to be answered.

He'd listened to me scream at him the entire drive back to Middlebury without saying a word. Wherever his mind had gone when he saw my ring, it stayed there. Nothing I said fazed him; no amount of begging got me an explanation for what had happened at the coffee shop.

Though he had been deaf to my questions, Micah had honored my request to be dropped off to Westley at the Thomases'. When he pulled into the driveway, he finally broke his silence. But instead of offering me the answers I'd pleaded for, he gave me an apology.

"I'm really sorry I've upset you so much, Cosette." He was sincere but frustrated. "Somehow, I think I really messed this up."

"Yup, you did," I retorted, pretending to know exactly what he was talking about. "Apology not accepted."

Tired of waiting for someone to let me in the door, I turned the knob and welcomed myself into the Thomas house.

The main floor was quiet, but I could feel heavy bass vibrating the stone tile under my feet, so I knew the guys were somewhere in the house.

I'd never been inside their house before, but I was sure that their cleaning service was owed all the credit for the tidy state of the house and not the four, spoiled, quasi-adult sons or their absent parents.

I stepped over piles of shoes, following the vibrations through their kitchen to a door leading to the basement.

Sighing with relief, I descended the stairs, knowing I was only seconds away from seeing Westley.

The music drowned out my footsteps, so no heads looked up as I emerged at the bottom of the stairs and scouted the room. The party was bigger than I'd expected, especially for being so early in the afternoon. After scouring the crowds around the hot tub and pool table, I spied Westley sitting at a card table with Trevor and a few of the other players and their girlfriends.

I approached Westley from behind. I wrapped my arms around his chest and rested my head on his shoulder.

"I'm not sure I've ever been happier to see you, Westley." I spoke directly into his ear to be heard above the music. Then I leaned over to kiss him on the lips.

Immediately, I knew something was wrong. I pulled away and stared my fiancé in his half-closed eyes.

"Westley!" I scolded. "Are you drinking?"

One glance around the table answered my question for him. Red plastic cups, shot glasses, and quarters cluttered the space between liquor bottles.

"A little." He smiled sleepily—or drunkenly—I didn't have the experience to differentiate.

"Whoa, what happened to your face, Cosette?" Trevor asked bluntly, pointing at my nose. He wasn't nearly as far-gone as Westley was but drunk enough apparently that tact didn't matter. None of the faces now staring at me from around the table looked even near sober.

"I fell," I responded, annoyed. "How much has he had?" I asked the group collectively.

"I dunno," Trevor answered. "We started about noon. For as big as he is, your boy's a lightweight." The party host took a long drink from his plastic cup and then sent some sophomore who'd been sitting on his lap for a refill.

"C'mon." I tried to pull Westley to his feet but lacked the strength to carry his dead weight.

"Let him have some fun, Cosette. Can't you let him off his leash for just one night?" Trevor ran an evil finger up my leg, and I swatted it like a fly.

"He looks like he's having a blast drooling on himself like this," I retorted, and a few of the guys simultaneously made angry cat noises at me.

Westley seemed to be fading in and out of sleep or consciousness. His lethargy reminded me of how he'd been at Julia's funeral. If he was going to be as physically useless as he was that day, I wasn't sure I'd have any luck getting him to go anywhere alone—and I doubted I'd find an ally in the crowd eager to help me remove him from the party.

I tried again to rouse Westley. "Hey, babe. Let's go get some air." I tapped Westley on the cheek. He flinched awake for a moment.

"Knock it off, Cosi," he mumbled.

"You heard the man, Cosi. Now be a good girl so Westley doesn't have to lay down the law again." Trevor reached for my face, pointing at my eyes, and I slapped his hand away.

"If you touch me one more time, Trevor, your face is going to look worse than mine."

I couldn't tell whom I was annoyed with more at that moment—Trevor or Westley—but both of them in this situation made my afternoon with Micah seem like a day at the park.

I thought of Micah. Despite our afternoon, I wished he were here to help me with Westley again, just like he'd done at the funeral. And also to fry Trevor's brain with his possible mind-control powers.

"Please, West. Let's get out of here." I bent down to plead with him out of earshot of the others, but Westley was completely asleep.

I could feel my stomach twist into knots. Westley had never drunk before, and while he may have arguably had a good reason to after all he'd been through the past few weeks, there was an even greater reason for him not to.

To play baseball for Camden High School, Westley signed a morality contract with the school. Per this agreement, athletes caught even in the presence of underage drinking would be suspended for at least a third of their sport season. If it could be proven that they were consuming alcohol, they would be kicked off of their team for a whole season.

After all the trouble the Thomas boys have had with the law, I wouldn't have been surprised if the Middlebury cops had their house staked out for New Year's Eve. I needed to find a way to get Westley out of there.

Mustering all my strength, I wrapped my arms around Westley's core and pulled him to a standing position. Mouths all around the table dropped opened, including my own, when I'd been able to lift him to stand. But quickly the looks of surprise turned to gasps as—not having planned on what to do with Westley once I'd removed him from his seat—I quickly lost my grip and he fell backward on top of me, knocking us both to the ground.

I barely heard the giggles at my expense because my nose throbbed so intensely that my other senses stopped functioning.

I wanted to cry or to scream, but when I opened my mouth, all that came out was a sputtering of blood.

Trevor had stood up when we toppled and was staring at us from above. "Oh shit, Cosette! You're bleeding!"

"I'm sure she doesn't know that, Trevor. Thanks for pointing that out to her," a familiar voice barked. Out of the corner of my eye, I saw someone had extended a hand to help me up, and I accepted it.

"You all right, Cosette?" Patrick stood me upright and examined my face. He grabbed a nearby box of tissues and handed me a wad of them. "What happened to you?"

"Are you drunk?" I asked, not wanting to waste a syllable trying to talk through the excruciating pain if Patrick would be useless to help me in the end. The tissues weren't enough to catch the blood pouring out of my nose, and he handed me another fistful of them.

"I haven't had anything. I just got here and saw Westley fall on you." Patrick turned his attention to Westley. "How much has he had?"

"No idea," I forced the words out, the taste of blood making me sick. "But can you help me get him to his car? I need to get him out of here. He can't get kicked out of baseball for this."

"Yup, I'm leaving too."

I was so grateful, I could have kissed Patrick—though I doubted he would have accepted any such gesture from a girl who looked like she'd just gone nine rounds in a boxing match.

No one offered us a hand in lugging my drunken giant of a boyfriend up the stairs. Patrick was definitely in shape, but he didn't have Micah's height or hidden strength, so I was left with more of the weight burden than I'd had when previously carrying Westley.

With each step we cleared, my nose throbbed harder. It was as if my brain assumed that my neglect to stop the bleeding meant I hadn't noticed I had a serious injury that needed attention, so it started signaling my pain sensors to work double time. My face's pulse beat like an agonizing metronome as we dragged Westley up one stair after another.

A steady trickle of blood dripped from each nostril and oozed down my arms. I didn't bother wiping it away, watching with satisfaction at the trail I was leaving all over the Thomases' white carpeting.

By the time we brought Westley into the foyer, my shirt was soaked a sticky red. The pain was so extreme that I was angry at it.

"Seriously, are you OK?" We propped Westley up against the door to take a break. "You look like a gunshot victim."

"I'll be OK, I think," I replied. "But if I pass out, please stick my body in Trevor's closet. Then call the cops and report me missing. Suggest foul play."

He laughed. "Yeah. Trevor's a bastard."

Patrick bore the brunt of strapping Westley into the passenger's seat of his Mustang while I leaned against the car and tried to keep the ground from spinning.

"Maybe I should just drive us all to the hospital?" he suggested after shutting West's door.

"Absolutely not," I tried to say with conviction. "There's no way Westley wouldn't go to jail."

He put a thumb on my forehead and tilted my head up to get a look at my damage. "Well then, let me see what I can do to stop the bleeding." Patrick ran to his jeep. I used my coat to cover my profile, in the event the police actually were planning a sting operation on Trevor's house.

Moments later, he returned with a catcher's mask, the front of it stuffed with a clean sock.

I looked at him skeptically. "This should work to apply pressure and still allow you to drive." He gently placed the mask over my head and did his best to tighten the cage so that the sock would serve its purpose to catch the blood still pouring from my nose while not impairing my vision. The pressure, at first, evoked some involuntary swearing, but after a few seconds, I felt a slight relief from the throbbing. He handed me a prescription bottle. "And this will get you through until tomorrow. Leftover pain meds from when I injured my rotator cuff last summer."

I hesitantly accepted the bottle and read the label through the wire frame of the catcher's mask. As a general rule, I didn't use other people's prescription medication. However, I also didn't typically find myself in the precarious situation of having my nose accidentally broken twice in the same week, so I made the exception.

I recognized the medication as one Bronwyn had been prescribed for menstrual cramps, so assumed it was mild as far as pain meds were concerned. Still, I decided to wait until Westley was down for the night, just in case it knocked me out.

"Well, when I left the house tonight, I was hoping for something to bring me out of my funk," Patrick commented.

"I didn't really picture it like this, but hey, at least I'm not bored."

"I guess not." I tried to ignore how much my voice resembled that of a cartoon telephone operator's and continued. "But how come Westley's the one passed out in the car and you're the one out here taking care of him?" The situation made much more sense reversing Westley's and Patrick's roles. Patrick was the one who had just buried his girlfriend, after all. "How are you keeping it all together?" Although it pained me to speak, I had to know the answer.

Patrick shrugged, more serious now. "It's amazing the perspective you can find when you got nothing left to lose, Cosette." He paused. "I don't know if you'll understand this, but in Julia's death, I found this clarity about life I never had before." He swallowed hard. "I feel like I love her even more now than ever because losing her has opened my eyes to so much."

I didn't understand. "Well, you're a stronger person than I am, Patrick. If I ever lost Westley, I'm pretty sure it would end me."

Patrick shook his head. "You know, I think I would have said the same thing before all this. But you only get the strength you need when you need it." As he spoke, he led me to Westley's driver's side and helped me in. "Still, I hope you never have to find out."

Since there was a long line of cars blocking me from backing the Mustang out of the Thomases' driveway, I had to drive through their yard to get to the road. What I didn't have to do was put the car in neutral in the middle of their lawn and spin my tires, but I did that also.

Patrick drove a car length behind me the whole way to my house to make sure we arrived there safely.

We'd almost made it through the S curve that led to my neighborhood when my sleeping passenger sat up so quickly that I jumped. "I'm gonna be sick!" West barely got the words out before the contents of his stomach followed them.

I thought about what Patrick had said, and I wondered how much strength would be given to me so that I could survive that night.

◆◆◆

I was as overjoyed as a girl wearing a catcher's mask full of bloody sock could be that Patrick was able to help me get Westley up to my room without anyone noticing we were home. He offered to stay long enough to help me strip Westley of his vomit-soaked clothing, but I declined the offer.

"You've probably already done enough tonight to get yourself sainted." I offered a million thanks to Patrick and sent him on his way.

Before attempting to clean Westley up, I set to work on assessing my own damage.

In the bathroom, I carefully removed the catcher's mask. The pain had been slightly dulled by the mask's pressure, but it instantly returned the moment I removed it. I quickly popped opened the pill bottle Patrick gave me and chased a dose with a Dixie cup full of water.

Though the pain rushed back, my nose had stopped bleeding. Any false move would likely restart it, I figured, so I moved delicately as I pulled the bloodied sock from where it was jammed in the mask and tossed it into the trash can. I then grabbed a pair of scissors and cut my bloodied T-shirt from my body rather than take the risk of pulling it over my head.

Midway through this process, I caught a glimpse of myself in the mirror.

Standing shirtless, holding a pair of scissors and a bloodied catcher's mask beside me, I looked like a victim from a horror movie.

Or a killer from one. I couldn't decide.

My nose was moved completely out of its original place, set crooked and bent, as though someone had removed my own and replaced it with some spare Mr. Potato Head part.

I was disfigured.

The shock of seeing the unrecognizable girl in the mirror numbed me more than pain meds ever could have.

I looked over at my bed where Westley lay, heaped in a pile and covered in his own vomit.

This was not my life. This was not my normal.

Without trying to remember them, the words I'd read earlier that day pushed their way to the forefront of my mind.

> We look not to the things that are seen but to the things that are unseen. For the things that are seen are transient, but the things that are unseen are eternal.

I stared once again at the mirror. My outer self certainly seemed to be wasting away.

Patrick's words echoed after the Bible verse. *"It's amazing the perspective you can find when you got nothing left to lose..."*

Did I have anything left to lose?

I put down the scissors and sat on my bathroom floor. My eyes closed.

"God...please help me."

◆◆◆

An hour later, Westley was cleaned up and snoozing soundly. I cracked the window in my room to let out the smell of vomit and liquor and let in the sharp freshness of a winter's night.

I pulled the extra quilt out of my closet and tucked myself into bed on my love seat with the Bible and a flashlight. The medicine had quieted my throbbing enough for me to concentrate on the words in front of me.

This time, I started at the beginning.

Genesis 1

"In the beginning, God created the heavens and the earth..."

CHAPTER 23

I awoke suddenly gasping for air, the wind knocked out of me.

I was lying on the floor in the dark. Someone was kneeling over my body, pressing his arms against my chest.

I involuntarily groaned as my lungs tried to inflate on their own, when suddenly a weight bore down on my chest, forcing them flat again.

This pattern continued rapidly, unrelentingly.

Gasping, pressing—repeat.

I couldn't collect my bearings or catch my breath.

"Help!" I mouthed futilely, having no air to produce a noise.

My arms tried to push the weight from my chest, but it was too strong.

"Help!" I heard a voice shout the word I was desperate to scream. It was a man's voice, not my own. It was Westley! He was there to save me. "Someone help us! Julia is dying!"

My shortness of breath was making me dizzy.

I could hear a door open.

"Westley, what are you doing? Stop!" another male voice shouted. Suddenly, the room was filled with light.

Blinded by the brightness, I jerked my head to the side to shield my eyes. Just then, the pressure bore down upon me again, off-center from where I'd felt it before.

There was a loud cracking sound from within my body.

I could not satisfy the need to scream with so little air.

And then there was darkness again.

CHAPTER 24

My eyes opened.

His face was near mine. Eyes closed. Lips moving.

"I ask for healing..." was all I could make out.

Those weren't the words he spoke, but I understood them as if they were.

I closed my eyes again.

Maybe I was dreaming. I felt a cold numbness setting in...

He ran his fingers over my clothes and rested upon my chest.

At his touch, a familiar electricity poured into me—a pleasant warmth penetrating deeply through all the layers of my flesh.

The warmth intensified; it reached through me, into the still cavity of my chest. Suddenly, I could no longer feel the heat outwardly—it was only inside me.

It moved within—spreading, tingling.

I could feel the warmth flooding around my heart, its temperature rising rapidly.

Hotter and hotter it grew, and I welcomed it.

Suddenly, the heat gripped me at my core, and its sinewy fingers wrapped around my ribs.

My concentration on the warmth was interrupted by a loud whipcrack, and then involuntarily, I gasped.

My lungs inflated like an emergency life preserver, and I became aware that just moments before, they were collapsed and airless.

I drew in several deep breaths, my body starved for air. When the hunger was satisfied, my intake steadied, and it was then I could feel that the heat had transferred to my head.

The center of my face where my nose had caved in grew hot. Suddenly, the displaced cartilage snapped back into place, straight and strengthened, welded by the heat. My sinuses cleared, and I was no longer forced to breathe through my mouth.

My lips closed, and I inhaled deeply through my nose.

The heat departed me.

I was filled with a peace I'd never known.

CHAPTER 25

The sun had already risen by the time I awoke in the New Year.

I'd been asleep a long time, and my body felt better rested than it had in weeks. But despite being reenergized, I couldn't convince myself to leave the comfort of my bed to start the day.

Wait. My bed?

I opened my eyes.

How did I end up in my bed? I had purposely slept on the love seat to give Westley his space.

Westley.

I sat up straight, surveying the room for him.

I was alone.

In my mind, I rewound the previous evening's events. Westley had been here, hadn't he? Was that really the night before, or had my first real night's sleep in weeks confused my internal time line?

Peeking behind my bathroom door, I saw the catcher's mask propped on the sink and a tied-off trash bag of Westley's vomit-soaked clothing.

I scratched my head. Most of the previous night was still clear as a bell—drunk Westley, jerkface Trevor, compassionate Patrick. But something must have happened between the time I fell asleep on one side of the room and when I woke up on the opposite.

It was then I noticed Patrick's orange prescription bottle sitting on the counter next to my sink, and I filled in my own blanks.

The obvious answer was that I had been dead asleep; Westley had awakened sober enough to be embarrassed and angry at himself for his behavior—if he had remembered it at all—and driven himself home.

A solemn thought entered my mind—what if Westley had woken up and was *not* sober enough to drive home but attempted it anyway?

I dashed back to my bed to search for my phone.

I found it on top of the Bible on my nightstand and picked it up to dial Westley, my heart racing.

"(1) Missed Text," the screen alerted me.

I unlocked the screen to read it.

I was happy to see that it was from Westley's phone, but the content of the message didn't alleviate all my worry.

Westley is at 23200 County Road 121.
Phone battery going to die.

I studied the message as I threw on a pair of jeans and a sweatshirt. The address was foreign, and the message was in third person. That meant that someone else had Westley's phone—and apparently, Westley—but who?

Patrick and Southeby both came to mind as the likeliest of heroes, or at least the two people Westley most likely would have called when he woke up and wanted to go home.

But he hadn't gone home.

I programmed the address from the message into my phone's map feature and saw that my destination was only a few miles away.

Westley's car was still sitting in the driveway, and I released a sigh of relief that however he'd gotten to 23200 County Road 121, he hadn't driven there himself.

As I backed around the Mustang and drove toward the mystery address, memories from Trevor's party replayed in my head.

My stomach knotted as I remembered Westley, sitting at the card table, falling over himself. I wanted to give him the benefit of the doubt that he hadn't meant to lose control like he did. After all, he wasn't a drinker, and even someone his size would be a lightweight his first time, I guessed.

Then I remembered the Valium.

He'd known what he was doing at Julia's funeral when he ingested twice an already generous dosage of the drug. He'd done it on purpose, to escape.

Something told me he knew what he was doing at Trevor's too.

My mouth went sour, and I tried to swallow the taste. I shoved the thoughts from my mind and punched the gas pedal.

I had no personal experience with hangovers, but I assumed that with the quantity Westley had consumed, he would have one. Perhaps the upside, if there was one to having thrown up all that he did in his car on the way to my house, would be that he wouldn't feel as sick when he woke up—though he was sure to at least be nauseated when he saw that my face looked like a pulverized eggplant.

I cringed at the thought of my reflection and swatted at my rearview mirror, pointing it at the passenger seat. I knew I would be beyond horrified if I caught a glimpse of myself. The image of the girl in the mirror from the night before disturbed me; I imagined she would look even less human today beneath the fresh purple and swelling, and I couldn't afford the distraction she would cause me. I would just wait and face her with Westley, and we'd figure out what to do with her together.

And I wanted to do that before the pain meds wore off.

I planned to sneak into Bronwyn's medicine cabinet for more pills when I got back home. Because she seemed to be in a constant state of PMS, I had no way of knowing currently how close on the calendar she was to her period. It was a gamble to take her meds away when they were probably the only thing keeping her from killing me in a menstrual-cramp rage, but then I remembered how I'd felt the night before and decided it was worth the risk.

The country roads were void of cars, but the buggy traffic was heavy because it was Sunday and the Amish were all en route home from church. I drove almost the entire length of the road on the wrong side to pass the convoy of horse-drawn vehicles in my way. As I passed, I sank low in my seat so that my face wouldn't spook one of the horses and cause a seven-buggy pileup on County Road 121.

Half a mile past the wagon train, I slammed on my brakes next to a rusted tin mailbox with the faded, hand-painted address of 23200 scrawled across the lid.

I looked up the gravel drive, but a thick of tall pines obstructed my view of the house. My eyes darted back to the screen on my phone, which displayed the address, and then suspiciously back to the mailbox.

This had to be the wrong place.

My stomach grew tight, and the sourness returned. Through the rust holes burned into the mailbox, I spied the faded-yellow pages of some partially biodegraded newspaper blowing in the breeze.

Though I had never been to Patrick's house, something told me that this was not the entrance to the Wellman residence.

I debated calling Westley's parents, explaining everything and asking them to come help, but I could only imagine the grave I'd be digging for him as I detailed his drunken night of accidental physical assault on my face. And what if they showed up here only to find Westley inside some baseball player's grandmother's house, safely drinking black coffee and nursing a headache?

I gave that scenario much more credibility than it deserved and pushed the idea of calling the Greenes back to plan B.

The rumble of dozens of horseshoes scraping the asphalt grew louder as buggies steadily inched closer to where I'd stopped. I waited until I was sure the drivers of the first few in line might notice my car, and then I gave my Element enough gas to creep up the driveway. If the locals were ever asked what became of me later, I wanted there to be witnesses to my last whereabouts.

I quickly rounded the pines, and a two-story farmhouse came into view. It was just as old and neglected as its mailbox suggested it would be.

The house looked condemned. Large areas of white paint had peeled from the exterior, exposing the gray, rotting wood underneath. A few hundred yards behind it stood an equally dilapidated, formerly red barn, leaning off to the side much less spectacularly than the tower in Pisa.

Old farms like this one were not uncommon to Middlebury, but I imagined they were rarely homes to grandmothers of high school baseball players. Or to anyone else.

Plan B was about to become plan A until I saw the familiar tailgate of an old truck sticking out from behind the tilted barn.

Micah.

Suddenly, it made sense that nothing made sense.

I slammed my car into park and hopped out of the cab, annoyance replacing my hesitancy about the setting I'd been led to.

"Good morning, sunshine," Micah said, greeting me with cheerful sarcasm from a rickety swing on the front porch. He'd been waiting for me.

"I'm not even going to bother to ask how or why you have anything to do with this situation." I made my impatience known with both my words and my tone. "Skip the mind games and tell me where Westley is."

His expression was feigned innocence as he pointed to the door. "Inside. Asleep in the back room."

"Oh."

Now I wanted to know how and why. But I said nothing else as I pushed by him and into the house.

"You'll probably want to keep your coat on." Micah followed me in with a warning and indicated a dark fireplace in the wall. "I haven't turned the heat on yet this morning." The room was chilly, but I was warmed by my anger.

"Yeah, fine. I don't plan to stay."

"You're in a mood." Micah laughed at me. "I figured you'd be feeling pretty happy this morning after last night. I gotta say I didn't expect this reaction."

I set my jaw. "Unless you're only going to say things I understand the first time, then don't talk and just take me to Westley," I demanded, refusing to be distracted.

"Are you kidding me right now, Cosette?" Micah shook his head at me in disbelief.

"I'm not falling for it, Micah." I stormed past him. "Show me where he is, and go philosophize to yourself."

"Whoa!" He looked hurt and then skeptical. "Do you seriously not remember what happened in your room last night?"

I felt my face go white. "What are you talking about?"

Micah rolled his eyes in disgust and stomped toward the kitchen. He threw open some squeaky-hinged cabinets, and there was a clanging of metal. He examined a silver mixing bowl and then held it out for me. "Here."

"What am I supposed to do with this?" I asked angrily, hoping he wasn't anticipating I'd need something to throw up in after he jogged my memory.

"Look at it. Your reflection."

I sighed. "Yeah, I'm well aware, Micah. I don't need you to point out my—"

Micah held the bowl to my face.

I couldn't finish my sentence. My reflection was distorted like in a fun-house mirror, but I could make out my face clearly enough.

The girl I'd seen looking back from my reflection the previous night was gone, and a familiar one stared back at me. Her mouth dropped wide open.

The skin below my eyes was clear, no bruising, no swelling. My nose, which I expected to be puffed up three times its normal size by now, was realigned—even straighter than it had looked originally.

I watched my hands hesitantly reach toward my face as I winced in anticipation of the throbbing.

162

"It's not going to hurt, Cosette," Micah stated matter-of-factly.

He was right. As my fingers grazed my skin, I felt no pain. I pinched my nostrils together and grasped the cartilage. It was intact.

This was impossible.

I shifted the focus of my eyes from my reflection in the bowl to the boy holding it out in front of me.

My eyes welled with tears.

I was better. My eyes, my nose, my face—no trace remained of the trauma I'd endured at Westley's hands. I would need no surgery or medication or makeup. No one would ask me what happened and not believe me when I covered up for my boyfriend. Westley could look at me again without being crippled by guilt for dropping me down the stairs.

With each new realization, I felt lighter, freer. My tears spilled over my cheeks, but they weren't the same bitter ones I'd become so used to crying. They were tears of release. Tears of gratitude.

My celebration was cut short by the questions swirling around my good fortune. "What happened?" I managed in a whisper.

Micah suddenly seemed as awestruck as I felt. "You were healed. Your face and everything else."

"Everything el—"

The piece of the night I'd lost through my medicated sleep came flooding back to me.

The pressure, the breathlessness, the cracking.

My noiseless screams.

They had all really happened.

I could see Westley above me; I could feel him crushing my bones.

He had broken my ribs. I'd heard it. I'd felt it. But he'd done worse than that too. Because he couldn't stop himself, trying to save Julia.

I dropped to my knees.

I'd been drowning, suffocating. He'd pumped at my chest, snapping my ribs, the jagged bones tearing holes in my lungs—each compression a desperate attempt to bring life back to Julia's body, each compression taking it out of mine.

And just before he'd squeezed the last ounce of breath from my body, Micah showed up. He touched me, warmed me. Melted away what was broken. And with the same hands he'd used to stop time at the coffee shop, he sewed back together what Westley had ripped apart.

"Are you OK, Cosette?" Micah's words were gentle.

I shook my head. How could he ask me that? How could anyone be "OK" just having been almost murdered by the man she was supposed to marry? And to top that, there was the inexplicable healing performed on me by my supernatural English partner. No, I may not have been certain of much else at that moment, but I was positive that I was *not* OK.

I didn't know who Westley was anymore. I couldn't figure out *what* Micah was. I panicked. "I have to get out of here."

I rose from the floor and dashed for the door. Micah could handle Westley, likely better than I would be able to at this point. I needed to run away from the insanity that kept closing in on me, if only long enough to catch my breath.

"Please don't leave," Micah pleaded, a step behind me as I yanked opened the door and stepped onto the porch. "I'm freaked out too, Cosi."

"Really?" I stopped on the gravel drive and turned to Micah. "What's freaking you out the most right now? Did *your* drunk fiancé almost kill you last night too? Do you *also* have some weird superhero altering your universe with time control and magic healing powers? Because that would be *some* coincidence, Micah." I hoped my tone was cool enough to freeze him in his place while I stormed the rest of the way to my car.

He stayed put but called after me. "It wasn't magic, Cosette!" he yelled as I reached for my car door. "It was a miracle!"

My hand gripped the door handle, and in my mind, I yanked it opened, squealed my tires, and sped as far from the farmhouse as space allowed. Miles, countries, oceans apart. I ran away from my questions. I ran away from their answers.

But in reality, I stopped, my reflection staring me down from the driver's-side window.

A miracle?

The girl in the glass with the perfect nose wanted to know what that meant.

I spun around on my heel. "I am only agreeing to stay if you are ready to give me some answers."

Micah exhaled loudly. "All right...Some."

CHAPTER 26

Micah sat back on the porch swing and pointed for me to join him. "I hated how we ended things yesterday afternoon, and I was feeling awful. So I came back by Trevor's to apologize, but everyone said you were gone. Some girl told me that you and Patrick had to carry Westley outside, and that you'd had some nosebleed. It was late by then, but something kept telling me I needed to go to your house, to make sure you were all right."

I shivered. Micah had been prompted.

"I kept praying for you and West, but things didn't feel right. I sensed I needed to get to you fast. I made it there just in time to see him standing over you—," Micah noticed me wincing and rethought his next words. "And I knew you were in trouble."

I buried my face into my hands and sobbed.

"Cosette, you have to understand—Westley would *never* hurt you if he knew what he was doing. He was so out of it that when I shoved him off of you, he immediately passed out again. He's not even going to remember any of this happened. Not that being drunk justifies his actions." He lowered my hands from my face and forced our eye contact. "But *this is why I came.*"

In six years, Westley had never laid a finger on me, but in one drunken, grief-stricken night...

What if Micah hadn't shown up when he did?

How had Micah shown up when he did?

My tears returned. I shed them for Westley, for his pain. For myself and how frightened I was by having come so close to dying at his hands. And for utter gratitude that I hadn't.

But *why* hadn't I? *Should* I have? *Would* I have? *Why* hadn't I?

My questions swirled in circles, one unanswerable hypothetical leading to another.

"You saved me," I choked out when I finally calmed down enough for my words to be understood. For as long as I could remember, I only ever had one person looking out for me, and he'd been all the hero I'd ever needed. Westley protected and comforted me faithfully, and I never doubted him.

Yet, it was from him that Micah had rescued me.

Through my blurred vision, I could see Micah smile at me genuinely. "You're wrong. All I did was have faith, Cosette. God was the one who saved you."

At this, I began to cry harder. Everything was already so confusing, and he'd just made it worse.

It was complicated enough to accept that Micah saved my life—that my life had *needed* saving. He somehow knew I was in trouble, and for some reason, he wanted to help me. But beyond just rescuing me from the situation, he *physically* healed my body—not with medicine, not with machines, but with his bare hands. I couldn't wrap my mind around how or why Micah did this when I barely knew him, and I certainly couldn't accept that a god unknown to me had any part of it.

Micah enveloped me as I cried, and just as at Julia's funeral, I needed it—so I let him.

"I came back to Middlebury for a reason, Cosette. And when I was asked to come, I had no idea you were going to have any part of what I was to do here."

I sniffled, forcing myself calmer to listen.

"There is something bigger for you, Cosette. Bigger than the plans you are making for yourself." His smile widened. "Opportunities."

As usual, Micah was jumping from one topic to another and leaving me behind. "What are you talking about?"

"Isn't it obvious, Cosi?" an unexpected voice from behind bellowed, and I turned to see Westley fuming. "He wants you," he growled, pointing at our embrace. "And you seem to be pretty open to the idea."

I blushed the reddest shade of guilt. "Westley, I—"

"Save it," he snapped at me, his tone as harsh as his appearance. The dark circles under his bloodshot eyes were a telling reminder of his previous evening's bender. "We're leaving. Now."

"Westley, we have to talk about what you did last night." Micah's voice was firmer than I knew Westley, in this mood, would tolerate.

"Who are you? My father?" he growled. Then he looked at the driveway and back at me. "Gimme your keys."

I was afraid to argue with him but equally afraid to comply. In the past twenty-four hours, Westley had become a stranger to me. I couldn't predict him, and at the moment, I certainly didn't trust him behind the wheel of a car. "Can we just talk first?"

"What's on your mind, Cosette?" he said with a sharp snark. "Because I'm guessing it's not setting a date for our wedding." Westley stomped toward me, and I cringed. He grabbed my left hand and jerked it up to my face; he pointed at my engagement ring, and then let it fall back into my lap.

His breath still smelled of stale liquor and vomit. I looked into his eyes; they were dull and distant, and I was relieved I hadn't handed over my car keys.

Micah immediately stood. "You need to back off her, West."

"I was going to say the same thing to you, Mic."

Things were escalating fast. "OK, Westley, we can go." I nodded at Micah, hoping I appeared more confident about my suggestion than I really was. "But I'm going to drive, OK? We'll go back to my house, and you can sleep this off." I hesitantly wrapped my arms around his middle, unsure if he'd accept any of my affections or cast me off.

When I hugged him, I could feel his stiff core loosen. He halfheartedly rested his own arms around my back, and I was washed with relief.

I didn't want to leave when my conversation with Micah was still punctuated with so many question marks, but we weren't going to make any progress toward the truth with Westley in this state. And any attempt to convince West to stay would at this point only make him more suspicious about Micah and me.

Westley didn't verbally acknowledge that he agreed with my plan but instead kicked at the gravel all the way to the car.

"I'm going to follow you home," Micah said once Westley was out of earshot.

I wanted to tell him that his offer was unnecessary, but I wasn't sure that I believed Westley would behave. "Thanks."

He agreed to give me a head start, and I thanked him again as I ran to catch up and unlock the door for West. My debt to Micah had grown beyond what I would ever be able to repay, and I hated owing so much to someone I knew so little about.

CHAPTER 27

When I got into the driver's seat, I mechanically put my seat belt on and began adjusting my mirrors, uncomfortably aware of Westley staring at me.

"Do you have something you want to say?" I tried to break the ice gently, looking at him from my periphery only. He was still frightening me, and I didn't want him to see in my eyes just how much.

"There're a lot of things I want to say, Cosette." His voice sounded calmer than it had inside the farmhouse, but he was still not quite himself. "But first I want to know what happened last night."

I put the car into reverse and pulled out of the drive. "Maybe you should tell me what you remember, and I can fill in the holes." Images of drunk Westley flooded back again, and an edge crept into my voice.

"It wasn't a big deal, Cosette. I went to a party and had a few drinks." Westley's tone didn't convince me that he believed his own words. "Kids do that stuff all the time."

"Kids might. Westley Greene does not," I reminded him. "And trust me, you had more than just a few."

He changed the subject. "How did we end up...wherever the hell we just were? And whose clothes am I wearing? I feel like the freakin' Hulk." He pointed at his outfit, which until this moment I hadn't noticed. He was dressed in a too-tight flannel shirt and sweatpants that cut off midcalf. I added Westley's ensemble as another act of charity for which I owed thanks to Micah.

I swallowed, unsure of how detailed I needed to be with Westley at this point. My own questions about how he'd gotten to the farmhouse were yet unanswered, as were the dozens regarding the events that prefaced his removal from my house.

Without the buggy traffic, I was able to speed along the road. My side mirror reflected a truck behind me in the far distance.

"Wow, you really remember nothing." I hoped this answer would conjure enough feelings of guilt about his behavior that he wouldn't press me further.

"I'm sure it will all come back to me," Westley defended himself sheepishly. I could still feel his eyes on me. He raised a hand and slowly moved it toward my face. I instinctively cringed when he traced the bridge of my nose with his finger, but then I remembered that the pain was gone. "Your face looks...perfect?"

I said nothing and turned the car into my neighborhood.

I hoped that Westley was tired enough to nap the rest of day away. I needed time to figure out an explanation for everything he would ask me when he got back to his old self, and simply ignoring his questions wouldn't suffice.

We pulled into the driveway, and I ushered Westley in quickly so as not to risk him seeing Micah's truck drive by.

I hadn't had time to sigh in relief after shutting the door behind us when Bronwyn appeared at the top of the stairs. "What the hell happened last night?"

I panicked and groaned. What had she heard? Or worse, seen? My eyes shot to Westley. He was already staring her down. "Everything's fine, Bronwyn. I'm sorry if we woke you up." I knew this wouldn't diffuse her, but an apology was all I had to offer.

She kept her eyes fixed on me while she held up Patrick's catcher's mask in one hand and then a wad of bloody sock in the other.

Westley's eyes widened, and his head turned to me. "Everything's fine," I said to Bronwyn as the color drained from my face. Then I turned to Westley and repeated, "Everything's fine."

"What did he do to you, Cosette?" Bronwyn demanded as if Westley weren't in the room.

I didn't know what to say because I didn't know what she knew.

"You do *not* have to protect him," she growled, locking her glare on Westley. She descended the stairs quickly, and I moved in front of him to head her off.

Both my sister and boyfriend were working to connect the dots about the night before, and I feared one of them soon would. My life had become a game of Clue. I held my breath as I imagined Bronwyn screaming out, "It was Mr. Greene, in the bedroom, with the pair of bloodied scissors!"

Westley spun me around to face him, his eyes narrowed again at my face. He traced me downward to my chest and placed a hand over my heart. I swallowed hard.

"Do not touch my sister," Bronwyn hissed, each word dripping with venom as she stepped around me. She stood on tiptoes and tilted her head in a futile attempt to put herself nose to nose with Westley. "If you ever lay a hand on her again, I swear on my mother's grave, I will slit your throat." She pointed at his face with the hand that held the sock.

"Bron, look at me. I'm fine." I squeezed between them, my back to Westley. Then in a lower voice, I asked, "And anyway, since when do you care what happens to me?" I hoped that this question would remind her that she hated me and she'd walk away.

"Since I now have physical proof of the extent he'll go to control you." She pointed at the mask.

"But I'm fine," I argued, almost now completely sure she hadn't witnessed what Westley had *actually* done to me. Her evidence of miscellaneous baseball equipment and a bloody gym sock were surely circumstantial now that there was no wound to link them to.

"I was about two seconds from calling the cops when you walked in, Cosette," Bronwyn seethed. "Your bedroom is covered in blood, Westley's car is in the driveway, but you're

172

both missing. I was sure he'd taken you somewhere to dump your body."

"OK, Bronwyn, this is all a misunderstanding. We were at a party last night, and I got a bloody nose. See?" I raised my chin to allow her to examine my face, grateful even more now that Micah had healed all of my injuries and not just those that were life threatening.

She stared at me skeptically. "Liar."

"Cosette, we need to go somewhere to talk," Westley said quietly from behind me. He reached forward to grab my hand.

Bronwyn slapped it away. Her eyes dared him to react.

I turned my body so that I was now facing Westley in a defensive stance of my sister instead of the other way around.

"Please, just go upstairs. I'll handle this," I whispered to him.

He was intentionally taking slow, deep breaths to calm himself, and I prayed he was sober enough to walk away from Bronwyn. After a few moments of jaw clenching, he stepped around us and headed up the stairs. I closed my eyes, relieved.

"What the hell is wrong with you?" Bronwyn spat at the back of my head, the concern in her voice replaced with her usual disdain. "I know he did something, Cosette. Otherwise, Micah wouldn't have had to drag him out of here half-naked in the middle of the night." I turned around to try again to convince her, but she wasn't finished. "You'd better be careful. I mean, he did already kill Julia Davis. What's to stop you from being next?"

There was a shattering of glass. I didn't even have time to wonder what Westley had thrown that broke the window beside the front door before he was standing over us both, his eyes wildly fixed on my sister. "You horrible *bitch*!"

"Walk away, Westley," I tried to say firmly. I had no way to predict his reaction, not now, and Bronwyn had pushed the one button that even on a better day could detonate him.

"I'm not afraid of you, Westley," my sister stupidly said from behind me. But for every step he took toward us, she took two back.

"I didn't kill Julia Davis," he said flatly. "But if I knew I could get away with it, I would *murder* you, Bronwyn! And the thing about it is—everyone would be better off. You already have no friends, so no one would miss you. It would sure as hell make Cosette's life a lot easier. Oh, and I'd be sparing your daughter growing up with a stupid slut of a mother. Cosi and I could raise her together and pretend you never existed. I'll be the father your bastard baby never had."

I couldn't believe such hateful words were coming out of the man I loved. "Westley, *please* stop."

"That sounds like a threat, Westley," Bronwyn piped up. "Guess I'm really calling the police now." She pulled out her phone and dialed three numbers.

I rested both hands on Westley's chest and pleaded for him to step back.

Bronwyn's shaky voice spoke from behind me, and I couldn't tell if she was genuinely afraid or acting. "Yeah, hello—there is someone in my house threatening me with physical violence. Please send someone...oh, and my baby is here with me."

Just as Westley shook my hands off and lunged past me at my sister, the front door flung open.

It took Micah less than a second to assess the situation. He jumped in the path of Westley's rage and bore the brunt intended for Bronwyn.

"Are you kidding me, Micah? Get the hell out of my way!" Westley barked as I pulled at him from behind.

"You need to leave, Westley!" Micah spoke with an authority that made me stand up straight. "Right now, walk away."

"You seriously think you can stop me from doing anything? I could kill you. And if I find out you laid a hand on Cosette, I will!"

"And now he's threatening to kill someone else..." I heard Bronwyn whisper into her phone.

174

"You need to get some help. And if you aren't going to make that realization the easy way, then you are going to have to do it the hard way." Micah set his stare into Westley's eyes.

Westley attempted to push around Micah, but he reached out his arm and—in a gesture that seemed to break laws of physics—pushed Westley with such force that he flew backward from the hallway and into the living room wall, knocking over everything in his path.

Micah shook his head. "He always picks the hard way."

My mouth dropped in a mirror image of my sister's.

"You're dead!" Westley immediately stood and charged toward Micah again. He stood firm, and when West was in arm's reach, he grabbed his hand, swung him around into what looked like a wrestling hold, and pinned him immediately to the ground, his face planted into the hallway tile. Westley struggled to flip back over, but Micah crouched over his back, a grip so strong around the back of Westley's neck it was as if he'd been nailed to the floor.

I'd never seen anyone so easily take Westley down. My brain couldn't make sense of the scene before me. Micah was so clearly smaller than his opponent. I was pretty sure that *I* could have knocked him over with the head start West had, but there they were on the floor, Micah one-handedly holding him fixed to the ground.

The room was still other than Westley's struggle to escape Micah's grip. "Did he hurt either of you?" Micah asked, pointing to both of us with his free hand.

"How the hell are you doing that?" Bronwyn read my own thoughts.

"He's not as strong as he looks," Micah explained unconvincingly.

"Thank God for us, neither are you," Bronwyn snorted.

It was then we saw a red light dart across the wall to the entranceway. It was quickly followed by a blue one that chased it along the back wall where Westley was plastered only moments ago.

The police had arrived.

CHAPTER 28

At any given time, there were a total of six police officers on duty in our tiny town. We, fortunately, did not have enough crime in our community to warrant our own SWAT team, but for that very reason, every officer working a beat had nothing better to do that afternoon. They all showed up at my house within two minutes of one another.

Bronwyn and I were taken into our kitchen by one officer, while Micah and Westley remained with another in the hallway.

"Are your parents home?" the policeman asked us.

"No one is here but us, and my daughter who is asleep upstairs," Bronwyn answered while I rubbernecked to see what was happening in the hallway. I could hear Westley's heated voice arguing, and I sighed.

Someone needed to defend Westley, and since his behavior was likely adding insults to his own injuries, I decided I would have to do it. "This is all a big misunderstanding—"

"I don't know how anyone would misunderstand Westley threatening to kill me," Bronwyn raised her voice.

"Westley? That's Tim Greene's boy?" The officer arched both brows. I nodded, and he dropped his guard, scratching his head. "Did he actually touch either one of you?"

I shook my head, but Bronwyn, sensing the change in the cop's demeanor, reminded him loudly, "He threatened to *murder* me, and I'm pretty sure *murder* is a crime no matter who your father is."

The officer sighed loudly, debating. "You ladies stay here. I'll be right back." He left us in the kitchen and joined the others in the hallway.

"You are kidding me!" Bronwyn was incredulous. "Well, if you are in the market for a new house, maybe my dad could buy me some justice too!"

The policeman ignored Bronwyn's accusation and joined the others in the hallway.

I followed him with my gaze to avoid my sister's eyes.

She grabbed my chin and pointed my face back toward hers. "You'd better start explaining what the hell has been going on around here, Cosette."

I slapped her hand away. "I told you, I got a bloody nose last night at a party. Aside from that, I have all the same questions you do." I peeked back toward the hallway and saw our officer making a call on his phone.

"Liar."

"What do you want me to say, Bronwyn? Westley is going through a lot right now trying to get over Julia's death. You getting up in our business isn't helping things."

"I thought you were dead, Cosette. Your room has all the makings of a crime scene—empty pill bottles, bloody scissors, and God knows what's in that bag in your bathroom that smells like death. It doesn't take a CSI to know that there's more to the story than a bloody nose."

"Things are just really complicated right now, Bronwyn."

"Complicated? Watching David manhandle Goliath in there was more than complicated. *This shit is crazy.*"

Complicated, crazy. Magic, miracles. Tomato, to*mah*to. "OK, fine—I get it. None of this makes sense to you, but trust me—everything that's happening here makes even less sense to me. And I don't know what you expect me to do about it!"

Something caught her eye from the hall, and she stood, smiling smugly. "I guess maybe I don't need you to do anything."

I jerked around to see what had suddenly made her so glib and saw Westley, now standing with his face against the wall, arms behind his back, being handcuffed.

CHAPTER 29

"Here ya go," Eastlyn said as she handed me a Styrofoam cup of coffee and seated herself in the stiff, plastic chair next to me in the waiting area of the Middlebury Police Department.

"Thanks."

Southeby took the seat on Eastlyn's other side and occupied his hands by bouncing an empty soda bottle on his knees.

Mr. and Mrs. Greene had been in a room with Westley and Officer James, the policeman Bronwyn and I had talked to, for the past half hour. Before that, I was in a separate room with his female partner, Officer Detweiler. She asked me twelve different variations of the same question—Was Westley an abusive boyfriend?—and jotted down my version of what had happened between Micah, Bronwyn, and West.

"So *how* exactly was Mr. Quinn able to restrain Mr. Greene from attacking your sister?" The officer wanted more details surrounding the most unbelievable part of my story. She had no doubt sized up the boys herself and found my explanation lacking.

"I don't know," I answered truthfully, remembering the ease with which Micah had carried Westley to his truck at Julia's funeral. "Maybe he takes steroids."

When my questioning was done, Officer Detweiler took Micah behind closed doors for his, and he had yet to come back out.

Bronwyn had been allowed to give her statement at the house so that she didn't have to bring Ginger down to the station, which was just as well since she didn't typically mix well with my present company.

"Is Westley going to jail?" Southeby asked quietly.

Eastlyn was quick to ease his worries. "Dad wouldn't let that happen. And anyway, I'm not sure what exactly they'd charge him with. He's a minor, and from what you said, Cosi, he didn't actually touch anyone. My guess is worse-case scenario, they'll offer Bronwyn a restraining order."

My stomach fell. If indeed that was an option, there was no way she would refuse it. I guessed I'd be moving into the Greenes' guest room since Westley wouldn't be allowed within three hundred feet of my house.

"The bigger issue here is how Westley gets better, though. He hasn't been the same since Julia, and things are only getting worse." Eastlyn looked over at me with narrowed eyes, her out-loud analysis of her brother's condition reminding her of my fall. "How's your nose feeling, Cosette?"

"Amazingly better," I responded honestly. "I feel as though it never happened." I still hadn't had the opportunity to process my healing. Or my need for healing. Or really anything else that had happened in the past two days. But even if I'd had the time to sort through it all, I knew that I wouldn't be any closer to the truth of what was happening unless Micah was willing to help me understand it.

I allowed Eastlyn to feel for herself. "Wow, that's really incredible..."

The sound of a door opening down the hallway made all three of us jump. Mr. Greene emerged from one of the rooms and called for us. "Kids, can you join us here for a minute? You too, Cosette." Westley's father's tone was firm, and the three of us obediently filed down the hall.

We followed Mr. Greene into a room with a long conference table. At the far end sat Officer James, a tearful Mrs. Greene, and a somber Westley. His handcuffs had been removed, and his arms were folded across his chest.

The Greene children seated themselves on both sides of their mother, while Mr. Greene offered me the seat next to Westley. He remained standing as he spoke. "So, we've reached an impasse here with Westley, and I thought I'd call everyone in to get their input on what needs to happen next."

I hesitantly put my hand on West's knee. He wouldn't look at me.

"As we've all seen, Westley has not been himself these past few weeks since Julia died. His mother and I have been trying to give him a chance to grieve this on his own, but he's showing us that he needs professional help."

Westley sighed.

"Officer James has agreed to drop any charges against Westley if we admit him to an inpatient treatment facility to help him get better."

My heart sank. Inpatient. Mr. Greene wanted to send Westley away.

"The nearest one that specializes in young adults is called Maplecrest and is about ninety minutes away in Fort Wayne. I spoke with one of the doctors there, and they are confident they have a program that could help him."

Tears filled my eyes again. I'd lost count of how many times I had cried that day.

"So our options are these—we send Westley away to get better, or he stays here and faces some pretty serious charges."

"What would he be charged with exactly?" Eastlyn asked for the rest of us.

There was a long silence following this question. "I think he should tell you."

Westley rolled his eyes. "Well, there's the underage drinking, thanks to me blowing a point zero two on the Breathalyzer. And then there's assault with child endangerment for threatening Bronwyn while Ginger was in the house, destruction of property, disorderly conduct, and probably a few more Dad asked the cops to make up so my record will be ruined if I don't choose to go to the mental hospital." Though he copped an attitude, I could still sense his shame as he admitted his actions to his brother and sister.

I thought again of how close involuntary manslaughter was to being added to the list and shuddered.

"Well, this is an easy vote for me. Westley, I love you too much to see you hurting like this. I want my brother back. I vote you go to Maplecrest." Eastlyn was no-nonsense, which was easy for her to do since she was his sister and not his fiancée.

Heads turned to Southeby. "When would you leave?"

"Tonight," Mr. Greene answered. "We want him better as soon as possible."

I sank into the floor.

Southeby frowned and considered his options, but we all knew what he'd say. "I'm sorry, West. But I want you to go get better too."

Westley scoffed. "Well, Cosette and I have already decided that I can handle this on my own."

I thought back to what I'd agreed that day at the park, the pre-almost-killed-by-Westley promise. "West..."

"Scott, would it be too much to ask for us to give them a moment alone?" Mr. Greene asked the officer quietly. He nodded. I shot West's dad a grateful glance as the room cleared.

"We already discussed this, Cosi," Westley reminded me as the door shut behind them. "I'm not going."

I reached for his hand. "Things aren't getting any better, West."

"Your face is better." He pointed out suspiciously, and I wondered if he'd started to remember more about the previous night.

Fresh tears fell from my eyes. "*This* time, I got better."

"Cosette, I swear I can do this alone. Don't send me to some crazy house." Tears welled up in his eyes. "Don't give up on me."

"I feel like you are the one giving up on us, Westley!" Part of me wished he knew what he'd done to me, how close we'd been to losing each other forever. But even if there was a way to explain it to him, I wouldn't have been able to do it because it would have hurt him too badly. "Don't you want to get better for us? Don't you want us to have a future?"

"Of course I do!" He was crying now. "But I'm scared, Cosette! I feel like I'm broken inside. Like I'm unfixable...What if I go to this hospital and they find something really wrong with me?"

I reached my arms around him to comfort him, and he pulled me into his lap and buried his face in my shoulder.

I felt his pain. I felt his heart breaking. I felt everything he felt.

"I'm afraid to be away from you, Westley. But I'm more afraid of what happens if you stay." I treaded lightly, hoping not to jog a memory. "The pills, the drinking, those awful things you said to Bronwyn. That's not you. And I'm worried it's who you'll allow yourself to become if you don't get help. I'm worried that next time...maybe you'll hurt me...and I *won't* get better."

He started crying harder. "I know, Cosette. I've thought of that too...I'd never forgive myself..."

I kissed his forehead and stroked his hair. I hated to have to be the one to convince Westley to leave me. "Does that mean you'll go?"

He sniffed. "Do I have a choice?"

My thoughts went back to the conversation Micah and I had had in class, the one about soul mates. "There's always a choice, Westley. And you're mine."

CHAPTER 30

One of the conditions to Officer James clearing Westley was that Bronwyn had to agree not to press charges. They asked me to call and reason with her.

"So, if I press charges, Westley stays here but only has to stay away from me. But if I don't, he goes to the insane asylum and you won't see him either?" She was giddy. "Where do I sign?"

Mr. Greene rode with the officer back to my house for Bronwyn's signature, to pick up the Mustang, and to drop off a blank check to my father for the damages Westley had inflicted on my house.

With Bronwyn's consent to drop charges, all Westley had to do was finish paperwork at the station and he'd be free to leave for Maplecrest. His mom was going to stay with him while Eastlyn and Southeby went back to the house to pack.

"Go with them, Cosi," he instructed, still pulling himself back together after making his decision to leave.

Though I didn't want to leave him for a second—knowing we'd soon be separated indefinitely—I knew he wouldn't have asked for time alone had he not needed it. I rode in the Yukon back to the Greenes' home.

It was approaching dusk when we pulled into the driveway, and as our headlights lit the path up the hill to the garage, we saw Micah's truck parked there. He was sitting in the cab.

Eastlyn pulled the SUV up beside him.

"Hey," Micah said, all of us exiting our vehicles together. "I hope I'm not intruding. I just wanted to check on Westley."

"He's not here," Eastlyn responded, though I was sure his comment had been directed to me. "But you're welcome to come in anyway. I hear we owe you for keeping Westley off a murder-one charge."

Micah shot me a look.

It occurred to me that he'd now rescued both my sister and me from Westley coming undone, and he needed clarification regarding whose saving Eastlyn was referencing. "Yes, Bronwyn sends her thanks for saving her life. I'm sure she'll pick up a card for you tomorrow."

"No sweat," he smiled.

We entered through the garage, and as we approached the door to the house, we could hear Northrop barking hysterically from inside the house.

"What's up with our dog?" Southeby wondered out loud while punching a code into the keypad to disarm the security alarm. As he turned the doorknob, the Greenes' Labrador pushed his way out of the house. "Get back, boy!" He used his foot to block the dog from escaping into the garage. Northrop's bark was replaced by a desperate whine.

"Aww, you can let him out. I love dogs," Micah said eagerly, and with that, Southeby stepped aside.

Northrop bounded two steps out the door, his tail wagging furiously, and pounced at Micah, knocking him off-balance onto his backside. The dog immediately began licking his face.

"Calm down, McNally!" Micah scolded with a smile at the same time Eastlyn yelled, "Get back, Northrop!"

Micah and Eastlyn looked at one another and in unison said, "What did you say?"

Eastlyn smiled and answered first. She was laughing as she unsuccessfully worked to restrain her dog's enthusiasm. "I called him *Northrop*, which is his name. Why? What did you call him?" She bent down to lure her dog's affections away from the guest, but he was undeterred.

Micah blushed the way most guys did around Eastlyn. "Oh...I...uh...I called him McNally," he stammered, the dog still lapping at his cheeks. "He looks just like a dog I used to have. Name slipped out when he surprised me, I guess." Then to the dog he emphasized, "All right, *Northrop*, calm down." Southeby helped Micah up, and all of us made our way into the house, Northrop at Micah's heels. Southeby went into the basement to retrieve the needed suitcases while the rest of us filed into the kitchen. Eastlyn grabbed some bottles of water from the fridge and distributed them to us as we sat down at the table. The dog sat at Micah's feet.

We surrounded the table, fiddling with our drinks.

Micah broke the silence. "Does Westley hate me?" he asked, wincing in expectation of the answer.

"He didn't bring you up, actually," I related, remembering all we'd talked about at the station. "I think he's probably still embarrassed. But no, I doubt he hates you."

"Oh," Micah said, looking slightly relieved and disappointed at the same time. "When does he leave?"

"As soon as we take his stuff to the police station."

He frowned.

"How old are you, Micah?" Eastlyn's question was off the topic.

"Um...eighteen?" he answered her curiously.

"So, you're graduating this year," she stated before following up. "Where are you planning on for college?" Eastlyn twisted a lock of blonde hair in her fingers, her eyes locked into Micah's.

"I haven't given college much thought."

Eastlyn's smile lingered a touch too long on her lips.

Was she flirting with Micah?

This seemed impossible. Eastlyn Greene, after all, was her own league of woman. In the food chain, she was the sun. Micah, on the other hand, was less...extraordinary. I looked at him sideways and decided in the same scenario, he probably ranked somewhere around prairie dog.

I took the moment to size him up for really the first time. Micah had light hair, which was extremely blond for winter, and the greenish-brown eye color most people called hazel. He was built like a cross-country runner, lean and fit, and was wearing a too-tight T-shirt and faded jeans.

I supposed that he wasn't *unattractive*. He just wasn't attractive to me, and I couldn't imagine how Eastlyn could notice him over her own blinding radiance. I could understand how someone would be intrigued by Micah if she had experienced the things about him I had, but as far as I knew, Eastlyn only met him the one time at the funeral. Still, she appeared transfixed on him, seeing something that I didn't.

At the sound of clanging in the basement, Micah excused himself to help Southeby drag the suitcases up the stairs. Northrop followed.

Eastlyn's eyes followed Micah's exit, and then she turned to me and whispered, "I swear I know him from somewhere, Cosette. Does he have an older brother or something?"

I shrugged. We hadn't found time for chitchat about our family lives in between time-bending and miracles. In the two minutes we'd sat at the kitchen table, Eastlyn managed more straight answers from him than I had in all the time I'd known him. "Why don't you just ask him?"

"I don't know." The thought seemed not to have occurred to her. "I feel like I shouldn't, though. That I need to just figure it out myself."

I nodded. "Good luck with that."

◆◆◆

A few minutes later, the four of us trudged up the stairs to Westley's room.

Having never myself vacationed in a treatment hospital before, I was at a loss for what to pack for my fiancé's stay in one.

We stood in the middle of his room with two empty suitcases open on his bed.

Eastlyn quickly got to work collecting the necessities—T-shirts, socks, underwear, toothbrush. Southeby tossed in a few copies of *Sports Illustrated*. Micah looked at a bookshelf and suggested a photo album, and then pitched in one I'd made for Westley a few years ago for an anniversary.

As everyone buzzed around me, I sat down at the edge of West's bed. They didn't need my help, and I didn't have any to offer.

I wanted Westley to get better, to beat whatever it was about Julia's death that kept torturing him, but I wasn't used to him needing help overcoming anything.

I faced his wall of achievement—his baseball trophies, academic awards, and countless other medals and certificates recognizing his endless talents. All of this proof that he could accomplish anything he attempted.

Westley was gifted. He was fortunate. He was an invincible teenager with potential oozing from each pore of his body. It felt like all of this should have made him immune to the affliction that plagued him. But it didn't.

In scanning the wall, my eyes fell upon a team photo from the previous spring, framed in a plaque from their regional win. Westley stood in a huddle with his teammates, each raising a hand with an index finger pointed to the sky. At his side stood Patrick Wellman. Both of them were smiling ear to ear, a moment of happiness frozen in time.

I remembered that day. I'd been in the stands on my feet, cheering and hugging Westley's parents when the picture was snapped. Julia would have been no farther than a few rows away from me, equally excited, equally alive.

But now she was gone, and instead of her fall taking Patrick down, she haunted Westley.

It didn't make sense—why *wasn't* it Patrick? What did he have? What was it about him that he was spared the same breakdown as Westley?

It wasn't that I wanted him to suffer alongside my boyfriend. I just wanted him to share with Westley whatever antidote he was using to get him through each day.

My brooding was interrupted by Micah clearing his throat. "Are you gonna help us?" He pointed to the two now almost-full suitcases.

I shrugged and looked back at Westley's picture. I was still trying to figure out who was going to help me.

CHAPTER 31

The entire Greene family sat inside their SUV and patiently waited for Westley to tell me good-bye, which he'd requested to do inside the privacy of my car.

"You are *seriously* not letting me come with you?" I choked the words out. Had I known we wouldn't have the hour-and-a-half drive down to Fort Wayne together, I never would have gone back to his house to pack for him. I felt tricked, angry, and sad—a trifecta of unpleasantness.

"Cosette, *please*," he was fighting back his own tears. "I'm not doing this to hurt you. I have no idea what this place is going to be like, and I don't want you to see something that's going to upset you."

I wished he'd given me the same consideration a day earlier before getting hammered at Trevor's. The memory of him wasted was tattooed on my brain forever.

"Does that mean you aren't going to let me visit you while you're gone?" I stopped my tears only long enough to panic at this thought.

"Of course not! I just want to be able to brace you for what it's like before you see it." Westley stroked my hair, and my faucet turned back on. "No, you have to visit. If I have to go too long without seeing you, I'll really need a psych ward."

Our conversation, the past few days, every moment since Julia had died—it was all surreal to me. I didn't want to say good-bye to Westley long enough for him to go to baseball practice. I couldn't say good-bye to him now with no way of knowing when we could be together again.

Westley leaned in and kissed me, and I wrapped both my hands around his neck so that he wouldn't pull away. And he didn't.

He held me and comforted me, and for those moments, we were us again, the world beyond his arms nonexistent.

"So I have something for you," he said seriously. "I wrote it while you were getting my stuff." Westley pulled a white envelope from his pocket and handed it to me. "Those are my vows."

I was confused. "Like, wedding vows?"

"Of course wedding vows," he teased. "I was thinking about what I wanted to say to you on our wedding day long before I picked out your ring. Tonight, it felt like the right time to put it down on paper. But I don't want you to read them right now." He pointed to the envelope. "I want this to serve as my promise to you that I'm going to get better. I don't know how long this is going to take me, or what they're going to find wrong with me, but I'm sure as hell going to fight every day to get better so that I can come home to you. We are going to have that happily ever after."

At a loss for words, I nodded.

"You can open it whenever you need to, Cosette. The words I wrote in there were true six years ago, and they'll be true any time you ever need to hear them."

I doubted the envelope would stay sealed through the night.

Westley's lips met mine again, but this time our moment was interrupted by a tap on the window.

"Sorry to bother you guys," the voice on the other side of the foggy glass apologized, "but I need to talk to you, Westley."

Micah. Again.

When we'd parted ways at the Greenes' house, I could sense he was still uneasy about all that happened, especially the way things were left between him and Westley. But I didn't guess he was so distraught by them that he'd crash our last moments together.

"Really?" Westley rolled his eyes and lowered the window. "Come back to kick my ass again? I think I'm still good from the last time."

"Whatever, nobody kicked anyone's anything." Micah brushed off West's comment. "I wanted to come here to tell you..." His thought trailed into silence. He scratched the back of his head and looked away, and for the first time since I'd met him, Micah seemed at a loss for what to say.

"I haven't got all day. My nuthouse is waiting."

Micah groaned in frustration at himself. "OK, I'm *not* the villain that you think I am, Westley. Despite whatever it is you think I am trying to take away from you, I just want you to know that more than anything...I'm *rooting* for you. I'm...*praying* for you."

Westley was caught off guard and shot me a look out of the corner of his eye. "Um, OK. Thanks?"

"And I guess I understand if you hate me. I just wish you didn't." Micah nodded, having said what he needed to say. Then he turned and started walking back to his truck.

Westley closed his eyes and muttered under his breath, "Like I need this right now." Then he turned to me. "C'mon, Cosi," he said and jumped out of the car. "Micah!"

Micah stopped walking and turned around.

I ran behind the back of my car to join Westley.

"Listen, Micah...I'm not an idiot. I've definitely been *acting* like one lately, but honestly—I know I owe you big-time. I mean, I have no idea why you did whatever you did for me last night, but I'm guessing I didn't end up in that Amish motel from hell because of my *good* behavior. So thanks. And thanks for today too. As good as it would have felt to knock Bronwyn out...Well, I'm glad you stopped me...I don't understand *how* you stopped me, but I'm still glad you did."

I reached for Westley's hand and squeezed it. I felt as though he was already getting better.

Micah half-smiled. "Don't mention it."

"But as grateful as I am right now, I still think you're weird and possibly after my woman. So I'm going to be using all my spare time in the clink to bulk up." Westley spoke flatly so that Micah wouldn't know if he was serious. "So while you're saying a prayer for me, you might want to add on something about me never finding out you've been messing with Cosette."

Micah wasn't dissuaded. "I would expect nothing less from you." His half smile spread to a whole, and he extended a hand out to West.

Westley returned the handshake and the smile.

Having watched the scene unfold from the SUV, Mr. Greene decided that this was the opportune moment to remind his son they needed to go.

Seizing the chance to leave before my tears started again, Westley turned to me and whispered, "Happily ever after—I promise." Then he kissed me good-bye and took off across the lot.

Micah and I stood silently as he got into the car. We both gave halfhearted waves as the Yukon pulled out of the drive and headed south.

I watched the taillights until they faded into the night. I could feel when Micah's eyes shifted from the disappearing SUV and onto me, but I didn't acknowledge him. He wanted me to speak first; I could tell. But I didn't want to talk to him. There wasn't a sentence I knew how to start that didn't end in a question mark, and I didn't have the energy for the mental gymnastics he would surely put me through.

I stuck to my guns, and he broke first. "Have you eaten anything today?"

"No," I realized. "I didn't have time for a sandwich in between the 'miracles' and the mental demise of my boyfriend." I checked the time and found it later than I'd expected. When *had* I last eaten?

He stepped toward me. "Are you hungry?"

"Kinda..." I sniffled back remnants of my earlier cry.

"Let's go somewhere. I'll feed you."

CHAPTER 32

"I think I just lost my appetite." I rolled down my window to inform Micah. I pulled the Element next to his truck in the gravel drive of the farmhouse. "I thought we were going to a restaurant. Does this place even have a functional kitchen?"

"Haven't we been through this whole provision thing already?" He smiled. "I wanted to go somewhere we could talk without interruption. And I've got the food thing covered."

"If you say so..." I stared up at the house. Nightfall had painted it with several new coats of creepiness, and I didn't want to go in. "You don't really *live* here, do you?"

"No." He shook his head. "Just hanging out here for a while."

"I wouldn't hang out here as a ghost."

"Good thing you aren't a ghost then. C'mon." He started out toward the door and waved me to follow.

My eyes were still on the house, and as I thought of reentering it, a shiver crawled through me.

Then, I reminded myself what I knew of Micah and decided if there was something in the house to fear, *it* should be afraid of *him*. I got out of my car.

He held the door open but asked me to wait on the porch until he lit some candles and started a fire.

"I'll be right back," he assured me.

I wished I'd waited in the car. Rather than rock in the creaking swing, I stood stoically with my back against the peeling wood siding. My uneasiness in those few minutes prevented me from dwelling on the day's events, which was the only bright side to being left alone outside my vote for "house most likely to be haunted" in Middlebury. My short, quick breaths puffed visibly into the cold night air.

Micah's rummaging noises from within the house were replaced by the familiar crackling of a fire, and through the window, I could see small but growing flames from the fireplace.

"Ready for me yet?" The sound of my own voice in the silence spooked me, and I didn't wait for a response before entering the house. The screen door slammed shut behind me, frightening me further and sending a gust of wind across the room that threatened the life of the fire. "Micah?"

I looked toward the dining table where the flames of three candles bobbed their delayed response to the shift I'd caused in the air. "Where are you?" I beelined to the table and snatched up one of the candles to use as my own light source.

The candle holder was dirty pewter, and I held it low at my waist so that my eyes could focus on what its fire illuminated rather than the flame itself. The open room was not completely lit, but as far as I could see, Micah was not present in it. I decided he'd gone back into another room, perhaps the bedroom where Westley had slept, and was out of earshot.

When I felt some wax drip onto my hand, I realized I was shaking. I took slow steps to the fireplace. Drawing a deep breath, I called loudly in the direction of the bedroom hallway. "I'm pretty sure that this goes without saying, Micah, but if you are planning on jumping out to scare me, today is *not* the best day to mess with me."

Though I faced the fire, I felt a burst of warm air from behind me.

"I wouldn't dare," Micah answered from mere inches away, and I screamed so loud the glass in the windows shook. Spinning around in an about-face, I poised my candle as a weapon. "Calm down, Cosette. It's just me!"

I sighed in both anger at him for scaring me and relief that he'd stopped hiding. "Don't you *ever* sneak up on me like that again!"

"Deal. I'm sorry." Around Micah's shoulder hung a bulging burlap sack. "How hungry are you?" he asked, pointing to the bag.

"I'm more confused than I am hungry," I confessed, still shaken.

"One thing at a time."

Over the next few minutes, Micah scavenged for materials to prepare our dinner. He found the metal mixing bowl I'd previously used as a mirror and an iron pot in the kitchen, and then filled them with the snow from a bank that had drifted onto the side of the house. He then set it near the fireplace. In moments, it melted into water, and he used it to scrub the dishes clean on the porch. Soon, he returned with the pot empty and the bowl filled again with snow.

He pulled two wooden rockers up to the fireplace and opened his bag. "I didn't know what you were in the mood for, so I just grabbed what I could." He began to unload the bag's contents into the bowl.

He removed from it several plant stems with green, bulbous fruit still attached and a handful of seeds. "How do you feel about olives?"

My mouth dropped opened. "Those particular ones?" I pointed as he plucked them from their stems, shook them around in the snow, and dropped them into the pot. "Absolutely mystified."

He chuckled, threw some seeds into the pot with the olives, and set it almost all the way into the fire.

"Care for an appetizer?" He reached into his bag and removed what looked to me like two oblong plums.

"What are they?" I was skeptical for too many reasons to be an ambitious eater.

"Figs. Ever have one?"

"Only in Newton form."

"So, no, then. Here." Micah demonstrated how to pierce the fruit with his fingers and then tore it into two pieces. He handed one half to me and turned the other inside out, popped it into his mouth, and began chewing.

Watching him eat incited a deep growl from my stomach. My nerves were calming after a day of insanity, and my body was voicing its needs.

I watched Micah for a moment, and when he didn't immediately die, I followed his lead.

My teeth tore through the sweet flesh, and I swallowed the first gulp of its juice. I chewed eagerly through the skin, in hopes of satisfying my hunger with something more substantial than its liquid.

After I'd ingested the fruit, the aftertaste lingered in my mouth. I wanted more.

This time, Micah offered me the entire second fig, and I ate it all in less than a minute.

This pleased him. "Wow, you really are hungry!"

How had I never tried this food before? It amazed me. "Where in the world did you get these, Micah? This is the best thing I've ever put in my mouth."

He laughed. "I grew them. Or, at least, I helped."

"You *grew* them?" Having lived in Indiana all my life surrounded by soybeans and corn, I was sure that this food was *not* native to the Hoosier state. Not to mention—it was winter. "Where?"

He waited to answer me. "Back home."

I licked the last hint of fig from my lips and considered Micah's hesitancy. "Am I not supposed to ask what that means?"

"You can ask...but there are other questions I need to answer for you first." He used his bag as a makeshift potholder and pulled the olives out of the fire. "These are probably warm enough. Most people I know eat them raw." He lifted the lid and smelled. "Not sure the cumin had enough time to release...but I doubt you'll be disappointed."

They were warm to the touch, but not too hot to hold barehanded. As I bit into the first one, its bitterness was shocking to my taste buds, which were still grieving the ending of the figs. The cumin was more potent than Micah had thought, and the flavors complemented each other well. We both ate a few, and soon I found myself full.

Unlike the drowsiness I'd become accustomed to feeling after a big, satisfying meal, I felt reenergized by Micah's food. I was suddenly just as hungry for the answers he'd promised me as I'd been for the dinner he had prepared.

Micah read my mind because he sat back into his rocker and turned it to face me. I mimicked the movement. He looked strangely anxious, but I didn't let it deter me. "Thanks for dinner. Now let's talk."

He laughed at my enthusiasm. "So you really think you are ready to know everything?"

I didn't give myself the chance to back down. "No, but I want you to tell me anyway."

"Then so be it."

"Where do we start?" I asked. He'd mentioned something about needing to tell me certain things before others. I thought I'd just let him begin and interrupt to press for the details I would want but was sure he'd be vague about.

"Well, how about you tell me whether or not you are enjoying your Christmas present?"

"Oh, no," I was quick to argue. "I shouldn't have to do anything but listen to you explain away the last few weeks of my life. In full disclosure."

He made a face at me. "This is a conversation, Cosette. Not a lecture." Then he asked again, "So, have you read any part of it?"

"A little," I confessed. "Been busy with other things. Like almost dying. My boyfriend going to a mental hospital. Hanging out with Middlebury's answer to Superman."

He ignored my sarcasm. "OK, so of what you read, what did you think?"

I tried to recall the verse from Corinthians and the first six chapters in Genesis I'd made it through before falling asleep the night before. "It was good, I guess. Confusing."

"Did you believe any part of what you read?"

"I don't know? Is it supposed to be true?"

Mrs. Holloway had spent a lot of time teaching us about allegory. I didn't know if what I'd read was thought of as accurate or just a story used to explain how the world came to be.

"Are you open to that idea?"

Humans formed from dust. Talking serpents. I wasn't sure how much of a stretch all this was in light of Micah's time-bending, healing power, and super-ninja combat skills. None of it made any sense to me, but I had experienced for myself the impossibilities of Micah. "Honestly...I think that if *you* told me the Bible was true, then I would believe it."

He let out a low whistle. "Wow, that's dangerous, Cosette. Putting all your faith in a guy like me. What happens the first time I let you down?" He didn't wait for me to guess. "Then you doubt everything I've ever said or done. It would be very easy to convince yourself I'm the bad guy instead of the superhero."

My answer had been wrong. "Then what am I supposed to do? Fake it? Pretend it all makes sense to me when it doesn't?"

"Nope." He shook his head. "All you have to do is *try* to have *faith*. Read the book. Pray. Consider the things you experienced. And then decide for yourself."

"OK." This challenge didn't sound so hard. I would prob- ably need something to fill my extra time with anyway now that Westley was gone for the foreseeable future, and figuring out what I believed about the universe was a more meaning- ful use of time than sobbing into my pillow. "But what does that have to do with you giving me answers right now?"

"Everything." He didn't miss a beat. "I don't know if you are aware of this, Cosette, but the miracle you experienced doesn't happen every day. You were spared—saved. And it wasn't randomly or accidentally. You have a purpose. There is a plan. And you're going to want to be fully equipped before you're asked to make a choice about whether to participate in it."

His words were weights upon my shoulders. "You healed me, so I could take part in this plan for my life? You saved my life, and now I owe you?" I tried to explain why I found what Micah was saying so foreboding.

197

He buried his face in his hands, losing patience with me and himself. "No, of course not! *I* didn't heal you. You were healed *through* me. And no one's charging you anything for that. But you do have the responsibility of figuring out how you believe it happened to you, right? Don't you want to know why?"

Of course I wanted to know. But I couldn't imagine I'd stumble upon the answer reading a book thousands of pages long alone in my room. I wanted Micah to give me the answers. "How am I supposed to figure that out?"

My question hung in the air.

Finally, he raised his head. "Come home with me."

"Right now?" I checked the time on my phone. It was already late in the evening of the longest day of my life; school was to resume the next day and bring with it several fresh helpings of drama. I would need to prepare my response to the rumors that were sure to surround Westley's absence. But at the same time, I needed to know the truth. I couldn't imagine trying to go to sleep that night without at least one of the giant mysteries closer to being solved. "How is that going to help me understand all this?"

"If I could explain that to you, we wouldn't need to go there."

"Fine." I accepted this as true, though it annoyed me to do so. Nothing was simple with Micah. Nothing was normal. After what I'd experienced with him, I should know better than to expect anything else.

At that moment, something occurred to me. All of Micah's paranormal behaviors had to have originated from somewhere. And if I couldn't expect easy answers about who he was, I doubted I could about where he came from, either.

I asked him skeptically, "Where exactly would we be going?"

The implication in my tone pleased him. "Not far."

"How would we get there?"

"Unconventionally." He smiled as he volleyed these vague responses at me as though they were breadcrumbs on a trail to an answer I was close to discovering for myself. He was leading me somewhere, but I was too confused to follow.

"So what am I supposed to conclude from this conversation about where we're going, Micah? That you're going put on your cape and fly us to Candyland? The merry ol' land of Oz?" My frustration with his intentional obscurity was rising.

"Sure. Expect those things. And then decide if you're still ready to come with me. Because any scenario you come up with, no matter how farfetched, is nothing compared to where I will take you."

I dropped my jaw, and my attitude did the same.

"Cosette, I always told myself that if I was ever given the opportunity to bring someone home that I would do everything I could to let them know what they were getting themselves into first." He flipped his hair from his face and fidgeted. His uneasiness was contagious. "It's like this. I know there is no way for you to know *how* where I'm taking you will change your life. But, trust me, it will. After you see this place, you'll never be the same again. I want to be clear about that before you decide whether or not to go."

I stood abruptly and walked away from the fireplace, needing to put space between us. My world was unrecognizable compared to before Julia's death, and now Micah was proposing I play Russian roulette with the remnants of normalcy in my life. "How can I go after hearing you say that?"

"How can you not?"

I felt hot tears spring into my eyes. The weight on my shoulders was becoming unbearable. My mind had overloaded and shut off from a day of intense madness. Suddenly, I didn't care about answers or going to Micah's home anymore. I wanted to go to mine, crawl into bed, and pull the sheets over my face. I wanted to lie unconscious for hours and hours until my world became a more rational place again. "Micah, I think I need to leave..."

He stood and walked toward me, disappointment clouding his face. He was quiet for a long time. "OK, I respect your decision. The invitation is open." I was relieved he didn't try to convince me to go with him. "Can you wait here for one minute while I get something for you?"

Knowing I was only moments away from an escape, I agreed.

"I'll be right back."

I nodded and then used the sleeves of Westley's jacket to dab the tears from my eyes. "I'm really sorry, Mic—," I began an apology but cut myself off when I realized I was again left alone. "Micah?"

The fire had grown significantly from the size it was when I'd first entered the house, and it now shed its light all the way to the four corners of the room, as well as to the fact I'd just witnessed another impossibility: Micah disappeared into thin air.

I held my breath as I searched for another explanation. In the brighter lighting of the room, I noticed the distance from me to the hallway down which Westley slept off his hangover. It was too far away for Micah even to have run to in the moment I'd closed my eyes, and I didn't recall hearing any footsteps in that direction. The day's traffic on the floor was easily traced by the dust that was disturbed; there was no path of footprints leading away from me. In the part of the room where I stood, there were only mine and Micah's leading up to me.

Up to this point, none of Micah's powers had frightened me. They'd intrigued me, freaked me out—sure. They'd also saved my life. But as I stood frozen in the middle of the farmhouse, Micah now one with the invisible air, I was terrified. The part of me that reasoned with the part of me that wanted to wig out threw up her hands. I'd had enough.

The only sense I could make of what had happened was that this house *was* haunted. And I didn't want to wait around for its ghost to return—no matter how friendly he'd proven himself to be.

Once my feet started moving, I darted for the door.

Just as my fingers touched its knob, I felt a hand on my shoulder.

"Cosette, I told you I'd be right ba—"

Once again, his return to the room sent panic through me. As he spun me around to face him, instincts and adrenaline overtook me, and my fist met his cheek with a crack that would have been loud had it not been drowned out by my scream. Micah dropped to the floor.

He groaned in pain from below me, clutching his eye. A moment later, my hand started to throb, and I realized I was still clutching my keys in it.

He struggled to stand as I doubled over from my own pain. "Why did you do that?" he winced as he spoke, and I saw blood oozing from a scratch I'd no doubt carved into his cheek with my Honda switchblade.

"I told you not to scare me like that!" I managed to squeak out my lame justification for domestic abuse.

"Well, I guess I learned *that* lesson the hard way," he retorted. Then he picked something up from the floor he must have dropped when I punched him. "Here, I brought this for you. I was hoping it would give you some peace about your decision. Whatever you choose." He extended his hand to me, still reeling from my sucker punch. "It's from home."

With my good hand, I hesitantly accepted his offer of a single white tulip.

At first glance, the flower appeared to be plastic—too pristine and too off its growing season to be real. However, as its fragrance made its way to me, I noted the veins in the leaves and the velvety petals. There was nothing artificial about it.

"Did you help grow this too?" The figs and olives had appeared to be equally perfect specimens.

"I did." He cringed as he pulled away the sleeve he'd been using to apply pressure to his face and saw it bloodied. The scratch now appeared to be more like a gash, and tissue from the inside of Micah's cheek was exposed.

I covered my mouth with my hands. "Micah, I'm so sorry!" I reached for his face, but he pulled away.

"I forgive you. I had it coming anyway. You warned me." He covered his cheek again. "But I probably should go get this looked at. And you've got some thinking to do anyway."

I nodded as he opened the door for me, and I stepped out onto the porch. "Do you want me to drive you to a clinic or something?"

"No. Won't be necessary."

"Oh, yeah." If Micah could heal broken ribs and punctured lungs, a scratch on the face was probably the healer's equivalent of a cakewalk. "See you in school tomorrow?" I turned to ask him before heading for my car.

"See you in school."

CHAPTER 33

Eastlyn's text message came through on my way home from the farmhouse:

> We made it to the hospital. Doctors took Westley's phone. Says he loves you and will get a hold of you soon. TTYS Sis—Love, E

While I was sad I wasn't going to get to talk to Westley that night, I understood it probably was for the best. He and I both had a lot to sort out separately, and I had no idea how or what I would even tell him about my evening if given the chance.

I arrived home to a dark house. The window beside the door was taped off and sealed, but there were no other signs of the day's altercation remaining. I'd have to remember to thank Grandma, next time I saw her.

I grimaced at the thought of my grandmother, shaking her head in disappointment as she swept up broken glass. Of course, both she and my dad would only have Bronwyn's side of what had happened, and I was sure in her version Westley had horns and carried a pitchfork.

But as currently no one was awake, I didn't have to think about how to reconcile the truth to either of them.

Once I got to bed, it didn't take me nearly as long as I expected to fall asleep. I placed the tulip in a vase on my nightstand and stared at it until my eyelids became too heavy to keep them open. Perhaps Micah's hope for the flower had come true. It had brought me peace.

◆◆◆

The next morning, I arrived at school early in hopes of avoiding as many people as possible in the hallways. The first day back to school after the holidays was always dreadful. Aside from Westley's birthday on the fourteenth of January—which this year he'd likely spend in the hospital—there was nothing to look forward to until Valentine's Day. With the excitement of Christmas worn off, the first weeks back always seemed years long. Now with Westley gone indefinitely, I was sure this month would never end.

As I approached my locker, I imagined things differently—the way the first day back should have been. Westley and I would have arrived at school and been surrounded by the buzz of our engagement. His friends would have congratulated us; Westley would have held my hand out to flash my ring at the baseball players' girlfriends. Life for us would have changed since before break, but for the better. Our new normal would be full of the excitement and possibility of our future.

As I walked down the senior hallway, deep in my daydream, I noticed a locker covered in flowers, cards, and photographs. It wasn't uncommon to see lockers decorated for birthdays or homecoming, but this display was more over-the-top than the typical balloons and ribbon streamers that usually marked a special occasion. Maybe someone else had gotten engaged too? I drifted off course for a better look.

When I got close enough to recognize the girl in the photographs, the fantasy I'd been enjoying shattered. This had been Julia's locker. It hadn't been decorated for a celebration—it had been turned into a shrine in her memory.

I stopped in my tracks. Westley's absence wouldn't be the only one clouding the restarting of school. And it wasn't the only reason why my daydream couldn't have come true.

I shifted my eyes to the ground and hurried to my locker. I filled my backpack with the books I needed for my first three classes so I wouldn't have to return to it before lunch and quickly headed for my first period.

School was going to be pointless today. Between missing Westley and trying to figure out what to do about Micah's invitation, I was sure to learn absolutely nothing. I contemplated leaving, but I knew the day would drag no matter where I spent it. Better to pass the time alone in a crowd than have the crowd pass its time speculating about me.

I parked myself in the back row of my first-hour history class. I'd beaten all the other students—and the teacher—to the room. My backpack slid off of my shoulder and onto the ground with a loud thud, and I bent down to remove my textbook and a blank sheet of paper—the props I would need so as to appear to be paying attention after the bell.

A few minutes later, as I was intently focused on writing the date at the top of my paper, a shadow darkened my desk. I slowly looked up to see a familiar girl whose name, not surprisingly, escaped me.

"Can I help you?" I attempted a friendly smile.

"Yeah, what happened to your face?" she asked bluntly. A few rows behind her sat a silent group of four others staring at us. Her tone was harsh and expectant, and I guessed that was at least partly why she'd been elected as the one to confront me.

"Um..." The girl crossed her arms over her chest to bully me with body language. This was a tricky question for me because I didn't know what exactly she'd noticed—had she been at the party two nights before and seen me disfigured? Or was she commenting on how I looked inexplicably better than before Christmas break? Her tone was definitely accusatory. And whatever she was charging me with, I was sure I looked guilty.

"I got beaten up by a girl," a voice from beside me answered.

I turned my head to see Micah set his backpack down one desk over, a large, adhesive bandage covering the majority of his left cheek.

"Go ahead and tell everyone. Make sure you get my name right though, or it's no fun." He went on to introduce himself to the confused mean girl.

"Weirdo," she mumbled under her breath and turned to rejoin her clique.

I ignored her and stared dumbfounded at Micah. "What are you doing here? We don't have this class together..."

"My face is feeling better; thanks for asking, Cosette," he answered with his trademark snark, and I blushed for not thinking to ask how he was. "And you're welcome for that, by the way." He pointed to the group of girls who all looked away in unison.

"I'm sorry," I apologized. "I guess I'm just surprised to see you. And hey..." I pointed at his bandage. "I'm surprised to see that too."

"Yeah..." Micah shrugged.

"Couldn't heal yourself?" I asked, just above a whisper.

Micah rolled his eyes. "You don't listen to a word I say. It's not up to me," he reminded me. "But no, it's still there."

"So what does that mean then?"

"That it has a purpose," he stated matter-of-factly, settling in his seat. "Who knows? Maybe God's whole plan for you gutting my face with your car key was to keep the attention off you today. Might have been his plan for this too." He slapped a paper face up onto my desk.

I looked down at the document. It was Micah's class schedule.

"Look familiar?"

I read it. It did. It was also *my* class schedule. "You know that it does. What's the deal?"

"Dunno. There was a note on my locker to go to student services. The secretary said there was a problem and they needed to switch some of my classes around."

"Why?"

Micah chuckled. "You sure ask me that a lot."

"And you never answer it."

"So, stop asking it. And start taking advantage of the opportunities placed before you. Maybe you'll figure out these 'whys' for yourself."

The bell rang, signaling the start of class.

Eight o'clock in the morning and my brain already hurt.

"Seriously, man? A chick did that to you?"

It was third period, and apparently word had gotten around about Micah. We were sitting together in physiology waiting for the teacher to start a movie on the evolution of diseases when the football player in front of us turned around to get the story.

"Seriously. Wanna see?" Micah pulled the bandage away from the skin to reveal the scabbed gash.

"That's nasty." The guy made a face. "Looks like you should have had stitches."

He was right. It looked awful.

"Nah," Micah responded. "I doubt it will even scar." He winked at me with his good side.

The lights in the room dimmed, and I poised my pencil to pretend to take notes.

My first two classes of the day went by faster than I'd predicted, thanks to Micah.

He somehow managed to keep me out of the spotlight. In all three periods, the teachers introduced him to the class, inquired about his injury, and chitchatted with him. Though the details he revealed were superficial ones, most of them were still news to me: he'd grown up nearby, but he doubted anyone would recognize him; he had brothers and sisters whom he didn't talk to much; and he loved working outside.

In all three periods, as Micah finished talking, the same word could be heard under the collective breath of the class: jerked-over.

It was Amish tradition that when a person in their community turned sixteen, he or she entered into what's known as Rumspringa. During this transition from adolescent to adult, the Amish kids, as far as the non-Amish kids understood it, did whatever they wanted—much like regular teenagers. Some partied, some dated, some used technology created after 1850.

After a couple years of free-for-all, they had to make a decision—return to their strict, religious sect or be jerked-over to the other side. Because choosing to leave their church meant, ultimately, leaving their family and friends, most kids went back to their traditions around the age of eighteen. Those who didn't were shunned by the Amish community and left to make a life for themselves, alone.

After hearing Micah introduce himself first period, I felt like an idiot for never considering him as a JO. He fit all the criteria—no family, no cell phone, dressed constantly in thrift-store flannel. He kept referring to a "big decision" he'd made.

I couldn't believe I'd missed the obvious answer.

Although, the obvious answer still wasn't a complete one.

As far as I knew it, Amish kids didn't acquire superpowers during Rumspringa. If they did, there would have probably been a lot more JOs running around Middlebury. Or flying around it.

But even though he omitted his special abilities from his bio, Micah was still turning heads. And the heads that were looking at him were ignoring me.

Shortly after the movie started, Micah discreetly slid a piece of notebook paper across our lab table to me. He'd written something on the top line of it.

Think at all about last night?

I let my eyes linger on his question, unsure how to respond to it. Then I scribbled a short answer.

Of course.

When I offered nothing more, he took the paper back. When he returned it, his question was rephrased.

WHAT have you thought about last night?

I tapped my eraser against the table. I was a little upset to be on the receiving end of Micah's questions once again when he continually evaded mine.

I don't know.

Micah took the paper back and frowned. Then he stared forward at the screen. I did the same.

A few minutes later, he was writing again.

OK, so I think I might understand why no one "warned me" before I accepted my invitation. I scared you, and I'm sorry for that. And while I respect your decision, I feel like you are missing out on something great, and that it's my fault.

I sighed. In a way, he was right—he had scared me. But I was also grateful that he had. I didn't think I was ready to see what he had prevented me from seeing.

What if I tell you that I'll pray about it?

He smiled.

It's all I ask.

◆ ◆ ◆

When class was over, I lugged my backpack across the school to my locker. My lunch period was starting, but my mind was too full to notice whether or not my stomach was empty.

Micah disappeared after physiology, or at least I didn't know where he'd gone. He'd been my shadow the entire morning, but when third period ended, he left without a good-bye.

The weight of my books in my bag was enough to put my arms to sleep as I dragged through the hallway, pins and needles shooting through my extremities. I decided then and there never to argue with Westley again about carrying my books.

Westley.

After cramming my bag into my locker and shaking the blood back into my arms, I dug my phone from my purse and dialed Eastlyn's number.

"Hey, sweetie. I was just wondering how you were doing?" Her chipper tone made me hopeful she'd heard good news about Westley, like he'd blown the doctors away with his record-speed recovery and was in transit back home already.

"Been better. How's West?"

"Well, the doctor said we shouldn't expect to hear anything for the first forty-eight hours."

I frowned. *First* forty-eight hours? I hated being reminded that my time away from Westley wouldn't be short.

She went on, "I guess he has to have an extensive evaluation before they decide what sort of contact he should have with the outside world."

My hopes dropped through the floor. I hadn't considered his communications being so restricted while he was away. Westley was right—this did feel like prison.

Eastlyn tried to cheer me up with promises of more dress shopping and an invitation to spend a weekend with her at Purdue after she returned there in a few days.

I told her I'd think about it.

"So..." she began her question as if it were just occurring to her to ask. "Have you run into Micah today?"

Eastlyn Greene was good at many things, but acting was not one of them.

"You're *still* thinking about him?"

"I'm sorry, Cosette; I know there's other stuff I should be more worried about right now. But there is just *something* about that kid. I dunno...It's driving me crazy that I can't figure out where I know him from."

"Well, I don't know if this helps, but apparently he's a JO. Maybe you were his Rumspringa fling?"

"What? He's not jerked-over; that doesn't make any sense."

I knew why *I* didn't think Micah made any sense, but it wasn't clear to me why she would make that call. "How so?"

I heard a soft sigh on the line. "You're going to think I'm crazy."

"Try me."

"Cosette, Micah knows something. He remembers me. I can tell that he does, but he's pretending not to." She spoke with such confidence I knew that she believed what she was saying. "And it's completely frustrating me! I mean, I know we didn't date, and I've asked around with my high school friends and no one remembers him. I looked in all my yearbooks back to elementary school, and I found no one with the last name Quinn in any of them."

"Well, if he's a JO, there wouldn't be any photographs of him anyway, even if he went to public school." Amish kids were always exempt from class pictures on religious grounds. I never knew why they assumed God would be upset by photography, as I was pretty sure cameras didn't exist in Bible times.

She thought about my point for a while but couldn't be swayed. "No, it just doesn't seem right."

As had the rest of my day, my conversation with Eastlyn had strayed from what I expected and became saturated with Micah.

I wrapped up our talk by asking her to let me know when she heard from Westley, and she in turn asked if I'd keep her posted on Micah.

I was glad Eastlyn wasn't there in person to see my eyes roll as I hung up the phone.

◆ ◆ ◆

The hallway was empty and quiet as I sat on the floor beside my open locker waiting for lunch period to end.

I'd contemplated heading to the cafeteria, but I kept picturing those nature shows where some stupid deer wanders alone into an open field and immediately gets descended upon by a pack of wolves. I decided to stay put.

With nothing better to do, I yanked my bag back out of my locker and began to pack it up for my two remaining classes. I pulled out my physiology book and stacked it inside when the note Micah and I had been passing in class fell out of it.

I picked it up off the floor and began crumpling it into a ball. I didn't need it as a reminder of what we talked about—Micah's invitation wasn't likely to slip my mind.

Thoughts of the previous night drifted back to me, and the heaviness I'd felt then returned with them.

In the clear of day, I was able to define the weight that bogged me down. All I'd experienced with Micah—the wonders, the miracle—it was mine alone. Bronwyn witnessed him take Westley down, which was impressive, for sure, but a long shot shy of the marvel of him restoring my life to me. She'd seen none of his other paranormal behaviors, which would make his fight with West seem like nothing more than an adrenaline rush paired with a little luck.

I knew better. But I still knew nothing. I had no answers and no one other than Micah to talk to about what was happening. Even if I did have any friends around, I couldn't imagine anyone believing what I had to tell them. Trying to tell anyone the truth about my healing would likely land me next to Westley at Maplecrest. While that idea seemed appealing, there were probably some downsides to being locked up in a mental hospital with my boyfriend that weren't clear in that moment.

A deep sigh escaped me as I tossed the paper ball into a trash can. I hated being alone. I really hated being alone with all these secrets. But I felt there was absolutely nothing I could do about it.

I glanced down into the wastebasket at the paper I'd just tossed in, remembering the last line I'd written on it.

Walking back to my locker, I checked the hallway up and down before leaning my back against the door. I closed my eyes.

"God? I need your help again..."

CHAPTER 34

The weight I'd been carrying around wasn't gone by the time the fourth period bell rang, but it did feel lighter. In place of the heaviness, I felt the shadows of the peace that had filled me after my healing.

I wondered if I should have been surprised by this. I wasn't. And I think that because I wasn't, deep down, I must have always believed God was real. Or at least, I'd never been convinced he was made up. But just because I believed he was real, it didn't mean I knew anything about him. I'd never made any attempt to learn who he was. I guess I'd never felt the need to.

Now that I was beginning to want to, I wasn't sure where to start.

At the very moment I was considering this, my trig teacher was explaining derivatives and antiderivatives, and I found that I felt the same way about them as I did about God. They were elusive and mysterious—and way too complex for me to figure out on my own.

I looked over at Micah who'd been assigned a seat three rows over. His book was opened, but his arms were folded over his chest; he appeared contemplative, but in a nonmathematical way.

I couldn't help but wonder what he could teach me about God if I would let him.

◆◆◆

When the bell rang, Micah was immediately at my desk. "Hey, Cosette—my cut is really bothering me; I think I'm going to go have the nurse look at it before fifth period."

"Oh, OK," I answered. The area of his cheek surrounding his bandage looked pinker than it had earlier in the day, and I felt bad. "Did you need me to take you down there or something?"

"No, I can manage that," he said before clarifying. "I just wanted to make sure you were going to be able to handle your first time back in Mrs. Holloway's class without me."

"Oh..."

I froze. It had not occurred to me that I should be dreading fifth period.

Truly, I didn't know how it would feel to walk back into that room—the last place I'd seen Julia Davis alive. My mind flashed back to her attempting to stumble out of the classroom and falling in front of my desk before Westley swooped in and raced her down the hallway. I thought about how confidently my boyfriend had reacted at the first sign of his friend in trouble, and I knew that Julia's death wasn't all I mourned when remembering that day.

"If it's a big deal, I can wait until after school. I'm just wondering if there's some reason it's getting infected," Micah offered.

I shook my head. "I'll be fine."

He attempted his half smile, but flexing his cheek made him wince. "I'll catch up with you soon."

Micah took off for the office, while I headed the other direction to Mrs. Holloway. The significance of her first class following such a tragedy would definitely not be lost on my teacher, and I was sure she would have a plan for helping all of her students cope with returning to normal.

As I approached the classroom, I noticed a larger crowd than usual had congregated around the doorway. Mrs. Holloway typically stood in the hall during passing periods, chatting with students commuting from one class to the next. Today, however, she was a one-person receiving line for all the members of our fifth-period class. I took my place at the end of it.

The bell rang before it was my turn to enter, but Mrs. Holloway was undeterred. Her considerations for her students were not subject to the law of time, and she would continue greeting us individually until each had a turn.

When I finally came face-to-face with my teacher, her cheeks were wet and rosy. As our eyes met, her face washed anew with sincere sympathy. "Oh, Cosette..." She pulled me close and stroked my hair, the way I imagined a mother might do for her hurting daughter. "Of all my students, I've been the most worried about you," she said in a low voice, still holding me tightly. "For some reason, even before I heard about Westley's hospital visit, you weighed on my heart. How are you holding up?"

She pulled away far enough to look at me. Tears sprang to my eyes at the genuineness reflecting back from her gaze. "I'm alive," I managed, and the thought crossed my mind that if there would be anyone on the planet to whom I could explain the truth behind why that statement was a remarkable one—it was Mrs. Holloway.

She followed up by reading my mind. "I know that I tell this to everyone, Cosette, but I mean it when I say that you can talk to me about *anything*. I can't even fathom what you are dealing with right now, but please know...I'm here for you." Mrs. Holloway squeezed me again and allowed me a moment to ready myself before indicating I should take my seat.

The classroom was silent when I stepped into it. All but a few desks were occupied, mostly with students staring at their hands. I took my seat and joined suit until Mrs. Holloway shut the door to the hallway and began class.

"I want to say to you all that I'm proud of each of you. No matter your relationship with Julia, it couldn't have been easy to come back here today. But you all did." She walked slowly over to her podium and pulled a tissue from a full box and then dabbed at her eyes. "I didn't want to come back myself, honestly. But from my experience, confronting your fears is always better than running from them. This time proved no different for me." She wadded up her tissue and walked to the trash can, where she released it. "The anxiety I felt *about* coming was way worse than actually seeing this place again."

Mrs. Holloway opened her seating chart for attendance, pausing for a moment when her eyes landed on Julia's desk. "You know, I contemplated giving you new seats for today, but it didn't seem right. I don't want to give the impression that we should pretend Julia didn't die." She intentionally didn't sugarcoat her wording. "Shuffling you around doesn't undo what has happened—"

"Is this all we are going to talk about today, Mrs. H.?" a boy from a few seats in front of me interrupted. "Or can we just move on?"

A blondish girl seated behind Julia's desk answered his question, "Just because you have a heart of stone, Eric, doesn't mean the rest of us do."

Eric refuted, "Seriously? I don't want to relive a girl puking herself to death in front of the whole class, and that makes me insensitive?"

"None of us want to relive it, Eric," a football player chimed in. "We're all just trying to get past it."

There was a lull after this, and Mrs. Holloway waited out the silence. "Does anyone else need to say anything?"

After an uncomfortably long pause, a voice spoke up. "In ninth grade, I cheated off of Julia on a biology test and convinced the teacher she cheated off of me." This confession came from a very petite girl I thought was named Mindy. "I got an A, and she took a zero. I have felt bad about it every day of my life since then. I never told her how sorry I was..." She broke down into tears, and the boy behind her squeezed her on the shoulder.

Mrs. Holloway put down her pencil and closed her binder. "Anyone else?"

"Three days before she died, Julia pulled her stupid Volkswagen out in front of me in the student parking lot, and I screamed out the window that she was a bitch," a boy in the front row turned around to explain to the class. "But she wasn't a bitch. And pulling out in front of someone in a car...Hell, we've all done that..."

Heads bobbed up and down in agreement.

"I never really knew Julia, but I went to her funeral to support my friends who knew her," a pretty, tanned girl admitted. "And I was more of a mess than any of them were. All I kept thinking about were all the things Julia would never get to do. I mean, her obituary talked about all the things she was *going* to do with her life, but it's too late for that now. That's so depressing to me..."

"Don't let it be depressing, Myra," another girl interjected. "Let it inspire you to live each day to its fullest. None of us know when our time is up—we can only do the best we can with each day not to have any regrets."

Mrs. Holloway pulled a chair to the front of the room and sat down.

Our class continued this way for the full hour, like a group therapy session. No one else bickered; instead, there was a sense of unity among us. We were bound together by this tragedy we had witnessed, and there was a collective sense of responsibility to help one another get through it.

Everyone in the class spoke at least once, sharing his or her fears—both related and unrelated to death—and dreams. Confessing and philosophizing. Encouraging one another.

Everyone in the class spoke, that is, except for me. It wasn't that I didn't have anything to say; I just had been sitting on the sidelines of life for so long that I didn't know how to enter into the conversation.

For the first time ever, this bothered me.

As the class wrapped up, Mrs. Holloway expressed her appreciation for how all of us had handled ourselves. "Thank you all for sharing your hearts so honestly today. I can sense the start of a lot of healing. It is a very honoring thing to do for Julia to allow her loss to be used as a catalyst for good growth in you all."

I wanted to have been able to receive this compliment and for "good growth" to have started in me too. But I felt I had missed my opportunity, and I was already regretting it.

"Before you go, I have your *It's a Wonderful Life* papers to hand back to you. Please pick them up on your way out." The bell cut her off, and a line quickly formed in front of Mrs. Holloway for essay retrieval.

I didn't rush up, as I wasn't in a hurry to confirm my anticipated C. By the time I repacked my bag, the crowd had thinned, and only a few essays remained in her stack.

Mrs. Holloway folded my paper and held it out for me to take. "Read my comments on the last page before you get too concerned about your grade." She added a brilliant smile to her verbal instructions.

My eyes widened. Had I overestimated the quality of my work? I quickly turned to the last page of my essay, bypassing the red-pen corrections for grammar and punctuation. There, at the bottom of the page, was a letter I had not expected to see.

"I got an *I*?"

Mrs. Holloway gave me a side hug. "Like I said, read the comments."

I skimmed back over the first pages and saw nothing clarifying my strange grade until I noted a sentence near the end of my paper that was entirely underlined. It was in one of the paragraphs I'd written about Westley.

I already have love. What more is there?

Below my rhetorical question, my teacher wrote in perfect English-teacher cursive—

Go find out.

It was then I knew that the *I* stood for incomplete.

I lifted my eyes from my grade and saw Micah, a fresh bandage covering his cheek, standing in the doorway. I stepped quickly over to him.

"Micah, I'm ready to accept your invitation."

CHAPTER 35

"I don't understand why we have to keep coming back here," I complained, shutting my door and stepping up the gravel drive to the farmhouse.

"We don't *have* to be here. And we aren't staying anyway. This is just a good place to leave from because we're pretty much guaranteed not to be seen."

I refused to allow myself to ask what that meant. I was done asking Micah questions.

He held the door open for me, and we entered the house. In the daylight, I scoured the room for things I may not have noticed in the dark the night before—like some sort of magical time portal sticking out of the wall—but there was nothing out of the ordinary for an abandoned Amish farmhouse.

"And being seen would be a problem why?"

"Because we aren't really *going* anywhere, Cosette. We're just changing our perspective. And, well, it tends to freak people out."

He extended his hand to me, and I looked at it skeptically. Just about every time Micah touched me, the unpredictable had happened. Now that I was expecting the unpredictable, I was afraid to take his hand.

"Here's the deal, Cosette," Micah addressed my hesitation. "Just like with everything else, you have the choice of whether or not you come with me. And if you choose to come, you have the choice at any time to leave where we are to come back here. Instantaneously."

My nerves were torn as I tried to decide if this promise was nonsensical or reassuring. "Not that this is a surprise to you, but I don't understand."

"I know, but you will soon," he assured me. "In your current state, you aren't fit to be where we are going alone. The experience would be too severe. As it is, I'm going to have to buffer a lot of what will surround us to protect you from the intensity."

I gulped, wishing my imagination was less vivid. "Can you at least promise I'll be safe?"

"No," he answered immediately. "But I can promise it will be worth it."

I took a deep breath and accepted Micah's hand. He pulled me to him, wrapping his arm around my waist. "As long as we're touching, you'll stay with me. If you let go, you'll come back here, understand?" he whispered into my ear and held my head to his chest.

"OK."

His heart was pounding so violently against my cheek that it felt as though it were pulsing the blood through my own body.

But it was in this moment that I understood what Eastlyn had been saying.

Micah was...familiar. His scent. His embrace. The sound of his heartbeat. Everything else.

I knew him.

But before these thoughts could be sorted, Micah began to speak again in the words unknown to me.

His speech was short and ended abruptly. It was followed by only a moment of silence.

Then, I heard the music.

Bells. Chimes. Strings. Winds. Unusual and enticing melodies.

I perceived it, at first, as if it were coming from a car stereo miles away, but both its volume and intensity increased so rapidly that no vehicle could have maintained the pace at which it came upon me.

At the same time, the walls of the farmhouse began to dissolve into brightness—slowly at first, and then with equal velocity as the music had changed.

A fragrance filled the air—freshness. A breeze filled with lilacs and cherry blossoms. Pleasing at first, but then instantly so powerful it sickened me.

My senses overloaded.

"What's happening?" I demanded, but I couldn't hear my own voice above the noise.

I buried my face in Micah's chest to breathe in his smell instead of the pungent floral perfume and to shut out the light that had begun to blind me.

The environment had shifted so much that I couldn't even attempt to find my bearings.

Beneath my feet, the ground turned soft, then wet, and just as quickly, I could feel waves lapping at my legs. As the water ran past me, it cut through my legs like an acid burning away my flesh. I cried out from the pain, but the music had deafened me.

I screwed my eyes shut and used both of my hands to claw my way up Micah's body and out of the water.

The fragrance had become putrid, and with each breath I took, I felt bile rising into my throat. I fought back my sickness with all my will.

I tore at Micah like an animal—breathing into his clothes, his hair, using any part of him I could as a filter for the stench that was suffocating me.

Where had he taken me? Why had I trusted him?

I felt for his face and raised myself to where I knew we'd be eye to eye before daring to squint him into focus. I wanted to look into the eyes of my betrayer before whatever was going to become of me...became.

Westley had been wrong. Hell was real. And Micah had tricked me into going there with him.

CHAPTER 36

"Cosette? Cosette, can you hear me?"

Whoever was talking, I wished they'd shut up. I wanted to keep sleeping.

"Cosette, wake up!" Micah's muffled voice pleaded with me. "Can you hear me? Can you see me?"

I opened both eyes.

He gradually came into focus, inches from my face. We were outside, but I wasn't cold. Nightfall had come while I slept, and all around me darkness covered my surroundings.

Micah's face shone against the risen moonlight. He looked worried.

"Has the burning stopped?"

I remembered the water and how it felt like razors cutting through my clothing. I tried to sit up to examine my wounds, but I hadn't the energy. I felt as though my torso had been weighed down with sandbags.

But—I couldn't feel any pain in my legs, or anywhere else in my body. In fact, an odd sensation had overtaken my entire body.

I felt...nothing.

As my surroundings came into focus, I realized that they did not match up to what I perceived them to be.

We were sitting on the bank of a river, but I couldn't hear it flowing. There were flowers all around us, their blossoms closed in the nighttime, but I couldn't smell their fragrance or hear them rustle in the wind. I saw leaves overturn on nearby trees and the wildflowers mere feet away dance in the breeze, but I couldn't feel it upon my skin.

The only sensation my body was aware of was Micah's hand in mine. It was all I could feel, as if someone had injected Novocain into every other part of me.

"What happened to me? Where are we?" I was glad I could hear the sound of my own voice.

"What happened to you is entirely my fault, and I am so terribly sorry." Micah sounded genuinely regretful. "I have never brought anyone here before. I didn't know how to measure what your senses would be able to tolerate. In the time it took me to realize the pain you were in and pull back, you'd passed out." He was disgusted with himself, and I was relieved that whatever had happened, it had been accidental. "But how is it now? Bearable?"

"I don't know," was my honest reply. "All I can feel is you."

Micah shook his head at himself. "I still don't have it right." He squeezed my hand. "OK, I'm going to try again—slowly—to adjust your senses to the environment. I want you to tell me when what you feel seems normal."

I resisted the urge to argue about his use of the word *normal* in light of our completely paranormal situation and nodded.

Micah's eyes closed, and I knew he was in deep concentration.

Faintly, I heard a wave break against the bank. Then another, followed by the trickling of water flowing downstream.

As the volume increased steadily, I became aware of pine and other woodsy smells as well as the hard earth under my back.

I could almost feel synapses in my brain that had been misfiring attempts to read this new environment finally forming connections.

When I could hear, feel, and smell my surroundings with as much power as I desired to, I spoke. "OK, that's enough." The pain in my legs had returned with a vengeance, and I didn't want that particular sensation to become any more intense.

He opened his eyes, still gripping my hand. "Are you sure? Do you need me to dial back more?"

I sat still, listening to the sound of my own heart pounding. I hadn't been able to hear it before, and I didn't want it to fade away. "No, I'm fine," I assured him. "I just want to know where we are."

Micah's concern gave way to a smile. "Well, this is the place I've been telling you about." He looked around and then corrected himself, "Or, from your perspective, probably, *not* telling you about."

Micah's trite explanation for the earth-shattering *Earth* shattering that had taken place inside the farmhouse would have annoyed me had I expected to understand it. "You live in a forest?" I asked, a tad let down that everything around me seemed so ordinary after how much Micah had built up the mystery of his home.

"A garden, actually," Micah corrected with pride, looking around the creation.

The night didn't allow me to take in the environment as I would have liked. In the thick of woods where we sat, I could only see a few dozen feet around before everything faded into a black backdrop.

"I'm going to need some more details than that."

Micah was unflustered. "I can show you whatever you want to see."

There was no snow on the ground or wintry crispness in the air. The greenery and foliage suggested we'd fast-forwarded into a warmer season or transported to a southern latitude. However, it really hadn't felt like we'd "gone" anywhere, just that we'd transitioned from one place to another.

I didn't know if that was physically possible, but then, most everything that had happened with Micah had been equally out of the ordinary.

I gripped his hand tightly. "OK. Give me the tour."

Micah smiled brightly, happier than I'd ever seen him. "All right." He provided me the help I needed to stand. "Welcome to my home, Cosette."

CHAPTER 37

Micah and I traveled along the water's edge for some time, headed in the same direction as the river flowed.

His path seemed sure and intentional, so I assumed our journey had a destination. I didn't demand to know what lay ahead of us. I let him show it to me rather than force him into a dissatisfying answer. I followed his lead in silence and tried to take in all I could of this new environment.

The ground was bare underneath our feet at the shore, but otherwise, lush, hearty vegetation covered every inch of the earth around us. The trees of the forest towered stories high, their thick trunks and large leaves suggesting they'd grown here undisturbed for some time; how long, I couldn't begin to guess, but I had certainly never seen such matured woods anywhere in Middlebury.

While I found everything remarkably beautiful, something about my location seemed off. The grounds didn't look professionally landscaped—grasses were overgrown, bushes and shrubs were dense and unmanicured—but they still appeared too perfect. All the plants were healthy and filled in. There was no rustling of decaying leaves beneath our feet or snapping of fallen twigs and branches of trees that were commonly on the ground after a heavy rain or windstorm.

It was as if we were on a movie set, a replication of the outdoors created by someone who had forgotten that what made a setting realistic were its imperfections. That nature wasn't supposed to be flawless.

The river looked likewise impossible. The moonlight glinted off its crystal surface and was bright enough that from the edge, I could see clear through its depth to the riverbed.

I collected these observations and began forming them into questions to ask Micah when the opportunity arose.

"We're almost at our first stop," he called over his shoulder with notable excitement. His pace quickened, and I struggled to keep up.

Our path and the water separated slightly as we began an upward climb onto a hill.

Micah must have noticed me dragging my feet because he stopped a short distance into our ascent and turned to face me. "It may be easier if I just carry you." I agreed and climbed onto his back.

Micah's speed dramatically slowed after this. He kept stopping to shift my weight around and change my positioning. His steps became clumsy, and at times, he almost seemed winded.

He wasn't a body builder or a giant. But, in all fairness, neither was I. And I'd seen his hidden strength with my own eyes. I'd seen him manhandle Westley without breaking a sweat; giving me a piggyback ride should have been a cinch. "All right, what gives here, Muscles?" I finally commented at another pit stop. "Maybe I should be carrying you?"

He cut his break short. "Maybe instead of insulting the chauffeur..." He took a breath. "You could pray for strength for him."

I almost laughed. "Are you serious? I'm pretty confident I've seen you both carry and take down someone who is at least twice my size."

The incline beneath us steepened, and Micah's steps became more intentional. "You flatter me, Cosi." He chuckled. "I mean, you've seen me, right? I'm not exactly athletic. You think I really could have done those things on my own? It didn't seem weird to you?"

"Everything about you is weird to me, Micah."

"Touché."

"So, how *did* you knock Westley down then? Are you a black belt in some sort of guardian-angel jujitsu?"

"Of course not," he scoffed as if my suggestion were completely absurd. "It was provision. Evidently, when it comes to Westley, my own strength isn't enough to get the job done. You're a different story though. I don't *need* help to get you where we're going. So, the effort's up to me."

It took me a long time to digest this. As I stewed on his words, I recentered myself more squarely on Micah, repositioning my arms around his chest. His heart slammed against my hands. "So, you're telling me that God gave you the strength to beat West?"

He moved my hands off his chest and back to his shoulders. "I prefer to see it that God gave me the strength to protect you, your sister, *and* Westley. I mean, I know he's in trouble now, but can you imagine how much more he'd be in if he'd actually gotten a hold of Bronwyn?"

My face fell. I *could* imagine.

I had never considered my boyfriend being flung through my house like a fastball and then pinned to the ground an act of God, let alone one performed mercifully on all of our behalves. "So how did you know to pray for the strength to beat West? Or did it just show up?"

He stumbled slightly but caught his balance. "Prayer's not a guessing game, Cosette. God knows what we need even when we don't. Sometimes when you pray for food, you're gonna get bread. Sometimes you pray for food, and you get rain. I prayed God would use me to help you guys, and I became the Hulk."

I was overwhelmed. Some being in the cosmos had orchestrated the fight scene in my living room. It was a hard pill to swallow. Weren't wars going on in other parts of the world that were more deserving of his attention than some living-room brawl in the middle of nowhere, Indiana?

"I know I've said it before, but God has a unique plan for your life, Cosette. He has one for Westley too. And your sister, and your niece...and everyone else. But he's not going to force it on any one of you. You get to choose whether or not you want to be a part of it."

I thought back to Julia's eulogy. Pastor Brian said dying *wasn't* part of the plan for her. But it still happened, hadn't it? Did that mean he was wrong? That Micah was wrong? This was all so abstract to me, so confusing.

But also, so intriguing. And I wasn't scared. I was curious.

Here in the garden, my questions didn't feel so empty. I didn't have the same urgency for answers to them as I had felt before. Instead of being cornered by the unknowns, I felt freed by the possibility of what I would learn.

I continued to dwell on Micah's words as we climbed. The sounds of the water had long ago faded, as had the light the waves reflected from the distant moon. Everything around us now appeared only as inky silhouettes, and even those were only visible in our immediate surroundings.

Wrapped around Micah, I welcomed the darkness more than I would have even by his side. Although slow, I didn't doubt his footing up the hill. His protection had yet to fail me.

The incline finally flattened out, and when we reached the summit, I held on to Micah's arm, rolled off his back, and lay beside him on the ground until he caught his breath. The nature around us atop the hill transitioned from the forest into moors. Without trees to obstruct the pale moonlight, the sky lit a much further distance in front of me than before.

After resting a while, he helped me up. Micah and I stood together, and from our vantage point, we looked out over where we had journeyed. Even in the night, the view was breathtaking.

Everything I could see—the winding river, the thatches of woods, and the blurry beyond—was painted in various depths of the blackness and silver highlights from the moonlight frosting the treetops. I drew in a deep breath. I could only imagine that the beauty of this view in daylight would have broken me completely.

"It's almost painful," I admitted to Micah. "Seeing something like this. I feel like I shouldn't be allowed here."

"Why's that?" he asked shifting his gaze to me.

"I don't know." I had spoken from emotion and not yet worked through a way to explain these feelings. I processed my thoughts aloud, "I mean, what did I do to deserve to see this? Why would God want this for me when I barely know anything about him? This place should be reserved for, I don't know...priests, I guess. You, maybe, since you love him so much. Definitely not me." The more I talked, the more I felt unworthy of being in the garden. I cast my eyes downward, away from the landscape.

The joy I'd felt moments ago melted into discomfort. My questions returned. What *was* I doing here?

"Don't do that, Cosette." Micah sensed the change in my demeanor. "No one deserves this, especially not me. But that's just what makes the fact that I was given the opportunity so amazing. You wouldn't be here if God didn't know your potential and believe in your ability to use it. And if he believes that—so should you."

Micah spoke so passionately that tears sprang back into my eyes. There wasn't a trace of doubt in his voice, and I wanted his words to be true. But how could they be? Why would God believe in me? I hadn't until recently even accepted that I believed in him. Why would he care enough about me to have a "plan" for my life? Why had he sent Micah to heal me?

Micah's description of God was so different than anything I'd ever heard before.

I thought of the abstinence pamphlet, the message from Anonymous warning me how hellfire awaited me for sleeping with Westley. They'd signed their message with, "God loves you, and so do we."

Which of these interpretations of God was truth? The one who believed in me or the one who condemned me?

Neither? Both?

Micah cleared his throat and gently spoke. "I'm sorry I can't give you more time right now to process through this, but I'm afraid if we don't keep walking, we're going to miss something very important."

I nodded, secretly grateful that he'd interrupted my thinking. I wouldn't have come to a conclusion on my own, no matter how much time he'd given me.

"It's all right. Let's just keep going."

We turned in the direction of the moor and continued our walk through the garden.

CHAPTER 38

I could tell by his silence that Micah was trying to give me my mental space as we crossed the field.

Instead of using the time as I'd guessed he was intending, I tuned into my new surroundings.

We only traveled a few minutes from where we'd stood overlooking the garden, but already, I noticed the ground was shifting again.

The flat fields were soon interrupted by black bumps of knotted wood that at first intermittently sprung up through the dirt but as we continued along became thicker and longer—the apparent root system of another massive tree.

As the roots became larger, they impeded our path, becoming an obstacle course. Micah again offered to carry me, but this time I declined. I considered that it may have been easier to maintain a hold of him while on his back rather than trying to climb over roots hand in hand, but I didn't want all the effort of our journey to rest on him, and he didn't argue.

For some time, I'd had my eyes fixed on the task at hand, focusing on the immediate—climbing, balancing, holding on to Micah.

I became so consumed with our journey that when he pointed directly ahead of us and said, "There it is," it took me a moment to remember that our course had a destination.

I followed his gaze and almost fell backward in surprise when I saw what stood before us.

Ahead in the distance, I made out the outline of the most magnificent tree.

Still a few hundred yards away from its base, I could hardly fit it all at once into my line of sight. The trunk itself was easily the girth of several of the trees we'd seen in the woods braided together. Countless branches, broad and twisted, jutted out in all directions, giving the tree a seemingly endless limb span. It stood, mammoth and reaching, dwarfing even the tallest trees we'd seen upon entering the garden.

It was majestic.

"Can you run?" Micah asked me eagerly, and his desire to reach the tree only fed my own curiosity about what I would discover about it when we got there.

"Yes."

We took off in step, racing forward along the path of the roots, the tree growing increasingly bigger the closer we came to it.

I'd never encountered anything of this size, and when we finally reached its base, I found myself with a striking awareness of my own insignificance.

I was a speck. Dust. Inconsequential.

This tree held up the sky.

It was so massive that I had a hard time comprehending it. Looking at it made me dizzy and anxious—yet at the same time, it drew me in magnetically. I wanted to climb it, to rest in its limbs and listen to the wind flutter through its leaves. I would build a tree house or a nest and live in it forever.

Micah interrupted my housing plans by pulling me over to a low-hanging branch. He plucked a piece of its fruit.

I stroked the smooth bark of the branch, excited that the tree was also a food source. Once I moved into it, I wouldn't have to leave every time I got hungry.

Micah rubbed the fruit onto his pant leg to polish it. It appeared pearlike, plump on the bottom with a bulbous top, reddish and lime colored. He gripped it like a baseball and held it to his nose to breathe in its scent before choosing a part of its skin to bite into.

He closed his eyes for a moment and then sank his teeth into the fruit with the sound of a crisp, satisfying crunch.

Less than an arm's length away, I could almost immediately smell its fragrance.

And in an instant, it overtook me.

My mouth watered as though I'd been starving. My stomach growled loudly, painfully. My breathing quickened.

The aroma attacked me. It was fresh and pure, sweet and alluring, and completely new.

"Cosette, are you OK?" Micah asked me with concern, still chewing.

I swallowed and tried to answer, but I instantly lost my train of thought when he again brought the fruit to his lips and bit into it.

I could see its exposed flesh was a milky white. I yearned to taste it, to feel its soft, sandpapery roughness against my tongue. To swallow its juices and chew it into a thick, satisfying pulp.

I had never been so captivated by a food.

I wanted that fruit.

I needed it.

My eyes sought out another piece hanging nearby. I reached my hand out to grab it, unable to deny my appetite for it any longer.

In one broad swoop, I grabbed at the pear and brought it to my lips for a bite. But rather than fulfilling my craving, I discovered that I'd failed to grasp it and had come up empty-handed.

"Cosette," Micah called my name curiously, and I ignored him. "What are you doing?"

I swatted at the fruit again. And again, I failed to make contact.

Dragging Micah behind me, I took a few steps closer to where the pear hung and grabbed at it again, this time examining my actions as they happened.

To my shock, my fingers seemed to move right through the fruit as if it were nothing more than a cruel mirage.

My senses were not computing—sight and touch were not corresponding accurately. One, or both of them, was misleading me.

"What are you doing?" Micah repeated while consuming the last of his snack. He'd eaten every bit of it—the core, the stem, the sticky juice that had dripped onto his fingers—all of it was gone.

"Why can't I grab onto that?" I demanded in frustration, pointing at the fruit dangling inches in front of my fingers.

I was now so hungry that I was becoming angry, so when Micah chuckled in response to my question, I shot him a dirty look.

The fruit's scent lingered in the air, teasing me.

As I glared at Micah, the moonlight gleamed off a trace of drying juice that had dribbled down his chin.

Without the willpower to stop my longing for the fruit, I found myself forcing my mouth toward Micah's lips.

His eyes widened as he pushed me back to arm's length. "What's gotten into you, Cosette?"

"I'm sorry," I apologized, though my body still fought to get closer to him. "The smell of the fruit, it's literally driving me crazy!" My craving had become so intense that failing to fulfill it was causing me physical pain that rivaled the burning from the river. I lunged for him again. I'd completely lost control.

Micah dodged me and spun me around in a reverse bear hug. I twisted in his arms. In our closeness, I could breathe in his breath, and the fruit's aroma only fed my frenzy.

"Please make this stop!" I begged for mercy against my hunger.

"I'm trying!" Micah began whispering quickly to himself. I craned my face around to his reach his mouth, but he evaded me again. "Just let go of me, and you'll go home!"

I sent the signal from my brain to my hand to release Micah's, but I'd lost the ability to manage my own body. My craving had broken into my mind's control room and taken over. "I can't!"

We continued to fight each other, both of us in some way against our will, until suddenly, I was numb again.

No sound, no smell, no feeling. Except for Micah's hand in mine.

Relief.

After basking in the return of control over my body, I demanded answers. "What just happened to me? What *is* that?" I pointed to another piece of fruit nearby, quickly looking away from it so that I didn't kick-start another round of crazy.

"Honestly, Cosette, I had no idea you'd react that way." Micah was mortified. "I was never around the first fruits before I lived here. I was warned that they would be attractive to you, but I had *no* idea you'd react like that. I should have blocked all of your senses before we got this close. I am so sorry..."

"You're saying that a lot on this trip."

"It was completely irresponsible of me. I should have known when the river burned you that I needed to be careful. I thought preventing you from touching the fruit would be enough." Tears filled Micah's eyes.

"Lesson learned," I sighed.

Now freed from the spell of the fruit, I felt embarrassed by how strongly I'd reacted to it. It had been so primal, the need I'd had to consume it. I couldn't understand how quickly I'd become so desperate.

I didn't want to talk about what happened, though my curiosity about this tree was sure to nag at me. I decided that maybe it was best not to have that conversation on an empty stomach.

◆◆◆

When Micah offered to carry me through the maze of tree roots to our next destination, I didn't argue. And our time crunch to get to our next destination must have been cause for some good, old-fashioned provision, because he practically flew through the root maze that led away from the tree.

In half the time it had taken us to climb our way to the tree's base, we'd put enough distance between it and us that looking over my shoulder, I could no longer see it.

When we'd traveled far enough that the root system no longer impeded our path, I noticed that once again our

235

environment had changed. Micah's pace had quickened in the clearing; he was now nearly sprinting through a field of flowers—tulips, large and full like the one he'd given me the night before. Their blooms were closed in the nighttime; they looked like thousands of lips pursed together, holding in secrets.

Our wake sent ripples through the flowers, bobbing them up and down like the waves in an ocean. I drew a breath deeply, anticipating their sweet fragrance invading me.

Then I remembered that Micah had turned off my sense of smell.

As much as I hadn't wanted it to, the incident at the tree had dampened my mood and created awkwardness between Micah and me. Obviously, I didn't understand why the fruit had been so alluring to me, though I guessed that he did. And now that my hunger pangs had subsided, I contemplated asking him about it.

But he beat me to the punch.

"I really don't know what I was thinking back there, Cosette," he began, his breathing steadier than it should have been. "Are you feeling any better?"

"Yeah, I'm fine. Sorry for trying to make out with you."

Micah snickered. "Hey, I mean, I'm surprised it took you so long, honestly. I've heard most chicks dig scars." He looked over his shoulder and pointed to his bandaged cheek.

"Yeah, you're so hard core." I redirected our banter. "So what was that anyway? Some sort of heroin-laced pear?"

"They're called 'first fruits.' It's just about all we eat here. Well, all we *need* to eat, at least."

His answer sent my eyes wandering around the darkened field. "Wait...*We?*"

"You didn't think we were alone, did you?" he stated his question so matter-of-factly that I didn't want to let on that I *had* thought that, and I wondered just how much Micah was keeping me from experiencing in the garden.

"So what? There are others like you?" I wasn't even sure what it exactly meant to be "like Micah," but it had never

236

occurred to me that he wasn't a unique creature. Maybe all JOs *did* have superpowers.

"Cosette, I've told you. I'm no different—all of us here, *we're* not any different than everyone else. We just made a different choice."

"Seems to me like you were given different options than most people." I'd certainly never heard that a trip to a mystical garden was a rite of passage into adulthood.

"Maybe." He shrugged. "I only know my options, Cosette. You only know yours."

I couldn't argue with him.

Micah's pace was steady, and as he ran, the rows of tulips seemed to part before us.

I didn't know what my options were yet, but I hoped they included the opportunity to learn more about this place.

CHAPTER 39

I dismounted Micah's back where the tulip field edged up against a grass-covered, downward slope. Retracing our journey in my mind, I assumed that the tree and tulips had been at the summit of the hill Micah had climbed, and we were now standing at the start of the decline back down it.

"We've only got few minutes until daybreak, so we need to get started."

Daybreak? While our travels seemed long, they couldn't have taken us the full fourteen hours of darkness that equaled a winter's night, unless I'd slept longer than I'd thought after the transition. Of course, it didn't seem to be winter in the garden, so perhaps it was only daybreak here and not back home.

I reassured myself that my reasoning wasn't going to make sense, so I should stop trying to make it.

Still holding onto my hand, Micah sat down and motioned for me to do the same.

"Your senses are going to need to readjust to see something, so I want you to look at the sky and tell me when it's as intense as you want it to be." He lay down in the grass and closed his eyes to concentrate. I joined him, keeping my eyes obediently fixed upon the sky.

The depth of the darkness above me hadn't struck me until now when I had no landscape to distract me from it. The moon was no longer visible, and the sky had become pitch-black, appearing one-dimensional. An opaque, seamless cloud stretched over the real sky.

"Get ready."

As the words left his lips, the blackness shifted unexpectedly, and I flinched. In the exact blink of my eye, the blank canvas above me became illuminated with hundreds of thousands of stars.

The light shocked my system, and I screamed and shielded my eyes.

"OK," he whispered and squeezed my hand, tempering the intensity slightly so that I could look at the sky without being struck blind. "What do you think?"

When I looked upward into the heavens, the standard by which I measured all things beautiful shattered. They were brilliant, the stars. Brighter than I'd known possible, bursting with colors I couldn't define. And more numerous than I had the capacity to understand.

I felt Micah looking at me, but I couldn't take my eyes off of the sky to be sure.

As quickly as I'd reacted to the fruit with hunger, I responded to the stars with an uncontrolled joy—manifesting in the form of laughter. I felt like a child, giggling wildly with pleasure. And while he didn't join me, I could feel Micah taking delight in my enjoyment of what he was showing me.

I tried to take it in wholly and then by sections and individual stars. But all attempts at examination were overwhelming, and I had to keep shutting my eyes to regroup.

I was awestruck.

"This can't be real," I said to Micah in a low voice. "I've never seen stars like this before."

Their surreal light radiated a heat that even with subdued senses, I could feel. Its warmth filled me, invited me.

"You can be sure it's real, Cosette," he assured me. "But those aren't stars in the way you think they are. They aren't the distant celestial bodies that you see back home when you look up at the night sky. They are...something else."

I was relieved by this revelation—if I thought I could somehow see this in my own world, I may never sleep at night again and spend forever staring up at the sky. "So what are they then?"

He pointed generally. "We call them 'light webs.' They're like...maps. People maps."

"What?"

"The lights up there—there's one for everyone. Every person, everywhere." Micah scooted his head more closely to mine so that our cheeks touched. "I will show you mine. Watch." He closed his eyes in meditation. Slowly, the stars began to fade apart from a small section directly above us. One blue star in the center of a cluster brightened vividly; the light enlarged. It looked like a sapphire hanging in the sky. "That's me."

The sky had never been so three-dimensional, and I was sure if I reached out, I would have pricked my finger on the light beam from the blue jewel. "It's beautiful...but what do you mean that it's you?"

Micah searched for words. "It's like my status. Each person has one, and each color represents something specific." He didn't stop talking long enough for me to ask questions. "And this one..." The sapphire faded into the back with the others in the cluster, and a smaller, emerald-esque light shone brighter. "Is you."

I looked to Micah and then back at the lights.

My green star dimmed, but not so much that I couldn't still identify it among the group of lights that surrounded Micah's.

"Tell me what you notice. About our group of lights."

There were dozens of stars in the cluster, perhaps hundreds. They ranged in color, brightness, size, and proximity to Micah's center star. "What do you want to know?"

"What sets ours apart from the others?"

This question was equally tricky to answer. It was easy to define what set Micah's light apart—his was the largest and the epicenter of the grouping. His was also the only light that distinct shade of sapphire.

But my light was less exceptional. There were several in the group that were varying shades of green and many of similar size. In the cluster, I could see all colors of the spectrum present, but the red and yellow hues were the most dominant.

There was a yellow star very close to my own. Its gleam was duller than some of the others in the same color family, but I couldn't find a link to connect it to Micah's question, so I didn't mention it.

Just as I was about to tell Micah that I could find no comparison between our two lights, something changed.

My light flickered.

For a brief second, my star's color blinked from emerald to sapphire and then back again.

I gasped. Then I felt slightly ridiculous for reacting so strongly since I had no idea what any of this—the colors or the lights themselves—meant.

"You saw it then? Your light changing color?" Micah asked enthusiastically.

I nodded. "What's the significance?"

"That is why you are here, Cosette," he smiled triumphantly. "Because something is changing in your circumstances. Something is changing in you."

I sensed heaviness in his statement. "What?"

"Your options."

My light flickered blue again, sending a twinge of excitement through me. "What am I supposed to do with that, Micah?" I was on the fence between eager and terrified, and I needed him to tip me toward the one I should feel.

"Weigh them carefully."

I noticed movement above, and turned my attention back toward it. Slowly, the rest of the stars became unmuted, and the sky's beauty distracted me from our conversation. I was used to leaving things unsaid with Micah. And I was learning it wasn't always a bad thing to leave our conversations open-ended.

The lights were hypnotic, consuming my sight the way the fruit had my taste. I desired them—to be in their presence, to bask in their warmth.

Their warmth...

I flashed back to my bedroom, Micah's hand on my chest, the heat running through my bloodstream, melting away the pain of my splintered ribs and fractured face.

It was the same sensation.

Peace.

I surrendered to it.

◆◆◆

Micah and I lay there together until day broke a few minutes later and the sun's first rays of light outshone the stars. Strangely, the sun's heat felt cooler than had the stars', and I shivered. We stood up, and he draped his arm over my shoulders and rubbed away my goose bumps. "It's almost time to go back. There's just one thing I have left to show you."

For a moment, I didn't understand what Micah had meant by "go back." My time in the garden was so intense that it made everything before coming there seem unreal. It was difficult to imagine what home would feel like after experiencing this place. I dreaded leaving it.

I followed Micah across the grassy field to a rocky area. Red sandstone formations seemed to have grown straight up from the earth as if they'd been planted there along with the grass. I was sure I'd only seen such scenery in deserts before, and I was positive that their presence, between a lush pasture of grass and endless tulip field, was impossible.

But with the light of the morning casting new vision onto the garden—which until daybreak I'd only perceived cloaked in darkness—what should have been impossible was instead stunning.

As the sun rose and the day brightened, I could clearly see the exceptionality of my surroundings. The grasses on which Micah and I had lain stargazing were magnificent, each blade extraordinarily long and expressing every shade of green in the spectrum all at once. I'd never encountered a more intriguing plant in my lifetime; I wanted to sit and watch it grow.

Micah must have noticed me lagging again because he didn't even ask before he swept me up into his arms and carried me the rest of the way to the sandstone.

When we reached the rocks, he immediately began an ascent up stairs that appeared to have naturally formed in the stone; they were too imprecise to have been manmade, yet at the same time looked intentionally placed.

"You'll want to close your eyes until I say when," Micah instructed me as he continued his climb.

I reluctantly obeyed, having been engrossed in the composition of the stone walls and how the layers of red grit painted the rock with rust.

Had nature always been this beautiful and I just never noticed? Or was this garden just the most spectacular display of it to ever exist?

Micah's pace slowed at what I assumed was the final stop of my garden tour. He sat me down on the hard ground and took the space next to me.

"OK, before you open your eyes, I need to talk to you."

"OK."

"What you are about to see is true. I want you to remember that later when you are back at home and trying to convince yourself that the garden wasn't real—'cause that's probably going to happen. At least, that's what I did when I left it for the first time."

I couldn't fathom why anyone would want to deny this place existed, but I listened on.

"I also want you to know that it wasn't my decision to bring you here. It was my decision to be obedient in extending you the offer, and you were the one who made the choice. Do you disagree with any of that?"

I didn't understand what any of this mattered, but Micah's careful wording made me nervous. "No. I came here because I wanted to." I stated the words with as much confidence as I could, feeling as anxious as I did.

"All right. Remember that, Cosette. Don't be deceived later on."

I nodded, not knowing what words I could say to convince Micah more.

"OK. Open them."

Before my eyelids fully parted, I had vertigo.

We were sitting atop the stone structure, high above the garden, our legs dangling in the air.

I immediately plastered myself against Micah, screwing my eyes shut again, dizzy from the height.

"Hey, now!" He laughed. "Calm down, I've got you. Remember? If you fall and let go of me, you'll just be back in the farmhouse. No worries." Micah pried his arm free from underneath my grip and used his free hand to point my face outward at the scene before us.

I guessed he had a point, judging by the rules of the garden he'd told me—the ones I had no way of verifying without testing. I opened my eyes again.

I could see it all.

The forests, the river, the fruit tree, the tulips...and everything else.

Spectacular landscapes of all varieties—lakes, mountains, beaches, valleys—each its own original masterpiece.

I scoured them all, photographing them with my eyes.

I searched in my mind for words precise enough to assign to their appearances, but my vocabulary—language in general—was lacking. How many different ways could a field of flowers be beautiful? Every description I attempted was insufficient.

"There's so much more to see in the garden. I thought before you left, I'd give you a preview. If you come back, I have plenty more to show you up close."

I didn't like Micah talking so much about leaving the garden. I wanted to stay and count each leaf on the trees, each grain of sand on the beaches. "How could I not want to come back here? If you weren't going to make me leave, I'd stay here forever."

"You say that now, Cosette," Micah said wistfully. "But people are driven by what's in the field of vision. It's not

244

natural for us to make choices about what's best for us when something else we also want is easier to obtain."

My eyes never left the garden as he spoke. I rested my gaze upon the fruit tree. "So is this place what's best for me or what I want?"

"That's not for me to decide."

"Well, then I decide it is."

Micah chuckled. "Just like that?"

"How can I see this..." I gestured out at the magnificence all around us. "And choose anything else? I'm staying. I'll just hold on to your hand forever so I don't have to leave."

Micah smiled at me. "It's not that simple."

"Why not?"

"Because truth is always complex."

I didn't give up. "I've just simplified it. I'm staying in the garden."

"I venture to say that it would be easier to convince you to let go of my hand than you think."

I was adamant. "Impossible. Staying here forever."

"In fact, I think it would only take one word to get you to let go."

I fixed my eyes upon the garden. There was nothing in the world I desired more than to be in this place.

"You're wrong."

Micah drew in a deep breath and leaned in close to me. "Westley."

◆ ◆ ◆

The morning had not illuminated the farmhouse as it had the garden. It remained as cold, dirty, and uninviting as it was when I'd left it.

I stood alone in the middle of the room, my shoes still in the precise position they'd been at the transition, next to the empty prints Micah had left behind.

At this moment, I wasn't afraid of my surroundings as I had been previously. I didn't long for Micah to step out of the thin air to give me company.

Now, I welcomed the solitude it offered me as I fell to my knees and wept.

CHAPTER 40

My GPS predicted my ride to Fort Wayne would take just under an hour and a half. Of course, it didn't take into account the snow that started to fall about ten miles outside of Middlebury, so I assumed I wouldn't arrive at Maplecrest until much later.

The clock on the dash read 2:00 p.m., but that seemed impossible to me.

My trip to the garden had left me jet-lagged, and crying had only added to my exhaustion.

I tried to remedy my emotional hangover by guzzling a large gas-station coffee and rolling down the passenger side window to let in the winter's air.

But even the wind blowing into the cab of my car was a reminder of my journey through the garden. Any other time, the crisp cold would have blasted my senses awake. But now, my perception's tolerance had been raised to a new level, and no matter how deeply I breathed, my body wasn't satisfied.

I drove on autopilot, my mind clouded with confusion, the memories of the garden so fresh and vivid they distracted me. I tried to blink them away.

My transition back had been wrought with emotion. The moment that Westley's name left Micah's lips, I became paralyzed with guilt. I was ashamed of how I had so easily forsaken him without even realizing it, how I'd pleaded with Micah to let me remain in the garden without so much as a thought of the one I'd be leaving behind.

How I could have experienced something as incredible as the garden without Westley entering into my thoughts even once? I felt as if I'd cheated on him somehow, but with a place instead of another person.

When it had occurred to me to check my phone for messages, I was equally relieved and saddened to have found none from West—no voice mail, text, or e-mail. While I desperately wanted to hear from him, my shame would have been compounded had I missed his attempts to reach me because of the garden.

If it was Tuesday—and according to the date on my phone, it was—West and I were closing in on two full days without communication. The first forty-eight hours were almost over, and I wanted to be at the hospital the nanosecond Westley was given a window back into the outside world. Even if it turned out that he couldn't see me, I needed to make the effort to try as proof to myself of my devotion to him.

But despite knowing that I owed Westley repentance for my unfaithfulness, I couldn't stop myself from grieving the garden.

I ached to return to it. Its beauty, its peace—they had birthed something new in me that I couldn't bear to let die so soon. Micah was right. I couldn't imagine that I'd ever be the same again having experienced that place.

Micah.

I didn't know when I'd see him again, but I assumed that I would. His business with me was unfinished, and mine with him seemed just to be beginning. I had dozens of new questions to ask him; I wanted to know so many things about where I'd been, what I'd felt.

But more than wanting him to tell me, I wanted to *experience* the answers to my questions. I wanted to smell the tulips, taste the fruit, and be warmed by the starlight on the hill.

The midweek, daytime traffic was light on the highway, so I didn't have to slow my speed to compensate for the weather.

As the miles between Westley and me decreased, my anticipation to see him rose.

I wondered how much progress toward coming home he'd made in the past two days. I had no idea what criteria a doctor would use to determine when Westley had been cured of what he was going through. It wasn't like a physical illness that an antibiotic could fix, and after seeing what Westley did with his Valium, I hoped that they would steer clear of prescribing him any kind of medication at all.

From farmhouse to hospital parking lot, I made it to Maplecrest in just under two hours. Immediately, I became anxious at the size of the campus. I parked my car and walked toward one of the entrances, not knowing which of the four I saw from the lot was the one that would lead me to my boyfriend.

The door I chose led to a receptionist's desk and a bank of elevators. A middle-aged woman attended the desk, and I waited for her to finish her phone call before approaching her to ask for directions.

"Admitting or visiting?" she asked with a forced smile.

"Visiting. His last name is Greene. With an 'e' at the end. First name, Westley." The woman typed as I spoke.

"Are you family?"

"Fiancée." I blushed as I said the word.

The woman rolled her eyes. "Visiting hours begin at four o'clock. You can wait over there." She indicated a row of seats facing a flat-screen television.

I sighed. "Does it get me up there faster if I say I'm admitting myself?" In light of the garden, I wondered if maybe I would need some in-depth psychoanalysis.

Her stern expression broke, and she resisted a smile. "Unfortunately, no. We are slow as hell around here at admissions. You're better off catching up on your talk shows."

"Thanks, anyway." I trudged off to the waiting room, feeling almost as tortured by the hour I'd have to wait there as I had been by the first fruits.

CHAPTER 41

I stood inside the elevator tapping my foot. I couldn't take one more minute of daytime television.

At exactly four o'clock, I stepped into the elevator that lifted me up to the fourth floor where I was greeted by a pretty receptionist who offered me a smile without making me work for it.

"Who are you here to see, hon?" she asked cheerily. I returned her smile and told her. She picked up a phone receiver and punched a few numbers into her keypad. "Mr. Greene, you have a visitor."

There was a pause.

"No, sir. I don't think she's one of your parents."

The woman placed the receiver back into its cradle and informed me that West would be along shortly.

I found a seat in the waiting area and looked back and forth between two hallways for signs of Westley.

"Oh, thank God." My ears perked up at the sound of his voice. He emerged from a closed door behind me labeled "dormitory quarters." Before I could take him all in, he picked me up from off of my seat and embraced me in a bear hug.

I melted into his familiar arms.

Our moment ended abruptly when he pulled away and looked me in the eye. "Wait a minute...Why are you here so early? Didn't you go to school?"

My eyes widened.

In my disorientation from the garden, I had forgotten about school.

I tried to recover quickly. "Um, no. I just didn't quite feel up to it today. I'll go tomorrow."

He narrowed his eyes at me as if sensing I was holding back, but then he let it go. "Well, you do look really tired. I hope it's not because you are worried about this nonsense." Westley pointed with his eyes around the room.

I shook my head honestly.

He was a sight for sore eyes, literally. He had been out of baseball conditioning for almost two weeks now, and his T-shirt hung a little more loosely around his chest, but other than that, he still looked perfect. His cheerful demeanor gave me hope that our separation would be short-lived. I sighed in relief.

Holding my hand, Westley led me to a cafeteria area where other visitors and residents would soon gather. We found an empty booth and sat together on the same side of the table.

"So, how are things?" I began gently. West's arm was around my shoulders, pulling me in close. I leaned my head onto his chest, and he held my left hand with his, catching my ring in the light.

"I don't know, Cosi. This place is a joke." Westley's annoyed tone dampened my hope that he was excelling in the healing process. "I mean, aside from them observing my sleep, there's no reason for me to be here."

"So, what are they saying?"

"Officially, nothing. They are telling me that I have some sort of stress-induced sleep disorder, which I'm pretty sure we already knew." I sensed an increasing frustration in his voice. "And then they are giving me some bullshit about how I have a fear of mortality."

"So, like, afraid of dying?"

"So they say. The doctor thinks that's why I keep reliving Julia's death. He says that I'm projecting fears of my own death onto hers."

"Why would you do that?"

He sighed deeply. "Because I know that death is the end." He spoke this statement as a declaration.

This didn't seem like a viable medical diagnosis. "The end of what?"

"Existence."

This puzzled me. Westley and I had never engaged in an intentional conversation about death and beyond, but I guessed I'd always assumed he thought *something* came next. "So, you're saying that you don't believe in an afterlife?"

"Of course not, Cosette," he said flatly. "I would say I'm more doubtful now than before I got pent up in this place."

His answer hurt me, though I didn't immediately know why. "Why more so now?"

"All right, get this..." Westley began. He scooted back from holding me so that he could use his hands to gesticulate as he explained. "So, at my evaluation with the doctor, he interrogates me about 'beliefs.' I told him that I didn't really get what that had to do with my medical situation, but he insisted. So, I tell him that I don't really have any. I tell him that there's no scientific basis for any sort of higher power, so I don't buy into it." My stomach sank into the floor. I wondered if Westley realized that this was the first time he was telling me this. "Then he asks me about Julia, and I tell him what happened. He leaves for a while and comes back in with some pamphlets about different religions and tells me that it might be good to explore some different faiths. Then he basically tells me to pick one because if I believe in heaven, it might be easier to accept death. Can you believe that? Kinda hard to put stock into eternity when it's presented to you à la carte." He scoffed.

I didn't know what to say to him. I believed in God. I was actual, living proof of his existence. But even with seeing all that I'd seen, I had no idea how to put it into words to convince Westley. I didn't have scientific evidence—I had experience.

I wanted that for Westley. I wanted a miracle for him, so that he would know what I knew.

"You're quiet," Westley observed. "There *is* something wrong, isn't there?" He sounded expectant, not panicked. "What's happened?"

Healing had happened. The garden had happened. But I couldn't bring myself to tell him any of it. I had no idea what to say, especially now when I was sure he'd reject it. And then he'd reject me.

"I just miss you." It was the truth, just not completely.

"I miss you too." His tone softened, and he kissed my forehead. "But, hey, look at the bright side—the longest they can keep me here is until the fourteenth."

I perked up at this news. That was still longer than I wanted to be away from him, but I hadn't allowed myself to guess a time frame before. Because I'd considered "forever" to have been an option—ten more days was definitely manageable. "What happens then?"

Westley made a face at me. "Seriously? We're getting married, and you can't even remember my birthday?"

"Of course I know when your birthday is, West. I just don't see what it has to do with you getting out of here."

"I'm turning eighteen, which means I'll be an adult." Westley smiled triumphantly. "At which point, I'll be free to check myself out of this hellhole without parental consent."

This made me uneasy. "Doesn't that annul your plea bargain with the police? I mean, they said you had to come here to get better and they'd drop their charges, right?" I reminded him.

"Well, if the doctor's orders are for me to join a religious cult, I'm not sure I'll ever graduate this place." He frowned. "And speaking of graduating, I'd like to focus on that. And baseball. And college. And my hot fiancée. I'm starting to wonder if all I really need to get through this junk is my old life back." He shrugged. "I'm sure there's one sane doctor around here who'll sign a paper saying he agrees with that."

I had to admit, Westley's recovery plan sounded very appealing to me. However, if sweeping his feelings about Julia's death under the rug were a legitimate option, I wasn't sure we'd have been at Maplecrest having this conversation in the first place.

"What will your parents say about that?"

His expression instantly darkened. "I don't care. I'm not speaking to them until they let me out of here."

"Whoa." I had known Westley was upset with his parents for insisting on Maplecrest, but giving them the silent treatment wasn't his style. "That's a bit dramatic, don't you think?"

"Maybe. Or maybe it was a bit dramatic to ship me off to a mental hospital for sleepwalking." His observation failed to include mention of the results of said sleepwalking, namely a disfigured girlfriend. "Seriously, Cosi, I'm in here with some real crazies. That kid over there..." He indicated a short, thin boy sitting at a table with a woman, presumably his mother. "He's a bed-wetter. He's sixteen, and he pisses the bed. Oh, and that girl over there with the dude haircut—she has these scars on her hands and face. I've never seen anything like them. They look like burns, but they're blue."

I sought out with my eyes the girl I guessed Westley was talking about. A petite brunette sat alone on a bench seat against the wall, her hands folded in her lap. Her expression was solidly sad, a downturned mouth and creased brow. Her cheek and lips were speckled with dark markings.

"You mean like bruises?" My heart immediately went out to the girl.

"Not at all. They look more like her skin crystallized or something. Who knows? She probably got them cooking meth or something. She doesn't talk though, so no one knows her deal."

The girl lifted her eyes to meet mine, and I looked away. "She doesn't talk at all?"

"Nope. Not sure if it's choice or a disability."

Suddenly, I understood how Westley could justify downplaying his own condition.

"How sad."

Westley wrapped his arms around me once again and pulled me up onto his lap. "Yeah, it is. This whole place is sad. So let's stop talking about it."

"OK."

We spent the next few hours together as our old selves, joking and flirting, and I realized that I had been missing Westley—my Westley—for longer than just the two days we'd been apart. After we ate dinner, we headed to the recreation room to play ping-pong. Since this was one of the few sports where reflex trumped strength, I could hold my own against Westley. By the time an announcement was made that visitation was ending, Westley and I had found our normal again. My cheeks were sore from smiling so much, and the comfort of our familiar had returned.

He walked me to my elevator as the clock struck eight. "You sure you are up to driving back tonight? You could just pretend you're crazy and be my roommate."

I wasn't sure I'd have to pretend anything. I'd just have to start telling the truth about Micah and the garden, and I'd probably be given a lifetime pass. "You aren't crazy, and I'll be fine." In my haste to get to Westley, I hadn't considered that I might be driving back to Middlebury at night. I hoped it hadn't snowed too much.

Westley kissed me on the lips, and I felt my knees go weak. I loved this boy. "Still wanna marry me?"

I grinned. "Of course. Nothing could change that."

We said good-bye, and I held my tears until the doors to the elevator closed. Westley had said that starting the following day, he'd have access to e-mail and he'd write me to schedule my next visit.

Ten more days at most? I could do this for that long. It wasn't a lifetime.

When I got to the parking lot, I was surprised to see about four inches of powdery snow covering the ground. I groaned to myself, realizing that digging my car out from underneath it would add significantly to what would already be a long drive home.

But when I reached my car, I found that someone had already cleared away the snow and scraped the ice from my windshield.

I scoured the parking lot. Every other car was still buried beneath the snow.

Curious, I pushed the automatic lock to let myself into the cab of my car, but I stopped before taking the driver's seat.

There, on my dashboard, was a piece of notebook paper, the word *provision* scrawled across it in pen. Next to it lay another perfect white tulip.

◆◆◆

I made it home without incident, but my mind was so heavy that when I got there, I barely had the energy to get ready for bed.

I'd yet to examine the damage my rough transition to the garden had caused, and the pain in my legs had not gone away. I wanted to assess my injuries before I passed out for the night.

I tugged off my boots and rolled up my pant leg under the florescent bathroom light, expecting the patchy, red blisters of a second-degree burn.

But that was not what I saw.

There on my shins, right above where the top of my boots had cut off and the river water had burned my skin through my jeans, my legs were an unmistakable, shocking blue.

At first, I thought the denim from my pants had melted onto my skin, tattooing my jeans onto me like an iron-on transfer. But as I ran my fingers along the azure burn lines, a thought suddenly occurred to me.

The girl at the hospital. Westley's description of the scars on her hands and mouth—every word of it applied to my own incredible injury.

The one I'd received in the garden.

And all of a sudden, I wasn't tired anymore.

CHAPTER 42

"Where the hell have you been?"

Bronwyn awoke me with a start. She was standing in my doorway, her hand lingering on the light switch she'd just flipped on.

I automatically sat up and squinted at my clock. Six thirty. At least I hadn't overslept for school. "I've been right here. Sleeping. Geez!" I fell back into my pillow and pulled my comforter over my eyes to block out the light.

"You didn't come home Monday night," Bronwyn stated.

I didn't have the energy it would take to come up with any sort of believable explanation for where I'd been, so I avoided her accusation. "I don't spend a lot of nights at home, Bron."

"True, you *are* kinda slutty." I could hear her welcome herself into my closet and shuffle the hangers around on their racks. "But Westley's in the nuthouse, so you couldn't have been with him."

Sigh. Glib Bronwyn was worse than regular Bronwyn.

"So did you finally take my advice and hook up with Micah?"

I sat up and stared at her. "Seriously, give it a rest about him."

"What?" she asked innocently. "He's hot, *and* he kicked Westley's ass. What more could you want in a guy?"

"I don't want Micah."

"Your loss." She hadn't forgotten her original allegation. "So if you weren't with Westley or Micah Monday night, where were you?"

Had I said I wasn't with Micah? I was too tired to trace our conversation back even a few seconds. "None of your business."

"You're bitchy in the mornings." She slung a few items from my wardrobe over her arm. "But your secrecy only leads me to believe you're doing something shady." Her eyes sparkled. She was smug. "Grandma got a message on her phone yesterday that you ditched school. I told her it was a mistake."

I was hoping to neither confirm nor deny anything Bronwyn was trying to get out of me. She was definitely fishing for information, and I didn't know why she wanted it. "Why would you say that?"

"Leverage, why else?" She shrugged as if her evil line of thinking was how the rest of the world thought too. "You're going to need an excuse note from someone to avoid detention. I'll write you one if you tell me where you were."

I laughed and rubbed my eyes. "I'm not telling you anything." What was a few extra hours spent after school? Detention would be a great excuse to catch up on all the homework I was sure to have from skipping in the first place.

"That's fine." She shrugged, holding a sweater up to her chin and looking back at me in the reflection of my mirror. "But truancy gets you a Saturday detention. I thought you might want to keep your weekends free for cuckoo-boy."

I cringed. Bronwyn was right; I didn't want to miss out on any opportunity to see Westley. I was going to need someone to verify an alibi.

It felt ridiculous that trivial details, such as school rules, still had any bearing on my life considering all that was going on, but I didn't need any more attention drawn to myself there. If Bronwyn was willing to get me out of trouble—even for a price—it was probably worth it. "Write the note first. Then we'll talk."

Her reflection arched an eyebrow. "Fine."

I decided that a shower would buy me enough time to figure out what to say to my sister that would satisfy her enough to give me what I needed.

But as soon as I undressed and saw my scars, all other thoughts vanished from my mind.

They were still prominent, though they didn't hurt as much as they had even hours before. I took my body sponge and gently scrubbed at them, hoping somehow I could rub the markings away. The friction did nothing but irritate my burns, so I stopped before I tore through the skin and caused an infection.

I couldn't understand how the river had scarred me in this way, but I supposed I shouldn't expect my body to react to the supernatural environment the way it normally would. If it did, then Micah wouldn't have needed to temper my senses in the garden.

Then, as they had most of the night before, my thoughts shifted to the girl at the hospital. I hadn't really seen her markings, but by Westley's description, I thought it highly probable that they were the same as mine. And if that were true, then I needed to find a way to meet her.

After my shower, I redressed in my pajamas to conceal my bizarre bruises from Bronwyn and exited the bathroom.

She was waiting on my bed for me, dressed in the outfit I'd worn the night Westley proposed. She dangled my excuse note in front of me like a carrot. "So?"

My markings had distracted me from crafting my answer to her. "I don't know why you want to know this so badly."

She immediately replied, "Because you are trying so hard not to tell it to me."

"Fine." I sighed. "If you *have* to know...I stayed out all night to look at the stars."

She narrowed her eyes. "Oh, please, Cosette."

"No, it's the truth." I wasn't lying of course, but I knew that this by itself wouldn't satisfy Bronwyn enough for her to give me my note. "But I wasn't alone...I was with Micah." This was also true, but admitting it felt like a lie because I knew what my sister would assume by it.

A wicked smile spread across her face. "I *knew* it!"

I attempted to snatch the note from her fingers. She quickly pulled it away and then dropped it to the ground, out of my reach, before standing up to leave. "Might want to read that before turning it in, tramp."

I opened up the note, completely unsurprised that she'd found a way to have the last laugh.

To Whom It May Concern:

Please excuse Cosette Miller for her absence on January 3. She was suffering from a flare-up of genital herpes.

Sincerely,

Bronwyn Miller

CHAPTER 43

I used the note.

I could have forged one myself, but it would have been equally untrue, no matter what I wrote. I convinced myself that whoever discovered it would feel too awkward to call my house to verify such a personal excuse. And honestly, since having STDs probably wouldn't be the worst rumor about Westley and me circulating around the school, if whichever office attendant read it blabbed about it, I decided I didn't care.

When I arrived at school that morning, I dropped off my note in the correct tray in the attendance office and headed straight for class.

Just around the corner from my first class, I heard my name.

"Hey, Cosette, wait up!" My ears perked up, and I surveyed the hall to see who was calling me.

Patrick was jogging my way. "Hey! How are you—wait a minute. What happened to your face?"

This question was becoming all too familiar of a greeting. My hands instinctively reached for my nose. "Why, what's wrong with it?"

"Absolutely nothing." He sounded surprised, and I remembered that the last time I saw him, I'd been wearing his catcher's mask to keep my nose from sliding off my face. "What happened?"

"Oh, yeah...must not have been as bad as it looked." I felt a stab of guilt for being so casual about my healing. It wasn't that I didn't want to tell people about what had happened; I just didn't know what I was supposed to say.

"Cosette, four days ago, you looked like you'd been hit by a bus." He scrutinized my face with wide eyes. "This didn't just get better by itself."

I shifted beneath his stare and tried to change the subject. "I've got to get your mask back to you—you'll probably need it for practice soon, right?"

This time, he looked away and shrugged. "Yeah, maybe. We'll see if there's even a team left."

"What does that mean?"

Patrick furrowed his brow. "You mean you haven't heard? Half the team got suspended for the whole season because of Trevor's party."

I felt myself go white. "*What?*"

"Yeah—someone e-mailed a bunch of videos from the party to the dean. Sims is showing no mercy. I'm guessing today's my day."

I tried to keep from panicking until I knew how this was going to affect Westley. "Who all was on these videos?"

"You mean, was Westley on them?" Patrick understood my concern. "I don't know, Cosette. I didn't see them. I've been trying to get a hold of West since this all went down, but he's not answering his phone, and I haven't seen him around. He sick?"

"He's...out of town." I was far too worried about Westley's baseball eligibility to think of a story to feed Patrick regarding his whereabouts. I needed to find out how much trouble West was in, but I didn't know how.

"Out of town?" Patrick wasn't buying it. "He OK?"

I was torn about whether or not to tell Patrick the whole truth. He was, after all, Westley's best friend, but I still didn't feel it was my place to explain what had happened. "Is there anything in the bro-code about keeping secrets?"

He instantly looked worried and stepped closer to me. He lowered his voice. "Of course, Cosette. What happened to West?"

I took a breath and told Patrick a summarized version of the saga. I decided to echo Westley's own sugarcoated explanation of why he'd been sent to Maplecrest: he'd been diagnosed with a sleepwalking disorder and needed to be admitted for observation and treatment.

Patrick could tell I was leaving out a lot of details. "Wow...any idea how all that started?"

I looked down at the ground. I didn't want to say her name. Though he appeared to be coping amazingly well with his girlfriend's death, I was sure that the constant reminders of her at school didn't make working through his grief any easier.

"It's Julia, isn't it?"

I didn't know if I was more relieved or sad that he'd figured it out. I nodded.

There was a silence between us that I didn't know how to end, so I was glad when Patrick did. "Do you think it would help if I talked to him? I mean, he's got to understand that her death had nothing to do with him. No one holds him accountable for what happened."

"I don't know if talking to him would help, really," I said. And I didn't. Westley hadn't seemed much in the mood to talk to anyone about what was going on. I wasn't sure if he'd feel freed hearing Patrick release him from any responsibility in his girlfriend's death or if contact from him would rip open a scab.

"He's got to realize he's not in control of the whole world. It'd be a lot easier for Westley if he could just get over his pride and realize God's bigger than he is. Kid needs to get some faith."

Patrick's words gave me a strange sense of comfort. He'd come to, essentially, the same conclusion as Westley's doctor. I believed it too, but I didn't know what to do about it. Perhaps Patrick did. "Maybe it *would* help to have you talk to him..."

We decided to meet up after school after learning more about the future of the baseball team.

As I walked the rest of the way to class, I grasped at straws for a reason for Westley not to meet the same fate as his friends. The athletic administration would have to understand how much he was suffering from Julia's death, that what happened at Trevor's party wasn't typical Westley Greene behavior. I hoped his parents had informed the school that he had been admitted to Maplecrest because at this point, that could only benefit his cause. After all, his record prior to this was squeaky clean. Four years of high school without so much as a tardy had to count for *something*.

I walked through the door to my history class as the bell sounded and was surprised to meet Micah's eyes from his desk. Somehow, his schedule change had slipped my mind. He half-smiled and seemed relieved I was there.

Seeing him sent an unexpected rush through my body. The last time we were in the same place, it was the garden. I remembered the moments before transitioning back to the farmhouse—the far, outstretching beauty of paradise...

I wanted to go there again. I wanted to escape all the anxiety this day was sure to bring by indulging in the mysteries of another world.

Why had I wasted my herpes excuse on only one day of absence? Surely, that sort of outbreak could easily have bought me more time off.

Maybe they still could? All I had to do was go to the nurse and tell her I was having more flare-ups of the medical issue detailed in my sick note, and I'd be home free.

I darted for Micah to ask him to take me back to the garden before my brain had time to find the flaw with my plan, when my history teacher said my name. "Cosette?"

I jumped. His voice sounded ominous. "Yes?"

"You're wanted in Dean Sims's office." He scrawled his signature on a hall pass and held it out for me. "You should probably take your things with you." He made a face suggesting he knew something more specific than he was telling me. Or maybe he'd just received enough phone calls from the dean to know that most people who were sent there didn't make it back to class within the hour. I didn't know. I'd never been sent there.

The hope of the garden faded, and my anxiety rose. I glanced at Micah and wondered if his expression was to mimic the disappointment on my face or if he, too, had his own reasons to believe I wouldn't be returning anytime soon.

I reluctantly accepted the paper from my teacher and turned back toward the hallway.

CHAPTER 44

All six chairs in the waiting area of the dean's office were occupied when I stepped into it. All six sets of eyes simultaneously looked up from the ground and in my direction when I entered the room.

I recognized one of the girls as the one who'd been sitting on Trevor Thomas's lap New Year's Eve. The rest of the kids were also familiar, but not so much that I could tell them apart from the rest of the student body I'd allowed to become mere extras on the set of *The Westley Show* throughout my high school days. But I didn't have to put names to faces to understand we were all there for the same reason.

"Cosette, where's Westley been?" a guy I thought Westley had played Little League with asked me. "Is it true he's in jail?" Evidently, I was not as anonymous to these people as they were to me.

I rolled my eyes and shook my head, hoping my silence would deter the others from trying to engage me in conversation about my boyfriend or anything else. It felt incriminating to be in this room with people who had attended Trevor's party willingly and not only been there long enough to rescue their drunk boyfriend from self-destruction. I knew I hadn't done anything wrong, but I decided it was probably smart to follow all the legal advice I'd gleaned from television and do things like invoke my right to remain silent and if necessary, plead the Fifth.

Just then, a woman wearing a winter coat and a scowl opened the door behind me, almost knocking me over.

She was too distracted to apologize and stormed directly to Dean Sims's door. His secretary addressed the visitor from her desk in the corner of the room. "He's expecting you, Becca. Go on in."

The woman didn't acknowledge the secretary, but she followed her directions.

After several minutes of muffled yelling, Dean Sims's office door opened again. "Becca" made a loud exit with her son, whom I immediately recognized as Lucas Weiss, an outfielder on the baseball team. "Well, there goes your scholarship. And your car. And probably everything else you hold dear. You're lucky your father isn't here..."

Her voice trailed off as Dean Sims appeared in his doorway expressing a look that seemed both annoyed and smug. "Let's go, Mr. Millsap." He made the "come here" motion with his index finger, and the boy who'd asked me about Westley stepped into the office. The door closed.

This scene continued for the next hour. And for each seat that opened up, another student came through the door to fill its vacancy. Of the five kids in front of me, three of them were sent home with parents who were at least as angry as Becca had been. Two were dismissed back to class. I had no reason to believe I wouldn't fall into the second category of student, but I was still anxious to get whatever was going to happen over with.

"Cosette," Dean Sims announced my name from his doorway following another angry mother-and-son pair leaving his office.

I stood and walked in. He shut the door behind me.

"Have a seat, Ms. Miller." The dean indicated a chair for me that faced his desk before walking around it to take his own.

Dean Sims held dual roles at Camden—administrator of discipline and varsity football coach—and from what I could tell, whoever had hired him for these jobs had cast the parts well.

Even after sitting down in his chair, he still towered over me. He wore a military haircut and had one of those faces that never changed expression no matter what he was feeling. Before he'd even spoken a syllable to me, I was already terrified enough of him to run a hundred laps if he told me to.

"So, did you have yourself a nice New Year's Eve?"

There was no time wasted loading this question and pulling the trigger. I'd felt less intimidated at the police station.

"I've had better," I responded nervously. It was hard for me to qualify my own answer as fact or fiction. I had never had a New Year's Eve before where I'd been basically resurrected from the dead, so in that regard, it *was* the best one. However, the fact that Westley had broken my face and various other body parts rendering me practically dead made it difficult to rank it at the top of the list.

"Do anything special?"

This was a weak attempt to bait me, but I didn't know what he had up his sleeve, so I answered him carefully. "I helped out a friend who was in trouble." I knew withholding the truth wasn't going to help my cause—he already knew I'd been at Trevor's, or I wouldn't have been called to the office. But, I didn't want to identify Westley if his attendance at the party had not yet been confirmed.

Dean Sims gave me a look as if to say, *You don't really expect me to believe that, do you?* Then followed it up with, "I got a different impression from this video." He turned his computer monitor around to face me.

With a click of his mouse, the frozen blur on the screen came to life. Though the vantage point was some distance away from us, it was clear that Westley and I had starring roles in this feature. My heart sank to the floor.

The clip was queued up to the exact moment I'd discovered West's condition, and I watched my on-screen self attempt what looked like an awkward Heimlich maneuver on my boyfriend. As I clearly remembered, my efforts to remove him from his seat had failed. From the third-party perspective, I looked ridiculous. Not that I expected myself to have looked at all graceful, but reliving this moment as a bystander illustrated how in over my head I'd truly been trying to save Westley on my own.

I also noted that my face looked terrible despite my best efforts to hide my broken nose. It was puffier than I recalled, and my black eyes shown purple through my cover-up. Screen Cosette looked like a caricature drawing of myself, one that accentuated the center of my face in street-fighter fashion.

"Still sticking with your story?" the dean asked flatly, re-folding his arms across his chest. He'd no doubt been reviewing these videos for days and was bored by excuses.

I kept my eyes on the monitor long enough to see Westley tackle me; we exited the scene in a loud crash, stage bottom.

I shifted my gaze to Dean Sims, still confident I had nothing to confess that could get me in any sort of trouble. "Absolutely," I stated more confidently than I felt. "If anything, this video confirms it. My friend needed help. I was trying to help him."

He narrowed his eyes at me. "What I see here are two kids at a party where alcohol is clearly present." He sat up and pointed at bottles, cans, and the keg all in view on the monitor. "And they're too drunk to even stand up."

"That's not true, Dean Sims." I chose my tone, not wanting to seem defensive at his accusation. "I hadn't had anything to drink."

He laughed. "That's the same thing your boyfriend's parents said about him, but I'm pretty sure he didn't get sent to Maplecrest for being too *sober*."

I swallowed. He'd talked to Westley's parents. Did that mean they'd already reached a decision about his future on the baseball team?

I didn't know how to defend Westley, though I was pretty sure nothing I said would matter anyway.

"And even if you actually weren't drinking, we still have a problem," he said too casually and then clicked his mouse several more times.

I started protesting again that I wasn't guilty of anything when a new clip began to play. It was shot from inside Trevor's house, pointed outside at the driveway. I was standing there, my shirt covered in blood. Patrick's back was to the camera as he slid a catcher's mask over my head.

Dean Sims eyed me. I just shrugged.

"I got a bloody nose trying to carry West up the stairs. What's the big deal—?" I started to explain but interrupted myself.

I stopped talking, but my mouth stayed open. The unidentifiable person in the shot, Patrick, was holding up a prescription bottle. He offered it to the girl in the catcher's mask, and she hesitantly accepted it.

I answered my own question. A drug deal. *That* was the big deal.

I ran both my hands through my hair. "This is a complete misunderstanding. It's not what it looks like..." Even though I knew I was telling the truth, everything out of my mouth felt like clichés from television cop dramas.

"So you are telling me that this kid on the video isn't giving you prescription meds?"

I fell back into my chair. Was this the part where I was supposed to plead the Fifth?

"You know that this is illegal, right?"

No, I didn't. I wanted to change my plea to "ignorance." Would that make this go away?

"It was a few pills, and he only gave it to me because I got hurt trying to get Westley out of there." I looked down at the ground, my temper rising. How had I become the villain? Patrick and I were Westley's heroes. Who knows what might have happened to him had he stayed at that party any longer. We'd been looking out for him, and now we were both going to be punished for it.

"Who gave you the pills?"

Or maybe, just I was going to be punished for it.

Patrick hadn't been identified. From the video, he was just another kid wearing a Camden Athletics hoodie.

"I'm not going to nark someone out over a mix-up."

The dean raised an eyebrow at me. "You may want to reconsider playing the martyr here. Cooperating could reduce your consequences."

270

For the first time, I found myself thankful that trigonometry had been so boring to me. It was during that class where I had often busied myself reading the copy of the *Camden Student Handbook* attached to my daily homework planner. I knew my rights. "Nothing you are accusing me of happened on school grounds. So I don't see how you can punish me for any of this."

Dean Sims was amused by my strategy. "No, not technically. But according to Camden's discipline policy, I have the right to suspend anyone who I believe is a threat to the safety of her classmates." He sat up straighter in his chair. He enjoyed his power. "And I gotta say, when a kid is hopped up on pills...Well, who knows what kind of violence she's capable of?"

He stared me down.

"You're going to suspend me over this."

He raised a finger. "Only if you don't tell me who gave you the bottle."

Inside, I was furious. This hardly felt like the blind justice students should be able to expect from the people leading their school. All the evidence against me was circumstantial, and I was pretty sure what the dean was suggesting to me constituted blackmail.

But I knew none of that mattered. I had a choice to make.

Throw Patrick under the bus and save myself—maybe; I didn't trust Sims further than I could throw him. Refuse, and get suspended.

I sighed. I pouted. I fidgeted.

Then I stopped, and I smiled.

My thoughts flashed to the garden, the miles of unexplored beauty I hadn't had the time in my first visit to experience. Then, they shifted to Westley—an hour and a half away at the hospital—and how much time a suspension would free up for more frequent visits to him.

Suddenly, it was easy to weigh my options.

"I'll take the suspension."

CHAPTER 45

Dean Sims wasn't accustomed to losing battles of the will with his students, as evident by how he tried to bargain back my decision. He explained to me that I'd be doing the community a huge favor by getting a pill pusher off the streets, that I'd be helping my "team" by cooperating with them to identify the guy in the video.

It was then I understood that this, busting potential teenage crime, was how Coach Sims stayed sharp in the off-season.

But Patrick Wellman was not the dangerous pill peddler this video clip made him out to be, and I was not going to paint him as one in exchange for my own immunity.

Begrudgingly, the dean called my grandmother to come pick me up. It didn't matter that I'd driven myself to school that day; it was procedure that students being suspended needed to be escorted out of the building by a family member or guardian. This detail hadn't been in the student handbook, so it was news to me. Grandma explained to Dean Sims that she was sitting for her granddaughter who was sleeping, so she'd send someone else in her place.

While we waited, the dean typed up the paperwork regarding our meeting and handed me a copy of his notes. Knowing I wouldn't agree with anything on it, I folded it and held it closed in my hand. My suspension was for five school days, which didn't make me eligible to come back until the following Wednesday. With the time I hoped to split between the garden and Westley, I wondered if that would be enough or if there was something I could do—like maybe throw one of his football trophies through the window—to tack on another week.

I fantasized about this until there was finally a knock at the door. Having had no experience with my father in this kind of situation, I couldn't predict how angry he'd be at me. I knew I had to already be on thin ice with him after the damage caused by Micah and Westley's fight in our foyer, and he'd surely be at the very least annoyed at having to miss work because I'd been suspended for drugs.

But instead of feeling relieved when the door opened and Bronwyn walked in, I felt worse.

"Come on, you little felon," she said through a snide smile. "Let's get you home for your fix before you start having withdrawals."

I stared at my sister, expressionless.

"Excuse me." Dean Sims stood and addressed Bronwyn. "But she can only be released to a legal parent or guardian. You don't appear old enough to be either."

Bronwyn rolled her eyes. "Well, considering our mother is dead, and our father is at work and couldn't give a rat's ass whether or not Cosette actually *is* a druggie—which by the way, no one believes—our only other family member who *appears* old enough is at home babysitting my daughter. So, I'm going to be the only one who shows up, and unless you want to spend the rest of your day waiting on a second chance to unload her—she's coming with me."

The dean's face got red. "Now you listen here, young lady—"

"And another thing—I don't remember hearing you complain about me not looking old enough the other night at Rulli's after you'd had half a bottle of wine with your coaching buddies, *Dan*. So you go ahead and start all the shit you want with me and my family. All it'll take is one phone call to your wife, and I imagine you'll be in enough of your own trouble that you won't have time to be falsely accusing anyone of popping pills."

Both of our mouths dropped to the floor.

Bronwyn flipped her hair. "Let's go, Cosette."

I stood up and followed my sister out.

◆◆◆

Although Bronwyn was meant to be my escort, I had to run to keep up her pace as she stomped off to the parking lot.

"Would you wait up?" My backpack, still full of my morning classes' worth of books, was slowing me down.

"I feel like I've done enough favors for you lately. The least you can do is walk faster so I can get back to the office without Dad knowing I'm gone."

"What are you talking about?" I picked up my pace and took a breath. "You said Dad was too busy to come get me."

"I know what I said, Cosette." She didn't slow or look back at me. "I didn't tell him. And I made Grandma promise not to either."

I caught up to her. "Why would you do that?"

We'd reached the double doors to the parking lot when she finally stopped walking and turned to face me. "Because I need you to owe me. And if I've got a secret on you, then you'll have to keep the one I'm going to tell you."

This day was full of surprises. Bronwyn had never willingly told me anything about her life. I'd only learned she was pregnant with Ginger because at five months along, she came down to breakfast wearing a maternity shirt that said "Virgin" in huge font on the front and "Liar" written across the back.

I ignored the possibility that sharing in whatever secret my sister had might actually make me an accessory to a crime, and I immediately agreed to return her favor. "Of course, what's going on?"

Bronwyn made a disgusted face at me. "You really think I'm going to tell you a secret in the halls of a high school?" She pointed back toward the commons area where half of the student body could be seen headed for lunch. "I'll tell you later. Oh, and until then—I own you." She pushed through the doors and clomped off to her car.

CHAPTER 46

I watched through the window until I saw Bronwyn's Malibu peel out of the student lot before exiting the school. I took a deep breath of winter's air and exhaled thick clouds of steam, feeling not at all like I would have expected to feel after just being handed down my first-ever suspension. My nerves were still calming from the adrenaline rush evoked by my sister's verbal smackdown of the dean, and for the first time in a while, I felt immune to anxiety.

I used this moment of clarity to generate a game plan for the rest of my day. My first priority was to assess the Westley situation. As far as I knew, the only people up to speed on the latest decisions about his athletic eligibility were his parents. Though, if they did have bad news for their son, he wasn't accepting any communication from them to learn it, so whatever really was going on, I was sure Westley knew nothing of it.

I decided the "if" and "when" surrounding Westley being told were secondary in importance to the "where." He would have to be informed while at Maplecrest. I guessed there was no better place to receive such soul-crushing disappointment than one with amenities like padded rooms. This way, if the news was going to impede any progress he was making at the hospital, they could deal with it head-on.

But before any of this mattered, I needed to hear from Patrick. Surely he would know the full details surrounding the baseball suspensions by the end of school, and maybe together we could figure out how to break the news to Westley.

One glance at the time told me that I still had about three hours before the end of the school day when I would be able to talk to Patrick. That was unless someone else was willing to play informant and name him as the guy in the video, and he got sent home earlier. But my guess was that the dean was going to be hard-pressed to find anyone willing to throw a guy who'd just suffered the death of his girlfriend under the bus. The anonymous videographer had, whether intentionally or coincidentally, protected Patrick's identity, and I assumed everyone else would too.

I reached my car and was fumbling for the keys in my purse when I became aware of someone behind me.

"Think I could get a ride?"

I jumped and spun around, keys poised to kill.

Micah ducked, his hands over his face in protective mode. "OK, this time, I was trying really hard *not* to scare you, Cosette."

I sighed in relief. "Sorry, I must have been lost in thought." I withdrew my weapon and used it to unlock my door. I gestured for Micah to join me inside the car, and he jogged over to the passenger's side and let himself in.

As I was turning the key in the ignition, it occurred to me that Micah should have still been in class. "Why are you out here anyway?"

"I ditched to find you."

"Oh." I felt relieved. "I figured Sims must have suspended you too."

"You got suspended?" He looked surprised, which made me feel all the more justified for judging the decision unfair. I explained the drama in the dean's office, leaving out Bronwyn's cameo since it had ended with the promise of an impending secret I would be expected to keep. "On the bright side, though," I added upon seeing how concerned Micah looked for my situation, "I figure that this frees up my calendar for another trip to the garden."

A smile broke across his face. "Really? So you want to go back? After the way you left, I wasn't sure..."

I cringed with guilt at Micah's reminder of why I'd transitioned out of the garden, but I recovered quickly, promising myself that the next time I went, I would keep Westley near in thought the entire time. "How could I not want to go back there? I didn't want to leave it in the first place."

"But you did," he pointed out.

"I know," I agreed but felt the need to explain my position anyway. "I don't expect you to understand it, Micah, but the garden was the first time I'd experienced something so significant on my own. Not that I've been anywhere like that with Westley...but I feel like I've shared just about every important moment in my life with him. Once I realized how I'd barely even thought about him during my time in the garden, it felt wrong being there."

"I understand that more than you know, Cosette." His jaw was set. "But the garden is what it is, regardless of Westley."

By his tone, I couldn't tell if his words were supposed to bring me sadness or solace.

"What does that mean?"

He shook his head. "Let me just say that I don't think it's a bad thing that you were able to have your experience in the garden without your thoughts being occupied otherwise."

"Why?"

"There's just a lot more you have to learn there. Might be easier to do that with a clear head."

Though incomplete for sure, his answer made enough sense for me to move. I had questions. "You mean like what these are?" I propped my boot on the dashboard and unzipped it down to my ankle before rolling up my pant leg. The markings were still there around my calf, tattooed with the same bright-azure coloring that had been there the previous night.

"Whoa!" Micah's eyes widened with concern. "Cosette, I am so sorry that I did that to you. Does it hurt? I'm so sorry..." He repeated his apology several times until I stopped him.

"It's OK," I reassured him. The tenderness was minimizing, though the color hadn't faded. I assumed this indicated whatever these markings were, they were probably permanent. "What do you know about this?"

"They're scars," he replied with a frown. "They can happen when a visitor comes to the garden and isn't given the proper protection from the environment by their guide." He reached hesitantly to touch the blue patches and waited for me to nod permission for him to do so. He traced his cold fingertips over my skin. "You shouldn't have even been able to feel the river at all...I can't imagine how painful that was for you." Micah looked sick.

"Never mind that." I was excited to share with him my discovery from the hospital. "I saw a girl who had markings like this. One of the patients at Maplecrest."

He froze in shock. "Well, did you talk to her? Who was it?"

"No, I didn't—I mean, it was before I knew about my own markings," I explained. "And Westley said she was probably mute anyway. Do you know the person I'm talking about?"

Micah was thoughtful. "No. But I think you need to see her again. Find a way to communicate with her. There has to be a purpose in your paths crossing."

I shivered, but I wasn't afraid. I believed there was a bigger purpose too.

"I'm going to go home and see what I can learn about this girl. I'll be back soon. Do you know where you'll be so that I can find you?"

I considered going back to my house, but I was worried that once I was there, my grandmother might not want me to leave again. She'd never been a disciplinarian because I'd never done anything that would have required her to be. I didn't want to chance her feeling like she needed to punish me for my suspension. "I don't really know where *to* go."

Micah halfway smiled. "Well...there is one place I know of..."

CHAPTER 47

The more familiar the farmhouse became to me, the less creepy it seemed. The early afternoon sun shone through the dirty glass in the windows, and I found being there in the daylight felt simpler. Micah lit a fire and retrieved a blanket for me that I kept in the back of my car.

"You look like you could use a nap," he declared as I sank into one of the heavy wooden rockers. I wanted to argue with him, but I knew it was probably true. Until Patrick got out of school, I had nothing I really could do for Westley, and having had such restless sleep the night before, I found the idea of wasting the afternoon unconsciously very appealing.

Micah agreed not to transition to the garden until after I'd fallen asleep, which couldn't have happened too long after he spoke the promise, because it felt like only moments after I closed my eyes that my thoughts grew jumbled, and I felt myself drifting into darkness.

Always my most vivid dreaming occurred when I was sleeping someplace other than my own bed. I assumed that for me this was because my subconscious was suspect of the unfamiliar and wanted to stay on-guard, never fully allowing my body to enter into the deepest cycle of sleep. I remembered that the first few sleepovers at Westley's had been that way, full of silly dreams about driving underwater and only being able to run in slow-motion, ridiculous movies playing in my head to entertain the part of my brain pulling an all-nighter.

But the dream I dreamed that afternoon in the farmhouse was different.

When I became aware of myself, I was in the garden again, this time standing freely in the field of tulips, not tethered to Micah. In fact, he wasn't even present; I was alone. It was day, and for the first time, I could see the flowers in the light. They seemed to stretch for colorful miles in every direction.

I found myself wrestling with the same overwhelming sense of insignificance I would have felt had I been standing in one of the empty winter cornfields in Middlebury, only I wasn't terrified. Instead, I wanted the rows of flowers to be infinite so I could spend the rest of my life counting and marveling at each one of them.

I let my arms dangle at my sides and took several steps forward, grazing the velvety petals with my fingertips. Then I knelt on the warm earth and ran my fingers along several of their long stems.

While admiring their design, something occurred to me. In the same way that I'd heard the music when Micah and I had transitioned to the garden together, I recognized that my sense of touch was being experienced in a different capacity. Each individual tulip seemed to have its own distinct feel. Each leaf, each petal—though they all looked identical to one another—was still unique in touch; I found that could tell them apart simply by feeling them.

The differences were subtle, like observing chronological shades in the color spectrum, but the properties by which my fingers could read the flowers—firmness, smoothness, weight—were all unique in every part of every tulip I touched.

I'd never appreciated any flower this way before. Or anything else, for that matter.

There were so many of them, but they were each special. I wanted to know them all.

The beauty all around me felt alive, and I wanted to engage it. I ran up and down the rows of tulips, glancing over my shoulder to see them bending in my wake, chasing after me.

I may have kept running in that field forever had I not heard the laughter.

It came faintly at first, the way the music had seemed far away in the farmhouse.

"Hello?" I called out to it.

A breeze carried my voice away from me, but from behind me, I could hear giggling.

The sound of it was musical. "Who's there?" I turned a full three-sixty, searching out whoever had joined me in the field, but I saw no one.

There was another soft wind and more laughter on its tail end. I ran against it, hoping to find the owner of the small voice; it was a child's voice, I was becoming sure of that. Children's voices, I decided as I ran. I heard more than one.

The giggling became constant as I tramped through the field, the tulips bending now before I ran past them, pointing me against the wind to the voices' origin.

After running for several minutes, I came upon a clearing in the field. There was an opening in the flower bed, and in the middle of this space, there stood a little girl.

She was wearing a sundress, and her hair was pulled into dark braids. She smiled at me, and in a flash, I recognized her, though I couldn't place her name.

"Ginger?" I heard myself call, knowing that it would be impossible for this child to be my toddler niece, but hers was the only name that I could remember.

The girl smiled at me and shook her head. Then she covered her mouth and giggled again. Her laughter instantly carried to me, and again, I was shaken by her familiarity.

There was a rustling in the flowers behind her, and suddenly, two more children pushed through into the clearing. First a younger boy, followed closely by an even younger girl.

As we narrowed the space between us, I could tell these children were related. While they each expressed their brunette hair in varying hues, their features were unmistakably drawn with the same pen.

Upon noticing me, the smaller girl stopped running. She creased her brow and called for her brother. He went back to her and reached out for her hand before leading her to the older girl.

"Hello there!" I greeted them all together, taking slow steps forward. "I'm Cosette," I introduced myself with a smile before bending down to eye level with the oldest girl. "What are your names?"

The little boy looked at me with complete confusion. He scrunched up his face. "Cosette?" he scoffed. "I can *not* call you that."

His adamancy amused me. "Why not? That's my name."

The older girl protectively took one hand of each of her siblings. "He just knows *we're* not supposed to call you that."

"Well, what—" My question was interrupted by more rustling in the field to my left. "Oh, are there more of you?"

Emerging into the clearing was a silhouette of a man. One that took my breath away.

"Westley."

He appeared taller, stronger than last I'd seen him in the hospital. And against the backdrop of the garden, he was more handsome than ever. His gait as he approached us was steady, confident. His skin was tanned, the way it looked after a summer spent lifeguarding. His hair appeared a shade darker than I was used to, and his features seemed more defined, matured.

He flashed a brilliant, dimpled smile at me, and had I not fallen in love with him at first sight all those years ago, I would have in this moment.

"Westley..."

The three children began cackling together, the two younger jumping up and down, still holding onto the older girl's arms. They pulled her to the ground.

"Be careful there!" Westley called to them, joining in their laughter. "I knew I'd find you kids here!" He ran to us, knelt down to help the older girl up, and then kissed her forehead. The three children clung around his waist and knees.

"Westley, what are you doing here?" I was equally delighted and confused by his presence in the garden and his interactions with the children.

He laughed at me. "What are you talking about? Where else would I be?"

"I didn't know you knew about this place."

Westley scooped up the younger girl, and she threw her arms around his neck. "Are you feeling all right, Cosette? You aren't making a lot of sense."

"I don't think she remembers us. She called me Ginger," the older girl explained as she tugged on Westley's shirt.

I hated that in a place where everything around me was clearer, more enhanced, my mind had gone fuzzy about who these children were. Obviously, if Westley knew them in such an intimate way, then I did too. "I know she's not Ginger, Westley. And I feel like I should know her name, but I just don't..."

He looked sympathetically at me. "Maybe you should lie down. If you can help me get them back inside, then we'll all stay out of your hair so you can get some sleep."

I found myself nodding at Westley, agreeing to a plan that seemed like it should make sense but didn't. Maybe I did need some rest.

Westley extended the little girl for me to take into my arms. She, more than the older girl, reminded me of Ginger, but her hair was lighter and her eyes darker. Judging by her size, I expected her to feel the way my niece did in my arms, the contradicting soft and solid of a young toddler, and I was excited to hold her close to me.

But when I tried to take her from Westley, something happened.

As I reached for the girl, my fingers, in the same way they had that night with Micah and the first fruits, slipped through her.

I stopped and blinked and then tried again. I reached to wrap my arm around her waist to lift her onto my hip, but I could feel nothing. It was like she was a hologram.

Or I was.

I reached quickly for both the other children, and like with the little girl, my fingers couldn't grasp them.

Westley and I stared at one another in bewilderment.

"Westley, what's happening? Please, make it stop!" I began to panic and continued repeatedly to grab onto the children, each time returning my arms to my chest empty.

I could see them also becoming uneasy. "What's going on?" the older girl asked Westley.

"I don't know, honey," he addressed her and then reached out his hand for mine. "C'mon, Cosi. Stop messing around. You're going to scare the kids."

His attempt to touch me failed, and I watched as his fingers slid right through my hand.

Westley looked into my eyes. "Cosette, what did you do?"

"I...I...I don't know!" I stammered, trying repeatedly without any success to interlock my fingers with his.

Westley's face darkened. "No, Cosette. You know exactly what you did." The older girl picked up the boy, held him close to her, and then buried her face into West and started crying softly. He began taking backward steps to distance them from me.

"Wait, Westley! Don't go away." I narrowed the gap between us. "What did I do? Tell me! I don't understand any of this!"

He snapped, "You stay where you are, Cosette!" He stroked the older girl's hair, and I could hear her sobbing softly. "You are the one who did this to us!" Westley barked at me, and tears poured out of my eyes.

I felt frozen in place as Westley turned his back to me with the children and hurried back into the tulips.

"Wait! Please! Come back!" I called against the wind, but my voice was carried off in the direction behind me.

I could no longer feel the beauty alive around me. I could only feel insignificance.

◆ ◆ ◆

I awoke to find myself covered in sweat, my body twisted unnaturally in the rocking chair.

My eyes automatically searched the room for Westley and the children, but of course, they weren't there.

No one was there.

I was alone, again, in the farmhouse.

284

And again, I appreciated the solitude it afforded me, as I sat up in the chair and cried.

CHAPTER 48

By the time I needed to drive back to the school to find Patrick, I had pulled myself together.

It was just a dream, not reality, I convinced myself. I was overly tired trying to process the guilt I felt about the garden while at the same time missing Westley; there was no use in trying to psychoanalyze it beyond that.

And the children...well, I couldn't explain them. And since I couldn't, I forced myself to forget them.

I called out for Micah, realizing too late that we hadn't discussed how I was supposed to communicate with him while he was in the garden. The night Micah cooked for me, he seemed to have come back when I called him. But for whatever reason, this time, when I beckoned him, the only response that came was the echo of my own voice.

I left a note on my chair that I'd planned to meet up with Patrick, and I told him to come find me if he could.

I drove to the high school the long way so that I could enter the student lot from the back entrance. Students on suspension were not allowed on school property for the duration of their punishment, per the handbook, so I knew I was going to need to be low-key.

There was an empty parking spot a few spaces down from Patrick's car, so I slid my Element into it and waited for the end-of-school bell.

Less than a minute after it rang, a text came through on my phone.

Where are you?—Patrick

I responded with my locale. A few minutes later, he came out of the school and jogged toward my car.

He flung open the passenger's door and hopped in.

"Hi," I greeted him.

He stared at me, completely puzzled. "So...why, exactly, did you get suspended?"

I sighed. News traveled fast. "I'm pretty sure the official reason had something to do with a drug deal I got caught on video participating in," I explained to a dumbfounded Patrick. "But unofficially, it's because Sims is a jerk."

"But...you don't *do* drugs?"

"Exactly." I wanted to shift the attention off of me before Patrick had the chance to ask for more details. "But what about you? Are you off the hook?"

He shook off his confusion. "Yeah...it seems that way." He heaved a sigh. "I mean, I got called down today, but it was only to ask me some questions about the party. I guess a couple people mentioned I'd been there but that I hadn't had anything to drink and left after I saw what was going on."

I was happy that others had stood up for Patrick.

"So, anyway, explain this drug thing again—"

I interrupted him. "Do you know anything more about Westley?"

His face instantly fell. "Yes. It's not good, Cosi." He tried to break the news gently. "Talked with Coach Bowen today...He said that once Sims got a hold of the videos, there wasn't anything he could do about it." He put a hand on my shoulder, and I knew what was coming. "Westley's off the team. I'm really sorry."

I was surprised at how much the news stung, even though it had been what I expected all along. A big part of me had been holding on to the hope that mercy would be shown to Westley with everything he was going through. Taking baseball away from him when he was obviously hurting so badly already just seemed unfair.

Patrick continued, "If you don't mind, I feel like I need to be the one to tell him."

My spirits lifted slightly at the thought of him being the one to break the news to Westley. I would have told him if I had to, but I didn't think myself the best candidate for the job. "I think that's a great idea."

Patrick made a call to Mr. Greene. West's parents had also been informed of their son's fate but had not had the opportunity to tell him of it. Evidently, Mr. and Mrs. Greene had been down to Fort Wayne twice to see their son, and both times, Westley had refused to come out of his room. I felt terrible for his parents, especially his mother. Her son's rejection had to be killing her.

Mr. Greene was grateful to Patrick for his offer and gave him permission to talk to Westley. We decided to drive immediately to Maplecrest; there was no sense delaying the inevitable.

"So how exactly do you want to do this?" Patrick asked me as I pulled onto the expressway. "I hope you don't mind, but I feel like, initially at least, I need to talk to Westley alone."

This was also a relief to me. "Yeah, I agree." I was glad we were on the same page. "Not that he's going to take it well either way, but I think it's better for him to have a chance to react without me around."

He nodded.

I considered for a moment that aside from his family and me, Patrick was probably the person closest to Westley. Micah had proven himself a pretty accurate judge of my boyfriend for the length of time they'd known one another, but the two of them didn't have the history that Patrick and Westley shared. I was glad for the time alone with him to glean any insight he might have to offer into West's current situation.

"You know, Westley's wanted to be a doctor since he was little, and now he's afraid he won't be able to because of how he's handling Julia. It's not good timing for another one of his dreams to come crashing down around him. It's going to kill him."

288

I cringed at my own poor choice of words, but Patrick didn't seem to notice them. "It won't kill him, Cosette. Hopefully, it will break him though."

"Break him?"

"Yeah," he said matter-of-factly. "Some people have to hit rock bottom before they will surrender to the fact that they aren't the ones in control of everything. And with as stubborn as Westley is, I'm just afraid he's going to keep digging himself deeper into a hole until the shovel breaks."

"Wait a minute..." I was confused. "Are you saying that you hope getting kicked off the baseball team destroys Westley?"

He didn't backpedal. "Destroys him? No. But I hope this wakes him up," Patrick explained his position. "I don't know how much the two of you talk about this kind of stuff, Cosette, or even how important it is to you. But your boy has some serious hang-ups about God. And honestly, I feel like more than anything, *that* is what's causing his issues over Julia." He'd alluded to this before, but hearing him state this opinion so boldly made it feel true. "Generally speaking, Westley has had a pretty easy life—he's got money, grades. Comes from a good family. He's in a great relationship. He's never had to accept that he needed God before because he never needed God."

I wanted to tread lightly on this subject with Patrick because of his relationship to Julia, but I wasn't following what he was telling me. "So that's the difference between you and him, then? You know you need God, so then what? You get to keep your sanity while Westley gets punished by losing his?"

"I don't believe that's what's happening to Westley." He shook his head. "I mean, if we're going to accept that line of thinking, then we'd have to consider that maybe God killed Julia to punish me for something...and that's just not his character."

I didn't know enough about God to argue one way or another, but I wanted to believe that Patrick was right. "Then why *did* she die, Patrick?"

"Brain aneurysm."

"No—I mean, I know the medical reason. But bigger picture. Why?" I recognized that Westley's downward spiral was only one side effect of Julia's death and that with the number of lives hers touched, there had to have been others still suffering deeply because of it. It all just seemed so unnecessary.

"It's still the same answer for me, Cosette—brain aneurysm. Something screwed up in her biology. Nothing more, nothing less. That's why she died. I've accepted that." By his tone, I could tell he hadn't come to this conclusion lightly. "Now, if you want to talk about how God can *use* her dying for good...well, I think I'm at the point now where I'm hopeful about that. It's part of the reason I'm going to talk to Westley."

"You think God can use Julia's death to change Westley?"

"I believe God can do anything."

I thought about the garden with its endless possibilities. My healing. The wonders of Micah. I had experienced all these things for myself, and I didn't think I could have spoken those words with as much conviction as Patrick had—and he experienced none of them.

"Where does that faith come from?" Aside from Micah, I'd never had an open conversation with anyone about religious beliefs. I didn't know what I was allowed to ask without offending. "What do you base that on?"

Patrick didn't answer right away, and I began to worry I'd said something wrong.

"I'm new to this, Cosette. I wasn't brought up in a home where anyone really believed in anything beyond the Curse of the Chicago Cubs. And when I started trying to figure life out, God definitely wasn't the first place I turned for answers. But at that time, Jules and I had been dating a few months. She'd just started going to church, and I began seeing these changes in her." His expression brightened. "Good ones, you know? Like when I first asked her out, it was because I had a thing for redheads, but it wasn't until I got to know this side of her that I really fell hard. She was genuine. She really loved people. She was...happy. All the time." He laughed. "Got really annoying actually." I smiled, remembering how bubbly Julia was. "But...I wanted that. I wanted to *be* that."

Who didn't want to be that?

"So what did you do?"

"The same thing I did when I wanted to make varsity in baseball. I worked at it. I studied it." He chuckled to himself. "And I prayed."

"That's it?"

"Well, it wasn't a one-time thing, Cosette. It's an every-single-day thing. And like with baseball—I get out of it what I put into it. The days I really spend praying and listening, I almost feel like I know what I'm doing in life. Others, not so much. But now that I've seen my life with God in it, I can see much better what was lacking without him."

Why was it that when I asked Micah a question about God, I left the conversation more confused than when I entered into it, but when I asked Patrick, he threw in a baseball analogy and made everything seem so simple?

He went on without my prompting, "People ask me if I'm mad at God about Julia..." He stopped as if to reevaluate his answer before giving it. "And I'm really not. I'm sad about it. I miss her." Patrick's voice slightly cracked at the end, and I gave him the time he needed to finish his thought. "But I don't blame God for her death." He turned to face out the passenger's window. "And I don't have to stop loving her because we've been separated. Or because my life is going to go on without her actively participating in it. I didn't only love Julia because of things she did for me or because I liked being with her. I loved *her*. And nothing's ever going to change that."

Patrick's perspective amazed me. "I don't know how you can be this strong."

"It doesn't make sense, does it?" He laughed, still looking out the window.

It didn't. But I was becoming more and more certain that things didn't have to make sense to me for them to be the truth.

CHAPTER 49

We arrived at Maplecrest after visiting hours had begun. From the lobby on the main floor, I wished Patrick good luck and watched his elevator doors close. Our plan was that he would take his time with Westley and text me when I should come up to join them.

I decided not to anticipate a time frame for the boys' conversation because whether it ran shorter or longer than I predicted, I would worry it was going badly. So to distract my anxious thoughts, I thumbed through an outdated gossip magazine, realizing without any pride about it that I could successfully fill in over half of the blanks in the crossword puzzle.

I heard the sounds of a phone being hung up, and then someone cleared a throat from the direction of the front desk. I automatically glanced up to see the receptionist staring at me. I lowered my magazine to indicate she had my attention whether or not she'd asked for it.

"You're Cosette Miller?"

"Yes." I stood up. Perhaps Westley had called down for me instead of having Patrick text. "Is Westley Greene ready for me?"

"No, hon. Someone else is." She looked at me skeptically. "Ms. Avalon Brant." She typed a few keystrokes into her computer.

"Avalon Brant?" I half-whispered to myself.

"Yes, hon. Wanted me to tell you she's a friend of Micah's? Whatever that means..."

It took me longer than it should have to connect the dots. I had been so focused on matters with Westley that I had forgotten about the girl with the blue scars. "Oh, yes, of course."

Though I was curious how she'd learned who and where I was, I didn't need the details to recognize it as provision.

The receptionist nodded, and my heart raced as I headed for the elevators. "She's on the fourth floor, dear."

Avalon Brant had requested a visit from *me*. As I waited for the elevator, I focused on the entire meaning of that statement. Obviously, she knew about me. And she knew I knew about her. And now we both knew Micah. And I also understood why Micah hadn't come back to the farmhouse when I'd called him.

But even knowing all of these things, I still felt that I was seeing a small piece of a very large and complicated picture.

Riding up to the fourth floor, I wondered what I would say to Avalon. I hadn't anticipated an actual meeting with her so soon, and I hadn't sorted out all of the questions I wanted to ask her. Considering her mute state, I wasn't even sure how we were going to communicate in the first place, but I trusted that with all the details that had to have been worked out for us to have this meeting, we would find a way to say what was needed to one another.

I stepped out of the elevator and signed in with the same pretty attendant as I had for my previous visit to Maplecrest. "I'm here for Avalon Brant."

Before she could indicate where I might find the resident, I felt a hand on my shoulder. I turned around to see the girl from the cafeteria standing before me, her eyes wet with tears. Before I could take her in completely, she threw her arms around me and began sobbing silently onto my shoulder.

Instinctively, I enveloped the crying girl. She was shorter and more petite than I was, and I felt as though I were comforting a child.

"There's a private room annexed to the dorm hallway," the woman at the desk whispered to me. "We don't usually allow visitors in there with patients, but for Avalon, I'll make the exception."

She pulled a key on a lanyard from her desk drawer and led us to the room. As she unlocked the door, she continued, "I can give you two about ten minutes of privacy—then you'll need to rejoin the visiting area."

I thanked the woman as I practically carried a still-tearful Avalon to the room.

I flipped on the lights and closed the door behind us. The space was small, but it had enough room for a love seat and two chairs and was painted in friendly, soothing shades of green. There were pamphlet dispensers screwed to the walls with all sorts of literature about mental health, medications, and diseases, and I assumed that the room we were in was often the place where patients received their diagnoses.

I sat us down on the love seat as Avalon regained her composure. She pulled away, wiping her eyes with the backs of her hands. Under the florescent lights, the dark-blue markings on her fingers and palms looked almost purple.

"It's nice to finally meet you." I understated what I was feeling.

She nodded, still sniffling. She indicated her scars and then pointed to me.

"Oh, yeah," I answered her, quickly unzipping my boot and rolling up my pant leg. "I've got them too." In the same light, my markings were lighter than Avalon's, though still prominent.

As I readjusted my clothing, Avalon pulled a pen from her pocket and took a pamphlet from off the wall. She quickly scrawled a message in one of its margins.

I see you had a rookie guide, too.

I smiled. "Yeah, so it seems."
She started writing again.

At least he knew better than to let you eat the fruit.

Avalon glanced at the crosshatched glass window in the door before taking both of her hands and pulling down her bottom lip.

I gasped when I saw that her markings were not confined to the outside of her body. The entire inside of her mouth also bore the deep scarring visible on her fingers. She parted her jaw, exposing her tongue, which was the same indigo as the rest of her mouth.

"That's why you can't speak," I stated what was now obvious to me.

She pointed to her throat and then picked up her pen.

My vocal cords cauterized when I swallowed the fruit.

Cringing, I grabbed at my own throat. I flashed back to the river, the excruciating pain of the water ripping against my skin. Then I thought of the tree and how I'd hungered for the first fruits, how I'd attacked Micah for just a hint of its juice. At the time, I'd been so angry at him for dialing back my senses, for not allowing me to satisfy my desire for it. Now, I felt so grateful to him for sparing me that I could have cried.

"I am so sorry..."

She flipped to the next page of the brochure to find more white space on which to write.

My guide told me it's reversible if I live in the garden.

This was news to me. So far, my markings had been easy to conceal, but I imagined in warmer, shorts-and-skirt weather, that would become trickier. I was relieved to know that the scars may not have to be permanent.

But so far, that's not an option for me.

I found this puzzling. "Why not?"

Avalon's gray eyes were sad. She shrugged.

*It's been months since I've seen my guide. So much
time had passed I was beginning to wonder if I'd
imagined the garden. Most days, I'm thankful for
my scars because without them, I might actually
believe I'm as crazy as everyone else does.*

"But you aren't crazy," I assured her. "Is that why you got
sent here? Because you told people about what happened to
you in the garden?"
She nodded.

*My parents think I had a bad acid trip. It's easier
for them to believe their daughter is a junkie than
to hear the truth.*

My heart sank. It hadn't occurred to me until this point
that I might need to keep my experience in the garden a
secret from everyone forever. But with the ink still drying on
my permanent record from my drug suspension, I knew in
this case, like in Avalon's, the truth wouldn't stand up in the
court of public opinion.
Suddenly, the garden felt like a burden. What good was
the joy I had felt there if I could share it with no one? What
did the wonders of the light webs, the trees, and the view
from the sandstone matter if I had no one I could tell about
it?
There was a knock on the door, and the desk attendant
poked her head in. "Sorry to interrupt you two, but you have
another visitor."
She opened the door wider, and standing behind her was
Micah.
The woman continued, "It's probably best if you all continue out here now anyway." She pointed toward the
cafeteria.
Avalon scribbled one last note and handed the pamphlet
to me on her way out of the door.

I want to give you something. BRB.

296

She stopped at Micah and wrapped her arms around his waist. He returned the hug, and she stepped away and disappeared through the residence hallway doors.

"How are you, kid?" Micah asked as I joined him in the waiting area. I waited for the attendant to finishing locking the door and walk back to her desk before answering him.

"I feel spontaneously combustible, Micah," I complained. I needed to dump out my emotions on someone, and after my conversation with Avalon, my guess was that he would be the only one I could unload on about all I was going through for the foreseeable future.

"I thought you'd be happy to talk to Avalon?"

"No, I'm glad we connected," I explained. "I just don't even know where to begin sorting out what's in my head."

Micah's expression was sincere. "Do you want to pray with me about it?"

I looked at him blankly and wondered how long it would take before I would naturally come to this conclusion on my own. The limited experience I'd had with prayer was positive, and if nothing else, it had consistently given me moments of peace. "Yes, I do."

He led me to a pair of empty seats in the lobby where Avalon would easily find us when she returned. We sat down facing each other, and then Micah held his hand open and I placed mine in it. I looked around the room and saw that all the people around us were engaged in their own business and paying no attention to us, and for some reason, this relieved me.

We bowed our heads together, and he began to speak.

A moment later, we were interrupted.

"Well, this is just perfect," a voice some distance away growled. Micah and I both instantly jumped up.

"Westley!" I called, feeling a variety of emotions all at once, none of which were the peace I'd been hoping for.

Patrick stood off to his side, shaking his head in warning. West's face was red, either from anger or from crying or from both, I couldn't tell.

Westley walked quickly toward us, and I instinctively stood in front of Micah to greet him.

"What the hell happened to your face?" Westley glared and pointed at the bandage on Micah's cheek. "Am I not the only boyfriend around town looking to beat your ass?"

Micah sighed but didn't respond to West's accusation. Instead, he addressed me. "Cosette, I will talk to you later. I've got to get back home anyway."

I nodded, hoping my approval would signal his exit.

"Yeah, I think that's probably a good idea." Patrick's eyes were huge as he motioned with his head for Micah to leave.

"What's the hurry?" Westley jeered. "Don't let me interrupt you holding hands with my fiancée."

"We weren't holding hands, West," I explained. "I just asked Micah to pray with me about something."

He made a disgusted face. "Since when do you pray?"

"Since I have a boyfriend who needs prayer." I slowly reached for Westley's hand, but he rolled his eyes and stepped around me to position himself closer to Micah.

"I'm actually glad you are here, Mic, because I have something to settle with you." Westley stood close enough to him so that he had to look down to make eye contact.

Micah wasn't ruffled by this intimidation tactic. "What's that, West?"

"Well, it must be all this great rest and relaxation I'm getting here at the crazy house because I've started remembering some things about New Year's Eve."

I felt all the color drain from my face. Did Westley know what he'd done? Had he remembered Micah healing me?

Micah didn't flinch. "I'd love to hear what you've pieced together."

Our situation took center stage in the lobby, and the room became tense. The desk attendant looked concerned and poised her fingers over the telephone.

"You're a cocky son of a bitch, you know that?" Westley's language was threat enough for the receptionist to start dialing. He lowered his voice before continuing. "I saw you. I remember your hands all over Cosette. You can deny it all you want, but I remember you in her room that night."

"I won't deny that, Westley, because it's the truth. After what you had done to her, I—"

Before Micah could finish his explanation, Westley pulled back his fist and sucker-punched him in the jaw—hard.

"Westley, no!" I shouted as Patrick attempted to restrain him from behind. Micah hit the ground in a motionless heap.

"You stay away from my girl, you hear me, Micah? You stay the hell away from her!" Westley's eyes were wild in the way that was becoming painfully familiar.

I bent down over Micah and felt that he was still breathing. I guessed he should have been, having only been hit in the face and not say, had his lungs punctured as mine had been, but I was relieved to discover it anyway.

A man in a white coat and two others in scrubs flew through the residence doors.

"Mr. Greene, you're going to have to come with me," the doctor said to Westley calmly.

I backed away from Micah so that the men in scrubs could tend to him. Westley grabbed me by the shoulders and held me close to him, and I cowered in his arms.

At my reaction, the fire in his eyes died. "Cosi," he whispered.

"Please let me go, Westley." My voice shook, and he released his grip on me.

"You are all I have that matters now. Don't let him take you away from me," he pleaded with me. "I love you, Cosette."

"Why can't you see that *he* is not the one that is coming between us, Westley?"

At this, Westley's mouth dropped open.

Another white coat entered the room, and before either of us could say another word, the two doctors forcefully escorted Westley out of the lobby.

As I watched him disappear through the residence door, I thought about what Patrick had said, and I wondered how much further Westley could dig before hitting bedrock.

CHAPTER 50

Westley was taken to a private room, and I was told that for the time being, he wouldn't be allowed any more visitors. One of the doctors explained to me that I could call to check on him daily, but that he wouldn't be permitted any sort of communication with anyone besides his parents until further notice.

At some point during the boys' scuffle, Avalon had reentered the lobby. She waited until the doctor had finished his news before approaching me with a box of tissues.

As she gently dabbed my eyes, I was grateful that she was the one comforting me. Her kind gestures spoke louder than any words could have, and her silence gave me the space I needed to think.

Micah was transported via gurney to a room for examining, and Patrick accompanied him so he wouldn't be alone when he came to.

I replayed the day's events in my head, having a hard time comprehending that so much could have transpired in twelve hours' time. So far, I'd falsely confessed to carrying an STD, been suspended from school for drugs, had some sort of terrifying prophetic dream in the living room of a house I'd made of habit of breaking and entering into, become friends with a blue-stained mute, and watched my mental-hospital-patient boyfriend commit assault and battery on my potential guardian angel, who wasn't really an angel but just a regular guy who "made a different choice."

I considered the recap of my day as a pitch for a plot line in a television drama, and even I couldn't buy into it. My life had officially become less believable than a daytime drama.

Avalon waved her fingers in front of my face to get my attention. Once she had it, she pointed to the clock on the wall. Not much longer until visitation was over.

I frowned. The only thing worse than this ridiculous day continuing any longer was the idea that it would end with me back home, facing a million unknowns alone.

Avalon picked up a book from her lap and placed it in my hands. It appeared to be some sort of journal, bound in leather and held closed by a strap that buckled around it like a belt.

"You want me to read this?" I clarified.

She motioned her hand side to side, a gesture I unclearly interpreted as "kind of." Then she reached into her pocket, pulled out a folded note, and handed it to me. Before I could read it, she stood up and pulled me to stand beside her. She again threw her arms around my neck and squeezed me, and then she withdrew from me, waved, and exited the lobby through to the residence hallway.

Once Avalon disappeared from my sight, I unfolded her note and read it:

The funny thing about a mute girl...No one expects her to have a cell phone.

(555) 295-1022

Text?

I smiled as I refolded the paper and shoved it into my pocket.

◆◆◆

As it turned out, Micah had been moved to another floor of the hospital, one that dealt with injuries of the body and not solely the mind, and it took me some time to find him. When I finally walked into his room, Patrick was sitting in a chair beside his bed, fiddling with his phone.

"How is he?" I asked, peering over the bed railing. Micah's eyes were closed. The side of his face was puffy and reddish purple. His bottom lip had been split, and a few stitches had been sewn in to hold the skin together.

His latest injuries accompanied the cut I'd left on his cheek a few days earlier. At first glance, Micah appeared to be recovering from a car accident instead of two separate fists to the face.

"Well, I'm not getting much information since I'm not family, but I heard a nurse say something about a mandible fracture. Pretty sure that means West broke his jaw."

I shut my eyes and groaned. "Oh, no..." Westley's strength had always been an asset, but now, fueled by all of his unchecked emotion, it had become a weapon of mass destruction.

"I think he woke up once, but they gave him something to put him back out." Patrick looked from the bed to me with concern. "Do you think Micah will press charges against Westley?"

This hadn't crossed my mind as a possibility. I shrugged. "I don't know." I considered the conversation Patrick and I had shared on the way down to Fort Wayne and wondered if Micah felt the same way about Westley needing to be broken before he'd be able to get better. "It's possible."

Micah took a deep breath and shifted. Patrick and I both watched him stir and resettle.

In a quieter voice, he said: "You know, Micah didn't have any ID on him. No cell phone, no wallet—nothing. The nurse was trying to figure out who to contact about what happened. Do you even know how old he is? Is he over eighteen?"

I shook my head. "I think so? I don't know his birthday. From what I gathered though, he's jerked-over. So even if he's a minor, I don't think his parents have anything to do with him anymore."

"Oh." Patrick thought for a minute. "That's gotta suck. I mean, I like electricity and indoor plumbing as much as the next guy, but I don't know what it takes for someone to quit everything and everybody they've ever known and start life over alone. Poor kid."

I found it interesting the way Patrick interpreted being JO'd. I'd never really thought about why Micah had made the choice he had, but now I wondered.

He used the following moments of silence to segue our conversation, and had I known the direction it was going to take, I would have filled the quiet moment myself. "Cosette, what was Westley talking about before he hit Micah?" His tone grew more serious. "What did he remember about New Year's Eve?"

I was caught off guard again. Patrick was too perceptive. "He just said that he thought he remembered seeing Micah that night."

This did not satisfy him, and he waited for me to offer more explanation. When I didn't, he kept talking. "You know, several people reported seeing Micah at Trevor's party. No one knew his name, but by the description, I'm pretty sure they were talking about him. They said that he showed up late and was pretty concerned about West and you. Someone told him what had happened, about how much you were bleeding when the three of us left together." He eyed my nose with the same skepticism he had that morning. "Cosette, did Westley remember something about Micah that would have given him a reason to be jealous of something?"

I looked at the ground, not sure what response, if any, would be best. I couldn't tell him the truth, and there was no way with the handful of pieces Patrick had that he'd be able to solve the entire puzzle accurately, so he was filling in the blanks with some very false assumptions.

"Cosette, I know that Westley has not been himself lately. He's screwed up right now, and he's making some pretty horrible decisions. But he *loves* you. And you guys have an incredible history—"

"It's not what you think, Patrick. I can't really explain it all to you, but—"

He held up his hand and shook his head. "You don't owe me any explanation, Cosi. Just please, don't give up on

Westley, OK? I mean, I know it's not up to you to save him, but after tonight...I just think you might be his only tangible hope."

I chewed on my bottom lip and nodded.

"Knock, knock!" A woman in a white coat entered the room. She didn't look up from the paperwork in her hands before she started introductions. "I'm Dr. Bennett, and I'm guessing you are..." She pointed at me. "Cosette Miller?"

"That's me," I answered, not exactly proud about my increasing familiarity with the staff at Maplecrest.

"Then you are the person I was hoping to see." Her words seemed absent any real meaning. She still hadn't looked up at me from what she was reading. "I'd like to ask you a few questions about the patient here." Her eyes finally lifted, and she looked in Micah's direction. She clicked her heels against the tile floor as she stepped toward her patient to check his monitors. She then drew the curtain around his bed to give him, or us, privacy. Her eyes were cast downward again at the chart when she finally began interviewing me. "What's your exact relationship to Mr. Quinn?"

Patrick had basically just posed the same question, but in this phrasing, I found it easier to explain. "We're just friends from school."

"And he was down here visiting another friend of yours...Avalon—"

"Westley Greene," I corrected. "We were both here to see Westley." It didn't seem necessary to drag Avalon into what had happened between the boys, and I didn't want anyone working too hard to figure out a connection between the four of us—especially in front of present company.

She drew a line through something in her notes. "Do you know how we might get a hold of anyone in his family?"

"No...he's kind of a loner. I don't think he has much contact with them."

"So, I suppose then you would have no idea of anything in his medical history?"

"No, I wouldn't."

Patrick was taking his own mental notes of our conversation and assumed there was a deeper reason behind the doctor's question. "Why? Is there something wrong with him other than his jaw?"

"No, actually. And that's partly why I asked." She made additional scribbles onto the chart before finally looking up. "According to his blood work, Mr. Quinn is likely the healthiest human being I've ever seen in all my years in medicine." The doctor seemed both surprised and suspicious, but I found the news encouraging. Maybe Micah's body would heal much faster with a healthy head start. "Aside, of course, from the injury he suffered tonight. And that terribly infected cut on his face. Any idea how that happened?"

My cheeks burned, but before I could confess, Patrick piped up.

"Word at school is that some girl cut him with something."

"Hmm...Mr. Quinn seems to have a lot of enemies," she muttered. "Any idea if he has any siblings?"

I assumed this question was intended for me, though I didn't know the answer to it. "I know he has brothers or sisters somewhere, but it's not something we've ever talked about in depth..."

"Well, that's unfortunate," Dr. Bennett replied. "I'm still waiting for some tests to come back, but he may require surgery on his jaw."

"What does him needing surgery have to do with having siblings?" Patrick asked.

"For this type of surgery, it isn't out of the question that the patient may require a blood transfusion. When patients aren't able to donate for themselves, we like to ask family members to do it," she explained. "And Mr. Quinn's blood type is not the most readily available." She folded Micah's chart under her arm. "But we'll make do."

All of a sudden, the curtains surrounding Micah's bed shifted slightly to one side, as if caught up in a breeze. A moment later, I could feel the temperature in the room rise. I carefully glanced at both Patrick and the doctor to see if they'd noticed the movement, but it seemed they hadn't.

"Well, if you are able to find out any more information about him, I'd appreciate it if you'd contact the hospital. Tomorrow, we'll be deciding if Mr. Quinn needs surgery, and it would be best if he had a family member present who knew his entire medical history to discuss his treatment."

I took a breath to respond to the doctor when the strong fragrance of fresh flowers distracted me.

I glanced back in the direction of Micah's hospital bed. The curtains had stilled.

"I'll see what I can do, Dr. Bennett."

She thanked me and exited the room, and I immediately suggested to Patrick that I get him back home.

"What about Micah?" He was both confused and concerned. "Shouldn't someone stick around for him in case he wakes up?"

I had to think of an answer fast that would convince Patrick we needed to leave without sounding insensitive to Micah. "Maybe...but I'm not sure how it looks to Westley if I spend the night at the bedside of the guy whose jaw he broke because of his suspected feelings for me."

"That's true," Patrick agreed, and I exhaled quietly in relief. He picked up his jacket from the chair beside the hospital bed and slipped his arms through its sleeves. "Think you'll see him tomorrow though?"

"I wouldn't rule it out," I answered honestly. Though I was almost positive if I did see Micah anytime soon, it wouldn't be at Maplecrest. I didn't have to look behind the curtain to know he had already checked out of the hospital.

CHAPTER 51

I was grateful that Patrick slept all the way back to Middle-bury. I could handle his snoring much more easily than I could his questions about my relationship to Micah. It felt odd to be the person with the all the secrets instead of the one trying to uncover them.

Patrick awoke as I pulled into the Camden parking lot. Before getting out of my car, he made me promise to give him an update on both Micah and Westley as soon as I learned anything, and I agreed to be in touch. "Gimme a call if you feel like going to church on Sunday," he offered, and I told him I'd think about it.

The clock on my dash read just after ten when I pulled into my darkened driveway. I entered the house with my key through the front door rather than risk going in through the garage and waking Grandma.

A lamp had been left on in the living room, and I flipped off its corresponding switch in the hallway on my way up the stairs.

"Um, excuse me," an annoyed voice barked, and I jumped.

I turned the lamp back on. "I'm sorry, I couldn't see you there."

Bronwyn sat up from her reclined position on the couch and immediately shut her laptop. There were some old-looking papers in piles around her and on the coffee table, and she quickly gathered them into one large heap and stuffed them into her computer bag. "So, did you score any pills today with all your free time?"

"Very funny." I sighed, not having an ounce of energy left to waste in bickering with my sister. "I'll see you later."

"I left a list on your desk of things I need you to do for me tomorrow." She smiled sweetly at me.

My shoulders sank when I remembered my debt to her. "Of course you did, Bronwyn."

"Damn right 'of course I did.' You owe me. I did you a favor."

"No, a favor is something you do for someone because you care about them. What you are doing is called extortion."

"I don't care what you call it as long as that list is done by the time I get home from work tomorrow."

"Fine," I mumbled under my breath. Her list would provide me with a distraction from worrying about Westley and Micah, which without knowing how to help either of them at this point, was the only thing on my agenda for the following day.

Once upstairs, I turned my bedroom light on and locked my door. There was indeed a written-out list of chores taped to the shelf above my desk, and as I glanced through it, I noticed most of them were things I didn't mind doing anyway. After the past several days of nonstop insanity, I actually looked forward to the prospect of a day of mindless housework.

I tossed my purse onto my bed, and in doing so, the book Avalon had given me fell out of it. I picked it up and unlatched its buckle.

There were several blank pages to fold back before I arrived at a pencil sketch of a boy that looked so realistic, I at first mistook it for a black-and-white photograph.

The subject of the portrait was not someone I recognized. His features were sharp and intense: thin lips pursed together into a straight-lined expression, narrowed eyes hiding beneath a furrowed brow. He could have been handsome, I considered, if he didn't look so gritty.

But regardless of whether or not I found the subject of the picture attractive, I was captivated completely by the artistry in the drawing. The same pencil used to sketch this portrait would have been useless in my own hands, but in the artist's, it was a tool fulfilling the utmost purpose for which it had been created.

I glanced down to the bottom of the page. Beneath the drawing was the name "Gabriel" and Avalon's initials.

Having no comparable talent myself to know for sure, I could only imagine what I would do with it had I drawn this portrait, and at the bottom of that list was hiding it in a journal and giving it to a stranger.

But upon turning the page, I understood better why Avalon's art had gone unpublished. This second picture I *did* recognize, though it wasn't another portrait. Rather, it was a nature scene set unmistakably in the garden.

Again, the accuracy of the picture rivaled that of a photograph. It was drawn to scale from the riverbank and illustrated the towering forests Micah and I had walked through during our journey to see the lights. Avalon had evidently experienced the garden in the daytime because the silhouetted outlines of trees I had memorized were filled in with painstaking detail in the drawing: textured bark, coiling ivies, and blooming flowers of every kind.

A quick thrill of excitement shot through me. I longed to return to experience this picture for myself in the light of the day, when I could marvel at the scene in person.

But then, my thoughts quickly cut to Avalon sitting silent and alone in the cafeteria at Maplecrest, weighed down by the solitude of her secrets, and I remembered that even the garden had its consequences.

I turned the page, and immediately, the thrill I'd felt at recognizing the first landscape was replaced by an aching. This drawing was of the tree—the one that bore the first fruits—and as much of its majesty as could be translated onto the dimensions of a piece of paper, Avalon had captured.

The drawing triggered more emotion than I could have expected, and my eyes filled with tears. How could I miss the garden so much when I'd only been there once?

I didn't want to stop looking at the picture, but I forced myself to flip to the next sketch.

Several pages following the tree were filled with stills—the same image, a first fruit—repeated over and over again from varying angles as if the artist felt she hadn't been able to capture its exact essence. From what I'd seen of them in the garden though, her depictions were perfect. And as I studied the drawings, my mouth began to water.

Around the third page of these sketches, the pictures of the fruit changed to include a large bite taken from its center. Instantly, I remembered the pain I'd felt watching Micah devour fruit, each of my senses commanding me to consume it too. I thought of Avalon's hands and mouth and decided that she had experienced a similar reaction.

It struck me to consider if these pages signified something deeper than an artist's perfectionism. This object of desire was what had disfigured Avalon; it had robbed her of her voice. Maybe drawing it over and over was her way of trying to understand how something that she'd yearned for so intensely could have harmed her so badly.

There were several more pages of landscapes, some familiar and others intriguingly unfamiliar. I had not seen pristine beaches during my trip to the garden, and I had only experienced the mountains Avalon exquisitely detailed in her sketches from afar atop the sandstone. As illustrated in this book, there was so much left for me to explore when I returned to the garden. If I returned.

When I reached the final pages of the book, I found myself as curious about them as I had been about Gabriel. The pictures on every page to this point had looked real—fantastical probably to anyone aside from Avalon and me, but stylistically real nonetheless. Yet, on the last three pages, the sketches became dramatically less polished.

The first of the final pages was a drawing of a section of fence. There were two sets of large, iron pillars in symmetry with one another, and in between them was a wide opening. I stared at it puzzled. I considered perhaps she hadn't had time to finish it, but Avalon's initials appeared in the corner of this page as they had in all the others. It seemed to me that the artist's signature was usually the last stroke added to her work, like a stamp of approval. Avalon had considered this picture finished.

The final two pages were even rougher than the last. They appeared to be of the outline of flames, and for the first time in the book, I noticed several worn places where an eraser had been dragged over the page, wearing the paper thin. I couldn't find a signature anywhere on these pages.

I shoved my hand in my pocket, dug out Avalon's phone number, and grabbed my phone.

You're an incredible artist—CM

I didn't know how long to wait before I should expect a response, so I left my phone on my bed and changed into my pajamas. By the time I returned, Avalon had written back.

When you tell people with words about the garden, they think you are crazy. When you tell them through pictures, it makes you an "artist" ;)—AB

I smiled.
As I went to respond, another text came through.

New roommate tonight, not sure if she's cool with me having a phone.
E-mail me: ABRANT@SAIC.EDU—AB

I frowned.

I'll write you. Lots of questions.—CM

I didn't expect an answer to my final text, and I didn't get one.

As I stood to retrieve my laptop, an involuntary yawn reminded me just how long my day had already been, and I decided that since Sims had so graciously gifted me the next week off school, I could wait until morning before writing to Avalon.

I switched off my light, and amazingly, my brain turned off with it.

CHAPTER 52

I slept so well that I woke up with a clear head.

But it quickly filled with the onslaught of unresolved issues left over from the previous day.

I stood, stretched, and picked up where I'd left off the prior evening by starting up my computer.

Before delving into the barrage of questions I had for Avalon, I realized that Maplecrest might be the sort of hospital that would "monitor" its patients' e-mails, and I was glad I'd had the foresight to put off writing the e-mail until I'd slept enough to consider this. I needed my communication to Avalon to remain open, which meant I needed to choose my words carefully.

Avalon—

> *Loved the book. Brought back some fond memories and made me curious about some things you remember that I don't. Especially at the end. Would love to hear whatever you're able to tell me about it...In fact, I'd love to hear about anything "else" you think might be of interest to me.*

—CM

I hoped Avalon was sharp enough to crack my code; it would be nice to have someone keeping an eye on Westley in my absence, whether or not he knew it was happening.

I sent the e-mail, grabbed Bronwyn's list, and headed down the stairs.

The hallway clock confirmed what I'd assumed from the light streaming through the blinds in my room—it was late enough that the only person I'd have to face at the breakfast table would be Grandma.

As I descended the stairs, I heard a loud squeal and the pounding of what I assumed was a sippy cup on a high-chair tray, and I corrected myself.

I would also see Ginger.

◆◆◆

Grandma avoided lecturing me about my suspension, and I got to spend an hour with my niece while she readied herself to take Ginger to a well-child visit at the pediatrician. As we played with her new Christmas toys in the living room, I marveled at how fast she was learning new things. Just months before, I remembered watching her sit up on her own for the first time, and now she was taking independent steps. I was awed how quickly this tiny baby I'd met only a year ago was becoming her own person, and I was grateful even more for my unjust suspension now that it had given me extra time with her.

Ginger toddled to me and handed me a polka-dotted ball that jingled when shook. I bounced it on the carpet, and it clanged loudly. This noise fiercely pleased my niece, and she fell into a giggle fit. Her laughter was contagious, and I joined in, prolonging our happy moment with tickles and raspberries on her belly.

Ginger's laughter grew louder, and it echoed down the hallway. As her cheery sounds bounced back and forth, it triggered in me memories of the garden. Or, at least, it triggered memories of my *dream* about the garden.

Though I hadn't allowed myself to think much about it since I'd awakened from the nightmare the afternoon before, I could easily recall the details, especially those of the children I'd met there.

As my niece caught her breath, I traced the curves of her face with my index finger. There was no doubt that she shared similarities with the girls from my dream. She should have though, right? I mean, they were representing my children, and that would have made them Ginger's cousins. I knew a lot of cousins who looked related.

That was the obvious answer, of course, if the children in the garden had been real people instead of figments of my imagination.

I never put much thought into the meaning behind my dreams before because I doubted they meant anything significant. But as I crouched over my giggling niece, remembering how abandoned I'd felt when her imaginary cousins left me alone in the garden, I understood that the reason I hadn't put much thought into this dream was not because I doubted it had meaning; it was because I feared that it did.

◆ ◆ ◆

At the top of Bronwyn's list of chores was laundry. As I sorted the darks from the lights in her hamper, I discovered that most of the clothes I was being forced to wash were ones she'd taken from my closet. I took satisfaction that though I had to be Bronwyn's laundry wench, when they were done, I'd have my wardrobe back.

I started a load and then shut the light off in the laundry room when I saw that the pantry door had been left open. On my way out, I reached to pull it shut when I noted that something seemed different inside it. Had I not just inventoried the space in my search for wrapping paper the week before, the empty space on the shelf would have meant nothing to me. But I had, and therefore, I immediately recognized the vacant outline in dust in the place where my mother's box had been.

I scanned the rest of the shelves, but nothing else seemed to have been moved, and I regretted not having explored the box's contents when I'd had the opportunity. Someone must have noticed it had been cleaned off and moved it somewhere else where it would be less accessible to curiosity.

That someone could have easily been any of the other three adults in the house. Since I never talked about my mother with any of them, I had no way to guess which one would be most likely to want to keep all of her memories to him- or herself.

I tried to be relieved that the box was missing. It would be pointless to wonder about it now, since I no longer had a choice whether or not to open it. I'd been hesitant to learn what was inside it anyway, right? Otherwise, I would have gone through it when I saw it the first time.

But I wasn't relieved. In fact, I felt sad. Like I'd missed an opportunity I wasn't going to get back.

The comfort of routine had always seemed worth whatever it took to preserve it. But despite all my efforts, all the things I *didn't* do so that things wouldn't *change*...normal was gone.

And knowing now that it wouldn't have mattered anyway...I wished I would have opened the box.

CHAPTER 53

If it were possible for a room to physically sparkle with cleanliness, then Bronwyn would have needed sunglasses to shower. For over an hour, I put my current frustrations to use and scrubbed my sister's bathroom with such vigor I suspected I no longer had fingerprints.

Heavyhearted from the morning's thinking and dizzy from the cleaner fumes, I retreated to my bedroom and sank into my desk chair in hopes my e-mail inbox had something waiting in it to cheer me out of my lonely funk.

But before I could check it, my phone let out a short tweet, indicating I'd missed some communication—a text or a call—while I was off fighting the war on mildew.

(3) Missed Calls
Eastlyn Greene

Though fairly sure she was only calling because Southeby had shared with her the news of my suspension and Westley's latest crimes, I called back anyway.

"This is complete madness, Cosette," she greeted me. "It's like the universe is using you and Westley for shooting practice or something."

"Tell me about it," I groaned. But at the same time, I felt comforted by her sympathies.

"Southeby says Westley isn't allowed visitors anymore." I confirmed this.

"That sucks," she declared. "But I guess that frees you up tomorrow for me to take you dress shopping."

I instantly looked down at my ring, a tiny flutter of excitement hatching in my stomach. "Really?"

"I was going to head back to school tomorrow, but it doesn't feel right. My parents are having a hard time right now..." Her voice trailed off, and I could tell there was more she wanted to say. "So, what exactly happened with Micah?"

"Oh." My flutter was replaced by sharp guilt for not having spent more time wondering the answer to this question myself. "Um, I guess I'm not really sure. I haven't seen him since I left last night."

"One of the doctors Mom talked to said that West broke Micah's jaw, and then he just went missing. Any idea where he would have gone?" Eastlyn's voice was full of concern. "I mean, that's a pretty serious injury, right? He shouldn't be walking the streets like that."

I knew that Micah wasn't lying somewhere in a ditch, unless the garden had ditches, in which case, it was probably the most glorious and comfortable ditch in existence. But I also knew that just because he was in the garden, it didn't necessarily mean his jaw was better. Last I'd seen him, the cut my car key had dug out of his cheek had yet to heal, so I had no guarantee his more serious injury would be cured the way mine had. "Try not to worry about him, E," I reassured her, though I couldn't take my own advice. "Micah has a way of taking care of himself."

"If you hear from him..."

"I'll let you know." We wrapped up our conversation by confirming a breakfast and shopping date for the following morning.

Before I resumed checking my e-mail, I jiggled my mouse to wake up my computer and typed "broken jaw" into my homepage's search engine.

After twenty minutes of reading about the injury, both best- and worst-case scenarios, I felt confident that Micah wasn't at death's door, though he was probably in a lot of pain and very hungry since he likely wouldn't be able to eat much.

I debated driving over to the farmhouse to see if I could find him there. Maybe bring him a milkshake or something more nutritious that also came in liquid form. But I still hadn't figured out how exactly to communicate with him worlds apart, and I had half a page of blackmail to finish before Bronwyn returned from work.

As I sat at my desk, it occurred to me that while I might not be able to go to my friend physically to help him, there was still something I could do.

"God...Please, take care of Micah."

CHAPTER 54

I still hadn't received a response from Avalon when I finished praying. And I didn't have one by the time I checked the last item off of my chore list or by the time I completed the homework assignments that had been collected and e-mailed to me by Dean Sims's secretary.

When I couldn't take her silence any longer, I sent her a text message:

Everything OK?—CM

As I waited to hear back from her, I decided to thumb through my bridal magazines in preparation for the following day's trip with Eastlyn to Stephenson's. I hadn't spent any real time considering the type of gown I wanted for my wedding, and after the disastrous first attempt at finding my dream dress, I needed to do a little more homework before our second try. I wanted my wedding planning to be as magical as I hoped our actual wedding day would be. Fifty years from now, when all this Maplecrest business was long forgotten, I wanted to have an amazing story to tell our grandchildren about how I found the dress I would wear the day I married their grandfather.

I was reaching for the stack of magazines on my nightstand when I noticed the white envelope sticking out of the pile.

It took me a moment to remember the letter, but when I did, I was instantly mortified.

This was the same envelope I'd set on my nightstand after returning from the farmhouse the night Westley had left, the night Micah had scared me senseless by disappearing into thin air. It was the same envelope I'd been eager to open but didn't because I knew the night's insanity would have detracted from its meaning.

Westley's vows.

I gasped, horrified at myself. I'd forgotten about them. Absolutely, truly, and unforgivably forgotten about them.

There was no justifying my way out of the guilt that engulfed me. Westley had given these words to me for comfort while he was away, and I'd carelessly set them aside and not given them a second thought.

I felt ashamed, like I'd betrayed him. It was the same feeling I'd had sitting atop the sandstone with Micah when he'd whispered Westley's name to me in the garden.

And now that I'd rediscovered the vows, I was equally compelled by unworthiness not to read them as I was by desire to rip open the envelope and memorize each word.

How could I have forgotten them? His gesture had been so thoughtful, so...*Westley*. The real Westley.

I delicately ran my finger over the seal of the envelope, fighting back both tears and the urge to tear open the letter, but I knew in that moment I didn't deserve the comfort, the love I would feel from the words written inside. I deserved to be punished for my negligence.

Reaching again for my nightstand, I picked up my Bible and opened it. I placed the envelope between a few pages near the back and closed the book again.

I wouldn't forget them this time. Just like I wouldn't forget Westley when I returned to the garden.

◆ ◆ ◆

Half an hour later, I was still mindlessly flipping the pages of a magazine, unable to focus on fashion when I felt like such a traitor.

My thoughts had become so consumed with self-loathing that I forgot I was supposed to be listening for my phone to buzz. When it finally did, I picked it up and stared blankly at it.

It was Avalon, but she wasn't texting—she was calling me.

Unsure of the proper greeting when answering a phone call from someone unable to speak, I went with the traditional, "Hello?"

"Cosi...it's me," he said hesitantly. "Westley."

And all at once, my impatience with Avalon for not writing me earlier vanished. "Hi..."

"Listen, I only have a few minutes. One of the girls here—the one who can't talk—had a cell phone, and she let me use it. No idea why, but I'm not looking a gift horse in the mouth."

I had an idea why. "Is everything OK?"

"You were right, Cosette. About everything," Westley took a deep breath. "I'm the one coming between us, not Micah."

I resisted the reflex to be relieved by this; too many apologies had come prematurely lately. "Why the sudden change of heart?"

There was a pause. "One of the doctors came in here today and showed me an x-ray of Micah's jaw. I saw what I did to him." He cut himself off. When he spoke again, his voice was shaky. "What is happening to me, Cosette? I got put in this place because I couldn't get over not being able to save someone, and then I turn around and hurt someone else...badly."

Why had *I* not considered appealing to Westley's medical-mindedness? Of course, the only way he would respond to the writing on the wall was if it was recorded by a radiograph.

His remorse overpowered my resistance to forgive him, and I felt new hope for my boyfriend. "Yes, you did hurt him, but this isn't like last time. People don't die from a broken jaw. Micah's going to be fine. You have a chance to make this right with him." I decided to be confident in this belief since I had no indication contrary to it.

"People don't die from headaches either, Cosette. But here we are." Westley's tone was serious. "Did you know Micah left the hospital?" The way he asked, I could tell he assumed that I did. "Where is he, Cosi? Is he getting help somewhere? The doctor here said he probably needed surgery..."

My hopefulness for Westley was dashed out by my resumed worry for Micah. "I haven't seen him since last night. But I know him, and I'm sure he's getting whatever help he needs." This was true, wasn't it? Micah had provision, right? His needs would be met, however dire they were.

My self-soothing was interrupted by a sudden memory. The conversation I'd had with Micah the first day in English class. The one where we'd discussed our deaths...

Though I still didn't fully comprehend *what* he was, Micah had alluded to his own death more than once. He was not immortal. In fact, he'd had some very strong opinions about his mortality, about how he wanted to give his life for a greater purpose.

Somehow, I doubted that death by complications of a sucker punch in a mental hospital fell into the category of a meaningful death.

I shook off these thoughts. He wasn't going to die from his current injury. Westley only suggested that out of paranoia because of Julia. I pictured Micah in the garden, sleeping cradled in one of the branches of the first fruit tree, a white bandage wrapped around his head the way animators drew cartoon characters to indicate they had a toothache.

"Can you please just find him, Cosi? Make sure he's all right. Help him."

The urgency in Westley's voice touched me. His concern was genuine and familiar. And for the first time since he had been sent to Maplecrest, I felt like Westley was starting to heal.

"I will."

CHAPTER 55

I waited ten minutes after Westley and I said good-bye to text my gratitude to Avalon.

Thank you for that. I owe you.—CM

She responded immediately:

The way he moped around here today, I figured he needed it as much as you probably did.—AB

Before I could think of what to say next, she wrote again:

You know, Westley may not be allowed visitors—but I still am.—AB

I smiled.

I'll come soon.—CM

Knowing I was Bronwyn's indentured servant and that I hoped to see Micah, I didn't set a specific time to meet Avalon. I was curious to learn more about the drawings in her book—especially the last few sketches—but I also wanted to know more about *her*. So much about her remained a mystery to me, and I was anxious to hear her story.

I gathered up my magazines, having made zero headway in choosing my dream dress, and set them on my desk before jumping in the shower to get a head start on grooming myself for the next day. If I was going to spend the whole day next to Eastlyn, I needed to look my best.

While exfoliating, plucking, and blow-drying, I caught a glimpse of my reflection. On normal days, those that didn't include hours standing in front of a room full of mirrors next to Eastlyn, I didn't spend inordinate amounts of time scrutinizing my body—probably because the only person I cared to impress with it had no complaints. But as I watched myself in the mirror, my chest rising and sinking as I breathed, I suddenly had a new appreciation for it.

I ran my hand down my breastbone and over my ribs. They felt hard, solid. The way bones were supposed to feel. They weren't flexible like the cartilage in my nose. That was why *they* hadn't broken when I fell down the stairs.

It was hard to believe that Westley had so easily been able to shatter them like he did, that less than a week ago, my body had been broken beyond what would have supported me living in it. There were no physical signs, no scars remaining from what had happened that night. No proof or evidence to convict Westley of his crime.

The aneurysm that killed Julia was tiny in size. An invisible imperfection inside her body had ended her life.

My injuries had been massive. My body had suffered similar damages to those sustained during a head-on car collision. My wounds had been irreparable.

Yet I lived, and she didn't.

It made no sense.

People didn't die from headaches, but here we were.

So many times, Micah and I had begun talks of the plan for my life. An invitation. That I was part of something bigger.

I wanted now, more than ever, to finish that conversation. I wanted to know my purpose. I wanted to understand why I had been brought to the garden and who Micah was.

I was finally certain of this.

But each hour that passed without word from him made me less certain I'd ever get the answers I was finally ready to learn.

◆ ◆ ◆

Bronwyn was sitting on my love seat, thumbing through my bridal magazines when I reentered my bedroom.

"These dresses all suck," she stated matter-of-factly, though I hadn't asked her opinion.

Not wanting to engage with my sister in any conversation even on the fringe of my wedding, I changed the subject. "I finished your list," I said as I handed her the paper with each item checked off of it. "I assume you have another for tomorrow?"

She took the list from my hand and set it down beside her without taking her eyes off of the magazine. "I can't believe you marked this page." She made a face and scoffed before showing me a mermaid-style dress that I agreed would have looked terrible on me.

"I didn't mark that one. Eastlyn did." I'd meant my remark to defend my taste, but realized too late that it had entered me into the conversation I was trying to avoid.

"Why is she marking pages for you? What is she? Your maid of honor?"

This question felt like a trap. Unofficially, Eastlyn was most certainly my maid of honor, but since I couldn't see how revealing that to Bronwyn could benefit me in anyway, I chose not to. "I haven't exactly had time to make many decisions about those things."

She continued flipping pages in silence for long enough that I began to wonder if she was waiting for me to say something.

"Is Ginger asleep?"

"Of course she is. It's late." Bronwyn looked up at me annoyed.

"Oh."

There were a few more minutes of awkward quiet before she stood up and said with her usual sarcasm, "Well, it's been *real* great talking to you, Cosi. So glad we did this." Then she tore out a page from the magazine and shoved it at me. "This one. It's you."

Confused, I reached out to accept it.

"Oh, no list for tomorrow. I decided it's not fun making you do shit unless I'm around to enjoy watching you suffer. So, keep your weekend free." And with that, she left.

I looked down at the picture of the dress.

The bodice was a vintage-style corset with crystal detailing over the bust of the beautiful model who wore it. Her shoulders were bare apart from the loosely hanging cap sleeves that fell at her sides. At her waistline, layers of lace flowed down to her ankles in front and out to a short train in the back. This dress was the perfect mix of old style and new, youthful and classy, simple and extravagant.

It was gorgeous.

I felt my eyes brim with tears as I stared at the page.

Bronwyn had chosen my wedding dress.

CHAPTER 56

"How's it going in there?" Eastlyn called from outside the dressing room.

I knew it was killing her not to be inside, getting a first glimpse of all the dresses she had selected for me before I had the chance to refuse to step outside wearing them. But the scars on my legs weren't going anywhere, and I had no believable excuse for them. I convinced Eastlyn that I wanted a moment in each of the gowns to form my own opinion before I allowed her reaction to influence my decision, and she reluctantly agreed to give me privacy.

Not that my decision was going to be swayed—I already knew the dress I wanted. But there was no way I was going to rob my future sister-in-law of this experience.

She'd invited her mother to come along, but Mr. and Mrs. Greene were making another attempt to connect with Westley and had left for Maplecrest before we went to breakfast. I hoped that in light of his epiphany and the probability that he was in serious trouble for what he'd done to Micah, this trip would be more fruitful for Westley's parents. And though Westley had been on both of our minds as we ate our frittatas and drank our lattes, Eastlyn and I kept our conversation all wedding. She'd brought me a gift, a framed copy of her parents' wedding invitation dated almost twenty-two years ago. The Greenes had one framed in their foyer, and over the years, I'd read it dozens of times:

It is our joy as the parents of
Mr. Timothy Lewis Greene
&
Ms. Lillian Josephine Dequindre
to cordially invite you to the ceremony of their
marriage union
on the first of June
at the Basilica of the Sacred Heart
on the campus of the University of Notre Dame.

Many times, I'd listened as the Greene parents recounted the magic of their wedding day. I'd long ago memorized their photo album of the event. Mrs. Greene had been stunning, of course—she was, after all, Eastlyn's mother. And if I re-imagined Mr. Greene with a more modern haircut and tux, Westley was his spitting image. Their wedding had been every bit of what I thought a royal ball in a fairy tale would have been, very fitting for a princess and her prince.

"I love it," I gushed. And I did. My sister-in-law, so thoughtful.

Her gift was the deciding reason I would wait to reveal that I'd already made up my mind about my wedding dress. She was so deliberate in participating in our engagement; I didn't want to spoil her fun of dressing me up, no matter how different our tastes would turn out to be.

Each gown she chose for me to try on at the boutique was beautiful, no doubt, but all of them would have looked better on her than me. I was sure she hadn't consciously been trying to select her own wedding dress, but there was a distinct difference between the kinds of gowns that looked good on someone who resembled Helen of Troy and someone—like myself—who didn't. So, finally, after the fifth time parading through the room of mirrors in a dress I had no chance of pulling off, I snagged the page from the bridal magazine out of my purse and handed it to her.

"What do you think about something like this?"

Eastlyn cocked her head to the side and studied the gown. She looked back and forth from me to the page,

329

skeptically, and humoring me, said, "Guess we won't know for sure unless you try it on..."

She got the attention of our consultant and showed her the picture while I traipsed back to my dressing room to remove from my body what felt like twenty-five pounds of taffeta.

The boutique was slow that morning. It was Friday, after all, and most brides-to-be were off at their day jobs instead of enjoying a high-school suspension like I was. However, there were two twenty-something women walking around in white dresses, filing in and out of their respective dressing rooms just as I had been for the past hours, though their entourages were much larger than my own. Friends, sisters, and mothers accompanied them, oohing and aahing over how striking each looked in every single dress, shedding tears of happiness for the brides.

I stole glimpses of their moments, and I fought back the impulse to envy them. Sure, their fiancées were probably not being held against their will at a hospital after having quasi-murdered them. And sure, they had moms and supportive friends to share this special time with, as in plural, more than one person...

But I had Westley.

My thoughts were interrupted by the awareness of someone's eyes on me. With my hand on the dressing-room door handle, I noticed a woman seated across the aisle, staring intently at me. She smiled and nodded when my eyes met hers. I returned the gesture.

She was middle-aged, I guessed by the lines in her face. Her hair was very long and black, and from her dress and skin tone, I knew she was likely not native to Northern Indiana. Middlebury, especially, was not known for its ethnic diversity. And while nearby Elkhart was home to a broader mix of cultures, the presence of this woman still struck me as incongruous, unique. Her appearance did not immediately suggest she belonged with either of the other parties I'd seen in the store, nor did she seem as interested in them as her unbroken stare hinted she was with me.

I wondered if I should speak to her, at least say hello and offer her the chance to say something to me. But before I could think of how to address her, she stood and nodded at me and then ducked out of my sight.

I shrugged off the strange encounter and entered the dressing room. It took me a solid five minutes to remove the heaviest wedding gown in the history of clothes. But just as I hung the dress back on its hanger, Eastlyn knocked on my door.

"You are never going to believe this, Cosette, but they had the dress here—*in stock*. They just used it three weeks ago for a bridal expo in Chicago. It's already been tailored for the model who wore it, but I think with an extra inch on your heels we can make it work."

We exchanged gowns over the top of the door, and she brought me a pair of taller shoes to try on with the new dress.

I faced away from the mirror as I tried on the gown. Once I had my legs covered, I needed Eastlyn's help fastening up the back since it wasn't the larger, off-the-rack sizes of the other dresses. She was eager to join me in the dressing room and quickly tied up the corset before stepping in front of me for a look.

"Cosi...I think I might cry..." Eastlyn placed a hand over her mouth. Her reaction told me what I already knew—this was the dress for me.

Before I could turn around to see it for myself, she pulled me out of the dressing room and helped me up onto a pedestal in front of the mirrors where I could see every possible angle of myself wearing the gown.

Immediately, a consultant clipped a veil into my hair as though she were crowning me Miss America. And that's exactly who I felt like.

I took in the reflections of a dozen beaming Cosettes. If I hadn't *been* her, I would have *wanted* to be her.

The vision of who I was in the dress—a bride, Westley's bride—inspired me, reignited my hope for my future with him. Convinced me that no matter how bad things seemed right now, Westley was right—I was going to get my happily ever after.

"This is the one," Eastlyn whispered to me, dabbing at her eyes.

"Yes." I repeated her words, "This is the one."

◆◆◆

Before we completed our purchase, the staff seamstress came by to measure for alterations the dress would need. She was a pale, older woman who wore her glasses on a gold chain around her neck and spoke with a harsh foreign accent.

"This dress is good. No changes. Made for you. Just don't eat the Twinkies too much."

I promised I wouldn't. Eastlyn untied my corset and sent me off to the dressing room while she completed the sales paperwork.

A consultant took my gown from over the dressing-room door and packaged it into a thick garment bag so that it was ready for me by the time I'd re-dressed.

"You're going to make a gorgeous bride," she said as she hooked the hanger onto my hand.

I smiled.

Eastlyn had stepped outside to call her mother with the news that we'd found the dress, and I started in the direction of the exit to join her when I heard my name announced from near the front of the store. I made eye contact with another sales associate, who then repeated my name, "Cosette?"

"Yes?"

"Someone left this for you, honey." She stepped out from behind her workstation and extended something in my direction.

As I approached her, I could see what she was offering was an envelope with my name written in bold ink and a single white flower.

A tulip.

I gasped. "Who gave you this?" I searched the boutique for signs of Micah. "Did you see him? Did he seem all right?"

I laid my dress over the counter and took the envelope from her hands.

She seemed puzzled. "Well, it was a her, not a him. And she seemed fine. Older woman, dark hair...left about ten minutes ago. She just asked if she could leave this here for you because you were in the dressing room." She spoke fast, worried by my reaction that she'd inadvertently taken part in something she shouldn't have. "Is everything OK?"

I tore open the envelope and unfolded the paper stuffed inside.

Please come.

I swallowed hard. There were only two words on the page, but that was all it took to confirm my fears.

Micah was in trouble; that was why he'd been staying away. And because he'd sent a messenger to deliver his request, it led me to believe that the kind of trouble he was in was...serious.

Without another word to the clerk, I grabbed my dress and rushed for the door. Micah needed me to come, and there was only one place I knew to go where I might find him.

CHAPTER 57

To avoid worrying Eastlyn, I told her that my grandmother had called and needed me home immediately. I felt horrible lying, but if I'd even hinted that Micah had anything to do with the abrupt end to our girl time, she would have insisted on coming with me to find him.

I thanked her a dozen times for our morning together as we pulled into my driveway. I hoped that through my distracted state, she was able to feel my sincerity. After I was sure Micah was going to be OK, I would find a way to show Eastlyn just how much I appreciated everything she'd done for me.

Once inside, I hauled my dress and Eastlyn's gift up to my room and laid both of them on my bed. I then turned around and flew back down the stairs and out to my car.

As I drove, I tried to recall details of the woman from the boutique. I couldn't remember enough about her demeanor or expression to rate the urgency of the message she'd left for me. But in light of the events of the last few weeks, my default reaction was set to panic, so I pushed the accelerator hard on the open country roads.

The next time I touched the brakes was to park my car in the driveway of the farmhouse. I got out of the cab and jogged toward the front door announcing my arrival. "Micah? Micah! I'm here..."

But when I pushed through the door to the house, Micah was not the one awaiting me.

Sitting in the rocker next to the glowing fireplace was the woman I'd seen at the boutique. She had her hands folded in her lap and appeared to have been watching the door expectantly for my entrance.

"Welcome, Cosette," she said serenely in an accent I'd never heard before.

"Hi." I was too disappointed to remember my manners. "Who are you, and where is Micah?" I made a quick scan of the empty room.

She wasn't offended by my shortness. "My name is Sidona. Your friend remains in the garden."

Though she'd answered my questions, I felt she was leaving out a lot of details.

I pressed further. "Is he all right?"

"I'm afraid not." Her expression did not change with the deliverance of this news. "He is quite ill."

I swallowed hard. "What's wrong with him?" I stammered, my stomach churning.

"Much." Her eyes moved to the fire. "But most pressing to him is that he is starving."

"Starving?" I parroted. I was expecting bad news about Micah's health, but I hadn't predicted he would be dying of malnutrition. "You just mean he's having trouble chewing or something, right? Like, he's probably weak and sick of having to eat soft foods." I felt relieved. If needing a square meal was Micah's biggest crisis, I was happy to puree the entire food pyramid for him. Problem solved.

"He is not starving in that way, Cosette," she corrected.

How could I have misinterpreted what she'd said?

"How many ways are there to starve?" I was beginning to grow impatient the same way I did when talking to Micah.

"Have you not been to the garden?" she asked, still eventoned. "Did your experience there not teach you that there are truths beyond what you know in this world?"

Yes, I had. And yes, it did.

"Your friend has made a request for you to come to him. Do you accept it?"

An excited thrill shot through my body. "You are going to take me to the garden?"

"If you agree to come, yes."

335

"Of course I want to go!" I didn't hesitate in my response. I'd been preparing myself to return to the garden since I'd left it. Aside from a rocky transition into it, and a melancholic exit from it—which would *not* happen again, I reminded myself—I'd been dying to relive my time there. And with the added bonus of seeing Micah and hopefully convincing him to come back to Maplecrest for help, there was nothing that could stop me from going.

"I will take you, if that is what you wish," she agreed. "But be warned, my dear. What is happening to your friend will not be easy to watch."

Sidona underestimated me. I had seen my fair share of news footage of *actual* starving children in third-world countries. I was sure that whatever "starving" meant in the garden, it wouldn't be as painful to watch as that had been.

My new guide ran through the same instructions Micah had before my first transition: hold onto her and stay, let go of her and leave. I nodded that I understood, and she reached out her hand for mine.

As we prepared to transition, I could feel myself stiffen under Sidona's arms. It had been at this point the last time that I had begun to worry what I had gotten myself into by agreeing to go to Micah's home. The music started blaring, and the putrid flower stench overwhelmed me—and then I passed out. When I awoke in the garden, I'd been scarred for life by the experience—literally.

"So, this isn't your first time, is it?" I asked Sidona. "Because the last guy was a rookie, and I've got the blue shins to prove it."

For the first time since I'd walked through the farmhouse doors, her serene expression broke, and she smiled faintly. "Do not worry, my dear. I am a professional."

I felt her arms around me squeeze, and instantly, the room began to fade.

◆ ◆ ◆

My transition to the garden with Sidona was flawless. I noticed no change in perception—no overpowering smells or sounds. From our adjoined hands, I could feel a steady stream of warmth pulsing from her body to mine like an IV of energy. This experience with a seasoned guide was very different than it had been with newbie Micah. No pain, no nausea, no permanent changes in my skin tone.

We arrived in the garden near the base of the fruit tree, and in the light of the day, it appeared even more glorious than it had looked under the night sky. Before I could become too enraptured by its colors and grandeur, Sidona directed my eyes to movement in the distance.

There appeared to be a man maneuvering around methodically, raising something up high into the air and then pulling it back to the ground quickly. Moments later, a thudding noise reached my ears.

"Is that Micah?" I asked as we watched him fall to his knees for a moment and then stand back up and begin the same actions all over again. "What is he doing? Chopping firewood?"

"Yes. And no. Let us go to him."

Covering the rooted terrain with Sidona was also much easier than it had been with Micah, and I didn't know whether to attribute it to provision or how experienced she seemed to be in matters of the garden. Either way, we were soon within his earshot, and I eagerly called out to him.

Micah was standing in a level area of root, raised above the ground. Sidona effortlessly led me over the dips and bumps on our path, and soon, we were upon him.

When we locked eyes, my stomach dropped.

As I took Micah in, all the relief I'd felt in the farmhouse was quickly replaced by a deep aching in my chest. His jaw was swollen from just under his eye to the base of his neck; it looked puffy, but also heavy, as if he were somehow holding a water balloon in his cheek. A dark redness outlined the area but extended down past his shirt collar. His mouth was closed, but at each corner, a stream of drool leaked out from his cracked lips.

"My God, Micah..." I stepped toward him, pulling Sidona with me toward the monster-masked version of my friend.

337

Micah grunted in response, and I retreated with my guide a few steps.

"The infection is preventing him from opening his mouth. He cannot speak," she answered on his behalf. "Or eat."

It was only after she said this that I noticed the bulge on his good cheek where his jaw appeared fully clenched. "Oh..."

Micah's eyes fell to the ground and mine followed. Looking around, I now understood that the movement I'd spied from the distance hadn't been the chopping of wood. In his hands, Micah gripped a large stone, covered in a wet, white substance. Scattered around him, chunks of pulpy fruit flesh mixed with dirt in the crevices of the tree roots.

I was immediately grateful for the provision I had in Sidona; though encircled by a landmine of exposed fruit, I felt no reaction to them. She was fully protecting me.

Micah, however, was not as immune as I was.

From his stomach, a deep growl erupted, and a grimace wrenched the functioning side of his face. He doubled over to the ground, his knuckles gripping white onto the stone in his hand as he moaned in pain.

"Micah..." Again, I stepped forward. And again, he warned me away, this time shooing me back with his hand.

When he recovered, he quickly stood and ripped one of the pears from a branch and set it atop a raised place on a root. Lifting the stone high into the air, he swiftly thrust the rock down onto the fruit, smashing it into more of the wet bits scattered among the roots. He did this several times, until even the core of the fruit had been broken up. He then cast the stone to his side and dug into the exposed flesh of the pear with his fingernails. He squeezed the mush in his hands and brought it to his mouth.

With his jaw locked, he could not force the food past his teeth, so he tilted his head back and tucked it into his good cheek, cramming in all that would fit. Once full, he held his lips closed with one hand and then violently slapped his face in an attempt to push the fruit through to his throat.

For a moment, I thought he'd been successful. He closed his eyes, and I could see that he was trying to swallow.

But almost instantly, he began to cough, gagging on whatever he'd managed to get into his throat. Soon he was on all fours, a foamy vomit oozing from his nose and mouth onto the ground.

The aching in my chest swelled; I was unable to bear my friend's suffering. "We've got to get him to a hospital! He needs medicine! Doctors will find a way to feed him there..."

Micah uttered another sickening moan.

"Yes, he needs those things, I agree." Sidona nodded. "But he refuses to go."

"What? Why?" I looked back to Micah who was now shakily standing, picking another fruit from the tree.

"Because he doesn't want to leave the garden."

"That's crazy; Micah leaves the garden all the time." Her reasoning didn't make sense to me. "And anyway, the sooner he gets better, the sooner he can come back."

"You do not understand." She shook her head. "Your friend is not starving for nutrition; he is starving for what he needs to remain living here in the garden."

I watched as Micah shoved more pulp around his clenched teeth and tried to swallow it. "You're right. I don't understand."

Sidona explained her answer as Micah again coughed and sputtered. "When someone makes the choice to fully transition into the garden, to live here, they may eat of any plant in the garden...but there is only one food that our bodies *need* to survive here, and that is the first fruits."

She paused so as not to have to talk over Micah groaning. Again, I wanted to rush to his side, but I knew if I let go of Sidona, I'd be transported back to the farmhouse—and to an even more helpless position than I already felt I was in.

She continued, "Each day, we must choose to eat from this tree if we want to remain here, Cosette. This is a daily reminder of our covenant in the garden, but also the fruit sustains us; it keeps our bodies suited for the environment."

I swallowed hard. Though I was fairly sure the answer was in front of me, convulsing in the fetal position, I asked anyway, "And what happens if you don't eat from it?"

"We starve."

Sidona had said that Micah wasn't starving in the way I understood it, but watching him suffer in this way, I feared that however she defined the word, the end result was the same. "So he's dying? If he doesn't eat the first fruits, he'll die?"

"Your friend's health is in danger, yes. But more imminently, his body is becoming unable to support being in the garden. Right now, he is beginning to experience much of what you felt during your first transition before your senses were adjusted." My eyes shot back to Micah, a new wave of sympathies for him washing through me. "The sights, the sounds...the hunger. It's beginning to overtake him."

Micah attempted to stand again but fell this time, too weakened for another attempt to feed himself. His eyes were now screwed as tightly shut as his mouth, and he covered his ears with his hands.

"We've got to do something!" I pulled Sidona a step closer to Micah, but she planted her feet into the ground. "We have to get him out of here!"

"We cannot make that choice for him, Cosette. We cannot force him to leave the garden."

"You think he wants to be in this pain?" I vividly remembered the deafening music, the blinding lights, and my desperation for the first fruits. "We would be sparing him!" I again pulled forward, and my guide again resisted.

"He knows how to transition back into the world. He is choosing to remain here," she explained to me gently. "Your friend paid a great price to live in the garden. And he understands the cost of leaving it in this way. That is why he is fighting so hard to remain here."

I could hear my heart pounding in my ears so loudly that I wondered if Sidona had lost her control over my senses.

Micah found the strength to bring himself to his knees, his hands still clutching his ears.

I remembered how overpowering the music had been to me during my transition. I'd not forgotten any of the pain—the gut-wrenching floral stench, the piercing light, the cutting of the river against my shins...

My shins.

My scars.

In the brief moments I had been vulnerable to the elements of the garden, the river had permanently damaged my skin. Avalon had become mute and disfigured by the first fruits.

Through hot tears, I searched Micah's body. Faint, blue, spidery lines had already begun to form on his face beneath the traces of the juice from the fruit.

"What's going to happen to him if he stays here?" I demanded. I feared my time was running out. "Will he be burned to death?"

Sidona said nothing.

My tears came faster. "This is so unfair! This place...this place is supposed to be all about free will and choice. You won't let me take him out of here to save his life because that isn't his will, but don't you understand that not being able to eat the fruit is *also* not his will? It's his choice to stay here, not to starve himself from this place! This free-will double standard you are protecting is flawed!" I choked back another sob. "*Please*, let's take him away..."

Sidona did not hesitate in her response. "Free will is not flawed, Cosette. We are flawed. And there are far-reaching consequences for imposing one's will on another."

"*What are you talking about?*" I screamed. Why in the world did she think this was time for a philosophy lesson? We needed to take action, or Micah was going to die right there in front of us.

"It was not your friend's will that his face be cut and become infected. Nor was it his will to have his jaw broken." Sidona's tone became stern. "But those are the circumstances that have led him here."

My heart stopped pounding in my ears. I was sure it had stopped beating altogether.

341

I had done this to Micah. So had Westley. We were the reason he could not eat from the tree.

Instead of aching, my chest now felt hollow. Empty. As if upon learning of my crime, my soul had abandoned me.

"But I didn't mean for this to happen," I choked out. "Neither did Westley."

"I know this is true. As does your friend," Sidona comforted in her even tone. "He forgives you."

I didn't understand how Sidona was able to speak on Micah's behalf so freely. Micah had no reason to forgive me, especially if what I'd done to him played a part in getting him kicked out of the garden and possibly losing his life altogether.

Through Westley, I had experienced what happens to someone when he witnesses the death of another human being. Julia's death had not been his fault, and still it had almost destroyed him completely. What would become of me if I watched Micah die from wounds he suffered at my and Westley's hands? What would become of Westley?

The stains on Micah's face grew darker, and I could see blue scars beginning to form on his hands. His moaning was constant now, though I was sure no matter how loudly he cried out, he wouldn't be able to hear himself above the music that deafened him.

I watched Micah helplessly. Suddenly, my mind flashed back to my first conversation with him in Mrs. Holloway's class, the one about our eulogies. He and I had discussed how I wanted to die a cowardly death in my sleep of old age—quietly and painlessly. That hadn't been what Micah wanted for himself; he had wanted a more meaningful death. He had wanted to give his life, willingly, for a purpose...

I looked at Micah on the ground, surrounded by the gutted fruit.

No, this was not how he wanted to die.

"You are not required to stay here, Cosette," Sidona offered. "You may leave at any time you wish if this becomes too overwhelming."

I was confused. "So, this is why Micah wanted me to come?" I sniffled loudly. "He had you bring me here to watch him starve?"

She paused before answering me. "You will know better than I why he chose to invite you here."

Before I could argue angrily that I didn't, a light breeze blew, bringing with it the scent of the tulips from the fields not far away. Their aroma reminded me where I was. I'd almost forgotten that I was in same garden I'd walked in with Micah. The one with flowers of infinite beauty and light webs full of colors that didn't exist in the world I lived in.

While the wind had brought me a momentary reprieve from my grief, Micah flinched at it. Jaw and eyes still clenched shut, his back straightened. Quickly, he pulled his hands away from his ears and used them to cover his nose from the putridity he perceived, unable to temper his own senses.

Only seconds after his hands left the sides of his head, Micah flinched again, and soon, thin trickles of blood dripped from both ears.

"Micah!" I shouted in the utmost futility. If my voice had been a siren, he wouldn't have heard me. The music had caused him to go deaf.

It was at this, his latest injury, that something in Micah's demeanor changed. He faced upward, tears running down his face and streaming over the fresh, blue burns that covered his cheeks. His shoulders slumped, and he clutched at his chest with shaking hands. I watched as he gripped the fabric of his shirt and began to rip it apart, tearing it from his body.

All the while his lips were moving. Incoherent whimpers spewing from his mouth.

"What is he saying?" I demanded of Sidona. "Does he want our help? Does he want to retransition?" My hopes soared. Micah had many serious and some inexplicable injuries, but I believed that if we could get him to a hospital fast, he could still live.

"He is not speaking to us. He is praying to God. He is asking for provision."

Provision.

My heart raced faster.

Provision.

Provision.

The word echoed in my head.

I looked again to Micah, his hands raised into the air. His now-bare chest heaving and shuddering with his cries.

Immediately, my thoughts shifted to a day earlier in my bathroom, staring at my own chest's reflection in the mirror.

My body had been broken beyond what would have supported me living in it. There were no physical signs, no scars remaining from what had happened...

I gasped.

Maybe he didn't have to die.

Maybe I *did* know why Micah had asked me to come.

With newfound strength, I stepped toward him, dragging my surprised guide with me and narrowing the short distance between us before Sidona got her bearings. "What are you doing, Cosette?" she barked, no longer calm.

"Exercising my free will!" I shouted back. Before she could pull me away, I reached out and grabbed Micah's shoulder, letting go of her hand.

CHAPTER 58

Everything hurt, all at once.

I could not see.

I could not hear.

There was fire in the air I breathed.

Micah cringed at my touch, my dependence upon him to sustain me in the garden quickly draining his remaining strength.

I stumbled for the words. I'd never said them before.

"God, I don't doubt that you can heal Micah. You used his hands to heal me. Now I'm asking that you use mine to heal him..."

CHAPTER 59

I awoke to daylight. Morning.

The farmhouse was cold, especially the wood floor where I found myself.

I must have fallen asleep crouched on my knees, and as I stood—my body stiff and joints cracking—I almost regretted not having driven home when I transitioned back the night before.

But it was hard to maintain any regrets in that new day.

I rubbed at my eyes, finding they were still wet, and wondered if I'd continued crying in my sleep. I wouldn't have been surprised. After what had happened, I had no other way to express what I was feeling but to weep.

On the night of my healing, when Micah had laid his hands on me, the experience had been surreal—the heat, the peace, how my body was sewn back together.

But when the tables were turned, and it was I who prayed for Micah's life to be restored, the same experience had been...transcendent.

I closed my eyes again and tried to relive it.

The environment had become entirely overwhelming immediately after I released Sidona's hand and touched Micah. The pain was so great, so powerful and constant, it felt infinite.

And then I prayed the prayer; I asked for Micah's healing. And all of a sudden, that same, unspeakable pain was...conquered.

I didn't feel how the peace entered me this time. It had no point of contact, no external source as it had when Micah put his hands on me.

It was just there, within me. As if it had always been there, but something had awakened it.

And I welcomed it. I invited it.

And when I felt it growing, felt it consuming me—

I surrendered to it.

And when I did so, the music stopped. The light faded. The wind stilled. And then the heat came.

But it wasn't only warmth radiating from my fingertips and into Micah's body.

It was more.

The words, ones like I'd listened to Micah pray but did not recognize, poured from my lips. I heard them, spoken in my voice, and though I had not formed them on my own, I knew them.

And they were beautiful.

My reverie about the night before was interrupted when I felt new tears dripping from my cheeks and into my hands. I used my sleeve to dab them dry, but moments later, they were wet again.

When it had been me on the receiving end of the healing, when I'd come to understand what had taken place, I had been moved. I'd had questions. I'd been equally confused and grateful.

But now, on this end, having experienced the power...having been used to perform this miracle...

I was changed.

As soon as Micah had regained the strength to do so, he stood from his kneeling position and left me. Instantly, I faded back to the farmhouse.

My retransition into the world felt triumphant this time, not tragic. And as I wept those tears of joy throughout the night, I realized that I finally understood what Micah had been telling me all this time: there was a plan for my life bigger than I had for myself.

And now, I believed that I was ready to pursue it.

CHAPTER 60

The peace I had received in the garden lingered within me.

In faith, I believed that Micah was healed. I didn't need to see him to know it. And I also believed that I didn't need to hang around the farmhouse to wait for him to come to me. He would find me when it was time, when he was ready.

So I left to face a new day.

I stepped out of the farmhouse and into the winter morning, embracing the cold with deep breaths. Looking out into the seasonal gray and all the naked trees, I felt my mood tinge with disappointment. Surely not now, in the dead frozenness, did any of the scenery before me compare to the visions I'd had in the garden. But I couldn't imagine even in the birth of spring, the lush of summer, or the color of fall that I would ever again be impressed by nature. The garden had been the prototype, the testing ground for the natural world I knew. After experiencing it, now even my most vivid memories of sunsets and rainbows felt like cheap, acrylic hotel art next to the original masterpiece.

As I drove toward home, I wondered whether it was possible to spend so much time in the beauty of the garden that, like Micah, I would be willing to trade my life not to leave it.

◆◆◆

It was odd that my house would be empty on a Saturday morning. So when it was, I pulled out my phone to make sure it was, indeed, the day I thought. My latest trip to the garden, much like my last experience there, had seemed incongruent with time as I knew it. The visit had been short, I thought;

yet, when I transitioned back to the farmhouse, dusk had passed.

My phone confirmed the day as well as displayed a text I didn't notice had come in sometime overnight. It was from Avalon:

On Saturdays, visiting hours start at noon. ☺

A jolt of excitement interrupted the peace of the morning.

I had so many questions for Avalon. She had so much to tell me. And I couldn't think of a better way to spend the afternoon.

On my way.—CM

◆ ◆ ◆

I was only at home long enough to raid the kitchen, wash my face, change my clothes, and retrieve Avalon's sketchbook from my room before I was on the road again.

With my mind so full and the drive so familiar now, the distance between Middlebury and Fort Wayne didn't seem nearly as long as it had on my previous treks to the hospital. Knowing I wouldn't be seeing Westley likely added to the quickening of my trip—not that I wasn't anxious to see Avalon, but I didn't feel the same anticipation that made time drag like it did when I was going to visit him.

I hadn't spoken with Eastlyn to know how the Greenes' visit with their son had gone, or if West had even agreed to see them when they came. I debated whether to call to ask her, but I worried she would bring up Micah or ask what I was doing that day, and since I had no explanation to either line of questioning, I decided against it.

From my last conversation with him, I remained hopeful that Westley's attitude toward his treatment was turning around. Remembering his remorse about hurting Micah sent a wave of relief through me. Maybe he'd reached his rock bottom retrospectively and had begun crawling out of the hole he'd been in these past weeks. Once he saw for himself that Micah was better, which I was confident *would* happen, perhaps it would propel him further toward his own healing.

But since he wasn't allowed visitors, and I wouldn't be seeing him to know either way, I pushed Westley from my mind. It would be all too easy to get lost wondering how he was coping, and I needed to prepare myself for the real purpose of today's visit.

Though we were linked by our scars, Avalon was still essentially a mystery to me. I knew she'd been to the garden, but I couldn't even assume what circumstances led her there since I wasn't even sure of what about my own had earned me the invitation. I looked forward to learning about her journey to the garden, but I also hoped that by the end of our visit, I would understand a little more about my own.

By the elevator ride up to the fourth floor, the calmness of the morning had been entirely replaced with anticipation of the afternoon. And when the doors opened and I saw Avalon sitting in the waiting room tapping her foot anxiously, I knew I wasn't the only one ready for answers.

CHAPTER 61

After another affectionate and tearful greeting, Avalon practically dragged me to a booth along the perimeter of the cafeteria. She had been clutching something like a laptop to her chest, and when we were seated, she went about untangling a few sets of cords and plugging the computer device into the wall. She then handed me a set of headphones and motioned for me to put them on.

"What's this for?" I asked in an effort to fill the silence, though I was sure she wouldn't be able to answer me conventionally, and I would likely find out for myself moments later.

Avalon held up a finger to ask for patience, unfolded the screen of the computer from its locked position, and began to type on a keyboard.

With the screen facing away from me, I couldn't see her message, but when she struck the "return" key, I realized that I wouldn't need to see what she was typing at all.

"I thought this might be easier than trying to handwrite everything." The mechanical voice of a woman read her message through my headphones.

"Nice," I said, happy that the speed of our communication wouldn't be as hampered as I'd expected.

Avalon smiled with closed lips and lowered her eyes back to the keyboard.

"You've been back to the garden."

I felt my eyes widen. I couldn't tell by the inflection of the nonhuman voice if this was a question or statement, but by her face, I could see Avalon knew where I'd been.

She typed some more.

"No perfume smells that wonderful."

My mouth dropped as I quickly pulled a handful of my own hair to my nose and breathed it in. As I inhaled, I recognized a hint of the unmistakable scent of the tulips.

I blushed and smiled sheepishly at my friend and then nodded. Avalon returned my grin at first, but it shortly fell into a more thoughtful expression.

"Why you and not me?"

There was sadness in her eyes when they rose from the screen. She, no doubt, had just as many questions as I did about the garden. But unlike me, who'd only begun to explore their truths, she'd been tortured by them for months without anyone to discuss them with.

"I don't know," I answered, wishing I had a more defini- tive response. "But why don't we see if we can figure that out together?"

To begin this process, we took turns asking one another questions to try to stumble upon that which would link the two of us to each other and ultimately, to the garden. But with neither of us having ever conducted this type of inter- view, it was difficult to know what to ask.

From her contribution to our conversation I learned that Avalon was originally from Kansas, where she'd lived a fairly uneventful childhood. She'd moved to Illinois after high school to attend the School of the Art Institute in Chicago. She'd been in her sophomore year there when she first met her guide.

Avalon pointed a finger at her sketchbook, which was sticking out of my purse. I handed it to her, and she opened it to the drawing of the young man, "Gabriel." She laid the book between us so that his eyes were facing my own.

"I was waiting tables at a restaurant near my school about six months ago when this guy came in. He sat down in my section and was very friendly to me. He ordered a meal he didn't eat and sat alone at his table until my shift was over, then asked if he could buy me a cup of coffee.

"I would not usually agree to something like that, but this time, I did. And we hit it off immediately.

"Very quickly, we became close. It was as if he spoke my language, like he knew everything about me without me telling him. I'd never met anyone like him before. I'd had boyfriends in the past, but Gabriel was different. We had a connection I couldn't deny. I fell in love for the first time in my life. It was the happiest I'd ever been.

"Sometime around two months after we'd met, something changed. Our relationship was strong, but I could tell there was something troubling him. He seemed nervous, almost panicked at times, but he'd never tell me why.

"I began to worry that he was sick or in some kind of trouble, but he wouldn't explain anything to me. He just kept saying that he wanted to 'show me,' but he didn't know how. He became so distracted and angered by whatever was bothering him that I felt it best to put some distance between us until he was ready to share it with me or he'd dealt with whatever it was.

"The night that I told him this, he broke down. He confessed that he did have a secret. Then, he grabbed me by the hand, and the next thing I knew, we were in the garden."

I gasped, and Avalon looked up from her keyboard. It took me a moment to put words to my reaction. "So you didn't have any warning about where he was taking you? You had no idea where he was from or that he was...unusual...before he just took you to the garden?" Gabriel was proving to be less and less like Micah. My guide had been so thoughtful, to the point where it had annoyed me at times. Though I couldn't appreciate it then, he'd gone to great lengths to prepare me for what he was going to show me in the garden. Micah had given me glimpses, small doses of incredible provision. He'd gauged my reactions, been patient with me. Granted me choices. And even then, the garden had been overwhelming.

Avalon stared off thoughtfully and then shook her head.

"No warnings."

"And obviously, no warnings about the first fruits either?" I hated reminding my friend of her disfigurement, but I wanted a clearer picture of Gabriel.

She looked down at her hands.

"He said if I ate the fruit, I'd be able to stay with him there. He pulled a piece off the tree, took a bite, and handed it to me. I tried to refuse it, but I felt powerless against its scent. Even as it was burning me, I kept trying to eat more—which doesn't make any logical sense, I know. The pains in my mouth and throat were excruciating, but my hunger was worse."

Avalon didn't need to explain her actions to me. I remembered the animal I'd become around the first fruits, throwing myself at Micah to taste a hint of the juice. "I get it."

She smiled at me through her sadness.

"When Gabriel finally pried the fruit from me and got me away from the tree, I felt like I was dying. First because my insides felt on fire, but also because he had taken the first fruit away. It was like I'd become addicted to them after one bite, and my body was going through withdrawal."

I pictured Micah starving, desperately trying to force the fruits past his locked jaw. The more I learned of the fruits, the more curious about them and afraid of their power I became.

"I had no idea what was happening to me, but from the way Gabriel looked at me, I knew it was something terrible. He picked me up and started to run, apologizing over and over again. Then I blacked out."

There was a look on Avalon's face of both hesitation and determination.

"This next part...I've never told anyone. The tree and the fruit were enough for my parents to send me here, and I wasn't really sure if what happened next had been real or a hallucination from the trauma. But maybe you can help me to decide for sure."

"Absolutely," I said, eagerly awaiting the rest of her story.

Avalon flipped a few pages to the end of her sketchbook and pointed to the unfinished drawings.

"Do these mean anything to you?"

I studied the pictures of the gate and the large flames. "No. I'm sorry. I wondered about them myself. I haven't seen anything like them in the garden, and I thought maybe they were drawings of something separate. What are they?"

Avalon's face fell.

"I don't know. My memory is so fuzzy from the point I passed out, but I feel like I came to for about a minute sometime after Gabriel had stopped running. I remember feeling warmth and seeing a giant fire—flames as tall as the trees I'd seen in the garden. They frightened me, so I looked away from them. When my eyes adjusted to the darkness behind me, I could make out the gate in the distance."

She traced her fingers over the rough pencil marks on the page and then went back to typing.

"Gabriel was screaming, but I couldn't understand him. His tone was desperate, like he was pleading with someone. I remember hearing something like thunder, and there was a flash of bright light. Then I blacked out again."

As I listened, I tried to make this part of Avalon's story fit with any of my experiences in the garden, but it didn't. Just because I didn't relate to it though, I wasn't convinced it was a delusion.

"The next time I woke up, I was in a burn unit at a hospital near my hometown. Gabriel was there, but only long enough to promise that what had happened could be undone and that he would come back for me when he'd figured out a way for us to be together. Then, he disappeared—literally. And I haven't seen him since."

"So he took you back home and just left you there?" Again, I thought of Micah and was grateful.

"I don't know how I got there. We'd only been dating a few months when this happened, and we'd just briefly talked about my life back home. Both of my parents say that they received phone calls from him incoherently apologizing and telling them which hospital I was at. But considering everything else I had to process about the garden and my injuries, Gabriel teleporting me across state lines and tracking down my parents hardly registered as strange enough to wonder about."

355

The enormity of all Avalon had been through sank into me. She'd lost so much by going to the garden, and I now understood that the physical scars weren't the deepest wounds she'd suffered. I put myself in her shoes; had Micah abandoned me the way Gabriel had Avalon, I'd be at Maplecrest with her.

But, to me, what made her story even more heartbreaking was that Avalon was forsaken by the man she loved. Her guide hadn't been some weird kid from her English class. He'd been her boyfriend. Had Westley done to me what Gabriel had to her, I'm not sure I would have even wanted to recover.

I sighed. This was not the way I'd expected our conversation to go. Avalon and I were supposed to fill in each other's blanks, to help one another come to a better understanding about what we'd experienced. We were supposed to discover what linked us together, the common road that had led both of us to the garden.

Instead, what I learned made me suspicious.

The high I'd returned with from the garden was fading.

What was this place really?

It was beautiful yet painful. Peaceful yet terrifying. Healing yet scarring.

Of those paradoxes, Avalon had endured their worst. I looked at my friend sitting across from me, allowing myself for the first time to truly examine the markings on her face. Her scars were deep, dark. Permanently inked and out of place on a face otherwise so fresh and innocent.

And now, I understood that they weren't the most she'd suffered as a result of paradise.

It was then something occurred to me: I'd been warned that there would be a cost for the garden.

Micah had paid one, a price so high he would have rather died than done so in vain.

Avalon had paid one too, though hers had been stolen from her. And then, to make things worse, she seemed to have been exiled from the garden without explanation. And without a refund.

What did this mean?

I thought of my first journey to the garden, Micah and I lying in the grass, staring up at the nighttime sky, watching my light flickering from emerald to sapphire.

"Your options are changing...Weigh them carefully..."

Avalon's fingernails clicked on her keyboard.

"Why do you look so worried?"

"Because..." I thought for a moment before answering plainly, "I am."

CHAPTER 62

Our conversation didn't last much longer. I was too distracted.

"I'm sorry. I feel like I've got nothing to offer you." In light of Avalon's heartbreaking story, it felt cruel to follow up with tales of Micah's valiance and miraculous healings.

I needed to think. Or somehow find Micah. Maybe he had discovered more about Gabriel than he'd been able to tell me.

Avalon was disappointed, but she understood.

"I've waited for months to find someone to listen to what happened to me and not want to put me in a straitjacket. I figure one more trip to the garden for you, and maybe we'll end up bunkmates here anyway. Then, we can talk all we want."

I promised her I'd come back soon.

Avalon put her hand on mine and squeezed it.

I smiled. I'd finally found a real girlfriend. And it only took the oddest circumstances in human history to bring us together.

We said our good-byes, and Avalon headed to her room. I walked back through the waiting area and pressed the button for the elevator, still deep in thought.

The pretty receptionist was on duty. Our eyes met, and she greeted me. "Have a nice visit with Westley?"

Her memory was impressive. "No, actually, I was here to see another friend. Westley's not allowed visitors right now." It seemed strange that someone working on this floor would have the mind to recognize someone she'd seen twice, but not be aware that a resident of hers had broken the face of one of his previous visitors and been placed on lockdown.

"Hmm..." She furrowed her brow, struck a few computer keys, and then smiled. "Looks like you're in need of an update. Westley's visitation ban was lifted as of yesterday."

My eyes widened. "Seriously?"

"Seriously. Should I call him for you?"

With so much on my mind, it was nice to be asked a question that I didn't have to think about before answering.

"Yes. Definitely."

◆ ◆ ◆

Westley burst through the doors a minute later. He swept me off my feet and into his arms, greeting me with a kiss that ended only when the receptionist cleared her throat.

"Guys, there are enough depressed people here already," she half-whispered, smiling. "Save the love fest."

Westley pretended not to hear her but obeyed her wishes and led me by the hand back through the cafeteria. He walked backward, facing me, and rattled off questions a mile a minute. "Did you bring Micah back here for treatment? Is he going to be OK? Where is he? I need to apologize..."

I couldn't help but laugh at his enthusiasm. And because I couldn't have imagined a better greeting.

I looked into Westley's eyes, and for the first time since Julia's death, I recognized what I saw.

My Westley was back.

"He's fine," I was finally able to squeeze in a generic reply to the uninterruptible string of questions Westley had about Micah by the time we reached the couch in the recreational room.

"So you've seen him?"

"Yes."

"And he's healthy?"

"Yes," I started. "Well, I believe he's going to be."

Westley was confused and skeptical. "Well, which hospital is he in? This one? Can I go see him?"

359

"West, calm down," I tried to soothe his anxieties, but I knew I had no answers that would persuade him. I wanted to share everything with Westley—about my healing, about the garden, about God using me to save Micah—but I needed a better feel for how he was doing before I broached the subjects. All of it had been a leap of faith for *me* to believe, and I had experienced it myself. Knowing how fragile he'd been lately, I didn't want to make Westley feel crazier than he already did. "I don't know exactly where he is right now, but I *know* Micah is going to be just fine." The conviction with which I was able to say this made me smile.

Westley scrutinized my face. "You're sure?"

"Absolutely."

He stared at me a moment longer before allowing himself to heave a sigh of relief. "Thank god."

"Yes, thank God."

◆ ◆ ◆

With Westley's immediate concern for Micah assuaged, we both relaxed. Despite all that had happened, it was easy to resume what we'd always had with one another—our comfortable normal.

"So, how did it go with your parents yesterday?" I asked, trying to redirect our conversation away from Micah and other potential reminders of all I had yet to figure out about the garden.

Westley gave me a funny look. "Didn't they call you? I mean, that's why you're here, isn't it? Because they told you I'm off lockdown?"

I tried not to let my face show the panic I felt having overlooked this detail. "I haven't talked to them. They could have tried to call, though. I was having reception issues with my cell." So far, so true. At least I supposed there wasn't a cell phone tower in the garden, so any attempts made to reach me would have failed.

"So you just came down anyway?"

I paused a moment. "Can you blame me? I miss you. Thought it was worth a try." Still true...practically.

He shrugged. "No, I guess I can't." Then he added a wink.

I felt a surge of butterflies released in my stomach. Westley was being so...Westley. "So, tell me—how did you get your visitation privileges back? What's happened to you since the last time I was here?"

Westley showed his dimples. "Drugs, mostly." He waited for me to react, which I did in the form of a frown, before continuing, "But the right kind, this time."

He explained that he'd agreed to be put on a medication that would prevent him from acting out the dreams he was having about Julia. He assured me that it was a safe medicine usually prescribed for sleepwalkers, and by the second day he was on it, he'd stopped having "episodes."

"Now that I'm sleeping better, and I'm not afraid of what I'm *doing* in my sleep, I feel like everything else is really easy to cope with." West's confidence was back. "It's like what you said, Cosette. Even doctors struggle with death sometimes. I just have to move on with my life knowing I did everything I could for Julia."

I loved what I was hearing, and I wanted it all to be true, but it seemed like Westley had done a complete one-eighty in just three days. I'd learned the hard way—through several broken bones and a near-death experience—that Westley wasn't always aware of his own limitations. What was the expression? Once almost-involuntarily-manslaughtered-by-your-boyfriend, twice shy? "This is all great news, Westley. But, please, don't rush your recovery. I want you to take all the time you need to work through the emotions that got you here."

He narrowed his eyes at me. "Are you sure you haven't talked to my parents? Because you sound just like them." I shook my head, and he continued. "Anyway, I see everything more clearly now, Cosette. I can either let what happened destroy me, or I can let it make my life better. I choose better."

I was hesitantly hopeful. "So what does that mean?"

"It means I'm staying here until my birthday. I'll participate in every group session and meet twice a day with my doctor for the rest of this week." I could tell he felt like this was a compromise. "But come Friday, I'm checking myself out of here...and then we're getting married."

I'd tracked with Westley's series of events until the last item on his list, and then all I could hear was myself gasping. "What did you just say?"

He was taken aback by my reaction. "You do still want to marry me, don't you, Cosi?"

"Yes, of course but—"

"Then hear me out," Westley interrupted. "It's not as crazy as it sounds."

"You're serious?" My heart beat faster. "Because if you are, I might have to start really doubting your sanity, Westley."

He rolled his eyes. "I'm absolutely serious, Cosette." Westley was determined. "If this past month has taught me anything, it's that life is too short not to be with you every moment of every day. Being in this hospital, away from you...it's been hell, Cosi. Do you know we've spent more time apart in this week than we have in the past six years of our relationship?"

I nodded. I had realized this. However, I hadn't concluded that the answer to that problem was eloping.

"If I have to spend much more time without you, there's going to be a real reason to put me in a padded room." I knew he was exaggerating, but Westley seemed to believe what he was saying. "I'm done with all this, Cosette. I'm done having to say good-bye to you every night. I'm done with dealing with people trying to come between us. I want you to be my wife, and I see no reason to wait to marry you."

Westley laced his fingers in mine and kissed my hand.

He stopped talking, and I assumed he was waiting for me to respond, but I couldn't think of anything to say.

I felt like I should argue with him, give him a list of reasons why it made better sense for us to wait until we were older—at least until we were out of high school—to get married. I knew they existed, that there *were* logical grounds why eloping wasn't the best option for us. But in that moment, I could come up with none of them.

"I can take care of you, Cosette," Westley promised. "And I don't just mean physically. I mean, I can provide for you. I'm not asking you to marry me and then live with me in my parents' house."

I was confused. My hesitancy had had nothing to do with where we would live or how much money we would have, though I supposed those questions might have been ones I *could* have used to argue with him had my brain been cooperating. "What are you talking about?"

A sly grin spread across West's face. "So, you know how my grandfather left Eastlyn all that money for school when he died?"

I nodded like a bobblehead. I vaguely recalled some conversation about an inheritance around the time Eastlyn had been applying to schools, but I hadn't taken notes.

"Well, he left her more than tuition money, Cosi. And he did the same for me. My parents just decided not to tell me about it. They thought if I knew how much money was waiting for me when I turned eighteen, that maybe I wouldn't work so hard in school. But after all the bullshit with the baseball team..." Westley made a face. "They thought I could use some good news."

My face remained a question mark. Westley was full of the unexpected today.

"Cosette, come Friday, I will have access to a trust fund worth more than what it would cost me to pay for two medical doctorate degrees." When my expression didn't change, Westley translated the amount into a currency I could understand.

My face became an exclamation point.

"So, you see? We have nothing to worry about. We can get married and get our own place until we go off to college." Westley was beaming. "We don't have to wait. Nothing is stopping us."

I was speechless as it all sank in.

I'd been at a loss for reasons why we shouldn't get married before he'd said all this. And now, I not only couldn't think of an argument against eloping...the idea was beginning to excite me.

When Westley had proposed, it had felt unreal. But even in taking that step, actually getting married to him seemed like a fantasy—one that, in light of everything that had happened since Christmas Eve, I wasn't sure would ever come true.

But things had changed. Again.

Westley was back, and the future we always knew we'd have together could start now. The only thing standing in the way of it was me.

"What do you say, Cosette? Will you marry me?"

And just like the first time he had asked me this question, I answered it through tears of joy.

"Yes."

CHAPTER 63

Westley hadn't come to the decision for us to elope lightly, but because of his current circumstances, he wasn't able to do much research to plan it out. He did, however, know one thing for sure: we couldn't tell anyone.

This news threatened to extinguish my excitement. "Not even your parents?"

Westley's own smile faded. "No."

I frowned.

"It's not that I think they'll disapprove," he explained. "Because they love you, obviously. And you're already part of our family. It's just that my mind is made up, and I know they'll try to talk me out of it. We've already had enough 'disagreements' in the past month. In this case, I'd rather ask for forgiveness afterward than permission beforehand."

It didn't feel right to have to keep this a secret. I was already keeping quiet about so much else.

"Eastlyn's going to be really upset." I thought of my future sister-in-law's excitement during our dress shopping.

Westley shrugged. "I know. Mom was here when she called to say you'd found your dress. We'll just have to let her plan our reception after everyone gets over not coming to the wedding." He cupped my chin in his hand. "It's going to be all right, Cosette. It may take a while, but everyone will be happy for us."

I nodded, though I had my doubts about "everyone."

Westley's family would definitely come around. All they really ever cared about was whether or not he was happy. I was sure there would be some hurt, but we'd work it out. After all, they were the Greenes.

My family, on the other hand, was not. After their reaction to our engagement, I wasn't sure what to expect. They might not even notice I'd moved out until Bronwyn came to steal from my closet and found it bare.

"So, how do we do this?" I switched the course of my own thoughts to revive my excitement.

Westley's smile returned. "Well...I was thinking Vegas."

This time, he didn't wait for me to recover from my surprise before unloading all the details of his plan.

Westley would be allowed to check himself out at midnight Friday morning. He wanted me to book flights for us out of Indianapolis as early as possible. We'd arrive in Las Vegas sometime in the morning, get married that afternoon, honeymoon until Sunday, and be back in time for school on Monday.

"I figure I can call Mom and Dad after the wedding. By the time we come back, they'll have had some time to cool off. And if they don't, there are dozens of bed-and-breakfasts in Middlebury that would love to board some newlyweds until we find an apartment."

How was he making such huge decisions sound so simple?

Westley asked me if I could handle making the needed arrangements since he would be without unmonitored Internet for the rest of his treatment and didn't want to risk one of the doctors tipping off his parents. I told him that I would.

We spent the next hour the way I wished we'd been able to spend more of our engagement—happily planning the impending wedding of our dreams. Or, perhaps more accurately, trying to detail out the spontaneous, secret elopement we were settling for.

By the time Westley had to leave for a group session, I'd recorded a full list into my phone of prewedding tasks I would have to complete by the time I picked him up early Friday morning, my hands shaking as I typed.

When we were finally saying good-bye in the waiting room, Westley bent down to wrap his arms around my waist. "This is happening, Cosette. We are getting married."

"I know," I said, and I blinked back tears. "I can't believe it."

He kissed me one last time and told me that he'd call as soon as he could. Then, he disappeared through the double doors that led back to his dormitory.

I pressed the down arrow button and waited for the elevator, my mind's load now doubled.

"Have a nice visit with Westley?" the pretty receptionist asked once again.

This time, I flashed her a smile of my own. "Yes, thanks. It was wonderful."

CHAPTER 64

My drive home was a blur. Fortunately, I'd recently become experienced at driving while distracted. And today, with Micah's healing, Avalon's heartache, and an elopement to plan, I had a triple dose of emotion to sort through with my cruise control set to sixty.

By the time I arrived home, I'd decided that it was point-less to try to figure out anything more about the garden on my own. Without Micah or Sidona or Avalon or the Ghost of Christmas Future or someone else, I was stuck. Until my path crossed with one of theirs, I could make no progress in understanding the garden and my place in or out of it.

Planning my wedding to Westley, however, was some-thing I could do. So, I spent my evening in front of my computer screen, looking up flights to and hotels located in "the marriage capital of the world."

Westley had assigned me, among many other things, to choose the chapel where we'd have our ceremony. But with zero experience in planning weddings and more locations to choose from than I could count, I had no idea how to make a decision. In all the ways I'd imagined marrying Westley, it had never been surrounded by topless dancers or in the presence of Elvis. While excluding those options seemed to eliminate half my list, I still had an endless directory of flamboyant, kitschy faux-churches to sort through.

It was around the time that I stumbled upon a chapel where the ceremony was performed by a marionette puppet and the wedding cake was a three-tiered Rice Krispie treat that I started crying tears of frustration.

There was no doubt I wanted to marry Westley. And yes, I knew that it really didn't matter where or how I became his wife. Our wedding was just one day; we'd be married forever after. But there was just something about all of these places that seemed to cheapen what Westley and I had together. And not just the obvious stuff, like the fact that a large percentage of them had drive-through windows.

I gave myself an out that night; I decided that too much had happened that day for me to make any official decisions about our wedding. Yes, I knew I had a deadline, that we were to get married in only a few days. But it had become just too much for me to decide between "The Chapel of Love" and "The Real Chapel of Love." I needed to sleep on it.

As I logged off my computer and got ready for bed, I reassured myself that I wasn't wasting time. I still had half of my suspension left to wedding plan. It was only Saturday. I had until Friday. And it wasn't like every day was going to be filled with as much craziness as the last few had been.

Right?

I took myself at my word and went to sleep.

◆ ◆ ◆

"Wake up, skank. You've got another one downstairs."

Bronwyn's loud version of "good morning" woke me with a start.

"What?" I sat up straight in my bed, squinting at the light coming in through the window. Judging by the brightness of my room, I'd slept away most of the morning.

"My vote is still for Micah, but the one downstairs isn't too bad. If you like short guys." Bronwyn examined her fingernails as she spoke. "Which I don't. Though I think he's the one with the dead girlfriend, so that gives him pity points."

I stared dumbly at her. "What in the world are you talking about?"

My sister gave me a look that was both an eye roll and a glare. "There is a guy downstairs waiting for you. He says he came to take you to church." She laughed at the absurdity

369

and then added: "So, what's that code for? Hooking up in the back of his Jeep?"

Ignoring the Bronwynisms of her statement, I sighed as I realized whom she was talking about. "It's Patrick."

"So he was serious then?" She laughed condescendingly. "What, is it Whore of Babylon day? You'd better think twice about going to church, Cosette. They stone tramps like you there." She turned on her heel and stomped down the stairs where she announced to my guest: "You can go on up. But be warned, she looks like shit in the morning."

"OK..." Patrick's voice trailed off, and then I could hear hesitant footsteps ascending the stairs.

I sighed, reaching for my robe, and tossed my bed-head hair into a ponytail before greeting my unexpected guest in the hallway.

"Hi," I welcomed him with a forced smile from the doorway.

Patrick stood in the hallway by the top of the stairs, his cheeks burning red. Immediately, he burst into apology. "Cosette, I am *so* sorry." He glanced at me for a second before casting his eyes downward either out of respect because I was in my bathrobe or because Bronwyn was right and I looked like Medusa. "I know, I should have called, but it's just that...Well, I just really thought that with everything you've been through this week, it would be good for you to come to church. And I figured if I just showed up here to take you, it would be harder to say no. I didn't expect you to still be sleeping."

"It's fine, Patrick." I tried to speak casually to alleviate the awkwardness. "I didn't mean to sleep in this late. It's just that I had a late night...with West."

Patrick raised both eyebrows. "How did that go?"

"Um..." I drew out the syllable in search of the perfect adjective but was stumped. I wasn't sure the English language included a word that could precisely describe what it felt like to plan a secret elopement to Las Vegas with your high school boyfriend from the confines of a mental hospital.

Patrick frowned.

370

"No, it wasn't bad," I tried to clarify but was still at a loss.

"Was it at least an upgrade from how he was after I told him he was being kicked out of baseball?"

I nodded. "Definitely. He didn't punch a single person the entire time I was there."

He laughed nervously before recovering with the follow-up question I should have predicted, "Hey, so how is Micah anyway? Is he gonna be all right?"

"Yeah...I'm pretty sure he's going to be just fine." I chewed on my fingernail and then looked up to see Patrick no longer averting his eyes from me. His skepticism had helped him overcome his shyness, and he squinted at me sideways awaiting further details.

"So that means you've seen Micah?"

Now it was my turn to laugh nervously. Our conversation at Maplecrest had not eased his fears of Micah's and my relationship.

I knew I was bad at lying, but I was equally bad at concealing the truth. Bronwyn always knew when I was being dishonest, but she rarely cared enough about whatever I fibbed about to discover what I was keeping from her. Patrick, on the other hand, wasn't bored by my evasiveness; he was intrigued. Not that I could blame him. He'd been probing for answers ever since my face had healed so quickly from Westley's New Year's bashing it in. And while he was right to be dubious about a lot right now, I didn't know how to give him any one answer about me that wouldn't lead to a thousand more questions about Micah I wasn't prepared to explain.

The clock in the hall chimed, startling both of us, and my mouth worked faster than my brain to use the distraction to deflect Patrick's question. "I'd better get ready if we're going to make it to church on time."

He smiled, and for a moment, I felt my diversion had been successful. "You're right. You can fill me in about everything on the way there."

◆◆◆

371

Patrick was dressed more casually than I would have expected to be appropriate for a church service, but since just about all the assumptions I'd made about God had been proven wrong so far, I decided that he likely wouldn't strike me down for wearing a pair of nice jeans and a sweater to a Sunday service at Northridge Community Church. I grabbed the feminine equivalent to Patrick's outfit from my closet before locking myself in the bathroom to clean up and prepare for my impending interrogation.

What could I say to Patrick that would get him to back off of Micah? I'd assured him in the hospital that nothing was going on between us, but he was still suspicious. Not that I could blame him for thinking there was a lot he didn't know about our relationship—there was still a lot I didn't feel I understood about it either. And until Micah came back, things were likely to stay that way.

I finished getting ready without any epiphany on how to handle my most current conundrum, and when I emerged from my bathroom, Patrick was ready to talk.

"So, you said that you went to see Micah?"

I pretended to look for something in my jewelry box to buy myself a few extra seconds before answering his question. "Yup."

"So," he prodded, "how was he?"

I clipped on a pair of earrings and said the first honest word that came to my mind, "Hungry."

"Huh?"

"Yeah. He was really, really hungry. It's hard to eat with a broken jaw."

Patrick narrowed his eyes at me. "So, his jaw was definitely broken? There wasn't a misdiagnosis or anything?"

"No, not that I know of. Why?" I was relieved that the nature of his questioning had shifted from the direction I'd thought it was headed.

"That's too bad." He shrugged. "I read online that it takes anywhere from six to eight weeks for that kind of injury to heal. Looks like he's going to be hungry for a while. Right,

Cosette?" Patrick stared hard at me when he said this, and his scrutiny made me uncomfortable.

I chewed on my lip. He seemed to have an agenda I wasn't catching on to. "Yeah...I guess."

"I mean, it's too bad not everyone can have your genes." His eyes were still fixed on me. "You know, the kind where your boyfriend accidentally breaks your nose, and then three days later, you're as good as new."

I froze, the reality of our conversation dawning on me much too late.

"Unless...Unless that's not the whole story about how you got better so fast."

I held my breath.

This whole time, I thought Patrick had been suspicious of Micah's interest in me, that it was somehow a threat to my relationship with Westley. But I had underestimated Westley's best friend. He wasn't worried about us; he *had* believed me at the hospital. He knew better than anyone how solid we were as a couple. Patrick's reservations about Micah had nothing to do with his romantic intentions toward me. In fact, this wasn't really about me at all. Patrick was paying attention.

"Hmm..." I said as if he were suggesting something I hadn't thought of before instead of hitting the nail on the head.

"What are you hiding, Cosette? About Micah."

"Nothing." I cringed at his question, thereby sabotaging what little credibility my answer would have otherwise had.

"No." Patrick shook his head. "I'm not buying that."

I sighed. Was it too late to change my mind about going to church with him and crawl back into bed instead?

I was stuck, and I knew I had to say something. The more I tried to hide what truth I knew from Patrick, the more likely he would misinterpret my protection of Micah.

"All right, listen," my explanation began before I thought through what I would say next. "I know you think I have a lot of secret information about what's going on, but I don't. I've spent most of my time with Micah asking questions that I rarely get answers to. Do I agree that there is something unusual about him? That he weirds me out almost daily? That some pretty strange things have happened since he showed up? Absolutely. Do I know for certain anything else about him? No. So whatever pieces you are trying to put together about the enigma that is Micah Quinn, you can be sure I'm trying to solve the same puzzle." I prayed that my answer would be enough.

"I knew it! I knew you had to be wondering about him too!" Patrick looked relieved, and I in turn was also relieved—and surprised—that he'd been convinced we were on the same team. "Thank you for saying that. I was beginning to think I was going crazy."

"You're welcome," I accepted his thanks as if it were well deserved, but inside, I uttered my own gratitude at having escaped the hot seat.

"So what do we do now?" he looked at me expectantly, ready to hash out the mystery of Micah right then and there. "I really feel like we need to figure out who this guy is and what he has to do with your face getting better so fast. And what his deal is with Westley and—"

"Hold on," I interrupted. So far, our talk was going much better than anticipated, but I was not willing to push my luck. I needed it to end before I accidentally tipped Patrick off that I knew anything more than what he assumed I did. "*I* really feel like before we do any of that, we need to do what you came here for. Unless, of course, the invitation to church was really just a ruse to get me to talk about Micah?"

Patrick blushed. "No—it was legit. And you're right, we'd better get going." He pulled out his phone to check the time. "But we're still going to talk more about this later, right?"

"Of course," I assured him and then added what I knew was true. "At this point, it's unavoidable."

CHAPTER 65

Patrick must not have taken me at my word that our conversation would continue later because he brought Micah up every five minutes of our half-hour drive to the church.

"I feel like he just keeps showing up places he doesn't really have a reason to be. Like the funeral...and Trevor's party...and Maplecrest..."

"There's something about the way he talks to people, like he knows us all way better than we know him..."

"He reminds me of someone. I just can't put my finger on what's so familiar about him..."

I answered each of these comments with enthusiastic nods. None of it was news to me, but I was impressed that Patrick had noticed all that he had. And he'd also done some homework.

"No one I've talked to knows anything about him—where he came from, where he lives. And, unless he uses some online alias, he's not on any social media websites. And I can't find any evidence of a birth record in any of the local hospitals' public records."

To this, I responded with words. "Wow, Patrick. Stalk much?"

He laughed. "I know. I went a little overboard. But hey, I have a lot of free time now."

When we were about two miles away from the Northridge Community Church, there was a sports update on the radio, which, at least for the moment, was more interesting to Patrick than playing detective. The subject of Micah finally dropped.

We parked in the church's lot, which was nowhere near as packed as it had been the day of Julia's funeral, and walked in through the front doors.

The atmosphere of the church was different than I remembered it. Most of the cliques I saw chatting together in the vestibule looked cheerful instead of mournful. There were children running up and down the hallways wearing their winter coats like superhero capes, elderly couples holding hands and shuffling into the sanctuary, and almost every adult in my view held a paper, to-go cup of coffee with the church's name branded on its cooling sleeve by a trendy computer graphic.

We hung up our coats on hooks that lined the hallway before filing into the sanctuary and taking seats a few rows from the front of the stage.

"Is this okay?" Patrick asked.

"Perfect."

He sat and rested his elbows on his knees with his head bowed, and I assumed he was praying.

I also sat but focused my eyes forward on a drum set, keyboard, and several guitars littering the area where last I'd last seen a greenhouse worth of flowers and Julia Davis's casket.

This place didn't feel any more like a church to me today than it had then. Not that I had much to compare it to.

A few moments later, Pastor Brian walked out onto the stage followed by four others, who each took positions at the instruments.

"Good morning!" he shouted as he slipped the strap of an acoustic guitar over his shoulder. "Would you stand and worship with me?"

Seeing Brian excited me because I realized that Mrs. Holloway might be somewhere near. But as the crowd took their feet, I glanced around and didn't notice her.

The large screens that had displayed Julia's picture montage lit up with words, and the congregation, along with Brian and the band, began to sing them.

Around me some hands raised in the air, and some eyes closed. Patrick did neither of those things, so I didn't either. If he was new enough to the church not to know the motions to the song, I figured I was exempt from having to follow them too.

Westley was way more into sports than he was music, so I'd only ever attended a few concerts, and they had all been at an outdoor venue near Indianapolis. The crowds at those were mellow, as was the music. But there had been an enthusiasm in the audience from fans more devoted to the band than Westley or I. Standing there among the regular church-goers, I felt much the same as I had at those concerts: a little out of place and not sure what to do with my hands.

But unlike the debilitating discomfort I felt at Julia's funeral, I could handle this. I realized that I felt more now like someone new to something than someone who shouldn't be there.

After the third song, Pastor Brian spoke to the crowd. "It's great to have you all here this morning! Before you find your seats, take a moment to greet those around you."

Obediently, people all around us turned to each other, shook hands, and said, "Good morning!" and "God be with you!" Patrick turned away from me to greet those behind us, and I, wanting to participate in the parts of the service I felt I actually knew how to, looked for an empty hand to shake.

When one was finally extended to me, I grabbed onto it before looking up.

"Good morn—" I stopped my words short.

"Good morning, Cosette." Micah smiled radiantly. "Is this seat taken?"

I shook my head dumbly as he reached around me to shake the hand of an equally astonished Patrick before squeezing in to sit between us.

My first experience at a church was about to get a lot less comfortable.

CHAPTER 66

An older man replaced Brian at the microphone and directed us to turn in our Bibles to the book of Philippians.

Then, he began to talk—and kept going for a long time. Judging by the behaviors of everyone else in the room, this meant we were supposed to sit quietly and listen. This was a particular struggle for me considering a walking, talking miracle had just taken the seat next to mine, and I had a lot I wanted to say to him.

I guessed that Patrick—looking pale and stunned by Micah's surprise, injury-free appearance—had plenty of his own questions to unload too.

But before I could worry about what he was thinking, I needed to sort out my own feelings about what was happening. This was the first time I'd laid eyes on Micah since the garden where he'd been broken and starving to death, and seeing him here, his health perfectly restored...I was awestruck.

I believed that Micah had been healed through my prayers. I hadn't doubted that his strength had returned in those last moments before I'd transitioned back to the farmhouse. But seeing the difference with my own eyes was overwhelming.

There were no signs of any trauma on his face—no scar from my gouging him under his eye; no swollen, fractured jaw line; no spidery, blue markings. All that had been done to him had been erased, and his face had been resculpted to appear more beautiful than it had looked even before his injuries.

The pair of feet next to Micah's began to tap impatiently, and I shifted my eyes to Patrick to find he was also staring at Micah's face with disbelief. While I was sure both of our expressions read the same, we were having very different reactions to what had just happened.

But no matter the difference in the roots of our shock, Patrick and I were on the same page about one thing: the church service couldn't end fast enough.

CHAPTER 67

After forty agonizing minutes of waiting, the pastor ended the service, and without missing a beat, Patrick piped up.

"All right, what is going on?" He placed an arm on the chair in front of us and squared his body to signal our trio wouldn't be leaving with the rest of the congregation. "And don't tell me *nothing*." He spoke just enough above a whisper to compete with the murmur of the crowd dispersing. "Because this is twice now in two weeks that I've seen someone get their face bashed in one day and turn up looking like a movie star the next. What gives?"

Micah listened to Patrick's demands thoughtfully and waited before answering until the room was quieter. "What exactly is it about what you have seen that you don't believe is possible?"

"Um...all of it." Patrick became impatient with Micah's standard answering-a-question-with-a-question routine much faster than I'd been the first time he'd used it on me.

Micah took his time answering. "If you mean that, then you don't truly have the faith you claim to."

Patrick was exasperated, and he took a moment to recover his words. "What? Don't try to turn any of this around on me—this is about you." He wagged his finger at Micah. "And whatever secret you're trying to keep."

Micah's voice remained level, and he indicated our faces. "This is just as much about you as it is us because you profess belief, but you don't, actually, believe what you say you do. Otherwise, seeing what has happened to us wouldn't make you so defensive."

Patrick's mouth dropped open.

Micah didn't let up. "Once you've already ruled out the truth about what has happened as a possibility, then nothing I say and nothing you see will matter. When you can accept what you've already decided did *not* happen to us actually *did*, come talk to me. Until then, there's nothing I can do for you, Trick."

Patrick choked on his comeback.

Micah picked up one of the church's Bibles off an empty seat in the row in front of us and handed it to him. "There's a lot of stuff in here about miracles. There's also a lot about doubt. You might want to read up on both."

Patrick's mouth remained agape, but he said nothing.

Micah continued, "Now if you'll excuse us, I need to talk to Cosette about something." He motioned for me to follow him.

Patrick looked flummoxed. "I think I understand why Westley punched you."

Micah smiled. "Oh, I know why Westley punched me. That wasn't surprising. It's *you* I expect more from."

"You're just as cocky as he is." Patrick glared at him but then spoke to me. "You want me to wait around, Cosette?"

"I'll see she gets where she needs to be." Micah gestured me toward the exit. "We'll see you later."

I gave Patrick a squeeze on the shoulder. Having been talked in circles by Micah many times myself, I knew how he must be feeling. But my sympathy for him was not so great that it was going to keep me from leaving with Micah. I had my own questions that needed answers.

◆ ◆ ◆

"There's no way I'm as cocky as Westley," Micah muttered as I put my jacket on. "I mean, seriously? I'm living proof of what Trick already believes is true—miracles happen. I was calling him out on doubting God; I wasn't being cocky. Cosette, you don't think I'm cocky, do you?"

"Are you serious?" I asked him. "The last time I saw you, you were pounding fruit with a rock like a half-dead caveman and begging God to spare your life, and this is what you want to talk about?"

"No...not entirely." He smiled sheepishly. "I was also going to say thank you."

"That's not what I was looking for." We walked down the concourse toward the set of doors we'd dragged Westley out of after Julia's funeral.

"No, I know. But I still want to say it." His words were genuine. "I think I'm still coming to terms with it actually. I mean, I seriously thought I was going to die there and then...I didn't. All because of your faith. That's a lot to take in."

"Tell me about it," I agreed, remembering how I felt New Year's morning after realizing what Micah had done for me.

"Can I ask why you decided to do what you did?"

I found his question odd. "Well, I had to do something. You were in pretty bad shape. I couldn't just sit there and watch you die without trying to save you."

"Why not?" He shrugged. We'd arrived at the exit, but Micah appeared to want to finish our conversation inside. He crossed his arms and leaned against the window wall. "It's a fair question, right? I mean, you aren't a doctor or anything. You couldn't do a whole lot. Odds were that I was going to die. Barring some miracle..."

"I guess..." I started, though not totally satisfied I could explain myself. "I guess I believed that's what would happen. You would get a miracle." I shook my head as I spoke. "I don't know; does that make sense? Does the reason I did it really make that much of a difference to you?"

"To me? Not really." He smiled. "But bigger picture, I think it made a huge difference."

"What are you talking about?"

"If you feel like taking a walk, I'll show you."

I felt a flutter from within. "Would this walk, per chance, be in a garden?"

"Maybe."

I beamed. "Let's go!"

"Hold on, Cosette." Micah put a hand on my shoulder. "I'm glad you're excited, but there are a few things I need to tell you before we go."

My face fell. The last time Micah had given me warnings about the garden, he'd talked me out of going there altogether. "OK, what?"

"We're going to go back to some of the places I took you during our first trip to the garden, but there is also a part of it that will be new to you."

There was a hesitation in his voice that alarmed me, and my face showed it.

"I don't want you to worry about it." He was trying his best to reassure me. "But this place can be intimidating."

My thoughts went to the final pages of Avalon's journal. "OK." I was starting to get nervous again, but then I remembered something. "If it gets to be too much for me, all I have to do is let go of you and I can leave the garden, right?"

Micah smiled. "Exactly...except at that point, it won't be me you'd be letting go of."

I gave him a look.

"There's something you need to see, but I am not the one who is going to show it to you. You'll be with another guide."

This struck me as odd. "Sidona?"

"Hey, good memory," he said, as if she could have somehow slipped my mind. "Yes, Sidona."

"OK, that's fine. I liked her." I knew if I wanted to see the garden, I needed to consent to this. Though I was curious why this trip had stipulations the other hadn't, I knew it would be pointless to ask Micah about it. If whatever I needed to see could be explained to me, then we wouldn't be going to the garden in the first place.

And anyway, I reminded myself, I trusted him.

"All right, then." I took a breath. "What are we waiting for?"

CHAPTER 68

We needed a secluded place to transition, and since Micah had arrived at the church by means other than driving there, going to the farmhouse wasn't an option.

Most everyone had left the building by now, so Micah suggested that we could likely depart undetected from the place he had transitioned into the church: a stall inside the men's bathroom.

I shot him a look.

"What? I couldn't just materialize out in the open. I had to be inconspicuous."

I rolled my eyes, but then I thought about this some more. "Wait—how do you even know where you are coming and going to at all?" The complexities involved in transitioning were occurring to me in waves. "Like, how did you know you were going to pop up in the men's room at the church and not, like, a subway station in France?"

He chuckled as we walked down one of the hallways that jutted off from the sanctuary. "Practice."

"Yeah, OK, I get that. And don't get me wrong, I'm glad you've perfected at least some part of the process." I indicated my shins. "But I'm new to all this, and I'm going to need a little bit more of an explanation about the science of teleportation than 'practice makes perfect.'"

He laughed again, and by this time, we'd reached the restrooms. "Baby steps, Cosette." He poked his head around the corner of the men's room dividing wall and bent down to look under the stalls before motioning me to follow him in.

"You're going to have lots of questions today, I'm sure. I'll try to steer you toward the answers you need to know now."

I checked the hallway to make sure it was empty before ducking into the men's room behind Micah.

We entered the largest of the three stalls, and I locked the door behind us before assuming the position I had each time before a transition. Micah laced his fingers with mine, and I squeezed his hand tightly. "Try not to do any permanent damage to me this time, OK?"

"Got it," he replied.

"Good."

I stood there in the moments before the world melted away, my knees shaking with anticipation for what was to come, when I remembered something I thought I'd noticed right before the pain from my first transition had knocked me out.

Standing there, his arms wrapped around me, Micah felt familiar.

I suddenly shivered, and he released his grip on me.

"You OK?" He furrowed his brow and craned to the side to look at me.

"I'm fine, West," I mumbled, still trying to identify the feeling I was having.

"Are you sure?" Micah laughed. "Because you just called me Westley."

"I did?" I blushed. "I'm sorry. No, I'm fine, Micah. Just having déjà vu."

"All right," he said skeptically before resuming his position. "Let's go to the garden."

And then he began to pray.

CHAPTER 69

Our transition wasn't without turbulence, the way it had been when Sidona had taken me there, but Micah managed to bring me to the garden physically unscathed. While it took him a moment to adjust the sounds and smells of our surroundings, overall, my arrival was pain free.

"Are you hurt?" he asked anxiously after the environment had solidified.

"No." I shook my head, pulling an arm's length away from Micah to see all around me.

It was still daylight, and there wasn't anyone starving to death in front of me, so I felt like I had an opportunity to finally absorb the natural beauty of the garden without distraction.

But when I opened my eyes to find that we were standing in the middle of a wheat field, I was all but disappointed.

Not that it wasn't beautiful—the crops growing around us were hearty, lush specimens. It was just that I had spent my whole life surrounded by amber waves of grain, and there was much more to the garden I wanted to see than the part that looked like Middlebury 2.0.

"OK, where are we going first? The beaches we saw from on top of the sandstone? The mountains?" I pulled Micah along the path between the crop rows. "I want to see everything."

He resisted my leading. "Actually, today isn't about sightseeing." He smiled his half smile. "It's going to be more about education than recreation...Kind of like a field trip."

I grimaced. "So there's going to be some strict itinerary and a test at the end?"

"Something like that," Micah said before lifting me onto his back. "We've got some ground to cover." And with that, he set to running through the field.

His speed told me that there was provision being given to us, which meant he hadn't been joking about keeping a tight schedule. I kept my eyes opened as we rushed through the fields in case the scene changed to something more interesting than the farmland.

Eventually, we passed by all the ground crops and began breezing through a grove of trees, mostly fruit-bearing ones, though none nearly as impressive as the first-fruit tree.

It was amid a cluster of small, exotic-looking trees that Micah slowed his pace and allowed me to walk beside him.

"Anything about these look familiar?" He stopped beside one of the trees and pointed at its branches.

I stepped over for a closer look. "Oh, yeah. Olives," I noted. "Just like the ones you cooked for me at the farmhouse."

"Yep," he grinned. "Do you remember anything I said about them that night?"

I knew it was only a short time ago, but so much had happened in the days since then that it was hard to recall the details of our conversation. "Just that you grew them 'back at home.' Is that what you mean?"

"Actually, yeah. That is what I'm referring to." He patted the trunk of the tree. "That's what I do here. In the garden. It's my job, I mean. You know, when I'm not hanging out with you."

"You have a job here?" This was strange news to me, but all the same, I was excited to be learning more about the inner workings of the garden.

"Sure, work is important, Cosette. Everyone here has work they do."

Micah opened the door for me to ask a question I'd been wondering about since I'd first learned of this place. "OK, so obviously you are here. And somewhere there's Sidona. And at one point, at least, there was that Gabriel guy who brought

Avalon here. And you said before that there were others. So, where are they?"

"All over," he stated. "You just can't see them."

"*What*?" I gave an involuntarily shudder. "You mean there are invisible people hanging out all around us right now? That's so creepy, Micah!"

He shook his head and laughed. "You know it's not like that." He took a step closer to me as he explained, "It would be way too distracting for a visitor to see everything all at once. Kinda like how it's too overwhelming for your senses to feel everything we feel."

I saw his point but had my own. "You know what's also distracting? Feeling like you're surrounded by a bunch of ghost farmers."

He laughed again. "Man, you're becoming high maintenance." He extended his free hand for mine. "Here, I can give you a glimpse of them, but that's it."

I reluctantly accepted the offer, unsure if a sneak peek into the invisible would make me feel more or less creeped out by it.

Micah squeezed my hands, and a soft breeze began to blow.

The air was warm as it washed over me and trailed past us through the rows of trees. Then, as if faded into view by some cinematic special effect, I began to see with my own eyes what Micah had attested, and I gasped.

We were surrounded by people.

"It's OK," my guide reassured me. "It'll just be for a few seconds. Look closely, and then tell me what you notice."

I defied the instinct to bury my face into Micah's chest until the vision was over. I wasn't usually agoraphobic, but this wasn't a normal crowd.

The quiet olive grove, where we had moments ago stood in seclusion, was now bustling with life. People all over were working the fields, just as Micah had suggested—pruning branches, plucking olives, and carrying full baskets of the harvest to large wooden wagons parked in between the rows. They numbered in the dozens, both women and men, a mix

388

of races, and wearing dress the likes of which I couldn't differentiate.

And then, just as quickly as they'd faded in, the warm breeze and my vision of those around me departed. The grove became empty and silent once again.

Micah remained quiet for a moment before looking to me for a reaction. "So?"

Though I wasn't cold, the hair on my arms stood raised. "So, that was insane!"

"OK, but you had to expect to be shocked, right?" he rightly pointed out with a shrug. "This isn't your first time in the garden."

"True..." I agreed but was still uneasy knowing just how much was happening around me I was unable to perceive.

"Do you have any questions about what you saw?" Micah offered.

I looked at him sideways. He was being significantly more forthcoming with information than ever before, and this change of pace made me glad but also suspicious. "Of course," I stated. "But I'm only interested in asking them if I'm going to get answers."

He shot me a half grin. "Cosette, you act like I've been keeping secrets about this place to torture you." He went on to explain, "I promise you, that's not the reason I haven't always answered everything you've asked me." His grin changed to a smirk. "Although I'd be lying if I said I haven't enjoyed watching you squirm at times."

I rolled my eyes. "I'm thrilled my frustration could be so entertaining for you."

"Thanks," Micah chuckled, leading me along a path out of the groves. "But seriously, my hope is that someday when you look back on all this—me, the garden, how everything has been revealed to you in an order you can't yet understand— you'll appreciate just how intentional it's all been." He paused for a moment before adding, "And I hope you'll be able to forgive me."

"Don't worry about it." I brushed off his apology. I knew he hadn't been purposely trying to annoy me by withholding information. I was just excited that today seemed to be the day I would finally get some answers. "Eventually, I'll have a secret you'll want to know the answer to, and I promise to take extreme pleasure in making you wait for it." I laughed at my own joke, but Micah didn't join me.

Instead, he forced a smile, and it occurred to me that he may have been hoping for forgiveness for something other than taking pleasure in my pain. But at that moment, I had more pressing questions to ask than what he may or may not have been sorry about.

I wondered out loud to Micah about the people we'd seen. I wanted to know if they had always lived in the garden, or if they'd all moved there by the same mysterious means he had.

"Everyone here chooses to be here. That's really important to understand, Cosette," he stressed. "No one is born here."

I added this piece of definitive information about the garden to the growing file in my mind. I wasn't sure I fully understood why it was important, but I tucked it away for future application to questions that might arise when Micah wasn't feeling so chatty.

It was then I realized that the scenery had changed again. I'd been in such deep thought that I hadn't noticed we'd moved away from the groves and into the meadows of tulips.

After pausing to reflect on the fresh beauty before me, I continued with my questions. "So, is it possible that I know anyone else here? I mean, if this place is really that populated, there's a chance, right?"

Micah scratched his head and took too long to answer what I thought was a straightforward question. "You wouldn't recognize anybody."

"That's too bad," I replied. "I mean, it's a bummer only having you and Avalon to talk to about this place." I would have loved to know if there was someone else I could share my experiences with besides Micah and Avalon. They had both become dear to me, but there were unavoidable complications in those relationships that made spending time with them difficult. It would have been nice to have one garden-experienced friend who was both a verbal, non-depression-hospital resident and someone Westley hadn't tried to kill.

I gazed upon the acres of flowers bobbing like waves and felt like I was standing in an impossible sea of rainbows. This area of the garden felt familiar now, and I embraced the peace that gave me.

Micah interrupted my quiet appreciation for the flowers with a tentative question. "Can I ask you something, Cosette?"

My head bobbed up and down like the tulips, and he continued, "Why haven't you told anyone else about the garden?"

"Oh." It hadn't occurred to me to think about this. "Hmmm...I guess I wasn't sure if I was allowed to. Something this amazing seems like it should be kept a secret."

"Why?"

"I don't know..." My mind hung on that thought as we approached a clearing in the meadow.

Micah paused here and looked at me. "Please don't get mad at me for suggesting this, Cosette, but I wonder if the real reason you haven't told anyone about me and the garden is because of Avalon."

I wasn't mad at him for saying this, but I was confused. "What do you mean?"

"Well, obviously she told people about coming here," he pointed out, "and it landed her at Maplecrest."

"Yeah," I agreed. "I guess that did cross my mind. You know that if I told anyone what had happened to me, they might want to lock me up. Seemed like a pretty good reason to keep quiet."

"That worries me." Micah frowned.

"Why?"

"Because you shouldn't make a choice based on fear."

Micah's instruction felt very general, almost flippant. It also seemed like advice impossible to live by, one of those, "easier said than done" deals.

"OK," I started, my defenses going up. "But isn't it natural to explore the consequences of your options before making a choice? And anyway, what would I even say? It's not like I can put 'the garden' down on the short list for prom venue and not be labeled a whack job. What good does it do me to tell the world about it if all it's going to do is get me imprisoned in a mental hospital?"

"No good that I can see," Micah admitted. "But that doesn't mean it isn't what you are supposed to do."

"I don't really know what you want from me here, Micah." I threw up my free hand in frustration. "I don't necessarily feel like fear is a bad thing. I mean, fear tells me I'm not supposed to play with matches, and it's like you're telling me to set a fire."

"No," he corrected me. "Wisdom tells you that you aren't supposed to play with matches, Cosette. There's a difference. And all I'm asking is that in the future, you consider your motives when faced with a choice. We all have fear, but you can't allow your fear to become a roadblock when it should be a yield sign."

I sighed. "Yeah, well, wisdom also tells me not to go traipsing off into a magical garden with my partner from English class, but here I am. So, what does that say about me?"

Micah's eyebrows arched. "That's a good point actually." He grinned and patted me on the shoulder playfully. "Maybe I'm the one who needs to start trusting *you*."

"Yeah, maybe you do."

CHAPTER 70

"Not that I'm not enjoying the tour," I started, breaking a long silence. "But why is it that we can't transition into the garden to the spot we need to be in instead of clear on the other side of it?"

I held on tightly to Micah's back as he ran alongside the perimeter of the rooted moors.

"Hasn't anyone ever told you that getting there is half the fun, Cosette?" Micah responded in between patterned breaths. "There's joy in the journey. And, plus, it has given us some time to talk."

"I feel bad that you have to lug me around," I apologized. "I mean, I know there's provision and all that, but it still can't be easy."

While it was difficult for me to judge time in the garden, this was by far the longest piggyback ride I'd ever had. And much of the ground we'd covered had been off a beaten path, so Micah had to bear the brunt of a lot of uneven terrain in an effort to take us wherever we were going.

"You know, you're right. Why am I doing all the work?" His pace slowed as we cleared the last of the roots. He gently brought me down off of his back and onto the ground below us, panting to catch his breath. "Why don't you get us where we need to be?"

I gave him a look. "Very funny, Micah."

"I'm not kidding." He looked both amused and serious as he dabbed the sweat off of his brow with his shirt. "I think you can do it."

"How?"

He shrugged. "How do you think I do it?"

"I don't know. Practice?"

He laughed. "I know you're being sarcastic, but you're right. Kind of. But maybe a better word for what I've been calling 'practice' is really *discipline*," he noted before offering me encouragement. "It won't be hard. I won't make you carry me. We can run it together."

"Micah, I'm sure I couldn't even keep up with you running at a non-provision-enhanced pace, let alone a super-human-ability-infused one." I pictured trying to run a few steps alongside him with our hands clasped before he sped up beyond my ability and my body lifted off the ground like a windsock flailing in his dusty wake.

"So then, ask for your own provision-enhanced pace."

I stared forward. I probably should have thought of that on my own.

Micah offered his free hand to mine and remained silent as I attempted to pray.

"God...Help me get to where I need to be..."

◆ ◆ ◆

As it turned out, running with Micah was much more exhilarating than being carried through the paradise surrounding us had been.

Almost immediately after I'd finished my prayer, Micah took off into a sprint. At first, I'd struggled to keep up. In the morning, when I'd made my shoe choice of black leather dress boots, I hadn't anticipated I'd spend the afternoon running a marathon through the woods.

But, as I'd trusted, provision was made, and I soon found that my efforts to maintain the impossible speed Micah was keeping were greatly aided. We ran in three-legged-race fashion, bound together by our hands instead of our ankles, and we were *fast*.

Had I not been enjoying the thrill of our speed so intensely, I may have been disappointed that I wasn't able to take in the setting the way I had been when Micah was carrying me. But as it was, I didn't feel like I was missing out on the trees and landscapes that we passed by. I felt like I'd unlocked access to experience the beauty of the garden in a new way, and I loved it.

The sun was setting now, and with every passing moment, the speed we had available to us seemed to increase. When I noticed this, I asked Micah about it.

"Are we late for something?" I was breathing so hard that my syllables came out choppy.

He understood me anyway and responded in the same manner. "Must be." Then he added with a smile, "Quit slowing us down."

I held in my comeback to save my breath and ran so fast that I was sure my legs were going to detach from my torso and disappear over the horizon without me.

CHAPTER 71

We lay down on the grass to catch our breath.

I'm not sure how I knew we were where we were supposed to be, but I did.

We had crossed the unspoken finish line at the downward-slope of the grassy hill where Micah had shown me the light webs my first trip to the garden. As dusk finally settled in, I regulated my breathing enough to speak.

"So, what did you want to show me here?"

Micah was also recovering from our run and positioned his body closer to mine. "The same thing I did last time."

"OK." I had assumed this much. "Why?"

The darkness that had been chasing the sun across the sky had finally swept over our heads, leaving nothing but blackness above us.

"Remember earlier at the church when you asked me if it made a difference why you chose to heal me?"

I nodded.

"This is why I think it did."

Micah squeezed my hand, and the sky lit up with the brightness of day.

I shielded my eyes with my free arm and waited for Micah to readjust their intensity.

"I know you're special and everything," I remarked. "But how does light that bright not blind you?" The heat from the starlight warmed my arm through my sleeve. When it finally dimmed, I peeked through my fingers before completely uncovering my face.

"I've adapted to my environment," he joked, but I'd stopped listening to him.

My full attention was on the sky.

It was hypnotic. The stars astounded me as they had the first time I set eyes on them. The night was alive with movement, brightening and dimming like a million radiant Christmas lights.

Micah gave me a few moments to bask in it before dialing back my perception. "Cosette, are you ready for me to show you what we came here to see?"

My annoyance at him for censoring my view lasted only a moment before it was replaced by anticipation. "What is it?" I whispered.

Like he had the previous time, Micah manipulated the stars so that one section of the sky drew nearer while the rest faded to dark.

"Do you remember anything significant about your light the last time we were here?" Micah asked quietly, both of our sights transfixed before us.

"Of course," I answered, recalling my first experience on the hill. "It was flickering. But I don't think I ever really understood what that meant."

"Well, what do you notice now?" Micah asked, drawing a single light even closer to us than the rest of the cluster.

The star before me glowed with vivid radiance outshining all those around it. Its light was unwavering, steady, and unblinking. It seemed to have grown larger than I remembered it, and I couldn't be sure, but it looked farther from the light I'd thought to have been Micah's.

But the most significant change was the color of the star. It was no longer green. The light had transitioned from its former emerald to a brilliant blue, a sapphire hanging in the night.

Just like Micah's.

"Ours are the same," I whispered the only difference that I was sure mattered. "Why?"

"I don't know the reason it changed, Cosette. That's why I asked the reason you decided to try to heal me—I want to understand it myself," he said in awe. "I was hoping if I knew what made yours change, it would help me figure out why mine did."

I took in this new information. "You mean yours wasn't always the color it is now?"

"No, it couldn't have been." Micah shook his head. "None of the lights begin blue, and of the billions out there, only a small number become the color ours are now."

Billions? And *my* light was one of the few like this? I couldn't decide if this made my color change more or less impressive. But still, I was curious. "So what does a blue light mean?"

I could tell Micah was choosing his words carefully, as usual. "It means you have a decision to make. The same one I did a few years ago."

"The one that *changed everything*?" I remembered our conversation from English class.

He nodded.

I chewed at my lip nervously. I'd never been someone who welcomed even small changes to my life, so typically the prospect of an *everything* change wouldn't particularly excite me.

But this was different. This was the garden.

I returned my eyes to my light.

Regardless of whether I wanted more things to change, I knew a lot already had. Even if I were to let go of Micah's hand at this moment, I couldn't undo all that was different. And I was pretty sure I wouldn't want to, even it if were possible. And if I was being honest with myself, *that* was the change that scared me the most.

The sapphire burned its shape into my sight so that when I closed my eyes, I could still see its outline.

"Are you ready to hear more?" Micah asked carefully.

"I don't think I'll ever be ready," I replied honestly. "But I'm willing."

A slow smile spread across his face, "OK."

All of a sudden, I sensed we were no longer alone.

"Greetings," a woman's voice called out gently. "Welcome back, Cosette."

Sidona stepped out of the darkness and into view, and I wondered if she'd been with us the whole time and I just couldn't see her.

"Thanks," I said self-consciously, considering just how big my invisible audience might be.

"I am pleased to be meeting you under less dire circumstances than previously," she said evenly. "Speaking of which, I wish to express my gratitude for what you did for your friend." The corners of her mouth turned up when she glanced at Micah. "I have seen many miracles in my time here, but that may be one of my favorites."

I blushed at her compliment, and Micah cleared his throat.

"Sidona is going to take over from here, Cosette. There's somewhere else I need to go now."

Although he had warned me that I'd be handed off at some point during this trip, I was surprised that it was happening in the middle of a seemingly important and unfinished conversation.

Sidona set her eyes on him. "So you have not changed your mind then?"

I was surprised when Micah wouldn't look at her to answer. "You think I'm handling this all wrong, don't you?"

"You know that my opinions are meaningless in this matter, my dear," she answered him without expression.

My eyes shifted back and forth between them as they jumped into the second half of a previous conversation I had not been a part of. "Does someone want to fill me in?" I prodded both of my guides.

Micah stood, and I joined him, but he ignored my question. Instead, he extended our clasped hands out to Sidona and addressed her. "You could at least tell me if you think I'm making a huge mistake."

"It is not my approval you should be seeking." She steadily raised an open palm to us.

He stared at her hand and then back at ours and sighed.

"Micah, what's going on?" I quietly demanded. His anxiety was contagious; it had been rare that I'd seen him so unsure of himself. Even when he was dying, he'd been so determined about every action he made; he'd faced death with more certainty than he showed now.

Micah's eyes pleaded with Sidona's.

"I will not take her hand unless you give it." Her words were firm.

He closed his eyes and nodded slowly. "I know."

"What's stopping you?" If it had been his plan all along for Sidona to take over for him, I wanted to know why he doubted it now.

He opened his eyes and looked at me for a while before speaking. "Do you remember when we climbed up to the top of the sandstone together and looked out over the garden?"

This question caught me off guard. "Of course I do. Why?"

"Do you recall what I warned you about?"

I felt guilty whenever I remembered the way that conversation had ended, so I tried to avoid thinking about it altogether. "Not really."

His face fell. "I told you why you shouldn't put your faith in me."

This hint jogged my memory. "Oh, yeah." Now that I was speaking the words, I didn't like where our conversation was headed. "You said it would be easy for me to decide you weren't a superhero."

"Well, it's true. I'm not," he said seriously. "But I'm also not a villain. I just want you to remember that after tonight." He paused as if he wanted to say more, but instead, he released a tired sigh.

I found this answer unacceptable. "If you feel like you have to say that, then I wonder if you even believe it yourself."

Micah's eyes were pained, but he didn't argue. Instead, he placed my hand into Sidona's, and by the time I'd recovered from the shift in energy, he was gone.

After waiting enough time to know he wasn't immediately coming back, I spoke to my new guide.

"Well, I guess he was right," I declared. "Ditching me like this isn't exactly what I'd expect from Superman." I wasn't used to being disappointed in Micah. He always seemed to take the high road, but his abrupt hand-off and departure from the garden before we'd finished what had seemed a highly significant conversation felt like a cop-out. "I don't suppose you'll tell me what he meant, will you?" I inquired of my new guide as we walked in the darkness. "Why will I think he's a villain?"

"I do believe he claimed not to be a villain," she corrected me. "Not that he was certain you would think him one."

"Whatever." I sighed. "Either way, I don't know why everything's always so cryptic. I can't get a straight answer from him to save my life."

"I am fairly certain that he already did save your life," Sidona reminded me. "Does that not account for his credibility?"

Though I was mad, I knew she had a point. "Yes, it does."

"I know that your journey has been very confusing to you, my dear," she went on. "But I can attest that it has been equally complicated for your friend. He has met some very unique challenges along the way, and he has been most faithful to handle them with your best interest at heart."

I sighed again. "I'm sure that will all make sense to me someday."

"With hope," she said encouragingly, "that day will be today."

CHAPTER 72

I hadn't been able to see much of my surroundings since Sidona and I departed the hill, but even in the darkness, I could feel that something around us was different. We had set out back in the direction from which Micah and I had come, but nothing about the environment was familiar to me.

"Are we still in the garden?" I asked hesitantly.

"We are," she assured me but then added, "just not as you know it."

Sidona's words instantly conjured up the images sketched in the final pages of Avalon's journal. We walked on a while before I gathered the courage to ask about them. "Are you taking me to the flames?"

My guide froze in place. "How do you know of the fire?"

Her question confirmed mine, and I felt a strange victory that I'd guessed where we were going. "I met someone who's been to the garden. Her name is Avalon, and she was brought here by a man named Gabriel..."

Sidona listened to me explain about Avalon and her sketchbook without interrupting.

"Your lives have been uniquely woven together," she commented when I finished talking.

"Yeah," I agreed. Then, hoping to gather some inside information about Gabriel, I added, "So, do you know him?"

Her tone was intentionally blank. "I am aware of what this man has done."

"Do you know when he's coming back for Avalon?"

There was quiet between us for so long that I thought Sidona was ignoring me.

"I do not."

Her reluctance to talk about Gabriel made me want to know what more she knew about him. "Why did he take her to the fire?"

"He was attempting to heal the girl's scars."

I hadn't expected this answer. "With fire?" At first, this was both a frightening and impossible thought. But then, I reasoned, so was Avalon being disfigured by a piece of fruit.

"Yes."

I didn't doubt she was telling me the truth, but something wasn't adding up. "Gabriel told her that the only way she could be healed was to live in the garden?"

Sidona nodded. "Yes, that is also true."

"OK..." I urged her for more details. When she offered none, I grew impatient. "I don't understand what one has to do with the other."

As soon as the words left my lips, I remembered something Sidona had told me before, the reason Micah wouldn't transition from the garden to save his life when he was starving to death: *Your friend paid a great price to live in the garden...*

"Fire serves many purposes, Cosette."

It was my turn to be quiet. Of all the uses of fire that I knew, not appearing anywhere on the list was "admission fee for paradise." But the more I thought about it, I could see how being burned alive might be a cost that Micah wouldn't want to have paid in vain.

"So, what then?" I wondered aloud. "You have to walk through fire to live in the garden?"

"That is an oversimplified explanation," Sidona cautioned. "We are not discussing an ordinary fire, just as our home is not an ordinary garden. The flames do not consume us to ashes, my dear. They are not meant to kill those invited here. The fire *does* require a sacrifice, but only that which is necessary." She spoke with extreme reverence when talking on this subject. "It is a holy fire. One which purifies. Through its flames, our bodies are made right for our home."

"So that's why I can't be alone in the garden." I was grateful to be tracking with Sidona. "I haven't been through the flames."

"That is correct."

"Does it hurt?" I asked, already knowing the answer. "Walking through the fire?"

Though it was dark, I could still see the sorrow in Sidona's eyes. "The pain is unequivocal, Cosette." She paused long enough for me to shudder. "But, fear not. Humanity was designed in such a way that we cannot truly remember physical hurt. It is impossible for us to relive the bodily sensations we experience. Once it is felt, and the body has healed from it, it is gone."

As I considered this, my fears eased. I hadn't allowed myself to think about Westley dropping me down the stairs because of how painful that night had been, but Sidona was right—my mind wasn't avoiding what happened because it feared revisiting the physical pain of my nose breaking. Even if I tried to remember the impact of my face hitting the Greenes' staircase, I couldn't recreate the sensations I felt as it was happening. I only had the knowledge that it had hurt then. It didn't hurt me now.

But that didn't mean it wasn't excruciating to think about; Westley dropping me down the stairs had been the harbinger of all the bad that had happened over the past few weeks. And while I recognized that good changes had occurred in the aftermath of my fall, I couldn't forget the bad ones. Evidently, humans were not designed with immunity from reliving emotional pain the way they were physical.

"If this information is enough for you to decide you do not wish to continue our journey, please speak that now, and we will not go," Sidona offered.

I considered this. "Does that happen often?" I imagined what it would be like to have come this far and reject my invitation before I fully understood it. "Do people ever get to this point and then just leave without even seeing the fire?"

She pursed her lips together. "Absolutely, Cosette."

This surprised me maybe more than it should have, perhaps because my recent string of bodily injuries had afforded me a unique perspective. After enduring *a lot* of pain over the last few weeks, the prospect of more—even "unequivocal" pain—wasn't enough to deter me from continuing on. I'd survived my nose being broken twice, my legs burned to the bluest degree, my ribs broken, and my lungs punctured, and I was still standing. Miraculously, I acknowledged, but standing nonetheless. So, after all that...physical pain seemed a small price to pay for paradise.

"I still want to go," I said with as much confidence as I could. "But let's hurry before I change my mind."

◆ ◆ ◆

We continued walking in the inky darkness. Because I could see nothing of our surroundings to distract my thoughts from our intimidating destination, I filled the emptiness with words.

"I feel like I've learned a lot in this visit to the garden," I announced. "But I think I have more questions now than when it started."

"There will always be more to know, Cosette," Sidona replied. "You are mistaken if you believe any of us here have all of the answers. I have lived here a long time, and there is much that I still do not know."

"Really?" I was both comforted and disappointed by this. "Like what?"

She thought for a moment. "For instance, like most of my garden brethren, I do not understand why I, in place of anyone else, was invited to live here."

"Oh." I frowned. "I was hoping that would be cleared up during orientation."

"No, I am afraid not."

I used the moment to ask another question that had been nagging me. "So if I don't get to know why I was invited, do I at least get to know what I'm here to do?" Micah had told me about the importance of work in the garden, and after seeing a glimpse of the operating fields, I doubted that *I* was being asked to come solely to hang out and sip first-fruit juice by the tree. "I should add that I have zero experience in the agricultural realm."

"I have no doubt that you possess skills beneficial to our needs," she assured me. "But you must remember that occupation and purpose are not synonymous, my dear. Each of us has work to do in the garden, but our greater purpose lies in our interaction with the world."

"Like performing miracles and saving people's lives?" I could see how those things were valuable.

"Yes, for example," she agreed. "But our tasks are not limited to such grand gestures. In all that we do, our intentions are the same. We are an elect group of missionaries, Cosette. One with extraordinary privileges."

"Yeah, I'm a fan of your work." I pointed to my chest. "But if all those people I saw in the garden are also hanging out in my world, why don't I ever hear about the stuff they do?" It seemed unlikely that everyone else would be as mum as I had been about my healing. If there really were these kinds of miracles happening every day, I couldn't understand why I'd never heard about them.

"You did, all the time," Sidona assured me. "But you did not notice the provisions because you did not believe them possible. So often, people disregard our work as coincidence. They call us 'guardian angels' because they are grateful for our interventions in their lives, but they do not understand that the work done through us is by God because of his love for them."

I thought of Westley, and I was grateful—grateful to Micah for saving me from him and grateful to God for caring about Westley enough to send Micah to us.

"So how do we convince people of that?"

"Cosette, my dear," Sidona stopped walking and placed her hand on my cheek. "We cannot convince. We can only demonstrate. And as soon as you learn to find relief rather than frustration in that fact, the better off you will be." In the darkness, I could see the faintest outline of her face, smiling knowingly as she spoke. "But before that can happen, there is something I must show you."

"What's that?"

"The flames, my dear. We have arrived."

CHAPTER 73

I only knew Sidona was still with me because we were holding hands. The world was so black I couldn't tell if my eyes were open or shut.

I felt warmth, but unlike with the healings, this heat came from outside my body.

"Are we near the fire?" I called into the darkness.

I heard no answer, and the air grew hotter with each passing second.

"Turn around."

The words were so quiet I couldn't be sure they were Sidona's, but I obeyed them anyway.

I about-faced, and my guide followed suit.

"I can feel the heat, but I can't see anything," I declared to my guide in case she had forgotten to adjust my senses completely.

"Patience."

I waited in silence as the temperature climbed.

Eventually, the darkness began to thin. From behind me, rays of light rose from the ground, casting our shadows onto the stone floor beneath me. They grew taller, and the brightness amplified as if the sun were rising behind my back.

When our black outlines had stretched so long that they no longer looked like human silhouettes, the tops of their heads bent upward and continued to grow vertically in the distance. The light had thrown our shadows against a tall, metal structure ahead of us. I recognized it immediately.

The gate.

And because I knew where Avalon had been when she saw it, I was certain that the sun was not what I had turned my back to. My mind had only seconds to connect the gate's detail to the sketchbook before the voice called out again. "Turn around."

Sidona squeezed my hand tighter, and together, we turned to face the flames.

Before they came into full view, my knees weakened, and I fell to the ground alongside my guide.

So much more than in the empty cornfields of Middlebury, and with greater intensity than when I'd stood at the base of the towering first fruit tree, I was broken by my own insignificance.

The fire was massive. Its flames were silver and iridescent. It burned from no source and released no smoke.

Beyond that, it was unspeakably terrifying.

It wasn't until I heard the voice speak again that I understood that both Sidona and I were shrieking.

"Silence."

My mouth closed.

Unable to scream, my body involuntarily reacted to the fear that shook its every atom.

Tears. Sweat. Vomit.

I was drenched in my own terror.

But though I could hardly stand to be in the presence of this fire, I could not look away from it. My bones could have shaken to dust, and I would have remained. I would have stayed until the voice ordered me away. Or called me forth into the flames. Or struck me dead.

There was something familiar in the fire. It drew me in, captivated me entirely. This light—I recognized it. It was the power behind all of my provision, the true source of the peace in the healings. And here, in its presence, I was complete. Whatever the invisible force that fed these flames was, it was both all that I feared and all that I loved. It was *everything*.

It was holy.

"Turn around."

The voice spoke with such authority, we cowered at the sound.

Still on our knees, we again faced the gate.

A moment later, all was black.

CHAPTER 74

Sidona and I held one another and sobbed together.

Grief. Aching grief, like I'd never known, pierced my hollow shell.

"Why couldn't we stay there?" I bawled, utterly ungrateful for the beauty of the garden in the sunrise. "Why were we sent back here?"

My guide attempted to comfort me, but she too was anguished by the separation. "It is the way it must be, my dear. You have more to learn before you can truly choose what you want to do."

"That's impossible!" I protested. "Nothing could change my mind now!"

"Dear, sweet Cosette..." Sidona struggled to regain her composure. "Your passion moves me. Forgive me for always underestimating you."

When I realized she could not be persuaded to break protocol, I changed my plea. "Tell me what I'm missing." My heart pounded in my ears. My determination was fueled by the adrenaline coursing through my veins. "Then take me back." Then, I reminded her, "I already know the cost. And I'll pay it. I am not afraid of the pain."

"No, you do not know the cost entirely." She was calmer now; there was more caution in her tone. "You understand only the physical act of the sacrifice, not the extent of its consequences."

"So then explain it to me," I demanded. Each second that passed away from the flames felt torturous. "I'm begging you!"

Sidona was hesitant but ultimately relented.

After a deep breath, she began, "Cosette, we cannot predict who will become eligible for citizenship of the garden. Since the beginning, we've watched the skies for patterns, and there are none known to us. But while we do not understand the light webs completely, we know that they do not change at random." She fixed her jaw before continuing. "There is much diversity among all of us here, but we know we are linked together, without exception, by a few essential commonalities."

I was anxious to learn any part of why I'd been invited to the garden. "OK, what are they?"

"I must tell you that these are mere observations, not rules that have been imposed upon any of us. The possession of these qualities does not earn anyone a right to this place. It is not *we* who choose those who are invited."

I nodded that I understood, still shaking.

Sidona continued, "There exist four distinctions we have determined that are true for all invitees." She continued to draw out her explanation by pausing for long breaths, and I was unsure if she was still trying to calm herself or if she was reluctant to tell me the truth. "The first is that they must not either intentionally or by circumstance have a direct role in the ending of someone's life."

My eyes narrowed. I hadn't known what to expect her to say, but it hadn't been that. "OK, great. So I won't be in the company of murderers."

"You misunderstand the cause for this, my dear." Sidona shook her head. "For the same reason, a visitor may also not be responsible for creating life or even rescuing a life that would have otherwise ended."

"Oh." Then as I considered the two additions to the list, I gasped. "But what about what I did for Micah?" Had healing him somehow voided my invitation?

"Such an act performed to save a citizen of the garden does not disqualify you, Cosette."

I was relieved, though I didn't understand the exemption.

"The final qualification has been a source of complication in your case."

"What is it?" Without specific effort, I'd managed not to kill, save, or parent another human being. It didn't seem likely that a fourth item on a list like this would be something I was in danger of having done accidentally.

"At the time of transition, no person may have spoken a vow of marriage."

I looked at my engagement ring and was completely confused. "What? Why?"

"To be eligible for citizenship in the garden, these things must remain true of you. Otherwise, your decision would change the world too radically."

I suddenly felt as clueless as if I were talking to Micah. "What you are saying makes no sense to me."

"The sacrifice at the fire is more than a physical one, Cosette. The cost is much greater than you have counted it."

I was suddenly suspicious of what lay between the lines of this list of rules. "Are you telling me that I can't marry Westley if I want to come to the garden?" This matter had not once arisen between Micah and me, though he knew of my engagement, so therefore, I decided, it could not be true.

"It is more than that." Sidona closed her eyes. "If you choose the garden, Westley will no longer know you. Nor will anyone else." Her words were nonsensical, but she continued to speak them anyway. "To accept this invitation, you must relinquish your future as you have planned it, Cosette. Along with the past you have lived. This is the reason scars are healed by the fire. They erase the scars because they erase your history." She was solemn. "By making the choice to come to the garden, you are removed from existence. All that you lived would be unlived. All done, undone."

I blinked dumbly for a few seconds as I decoded the gibberish Sidona was spouting. "No. This isn't true..."

"It is, my dear." Sidona was gentle. "To do the work before us, and for the benefit of those we leave behind, and for many other reasons both known and unknown, it is true. It is merciful and true."

"Then start explaining some of the known reasons!" I demanded, my fear of the truth of her words now changing to anger.

She looked as though she'd expected my reaction. "Cosette, life on earth is connected together so intricately. Each individual person, through intention and circumstance, affects so many others. Only those whose absence would not alter too significantly the fate of others—their living and dying, their *eternity*—are invited to the garden."

"OK, fine!" I accepted these conditions. "But marriage has nothing to do with that! Why can't I marry Westley and bring him here with me?"

"You have an earthly perspective of marriage, Cosette," she informed me. "It is a covenant before God, two flesh becoming one. And as Westley is not eligible for the garden, as one with him, neither would you be."

The dam holding back the realization of all Sidona was saying finally broke. "Why?" I choked out through loud, angry sobs. "Why didn't someone tell me this before?" I felt my hopes draining out of me—dreams I'd only begun to imagine, dissolving to dust. "Why, after all I've been through and all I've seen, do you tell me that it's impossible for me to be a part of any of this?"

A tear rolled down Sidona's cheek, and she wiped it away quickly. "It is not impossible, my dear. It is just a most difficult choice. And I believe that is precisely why your friend revealed it in this way."

A new wave of rage washed over me when I thought of Micah. "You call him my friend, but he's not!" All this time, he knew what he was doing, what I'd eventually be asked to sacrifice. He knew how much I loved Westley, and he'd hidden that from me all along. He knew I wouldn't be able to choose the garden without giving him up. "A friend wouldn't have lied to me like this!"

"He never lied to you, Cosette." There was no room for arguing in Sidona's tone.

"He betrayed me, and that's worse!" I fell into a hopeless fit of tears. "Why? Why did he have to bring me here when he knew I would never be able to choose it?"

I no longer desired the flames. Or the garden. I would never again dream of tasting the first fruits. It was over. All of it. Dead. A cruel tease.

"It is not my place to judge his methods, my dear, but your friend was doing the work asked of him. He did not decide your invitation. He was just selected to guide you through it." Sidona raised our hands to eye level. "From the history he has with you, he determined that this was the only way you could see."

"Don't pretend like what he did to me was for my benefit!" I screamed. "If he knew me at all, he would have known that no matter what the offer, I would always choose Westley!"

"I understand your devastation, my dear. I have been where you are now," she reminded me. "But please allow me to say this: perhaps he knows your heart better than you do yourself."

"Why?" I argued. "Because he so easily tricked me into trusting him?" I was disgusted with myself. With Micah. With everything.

"No, that is not at all what I meant," she soothed. "But if you are as stationary in your position as you claim, and there exists no possibility for you to choose a life here in the garden..." She held aloft our clasping hands. "Why have you not let go and exited it?"

◆ ◆ ◆

I didn't care that I was on the floor of a men's room. I lay there and cried until my tears ran out.

415

CHAPTER 75

If anyone saw me storm out of the church that Monday afternoon, they didn't interfere.

I mindlessly scoured the parking lot for my car until I realized I hadn't driven it there, and then I just started walking.

It was snowing, of course. But I didn't care. Disillusionment had made me unable to feel the cold.

Or anything else.

I wandered slowly past the cemented property of the church to a patch of trees. The snow fell in such large, heavy flakes, and the wind blew over my footprints faster than I could make them. There was no path in front of me and no trail behind me. No proof I'd ever even been there at all.

I sat on a frozen stump of a tree that was as hollow inside as I was.

"I'm sorry." The wind carried my voice away. "I know you're disappointed in me," I confessed. "But I'm disappointed in you too."

I had no tears left to cry, so I just stared dry-eyed at the white earth.

◆◆◆

Twenty-seven missed calls and fifteen frantic text messages. All of them from Patrick.

I responded to them collectively with a text of my own.

If you can come get me, I'll explain everything.—CM

I sent him my location, and Patrick's Jeep tore into the parking lot twenty minutes later and screeched to a halt at the edge of the pavement.

I stood to meet him and shook off the inch of snow that I hadn't notice accumulate on me while I sat wallowing in my sadness.

"Are you OK?" he shouted as he ran to me.

"I'm fine," I chattered.

Patrick practically carried me to the passenger's seat. The heat from the cab stung my face, and I suddenly realized that I was freezing. This must have been apparent to him because he immediately stripped me of my soggy coat and bundled me in a dry hoodie and blanket from his backseat.

"I was worried sick," he scolded me. "Literally. I couldn't even go to school."

I'd forgotten about the existence of school. "I'm sorry."

"What happened yesterday, Cosette?" his demand for answers began.

"It's a really long story, Patrick."

"Well, I'm a really good listener," he responded sincerely.

I faked a smile. "That's good to know because I just can't do this anymore." I inhaled the artificially warm air from the heater deeply into my lungs to thaw my vocal cords. "You were right, Patrick. My nose didn't just get better on its own..."

He said nothing as I talked, and I didn't want to look at him in case it was evident by his face that he thought I was insane. Every word out of my mouth sounded ridiculous, I knew, but once I started telling my secrets, they all came pouring out. I couldn't carry the burden of the truth alone any longer.

I told him everything. About Westley. About New Year's Eve. About the garden and Micah's healing. About Avalon and Sidona. Even about the fire. And then, as a finale, I pulled off my boots and revealed the scars on my shins.

"I know that all of this sounds crazy," I admitted as I wrapped up my confessions nearly an hour after I'd begun them. "And I understand if you don't believe any of it, but I swear to you it's the truth." I held my breath and looked at him, awaiting his judgment.

Patrick was as white as a sheet, his eyes wide and unblinking.

I wanted to give him all the time he needed to react, but each second he was silent tortured me. "Listen, I know that it doesn't make a lot of sense—"

"No, it does." He buried his face in his hands.

"What?" Patrick's reaction baffled me, and I forgot that I should have been grateful that he believed me at all. "How in the world does any of what I just said make sense to you? It doesn't even make sense to me!"

"It makes sense because Micah was right yesterday—I know better." His words were wrought with emotion. "Cosette, I didn't tell you this, but on New Year's Eve, you were *really* bad off. I tried to play it down, but you looked *horrible*. I'm no doctor, but I've seen broken noses in baseball, and there was no doubt in my mind you were going to need surgery before you'd look like a human being again."

I shivered, remembering the catcher's mask and bloodied sock.

"When I saw you at school less than two days later, without so much as a scratch on you, I knew immediately that you'd been healed. I *knew* that, somehow, there had been a miracle," he confessed. "But as time passed, I talked myself out of it. I told myself that stuff like that doesn't really happen, and your nose must have just looked worse than it really was."

A stab of guilt pained my heart. Patrick hadn't entirely talked himself out of believing my miracle; I'd helped him do that by concealing the truth.

"The same was true yesterday when I saw Micah. I knew what had happened, but I wouldn't let myself believe it." He raised his head and revealed his eyes were damp. "But he knew that's what I was doing, and he called me out on it."

"The healings are one thing. You basically have the proof that they happened," I countered, apprehensive of how easily

Patrick accepted my story. "But you *did* hear me talk about the garden too, right?"

"Yes," he whispered. "And without the healings, I might not be able to believe a place like that existed. But how can I pick and choose which miracles are possible and which aren't?" He made a good point as far as logic could factor into this discussion. "I'm not saying that I understand how a garden the way you described it could exist, but I *want* to believe that it does." He looked hopefully at me. "I want to go there."

I had to remind myself why I didn't. "Well, maybe you can take my place because I'm not going back."

"What?" Patrick was shocked. "Why not?"

He must have misunderstood why I left. "How could I now that I know I'd be giving Westley up?"

This was the first time since I'd started talking that Patrick looked at me like I was crazy. "Cosette, you *did* just tell me that Westley killed you, right?"

I groaned. "Yes, but you can't blame him for that. He was sick and not himself, and besides—it's been undone." It hadn't occurred to me that Patrick would hold anything I'd told him against Westley. "You know he would have never done anything to me intentionally."

"That I'm sure of," he agreed. "But if this opportunity wasn't so important, then why was your life spared that night? You were given a second chance to live out an amazing life that the rest of us couldn't even imagine as possible. You're being offered the chance to experience God in a way nobody else even knows about. And you're going to throw it all away for your boyfriend?"

"I thought Westley was your best friend?" I was appalled by Patrick's betrayal. "How could you tell me to just abandon him like that?" I was beginning to regret telling him anything.

"I don't see it that way, Cosette," he tried to explain. "Think about it. You have no guarantees in this life. It's fleeting and fragile, and then it's over. You know the truth about God more clearly than anyone else on the planet, and you have a direct invitation to be used by him every single day for the rest of your life—and you won't even consider it as an option."

I looked down and clenched my jaw.

"If Julia would have come to me and told me what you just did..." Patrick's voice cracked at the mention of her name. "I would have told her to go."

"That's easy for you to say now, Patrick; you already lost her." I didn't care if I sounded insensitive.

"You're exactly right, Cosette." He nodded. "I did lose her. But not to being some awesome missionary. And I didn't have my memories of her erased. She died, completely out of the blue. No warning. And I will carry that pain of our separation for the rest of my life. Given the two options, I think it's an easy choice."

"So, just because Westley and I will eventually die, I might as well just leave him now?" How could Patrick be so irrational?

"No, but right now, you have the chance to do something great with your life that you are not going to have if you marry Westley. And if down the road anything happens to you two, will you be able to live with the regret of not choosing to go to the garden?"

"OK, so now you're implying we're going to break up? Which is it, Patrick? Is it going to be Westley dying or leaving me that sends me spiraling into regret that I didn't abandon him when I had the chance?"

We stared each other down. Looking back, I wasn't sure how I'd expected Patrick to react to everything I'd been through, but I certainly hadn't anticipated it pitting us against one another over Westley.

"Are you ever going to tell him about all of this?" he asked quietly.

I already knew my answer. "There's no point in that now, is there? Since I'm not going back."

"I know that's what you said," Patrick acknowledged. "But what if telling him isn't about that? What if what you've been through can help Westley?"

I'd already debunked this thought in my own mind. "I'm pretty sure that telling him the God he doesn't believe in asked me to forsake him isn't going to get him in church on Sunday."

"Maybe not that part," Patrick admitted. "But what about your healing? What if knowing what he did and how God saved you can help him accept that he is not in control of everything? What if God can use what happened to help Westley get over his grief about Julia?"

I held my tongue long enough to think through his suggestion. I was angry about a lot right now, and my mind was already made up about the garden, but what if Patrick was right? I knew that Westley thought he had his "sickness" under control, that all he needed were the sleep aids to be normal again, but history told me otherwise. The medication was treating only the symptoms of Westley's struggle to deal with his own mortality. Until he accepted the truth about God and was freed from the responsibility he'd claimed over Julia's death, he'd never heal. And the implications for Westley not getting better were frightening for someone who had experienced firsthand the way his grief could manifest itself.

I hadn't told Westley about Micah healing me before because I was afraid. I feared that he wouldn't believe me, or if he did, that he wouldn't be able to forgive himself for what he'd done to me. And maybe at the time, that had been the right decision.

But it didn't feel that way anymore. And I wouldn't allow my fear to be a roadblock where it was meant to be a yield sign.

"Visitation starts in an hour. I'll pay for your gas if you drive me down."

CHAPTER 76

The roads were terrible, and the weather forecast on the radio predicted that the wintry conditions would continue throughout the week.

"The ride home should be better than this," Patrick assured me. "The roads will be salted by then."

"Yeah," I mumbled, not in the mood for small talk.

He took the hint. "Should I leave you alone?"

"No, it's fine." I sighed. "Just a lot on my mind right now."

"I can imagine," he sympathized. "My head is swimming too."

"Oh," I realized, "I guess I didn't really give you a chance to ask any questions while I was unloading everything on you."

"No, it's OK," Patrick forgave me. "I've just been piecing something together myself that you probably already figured out."

"Really?" I wondered. "What's that?"

"Well, I'm trying to figure out who Micah is," he confessed.

I raised an eyebrow. "What do you mean who he is?"

He looked at me from the side of his eye. "Like, who he was before he lived in the garden," Patrick clarified. "I mean, you knew him then, right? But when he left, you would have forgotten him or whatever?"

I gasped so loudly that Patrick slammed on his brakes. "*What's the matter?*"

How could I be this stupid and live? How had I *not* realized this?

"Cosette? What's the matter with you?" he repeated.

"I didn't think of that," I mouthed through my shock.

He was right, though. I knew he was. In the way that something could make sense because it didn't, this did. And because I accepted that, I could see now what I didn't before. All at once, staring me in the face.

Micah said he had come "back" to Middlebury. He knew me at the sporting goods store when I didn't recognize him. At Julia's funeral, he knew who Westley's family was without anyone introducing them. He drove me home after his truck broke down without any directions.

But there were bigger clues I'd ignored.

Like Eastlyn. Somehow, she remembered Micah from before.

And Sidona. More than once, she had mentioned how my history with Micah had affected his decisions about my journey.

"I told you I thought it was weird how he seemed to know more about people than we did about him," Patrick reminded me. "I guess it makes sense why he called me 'Trick' now."

I nodded as I ticked through every piece of information I could confirm about Micah. "He knew us for sure, Patrick." My heart was pounding. "He most definitely did."

CHAPTER 77

"Hey, Eastlyn, it's me." Westley's sister answered her phone on the first ring. "Got a minute?"

I held my phone away from my face and put her on speaker.

"Yeah, what's up? Did you hear from Micah?"

"Actually, he's exactly the reason I'm calling." I was glad to find he was still on her mind. "I did see him, and he's going to be all right." She was relieved to hear it. "But I've been thinking a lot about what you've been saying about him, and I'm starting to think you're right. I feel like I know him from somewhere too."

"Augh! Finally!" she squealed. "I knew I couldn't be the only one!"

"Yeah, the only problem is I can't place him either."

"Well, funny you should call me today," she confided in a lowered voice. "Because I had a dream about him last night."

I glanced at Patrick, and my cheeks instantly blushed. I debated taking her off speakerphone. "What kind of dream?"

"C'mon, Cosi—it was G rated," she teased. "Actually, it seemed so meaningless that I wasn't even planning on telling you. But, hey—maybe you'll be able to make sense of it."

Patrick and I exchanged a look.

"What happened?"

"Well, it took place at senior prom. I was there with my date, Tyson Magyar, and this girl from school I didn't know very well was there with Micah."

I remembered Eastlyn's date only through the pictures the Greenes had taken before the dance, but I doubted that mattered.

"So I know that I'm not there *romantically* with Micah, but I am still very aware of him. You know, like he's somehow still very important to me."

I glanced at Patrick, who mouthed, "Ex-boyfriend?"

I shrugged.

"So anyway, instead of Tyson and I being announced prom king and queen, they call my name and a boy's name I can't quite hear, and when I look up, they're crowning Micah. I remember being really happy, and I went to congratulate him, but all of a sudden, he was gone. Like, vanished gone."

I could feel the hair on the back of my neck rise. "Then what happened?"

"I'm not really sure. At this point, I don't know if that dream ended and a new one began, but after that, until I woke up, all I remember was running through the woods with my dog." She laughed. "Pretty random, huh?"

"Sounds like it," I said, but I knew it couldn't be. "So that's it?"

"Yeah." Eastlyn sighed. "Except that ever since I woke up, I can't shake the feeling of how much I miss Micah." There was a legitimate sadness in her voice. "Which, I know, you'll never understand."

It made more sense to me than it could have to her. "I believe you, E. I really do."

◆ ◆ ◆

The rest of the drive to Maplecrest, Patrick and I dissected every fact we knew of Micah to determine who he might have been.

Patrick remained true to his original assumption that Micah and Eastlyn had dated sometime before he transitioned to the garden. And while I didn't want to rule that out as a possibility, the answer seemed incomplete to me. There was definitely something that connected Micah to Eastlyn and the rest of the Greene family, but I wasn't convinced what that was.

By the time the elevator delivered us to Maplecrest's fourth-floor waiting area, I had refocused my thoughts on the task at hand. I could decide who Micah was later.

We checked in with the receptionist, who picked up her phone to announce our arrival to Westley.

"Do you want me to come too?" Patrick offered. "I have no problem telling him that I believe you were healed."

"Thank you." I appreciated his support. "But I think I should try alone first." Westley had been under the microscope enough at the hospital that I wanted to give him what privacy I could to react to my news before bringing in an audience.

As we waited, I could feel myself growing nervous about the impending conversation. When I'd left Westley two days before, it was to plan our elopement. Now the wedding was four days away, and I hadn't confirmed a single detail.

Maybe I could use that as my icebreaker?

"Hey, honey, I'm sorry I didn't book a chapel, but I thought before I did that I should let you know that you kinda murdered me the other night in your sleep, and before we get hitched, I wanted to tell you about it."

Westley emerged from the dormitory hallway looking nervous. "Is everything all right?" He quickly made his way to us, wrapped an arm around my waist, and then kissed me on the forehead. "Why are you two here? Did the school decide it wasn't enough to rob me of my senior baseball season? Are they going to keep me from graduating too?"

"No, man." Patrick greeted Westley with a hug. "We just missed you."

He lowered his guard but still seemed more jittery than was normal. "Well, you won't have too much longer. Four days and counting."

I smiled though I was slightly saddened Westley hadn't changed his mind about checking out prematurely.

"What's in four days?" Patrick was confused.

"What? Have I been gone so long you forgot my birthday?" Westley joked and then went on to explain his exit strategy—*sans* wedding plans—to a disapproving Patrick.

"Hmm. Well, that's great." He feigned a supportive response, but I knew this announcement was more confirmation to him why I needed to tell Westley about my healing. "Cosette, didn't you say you needed to talk to Westley in private about something?"

"Thanks, Patrick."

His lack of subtlety was not lost on Westley. "Cosi?"

Patrick stayed behind, and an anxious me led an anxious West to an empty corner of the cafeteria.

"Is this about Micah?" he asked as we took our seats.

I couldn't hide my surprise. "What makes you say that?"

He shrugged. "I just figured you heard about all the trouble he tried to cause around here this morning."

"Micah was here this morning?" I asked before I'd allowed myself time to understand the full meaning behind this revelation.

Micah had been *here* this morning. At Maplecrest, visiting Westley, while Sidona did his dirty work for him in the garden. This was the "someplace else" he'd abandoned me for, and I was at once worried why he'd kept that a secret.

"What did he say to you?"

"What *didn't* he say?" Westley rolled his eyes, dug into his pocket, and then unfolded two photocopies onto the table. "He brought me these." The copies were the x-rays of a human face profile belonging to, according to the name in the corner of the papers, *Quinn, Micah*. "Do you see this?" Westley slid one of the x-rays closer to me and pointed to the figure's mouth where a dark, jagged line extended from the back molars to the ridge of his jawbone. "This shows what happened when I jacked Micah in the face four days ago. That crack in the white there? That's a jaw fracture. A pretty bad one." He gave me time to let the image sink in before directing me to the other photocopy. "This one is time stamped from this morning, and...can you believe it?" His question was both rhetorical and sarcastic. "Not a trace of an injury."

Of course, I *did* believe it, but I still found myself sweating nervously as I examined the papers side by side. "Wow," I responded with the one syllable I felt was both honest and ambiguous. Before I revealed what I knew, I needed a better idea of what exactly Micah had come here to prove.

This disappointed him. "Don't you get what's going on here, Cosette?"

I was so sick of trying to blindly navigate conversations without a road map. "You should probably just fill me in on what you're thinking."

"I'm being lied to," he revealed disgustedly. "The x-rays are fakes. Or at least the first one is."

"What?"

"Think about it, Cosette." His instruction hinted of condescension. "My doctor's convinced that the only way I'm going to truly get over my grief is by subscribing to belief in a higher power. So when he found out about what happened with Micah, he fudged the x-ray to make him look worse off than he really ever was." Westley spoke to me as if I were missing the obvious. "You were there, right? You know that I didn't hit him *that* hard." He pointed again at the crack. "Everyone knows that an injury as serious as a broken jaw can't heal overnight, so they set up a second set of x-rays and had Micah come in person to convince me 'God' saved him through some miracle." Westley was proud of his deductions. "But I'm not falling for it." He leaned back in his chair with his arms folded signaling that he was done talking about the subject. "So, how's the wedding planning?"

"Wait. Back up." Whether he wanted it to be or not, our conversation was far from over. There were so many holes in Westley's conspiracy theory that I didn't know which to poke at first. "You're accusing Micah and your doctor of teaming up to trick you into believing in God so that you'll recover faster?" I wanted him to hear how crazy he sounded. "Why on earth would they do that?"

Westley didn't appreciate me challenging him. "Doctors like results. Maybe I'm not progressing the way he wants, so he's trying to make it happen."

He had to have known how weak that argument was. "And Micah?"

"I don't know, Cosette." His frustration showed. "Everybody has a price. Micah seems like a poor kid, so it probably didn't take much money get him to go along with it all."

Now, I was disappointed. "C'mon, Westley—"

"I'm not saying I understand why they're doing what they're doing, Cosette," he barked. "But obviously things didn't go down the way Micah is claiming because that would be impossible."

I wanted to scream. "So, what? It's more reasonable to believe that Micah was pretending to be unconscious and fake bleeding from the mouth on the waiting-room floor? That doctors are forging medical charts and bribing patients to fool you into believing in miracles? That whatever happened when you hit him—and yes, I was there, and you did hit him *that* hard—left not so much as a bruise?" I forced myself not to sound as discouraged as I felt.

"Sure," he remarked snidely. "And you can go ahead and throw a unicorn and a leprechaun in there, and I'd still believe that over what they're trying to force on me."

All the hope I'd brought with me to Maplecrest crumbled into dust. "Why, West? Why are you so willing to accept these irrational explanations over the possibility of a miracle?"

He was just as let down by me as I was by him. "Cosette, I am not so pathetic that I need to believe there is some invisible man in the clouds saving and smiting people. And even if there were some divine being in the universe, why the hell would he spend his time fixing Micah's jawbone? Seems pretty insulting to assume God would waste a miracle on something so lame when there's world hunger to solve."

Westley's words cut me. He believed these lies that he was feeding himself, and I doubted there would be anything that I could say or do to change that.

And before the garden, I wouldn't have tried.

I'd already been to the crossroads once that day, and I'd chosen Westley. I was angry that I'd had to make a choice, afraid that I'd made a disappointing one to God. Still, I couldn't let all I'd loved and lost in the garden be for nothing. Regardless of my choice, and even if God was done with me, I wouldn't deny all that had happened.

"What if Micah isn't the only one who's experienced a miracle?" I treaded these waters lightly.

He looked bored of the subject. "What are you talking about?"

I sat forward and grabbed his hands, startling him into eye contact. "New Year's Eve."

CHAPTER 78

"So he just left?" Patrick was confused.

"Yeah." I was too. "He let me finish talking, and then he stood up and went through the back doors to the patient rooms."

Both of us knew Westley well enough not to expect this reaction. It wasn't that he was confrontational all the time, despite what his behavior from the last month might suggest. Westley was just never speechless.

Patrick put a hand on my shoulder. "At least he heard you out first." He was trying to be encouraging. "And it doesn't sound like he punched anyone."

I forced a smile. "At least there's that."

As we waited for the elevator, I analyzed Westley's abrupt exit. While I was reluctant to make assumptions, the more I thought about it, the more hopeful I found myself becoming.

From the sounds of it, Westley had argued with Micah about the miracle he described. Even though he'd come in prepared with medical evidence and a doctor witness, West wouldn't even entertain the idea that Micah could be telling the truth.

This wasn't how things between the two of us went down at all, and I had my guess as to why.

The day after I was healed, Westley had been trying to remember what all the alcohol from Trevor's party had blocked out. He had questions: How did he get to the farmhouse? Why did my face look so perfect? What had Bronwyn heard the night before that made her believe Westley had hurt me?

At the time, I'd offered him no answers. In fact, I hid what truth I knew from him. I'd thought I was doing it for his protection, but instead, I had just given him an out—time to convince himself that what he thought might have happened didn't. Today, I righted that wrong. I filled in all the blanks that I had to believe were still nagging at him. I'd answered all the questions he'd asked me that day and probably a lot more that he didn't.

That would have been a lot for anyone to take in, even Westley. And until I learned otherwise, I chose to believe his reaction was, in its own way, an act of God.

"Oh before I forget." Patrick pulled a paper out of his pocket. "I met your friend. The one with the scars."

We stepped inside the elevator.

"Avalon was here?" I don't know why this surprised me, considering she was a resident at the hospital.

"Yeah, she wanted me to give you this."

I unfolded the page:

Micah came here. He told me everything. Don't hate him, Cosette. He's not who you think he is.

Avalon's words stole my thoughts away from Westley.

"Did she say anything to you about this?" I asked, handing him the note to read.

"Not much of a talker, that one," he reminded me with a look and then glanced at the page. "Hmm."

"Yeah," I agreed with his monosyllabic response. "So who do you suppose he thinks I think he is?"

"Not a clue, but whoever that is, you're wrong. So think again."

I did. And I kept thinking about it until I passed out in Patrick's Jeep. I couldn't calculate how long it had been since I'd slept because many of those hours had been passed in the garden, but I knew it was a long time. I was grateful that Patrick didn't press me to play detective anymore that night.

He woke me when we pulled into the driveway and promised he'd be in touch the following day. I thanked him for all he'd done and said good-bye. It was late enough when we got to my house that most of the lights inside had already been switched off, and I made it into my bedroom without being noticed.

As I changed out of my two-day-old church clothes and stuffed Patrick's hoodie into my hamper, I noticed the white tulips in the vase on my nightstand table. Both the one Micah had given me at the farmhouse and the one he'd placed on my car at Maplecrest were still alive, looking as fresh and perfect as the day I'd received them.

Of course, that should have been impossible, I knew. Westley's roses hadn't survived nearly half as long shut up without clean water and sunlight. Yet these remained as beautiful as ever.

I considered throwing them away. My decision was made, after all—I wasn't going back to the garden. Keeping the tulips around would only serve to remind me of the life I didn't choose while I was trying to live the life that I did.

In that moment, I was grateful that the life I'd chosen came with one more day's suspension from school. I felt I would need the time to truly mourn what I was giving up by not going to the garden. While on some level, my choice had been an easy one, it wasn't as if I was staying here because I found the alternative undesirable.

In fact, I'd been willing to pay almost any price to experience it fully.

I let the flowers be, deciding that it didn't hurt to keep them around as long as they lasted and then crawled into bed and tried to sleep.

◆ ◆ ◆

I regretted napping in Patrick's Jeep. The ride home had recharged my brain just enough that it could no longer be tempted by the promise of sleep.

After about an hour of tossing, I gave up and powered on my computer. Where I'd left things with Westley, I wasn't positive he would think himself sane enough to check out of Maplecrest on Friday as planned, but assuming he did, I figured I should plan our wedding.

Three websites into researching Las Vegas honeymoon resorts, I was so engrossed that when I heard the knock, I answered, "Come in," without realizing two important things. The first was that it was the middle of the night when no one—especially Grandma, who would have been the only person considerate enough to knock before entering—was awake. The second was that the knock had come from behind my own bathroom door.

It creaked open wide enough for a voice to ask, "Are you decent?"

Had anything resembling this scenario occurred a few weeks prior, my reaction would have been entirely different. But after weeks of constant shocks and impossibilities, I'd become desensitized to the element of surprise.

I closed my laptop and faced the voice. "So bathrooms are the new farmhouse, huh, Micah?"

"You're speaking to me." He stepped into full view in the dim lamplight that lit my room. "I'm taking that as a good sign. After talking with Sidona, I had no idea what to expect when I saw you." He raised his voice slightly above a whisper, and I noticed right away that he sounded as if he'd been crying. "I'm so sorry. I screwed everything up."

"Sorry if I can't attend your pity party, but I'm too busy planning my own, Micah," I commented, refusing to commiserate with him. On the wide spectrum of emotions I'd felt toward him since we'd met, currently, I was indifferent. There were answers he owed me that I was no longer willing to wait to hear, and only after I knew them would I decide if he was worthy of my sympathies. "If that is even your real name..."

"So you know then." He chewed at his lip. "Avalon told you."

"No, she didn't. She told me that *you* needed to tell me," I retorted. "But even before that, Patrick and I had already figured out that you probably know us better than we know you."

Micah was surprised. "You told Patrick about me?"

"Isn't that what you wanted?" I reminded him.

"What did he say?"

"That I should go to the garden," I stated flatly. I was annoyed to be on the answering end of the Q&A again.

Micah was sad. "Sidona told me what you said. Why you won't."

"If it was any surprise to you that I am sticking with Westley, you haven't been paying attention," I pointed out.

"No, Cosette. I've had my doubts the entire time," he revealed. "I know how much he means to you."

This answer infuriated me. "Then why did you even take me to the garden in the first place? Why subject me to the pain of giving up something I never could have had to begin with?"

He ignored my anger and continued, subdued as before. "You have an opportunity to do something amazing with your life. I wasn't going to keep that from you because it put you in a difficult position." He sighed. "I'm sure my guide had doubts about my choice too, but I'm glad she was obedient to her mission anyway. Choosing the garden was excruciating, Cosette. But I don't regret it for a single moment."

I folded my arms across my chest. "Then you must not have had as much to lose as I do."

Micah looked like he was restraining himself. "If you really believe that, then I'm not the only one who hasn't been paying attention."

I tried to brush him off, though I was instantly curious about what he meant. "I'm not in the mood for your mind games, Micah."

"That's what I don't get, Cosette. This isn't a game." He was resolute. "I stopped trying to hide who I am a long time ago."

I looked him in the eyes and was struck by the same sense of familiarity I'd felt during our transitions to the garden.

435

I immediately shook it off. "Well, if what Sidona said is true, you wouldn't have to try very hard to hide it, right? I have no chance of remembering you anyway."

"Yes, that's right. The life I lived has been undone. There's no way for you to remember about me what I remember about you..." He paused. "But still, there's something about me you recognize."

I shivered—how did he know that? The closer I felt I was getting to learning Micah's identity, the more hesitant I was becoming. "Why do you say that?"

"You called me Westley," he said slowly. "That wasn't accidental, Cosette. There's a reason. You must have realized *something*."

The implication of his statement confused and alarmed me.

I *had* called him that. At the time, I just thought it was a slip of my tongue, but Micah was suggesting it was more than that...

Why had I called him *Westley's* name?

My mind raced.

From the beginning in English class, I'd noticed Micah's charm and confidence. He was easy to talk to, and I quickly came to trust him. Those were things also true of Westley—qualities that had been exclusive to him and his role in my life, actually.

So was that it then? Was Micah just familiar to me because he shared some personality traits with my boyfriend?

That was not what he was suggesting. Instead, Micah seemed to be implying the opposite: that the reason he reminded me of Westley was because of who he was before he chose the garden.

But I was either too dense or too blind to guess who that was all on my own.

"I give up, Micah." I threw up my hands. "Please, just tell me who you are..."

He ran his hand through his hair, looked away from me, and drew in a deep breath. "I'm sorry," he began. "I'm sorry that I didn't find a way to tell you sooner...but you were right, Cosi. My real name isn't Micah Quinn."

My heartbeat filled the silence as he got up the nerve to finish his confession.

"My real name is Northrop. I am Northrop Greene."

CHAPTER 79

"My parents were so 'clever' when they named us that even though Greene is a pretty common last name, I couldn't come back as Northrop—especially since they gave my name to the dog." He chuckled. "Poor McNally."

I needed to sit down.

I was sitting down.

I needed to *lie* down.

"Westley's actually why I chose the name Micah." A small smile crept upon his lips. "When we were kids, he was obsessed with this little orange Hot Wheels car, and I used to hide it from him in my pocket. He'd chase me around the house trying to get it back, yelling, 'My car! My car!' My parents thought he was calling me 'Micah.'" He laughed. "Pretty soon, it stuck. He called me that forever..."

I knew that car. It was in almost every picture of Westley taken before he was six.

"I took Quinn from Mom's maiden name." He pointed beside me on my desk to the framed wedding invitation Eastlyn had given me. "Dequindre."

I couldn't speak. I couldn't blink. This was a dream. The crazy kind where animals talked and I couldn't run because my body was filled with lead. Pretty soon, a penguin would waddle through my bedroom door, and we'd go fight crime together. Then I'd wake up and laugh at how ridiculous this all was.

Micah or Northrop—I had no clue which he was at the moment—reached inside his pocket and pulled something out, which he immediately offered to me.

438

When the lead in my arms prevented me from accepting it, he held a photograph in front of my face.

"This was in my wallet when I transitioned," he said. "It was taken when I was nine. Westley was seven."

The picture was of four children standing around a large, novelty compass against the backdrop of a kitschy store. Miniature versions of Eastlyn, Southeby, and Westley were positioned around it clockwise next to the oversized direction markers that corresponded to their initials—east, south, and west.

At the top of the photo with his head sticking out from behind the compass was a blond boy I did not entirely recognize, though he smiled just like the others. The giant, red orienting arrow pointing due north singled him out.

I shifted my focus from the boy in the photograph to the one holding it, refusing to admit they looked to be one and the same.

"You can't be West's brother..." I mustered only a whisper of protest. Patrick and I had decided that Micah's life had been intertwined with ours before his transition, but I couldn't accept that *this* had been how.

But while my logic fought to reject his claim, the rest of me argued that Micah being Westley's brother would reconcile many of the questions I had about him that I'd never been able to answer.

He'd recognized me at the sporting goods store because...

He knew *Westley's* parents at Julia's funeral...

He knew where I lived...

I stared at him now with new eyes—his blond hair, the shape of his face. I could see it now. More Southeby than Westley, but it was there. My consciousness was catching up to what my subconscious had been trying to tell me when I called him Westley.

Micah was a Greene. I couldn't deny it.

But I did anyway. "Nice try." And then I accused him. "You're just trying to trick me. You think if I believe you gave up the perfect life of a Greene kid, then it would make me giving up Westley seem like less of a sacrifice. This is just

439

your last-ditch effort to convince me to change my mind about the garden, so you won't fail your mission." I impressed myself with how quickly I'd created this lie.

Micah was hurt, but he didn't miss a beat. "I thought conspiracy theories were Westley's thing, not yours, Cosette." His words were heavy with disappointment. "You know, since this whole thing started, I've been trying to figure out why *I* was asked to be your guide. But it had to have been me, right? For you to have a fair shot at choosing the garden, you had to be taken there by someone who had given up Westley Greene and lived to tell about it."

The way he trivialized my relationship made me indignant. "Correct me if I'm wrong, Mic—whoever you are, but there's a big difference between losing a sibling and losing the love of your life."

He was equally angry with me for trivializing *his* relationship. "Maybe you think it wouldn't mean much to you to lose your sibling, Cosette, but I loved my brothers and sister more than you'll ever understand. I still do. Even though they don't even have a clue who I am." His words were pained, and he struggled to finish speaking them. "Even though my own brother hates me so much that he almost killed me..."

And with this, the boy standing in front of me dissolved into his own anguish.

I fought to hold my ground. I wanted to stay angry at him, to convince myself he was a liar, just like Westley had done.

But I couldn't. Because he wasn't.

It all fit together. As much as I couldn't bear for his story to be true, I knew it was.

Micah was Northrop Greene. He'd paid the price and chosen the garden, and in doing so, given up his existence. He was undone. Unknown. Unborn.

He was the real-life George Bailey, a stranger to the people he loved the most.

And now that I finally allowed myself to accept this, I could withhold my sympathies for Micah no longer.

"I'm so sorry." My own tears began to fall. "I believe you, and I'm so, so sorry."

My heart was broken. I wrapped my arms around Westley's brother, and together, we cried.

CHAPTER 80

We stayed that way a long time, but when he was ready to talk, I listened to Micah eulogize the life he'd sacrificed.

Northrop Greene was eighteen years old when he made his full transition to the garden. Before that time, he was the star pitcher on the Camden High School baseball team and an honor's student who had planned to study biology at Purdue University—the college he would have attended that fall with Eastlyn, his twin sister.

Another riddle was solved. "Is that why she remembers you when no one else does?" I asked when Micah exposed their relationship, which in the context of the crazy I now lived in, made Eastlyn's connection to him easier to understand.

"I don't know. There's no record of any other twin in the garden, so there's not a precedent to compare us to." He shrugged, looking sad. "I'm not even convinced she does remember me, though. She may just sense I'm familiar because I remind her of Southeby and Westley."

I confidently disagreed with him. "Trust me—she remembers something. She's even dreaming about you now. Something about senior prom..."

His eyebrows rose. "What did she say?"

I detailed Eastlyn's dream to Micah, and I could tell by his reactions as I recounted it that it held more significance than a meaningless dream would have.

"Was she upset when she told you?" Micah was concerned. "Did the dream seem to bother her at all?"

"No. In fact, she was almost happy about it," I recalled. "She seemed glad to have fit you into some context, even if it didn't make total sense to her. She's been pretty psycho trying to figure out who you are."

"E's dreaming about prom night..." This cracked the sadness his face had frozen into, and I was glad to give my friend a moment of reprieve from his grief. "When I made my decision to leave, I was grateful that no one would remember me. In many ways, I feel like that's one of God's greatest provisions in his design of the garden—that the sacrifice is known only by the person who makes it. Everyone left behind is spared from feeling the loss. If it had been any other way, I'm not sure I could have put the people I loved through the pain my disappearance would have caused."

I remembered Julia's funeral, the thousand mourners gathered together to grieve her death, and I agreed with Micah's conclusions.

"But it's hard though..." he admitted. "There've been times the last couple of years when I've missed people *so* bad that I've wondered if I would have felt better if I knew they were out there, missing me too."

I ached. "What did you decide?"

He sighed. "That it wouldn't. That I'm glad for them." He thought some more. "It's nice to know Eastlyn has some remnants of memory of me—especially after coming back here and knowing what it feels like to not exist to the people I spent my whole life with—but I'm not sure I want her to have any more than that. She doesn't have the faith that could help her to understand why I did what I did. Why I left her."

I thought about this and then asked, "Am I supposed to be able to understand it?"

"Yes." He shot me a knowing look. "You do understand it. And you want to make the same choice I did—you told me that yourself the first time we were in the garden." He was quick to point this out. "You just won't let yourself choose it."

Micah's analysis was partly true but also unfair. I clarified my position again. "Of course I want to live in the garden, but I can't if it means I have to give up Westley."

"You are looking at this decision all wrong," he countered patiently. "Choosing the garden means you'd be separated from him—not that you have to stop loving him. You *never* have to stop loving Westley." Micah looked away from me. "You're only thinking of this choice in terms of what you're giving up if you leave instead of considering what you sacrifice by staying where you are."

My mind flashed to the garden, the fire...

I quickly shoved the thoughts away.

"I don't want to live anywhere if it means I have to be separated from Westley," I stated. "I'm sorry you don't understand that."

"I do understand how you feel. You forget, Cosette. I've known you a lot longer than you've known me," he reminded me. "You've always had this amazing faith and devotion inside you—you've just never applied it to anyone but my brother." Micah stood up from his seat and then knelt before me. "Until you came with me to the garden." He reached for my hand and touched it to his jaw. "Your faith saved my life. Your light isn't burning blue by accident."

While my hand rested on Micah's cheek, I recalled every second surrounding his healing. I'd never been as afraid as I was when I thought he would die or more ecstatic than when I knew that he would live. I understood that God was the one who had healed him, but it was because of the choice that I made to try to save him that he stood in front of me now. And in that moment when I allowed it to, *that* made me feel like I did have a purpose in my life. That maybe, my life *could* have greater meaning than the plans I was making for it.

My eyes moved away from Micah's to the wall behind him where Westley's—from the dozens of pictures of him that lined my wall of accomplishments—stared back at me. Reminding me.

I pulled my hand away from Micah's face. "Maybe it wasn't an accident," I agreed with him. "Maybe it was altogether a mistake."

CHAPTER 81

It was shortly after that Micah returned to the garden. He said he wanted to go there to pray for direction about what to do next for Westley, but I could tell our conversation had further dampened his spirits.

"This conversation isn't over," he told me, discouraged. "As long as you are eligible, we're going to keep talking."

I nodded and felt secretly guilty that Micah knew nothing of my plans to elope with his brother. If he had, he would have realized—like I had—that my eligibility would be ending in three days when I spoke my vows to Westley.

We said our good-byes, and as I watched Micah transition from my world into his, my heart involuntarily sank.

As much as I didn't want it to be true, I longed to follow him. I yearned for the music, the flowers, the tree...I wanted to rest on the hill and stare at my sapphire in the night sky. I wanted the fruit and the fire.

But—I reminded myself—I wanted Westley too.

I looked down at my engagement ring; its brilliant emerald twinkled even in the dullest of lamplight.

Three more days.

◆ ◆ ◆

When I finally woke up the next day, Tuesday was halfway over. Despite having been unconscious for eight full hours though, I wasn't rested. My sleep had been filled with too many dreams.

Some had been of the garden—my real-life experiences mixed with all I'd still wanted to do there—my subconscious mourning the loss of all that wouldn't be.

Those dreams were bittersweet.

The rest of them were, not surprisingly, about Micah.

Now that I knew who he was, I couldn't stop thinking about all he remembered that no one else did. I dreamed of Christmases, a stocking for Northrop hanging from the mantle, and of Greene family dinners with another place setting at the table. It all felt so real, so very possible. But at the same time, his addition to these memories was also so...irrelevant.

I understood now that part of why people were chosen for the garden was because of how little their current life impacted the world around them. Had Northrop done anything so important in his life that he'd altered the lives of others "too radically," then he wouldn't have been eligible in the first place.

But there was no way this rule could have applied to me too. If no one else, my existence had impacted Westley's too much for it to have no long-standing effect if I were to all of a sudden not have been born.

Hadn't it?

I couldn't decide if I should be more insulted that this was why God had chosen me for the garden or if I should feel as though the way I'd lived my life up to this point had been an insult to him.

So I decided *not* to think about it and took a shower.

The hot water revived me enough to start mentally working through my plans for the day.

I decided that I should drive down to see Westley. Even if I wasn't ready to talk about what he believed or didn't believe about Micah's and my healings, there were other things—like our wedding—we needed to discuss, and I was eager to feel like I was making progress toward that future. I could spend a few hours this afternoon finalizing plans for Vegas and get to Maplecrest at the start of visiting hours.

446

Also, I wanted to see Avalon. I realized it might be the last time we could be together in person for the recognizable future, and there was much I had to tell her that I wanted to face-to-face.

I used a towel to dry my hair off before wrapping it around my middle and opening the bathroom door.

An unpleasant surprise awaited me in my bedroom.

I jumped when I saw my sister sitting at my desk. "Geez, Bronwyn, don't you ever knock?" I asked before remembering I needed to cover my shins.

As I pulled my robe on over my towel, I hoped I'd be able to come up with a believable explanation for my scars by my wedding night. "Oh, those old things? Those have always been there!" was presently my only alibi.

"Can I help you with something?" I offered her as I regained my composure. Then realizing the day and time, I followed up with a suspicious, "Why aren't you at work?"

It wasn't until she spoke that I noticed how solemn she appeared. Or that my laptop was opened to the tab of flights to Las Vegas I'd bookmarked the night before.

"So you're just eloping without telling any of us."

I was caught.

Westley had warned me to tell no one of our wedding plans, and "no one" probably meant my sister more than anyone else on the planet.

But she knew. And even if I could think of another plausible reason for why I would be looking to book a flight for two to Las Vegas, there would be no way Bronwyn would believe it.

So, I didn't even try. "Since when do you care what I do?"

"Since now." Bronwyn's face wore its trademark scowl, but she sounded more hurt than angry. "Since this tells me you are completely incapable of making a sane decision about your life on your own."

I rolled my eyes. "Why don't you just tell me what I'm going to have to give you to keep quiet about this so we can stop pretending you're actually upset that I'm getting married?" I pulled a pair of jeans out of my closet, eager to better conceal my scars, and then quickly put them on under my robe. "What do you want?"

It didn't appear that my sister was listening to me, but suddenly, her eyes widened.

"You're pregnant."

"What?" I scoffed and then corrected her. "No, I'm not."

"Save it." She put up her hand. "And get dressed."

"OK," I agreed since I was already in the process of doing what she was demanding. "But why?"

Bronwyn stood and stomped toward the hallway. "I'm calling in that favor you owe me. Be downstairs in ten minutes."

I sighed. There went my plans for the day.

But as much as I'd wanted to spend the last hours of my suspension planning my future with Westley, I knew that if I didn't comply with my sister's demands, it was likely I wouldn't have one. She had all the ammunition she needed to ruin my wedding, and I knew she wouldn't think twice about using it.

When I got to the bottom of the staircase five minutes later, Bronwyn was waiting there with Ginger, both of them already in their coats.

"Where are we going?" I asked, slightly nervous.

"Well, it's sure as hell not to pick out my bridesmaid dress," she growled. "Just go get in the car."

CHAPTER 82

I sighed as my sister parked her car.

"Bronwyn, I told you I am not pregnant!"

We'd driven twenty minutes into Goshen before Bronwyn pulled her Malibu into the lot of a small medical building that was an offshoot of the hospital. The brick sign in front read: Medical Testing and Laboratory.

"Just go inside." It was the first time she'd spoken since we left the house.

"OK, fine," I conceded, afraid to be too argumentative. "But can't I just go pee on one of those sticks instead?"

She ignored me and pulled Ginger out of the car. Then, to my surprise, she handed her to me.

"Coco!" my niece squealed.

Bronwyn's gesture confused me, but it had felt so long since I'd seen Ginger I didn't want to waste the opportunity to hold her, even if it ended up being some sort of trap.

We followed my sister into the building, and she pointed for us to sit while she talked with the receptionist. She returned a few minutes later with a clipboard and sat a row away from us while she filled it out, coming over only once to take my wallet out of my purse and remove from it my driver's license and Social Security card.

After a few minutes, a nurse called all three of our names, and we followed her back to a scale.

I was weighed, and my blood pressure was taken. It was "a little on the high side," which was no surprise to me. After the last three weeks of my life, I was surprised I hadn't had multiple heart attacks and a stroke.

449

Next, our trio was taken into an examining room, where the nurse handed me a cup and pointed me in the direction of the restroom.

"You are blowing this all out of proportion, Bronwyn," I said to her as I accepted the cup. "I am not pregnant."

The nurse looked at my chart and said, "We have to test anyone who is sexually active, and since you indicated that you've had…" She looked puzzled. "Eight partners in the past year—"

My eyes widened. "What?"

"That's not an eight," Bronwyn corrected. "It's the symbol for infinity."

The nurse rolled her eyes. "You two must be sisters."

I glared at Bronwyn, who just shrugged.

"This is ridiculous." I was furious. "I'm not marrying Westley because I'm pregnant. But even if I was, I don't see why it matters to you—"

The nurse interrupted me. "Would you two mind saving your argument until after the test? I'd like to get the results and prepare the cheek swab before punches start flying."

A cheek swab? I'd never taken a pregnancy test before, but considering all the advertisements for over-the-counter ones I'd ever seen seemed to boast perfect accuracy six seconds after conception by analyzing one drip of urine, this felt like overkill. "I have to do a cheek swab *and* pee in a cup?" I was incredulous. "How much proof do you need? Am I going to have to give blood too?"

The nurse was catching on faster than I was that I didn't know the full reason I'd been brought to the clinic, and started to eye Bronwyn. "You didn't tell her?"

"No," she answered lightly.

"Tell me what?" I demanded.

The nurse shook her head in frustration. "I can't perform this test on a person who has no idea why it's being done, Ms. Miller."

"So, tell her then while you're performing the test," Bronwyn replied without emotion.

I looked back and forth between them. Now I was angry *and* confused. "Someone should probably tell me *something...*"

There was a stare down between my sister and the nurse. Bronwyn won.

"The cheek swab is to test if your bone marrow will be compatible to your sister's. It's how we determine if you're an eligible donor for her."

"*What?*" I almost yelled, this new information not computing. "What on earth does bone marrow have to do with pregnancy?"

My sister was bouncing my niece on her knee and stopped to groan at my stupidity. "It has nothing to do with it, you dumbass." She sighed with exasperation. "It has to do with me needing a bone-marrow transplant because I have cancer." Bronwyn made this announcement with all the gentleness of a wrecking ball.

Which was exactly what I felt like I'd been hit with when she said it.

"What?" I croaked.

"I don't think I stuttered, Cosette. Now go piss in that cup. I haven't got all day."

CHAPTER 83

Bronwyn handed the nurse some papers from her purse.

"These are my mom's medical charts from her illness. The doctor wanted a copy of them."

I couldn't move.

Bronwyn. Cancer. Bone marrow.

"Seriously, Cosette, *go pee in that cup.*"

Bronwyn. Cancer.

"OK, so if you could open your mouth, I'm going to use this long swab to collect some of your saliva..."

Bronwyn.

"You're next little cutie! But don't worry. See? It didn't bother your auntie one bit..."

My sister was sick. My sister had cancer.

"We should have the results in a few days. I'll be sure to call as soon as we hear whether either of them is a match."

My body was filled with lead again.

"Oh, and by the way, the pregnancy test was negative."

CHAPTER 84

I was sobbing, "Why didn't you tell me? How long have you known about this?"

Bronwyn finished buckling Ginger into her car seat and then slid in the front seat behind the steering wheel. "Like you should talk, *Mrs. Greene.*" She rolled her eyes. "Ugh. Please, tell me you aren't taking that loser's name—"

"Bronwyn, I'm serious!" I choked out. "What are the doctors saying? Is it treatable?"

"Would you calm down!" she shouted back at me. "God, Cosette, you're acting like you're the one who was just told you're dying."

It felt like I was.

"You're dying?" I whispered.

"I don't know." She sighed. "It's still early. I wasn't planning on asking you to do it until I was sure it was absolutely necessary, but then I saw you were eloping and I panicked. You've been disappearing so much lately. I didn't want to run the risk that I would need you and you'd be God knows where with Dr. Cuckoo on your honeymoon."

I was awash with guilt. "I would have come back for this, no matter where I was," I promised, new tears falling from my eyes.

She looked at me skeptically. "Liar."

I was mortified. "Bronwyn, of course I would!"

"Whatever." She rolled her eyes. "We're not exactly BFFs, Cosette. I don't expect you to be the first person in line to help me."

My heart ached. "You're my sister. There's nothing I wouldn't do if it meant saving your life."

And as the words left my lips, it occurred to me how true they were.

I looked my sister in the eyes, past her hatred. In so many ways, Bronwyn was my greatest enemy. She was my oppressor, my adversary. In my lifetime, she'd caused me more hurt than any other person I'd ever known.

Yet, despite all that, I wanted more than anything to help her. I loved her.

I realized then that up until that moment, I must not have completely decided to forsake the garden for Westley. I'd told myself that was what I was going to do, but because I was still eligible, the decision hadn't felt final.

The conversation hadn't been over.

Until now.

I closed my eyes and imagined the garden one last time.

"I'm in," I said with resolution. "No matter what it costs me."

CHAPTER 85

Bronwyn dropped me off in our driveway with a warning.

"Not a word about this," she said seriously. "Or you'll learn a whole new meaning to 'wedding crasher.'"

I nodded that I understood, though I knew full well I would be telling Westley all about the events of the morning as soon as I could get to him.

I had to, I reasoned. I had to explain to him why we couldn't go to Las Vegas.

I would still marry him on Friday; it would just have to happen somewhere closer to home. I couldn't fathom going across the country right now without knowing the full details of Bronwyn's illness. If indeed I was a match for her—I prayed that I was—I wanted to be in near-enough proximity to donate the moment I found out.

The drive to Fort Wayne felt infinite, but my hands were still shaking by the time I arrived at Maplecrest.

I signed in on the guest record and waited for Westley to emerge from the dormitory doors.

When he did, I was grateful that he was smiling. I hadn't forgotten the ambiguous ending to our last visit. But knowing how serious the news I had for him was, I didn't allow myself to worry about all the ways this reunion could go badly because of it.

As he walked toward me, my mind inadvertently flashed to Micah—to Northrop. It occurred to me that this was the first time I was seeing Westley as his brother, and instantly, I felt like an idiot for not recognizing their physical similarities before.

They walked with the same gait. Their hairline was identical. And as Westley enveloped me into his arms, his familiar scent instantly reminded me of Micah's.

But, I quickly reminded myself, this visit was not about Westley and his sibling; it was about me and mine. I pushed Micah from my thoughts.

"I was worried I would never see you again," Westley confessed, still holding me tight. "After the way we left things, I thought maybe you were done with me."

"Of course not!" I found this reaction confusing. "I was actually kind of worried that the reverse was true. I mean, you just left..." Our conversation about the healings came flooding back, and I remembered just how unresolved we'd left that issue. "I was worried you thought I was crazy."

"I know a lot of crazy people, Cosi." He gestured around the room. "And you aren't one of them. But I know we still need to finish talking about what happened."

I nodded and put Bronwyn's sickness on the back burner for the moment. Westley sounded like he wanted to say something, and I wanted to hear whatever it was before I revealed my latest shocking news.

He led me to our spot in the recreation room, and we sat down facing each other on the sofa.

"I've thought a lot about what you said. About the 'healings.'" Westley used finger quotes around the word. "And I just can't buy it, Cosi."

My heart sank. "So, you think I'm lying to you?"

"No!" His eyes widened. "No, I would never call you a liar."

"OK..." I shifted in my seat. "Then what *are* you saying?"

He took a breath. "Just hear me out, OK?" This opening line made me tense, as I was sure it meant I wouldn't like what was to follow. And I was right. "I think Micah's the liar. I'm not sure how he did it exactly, but he's convinced you that I hurt you." Westley looked at me sympathetically. "But you know I'd never do that."

I stared at him without blinking.

"So I don't know if it was some combination of the pain meds you were on and the power of his suggestions to you, but there's no way you sustained the injuries you say you did and then were fine the next day—"

"Yes, there is one way," I interrupted to argue. "And that's by a miracle."

Westley's face showed pity for me. "I know you believe that. Just like you believe that you healed Micah through a miracle—but that's just because you were an innocent pawn in this horrible thing, Cosette. I'm sure the doctors thought that if they could convince you that some higher power existed, then you'd convince me, and I'd be cured." He explained this to me with the utmost seriousness. "But you've been tricked."

"No," I said firmly. "*You* have, West."

I considered all the arguments I could make, all the proof I had that there indeed was a God. But I knew that it would be pointless to say any of it. If Westley could look at Micah's x-rays and my face and still not believe, then nothing I could say to him would matter.

Westley's face fell. So did mine. This felt like an impasse.

"I'm sorry," he admitted. "I can't see it any other way, Cosette. I wish that I could, but I can't."

I started to sigh, but something in his apology stopped me. "Wait...Do you mean that?"

"Do I mean what?"

"That you wish you could see what happened different-ly," I clarified. "That you wish that a miracle had happened?"

"Sometimes," he answered me quietly. "Sometimes, I really wish I could."

I felt the birth of a small hope within me. "Then I'll just have to spend the rest of our lives together trying to show you what you're blind to."

A smile broke on Westley's lips, and I returned it.

Perhaps God had a purpose for me outside of the garden too.

◆◆◆

457

"So, I was afraid to ask when you first got here." Westley's voice was low and hesitant. "But are we still on for Friday?"

His reminder of the original purpose of my visit sank my spirits. "Yes..." I trailed off, and his face clouded over. "But we can't go to Las Vegas."

West was immediately alarmed, and his panicked look didn't dissipate as I explained to him my reason for the venue change.

"Cancer?" His eyebrows shot up. "My god, Cosi. I'm so sorry."

I was thankful that Westley was able to offer his sympathies despite his history with Bronwyn and the fact that his most recent run-in with her was partly the reason he was in a psych ward.

"Are you OK? Do we need to postpone the wedding or anything?" Westley's offer was sincere, and I appreciated it.

"No." I'd already concluded this. Since our marriage no longer impacted my choice about the garden, I couldn't think of any reason to wait. "As long as you don't mind getting married here."

"Well, I'm sure as hell not getting married *here*." He pointed around. "But anywhere else on this earth is fine with me, as long as when we go back to Middlebury, you're my wife."

I smiled. "Thank you."

◆◆◆

Westley and I said good-bye just minutes before visiting hours expired, but I knew that I still wanted to try to see Avalon one last time before Friday. After Westley was no longer a patient at Maplecrest, it would be tricky for me to visit my friend, and there was still so much I wanted to say to her.

The pretty receptionist was on duty again, and she greeted me with a smile when I approached her desk.

"Hi, I know it's late, but I was hoping to see Avalon Brant for just a minute. Is that possible?"

She didn't hesitate. "Anything for Avalon."

"Great! Thank you!"

After striking a few computer keys, she dialed Avalon's room.

Since time was limited, I would have to pick only the most significant news to share with my friend rather than tell her everything that had happened since the last time we'd spoken—and for her, that would mean what I'd learned in the garden.

I needed to tell her that the flames were real—she hadn't hallucinated them. And she needed to know that Gabriel had taken her to them to heal her scars. My hope was that hearing this small bit of news would lift some of what was burdening Avalon about her boyfriend.

"Oh." The receptionist's eyes were fixed on her computer monitor as she returned the receiver to its cradle. "Avalon's no longer in our care?"

She seemed to be as surprised as I was to learn this.

"What?"

"It appears she was discharged yesterday," she read from her screen. "Voluntarily checked herself out."

I didn't understand this. "Did her parents come to get her?"

"That wouldn't have been necessary since she wasn't a minor. From what I knew of her, she wanted to be here. Whatever had happened, she wanted to work through it." The receptionist was no longer smiling. "Wish I could have told her good-bye."

"Me too," I agreed, but I was too confused to let my sadness sink in yet. "Do you know if she'd had any other visitors lately? A boyfriend maybe?"

"I'm not sure." She made a face. "And that would be confidential information, even if I did."

"Of course," I realized. "Thanks anyway."

"I'm really sorry your friend didn't tell you she was checking out," she offered sincerely as I turned to the elevators. "I'm sure she'll be in touch soon."

"Yeah," I agreed. "I hope so."

CHAPTER 86

The heaviness of the day was magnified with the news that Avalon had left Maplecrest without telling me. Though it probably shouldn't have, I took that decision personally. Had I done something wrong?

I was so inexperienced at female friendships that I didn't doubt I'd somehow botched ours, and if I did, I wanted the chance to repair whatever I'd done wrong.

Before I left the parking lot, I sent Avalon a text.

Where did you go?—CM

The drive through the gusting snow was nerve-wracking by itself, but when I didn't have a response to my message by the time I got back to Middlebury, I felt even more unsettled.

I considered the possibility that Gabriel had come back to take Avalon to the garden with him, but I supposed the mere fact that I could still remember her made that impossible.

Since I couldn't know for certain what had become of Avalon without her telling me, I decided to put off worrying too much until she'd had more time to reach out to me.

I parked my car in the driveway and let myself into my house through the front door. I was tired from the emotion of the day, but I knew I wouldn't be sleeping anytime soon. Between scrambling to finish my remaining homework for my return to school and trying to replan my wedding a few thousand miles closer to home, I wasn't sure I'd even make it to bed before it was time to wake up.

I hung my coat on the rack and noticed that Bronwyn was in the living room.

In the same way that life had been made of glass after Julia's death, my relationship with my sister seemed even more delicate now that she was sick. I longed to walk over to the couch where she sat and give her a squeeze on the shoulder or kiss her on the top of her head the way Eastlyn always did her brothers. But even when Bronwyn wasn't so vulnerable, such acts would have evoked a violent response. And if she wanted nothing to do with me before, she'd for sure reject me when she could attribute any attempts to play nice with her to pity.

"You should take this since you're moving out. Nobody here wants it." My sister's voice startled me.

I quickly changed directions from the stairs to the living room, too happy she'd engaged me in conversation to wonder what the "it" was she was talking about.

Bronwyn was sitting on the couch, surrounded by piles of papers and stacks of photographs. There was a box on the floor half-full of more of the same. A box with the name "Corryne" written on it.

"You're the one who took Mom's box," I narrated my thoughts out loud.

"Mystery solved." She was sarcastic but quiet in her retort. "I just needed her medical records, but there's loads of other crap in here I'd forgotten about." She extended a photo album to me. "Like this."

I accepted the book. "What is it?"

"A wedding present." She made a face at me. "I have to give it to you early since I never received my invitation to the ceremony."

"C'mon, Bronwyn." Although I knew my sister didn't really care about seeing me get married, she was a pro at making me feel guilty. "It's not like you would have come anyway."

"Guess we'll never know." She shrugged. "Have fun in Vegas."

"We're not getting married there anymore," I revealed. "Last-minute venue change."

She looked up from her piles of papers. "Where to now? Some place even farther away so it will be impossible for me to reach you if I need help?" Her voice was a mix of fear and annoyance. "Thanks a lot, *Sis*."

Her accusation hurt. "Not at all. I'm probably going to end up having my wedding in the Fort Wayne courthouse because I can't stand the thought of being away from you when you're sick." There was more emotion in my voice than I would typically dare with Bronwyn, but I didn't care. "As long as you need me to, I'm sticking around."

My sister's expression went blank. "Cosette, I'm not asking you to do that."

"You don't have to ask," I stated.

"I'm not trying to ruin your wedding," she defended herself.

"You aren't ruining anything," I explained. "This is my choice."

This left Bronwyn speechless. I knew it was as close to a kiss on the head as I was going to get, so I accepted the small victory and turned to exit the living room.

I made it to the third step before my sister regained her words, and I debated plugging my ears so that whatever comeback she'd come up with didn't ruin our moment.

"If this cancer thing kills me like it did Mom, promise me you'll raise Ginger."

I stopped in my tracks.

"What?"

"I think you heard me." She forced an edge into her tone. "And spare me the obligatory 'you aren't going to die' bullshit because you and I both know firsthand just how possible it is that I will. Just promise me you'll take care of my daughter if it comes to that."

Tears spilled down my cheeks, and I was glad that my sister couldn't see them. "I absolutely will."

When I was sure she had nothing more to say, I continued up the stairs, completely overwhelmed with grief and love for my sister.

"One more thing though," she called out just as I reached the top of the stairs. "Don't let Westley be too involved in her life... or I'll haunt the hell out of you."

◆ ◆ ◆

Since I was already a ball of tears and hiccups when I got to my bedroom, I decided I might as well look through the photo album Bronwyn had given me right then, instead of trying to schedule a time later to have another emotional breakdown.

And it was probably a good thing I got it over with. Everything I feared it would have done to me when I refused to open the box weeks ago, it did now.

The pictures inside were of a family I didn't recognize and would never know. One with a doting mother who had Bronwyn's eyes and my smile. One with a loving husband and father, who kissed his wife on the cheek and cuddled his daughters. One with two little girls who held hands and played together in ways so beautiful that their parents captured the moments in photographs.

One that had ended just as it was beginning.

I thought of the dream I'd had about the garden, of the children yet unborn to Westley and me.

I thought of Bronwyn and Ginger and all the pages at the end of my book that my mother's illness had forced blank.

I thought of everything that is, everything that could have been, and everything I wanted to be from now on.

And then, I prayed.

God, please...Please let my bone marrow be a match for Bronwyn. Please, spare my sister's life...

CHAPTER 87

I didn't get any homework done, and I didn't make any wedding plans.

I did, however, spend a solid two hours researching bone-marrow transplants.

It was difficult for me to determine Bronwyn's odds for survival since of all the forms of cancer that required this kind of treatment, I didn't know which she had. And it was also difficult not to be discouraged that according to the Internet, even though I was her sister, there was only about a 50 percent chance our bone marrow was going to be compatible.

And with these odds and statistics floating around in my head, it was also difficult to fall asleep.

Eventually, though, I did, and the next morning when I woke up for school, my thoughts picked right back up where I'd left them. My five-day hiatus had not been so much time away from my morning routine that I couldn't get ready on autopilot, which allowed most of my brain power left to continue worrying about Bronwyn.

My thoughts were so deeply with her that it took Micah greeting me as I walked into my first-period class to snap me back to reality.

"Change your mind about the garden yet? Ready to ditch high school for a life of wonder and possibility and miracles?"

In spite of everything, Micah made me smile. "Whatever happened to respecting people's choices? You used to be all about that."

He grinned back at me. "I still am. I just want to make sure this is really the choice you are making."

My smile faded. "It is," I said with more confidence than I had when we last spoke.

He shook his head at me. "I hope you fully understand all you are sacrificing for Westley."

"It's not just about him anymore," I explained. "It's also about my sister."

"Bronwyn?" Micah was confused. "Why?"

"Because she's sick," I told him. "And I'm going do whatever it takes to save her." I quietly filled him in on the sad details that had cemented my decision in place.

Micah closed his eyes and shook his head. "Cosette, I'm so sorry..."

I nodded.

"You don't think you could magically heal her or something, do you?" I asked, only half-kidding.

He shrugged. "It doesn't work like that...A healing isn't something you can plan. It's an impulse. A call." Micah frowned.

"Yeah," I recalled how I'd felt just before laying hands on him in the garden.

"So you're for sure a match then?" he asked carefully. "You already know?"

I swallowed the lump in my throat so that I could answer him. "No, but I will be."

He hesitated before he asked his next question. "And if you aren't...does that change your decision about the garden, or are you still staying here for my brother?"

I hesitated back. "I don't plan on ever having to know the answer to that."

Micah's eyes remained on me, and I could tell there was more he wanted to say but wouldn't. Instead, he just sighed and whispered, "That right there, Cosette. That's the faith I was talking about."

◆◆◆

Semester finals were two weeks out, and my history teacher used every second of class blathering on about the Ottomans—no doubt because it was on the already existing exam that he didn't want to have to rewrite because we hadn't covered it.

When class finally ended, I was excited to continue any of the conversations still unfinished between Micah and me, but he quickly dashed those hopes by announcing he was cutting out for the rest of the school day.

"I'll see you soon," he promised. "Need to go home for a bit."

I was disappointed for him to leave. Though I tried not to think about it, I knew that after Friday, I'd likely not be seeing much of Micah, either because Westley would forbid it or because I'd be ineligible and his business with me would be over.

"Aren't you worried about getting a Saturday detention?" I teased. School felt ridiculous to me; for Micah, I knew it was absolutely meaningless.

"Not really." He laughed. "This is my first day here since you were suspended, and no one seems to have noticed." He winked.

"Of course they haven't." I shook my head. "How come I can't get provision like that?"

"Come live in the garden, and you can cut all the classes you want..."

I found his directness amusing. "You really don't give up, do you?"

"Of course not." He smirked. "Did you forget I'm biologically a Greene? We're relentless."

This was true. "You know why I can't now." I understood his intentions in keeping this conversation alive, but now more than ever, my answer was fixed.

"I understand where you're coming from, Cosette," he acknowledged. "But I also think you should consider what you would choose if you took your sister and my brother out of the equation."

"That seems like a pointless hypothetical situation, Micah," I argued. "Because clearly they are the reasons why I'm not going."

466

He turned serious. "If Westley and Bronwyn are why you are refusing this opportunity, then when you're considering your future, make sure you envision what it's going to be like to resent them."

He tried to deliver this warning gently, but it still struck a nerve.

I didn't hide my frustration. "You think I'm going to regret saving my sister's life?"

"You could. I mean, we're talking about Bronwyn here. There's a pretty good chance that even if you took a bullet for her, she'd complain about having to step over your body on her way out of the crime scene."

This would have been incredibly insulting if it weren't such a possibility.

"OK, sure," I relented. "Even if Bronwyn knew all I was sacrificing to help her, there's no assurance she'd appreciate it. Does that mean I'm just supposed to let her die?"

"Just because you choose the garden, it doesn't mean she dies, Cosette. Just like choosing to stay doesn't guarantee she survives," he tried to point out, but I wouldn't let my mind go where he was leading it. "Or that you and Westley get to ride off into the sunset together."

"You don't know what you're talking about." I tried to end our conversation by walking away, but he chased after me.

"You're not being fair to him, Cosette. You can't expect him to give you a more fulfilling life than you would have had in the garden, especially when he doesn't even know what you're giving up to be with him."

I kept walking. He kept chasing.

"If you choose to stay here for Westley, there could come a time when you resent that decision—when you resent him for it. And I don't want that for you." He gently tugged at my arm to slow me down. "I don't want that for him either."

I stopped and threw up my hands. "I thought this was supposed to be about what *I* wanted, not you, Micah."

"It is," he agreed. "Choose the life you *want*, Cosette. Not the one you're just afraid to let go of."

He left me then, and I was glad he did.

If he had stuck around any longer, he would have seen my tears fall.

CHAPTER 88

Somehow, I survived the morning.

I pushed my argument with Micah from my mind and feebly attempted to pay attention in my classes.

Having been out for a week and having done very little studying during that time, I was completely behind in all my subjects, which meant I was likely to spend my honeymoon catching up in order to avoid being the only newlywed in history forced to repeat her senior year of high school.

A thrill shot through me when I remembered my wedding, and I indulged it. In two days, Westley and I would be married. We would officially begin living our future, and nothing else would matter.

For a brief moment, I could recall the contentedness of life before Julia's death. It was comfortable and familiar. I thought those feelings had been lost forever, but maybe they didn't have to be. Maybe once my choice was official, I really could resume life as it was before.

That *was* what I wanted, right? For everything to be as it was?

Yes. I was almost sure of it.

When the bell rang for lunch, I decided I'd rather skip a meal than brave the cafeteria alone. Anyway, I had plenty of other things to do to keep my mind off of the food I wasn't eating, starting with checking for a response to the text I'd sent Avalon the night before.

As much as I hoped all was well for her, I couldn't convince myself that it was. She'd been so eager in her communication with me before, and I didn't understand why that had changed so suddenly.

When I saw that I'd missed no messages, I checked my e-mail through my phone. There was nothing from her, which was disappointing, but there was one new message in my inbox that brought an instant smile to my face.

It was from Westley.

Cosi,

Don't worry at all about Friday. Everything's taken care of.
See you at 12:01 ☺
Take care of your sister.

I love you,

—W

I must have stared at the e-mail for a full ten minutes.

Somehow, from the confines of the hospital, Westley had managed to plan our wedding for me. He'd taken the burden on himself, without any sort of real privacy to do so, all so that I could concentrate my attention on the sister who'd helped to get him locked up there.

I breathed in deeply and then released it.

I would take Westley's advice. I wouldn't worry at all about Friday.

◆ ◆ ◆

Before fifth period began, Mrs. Holloway stood in the doorway and welcomed me back into her class with an embrace. "I want to talk to you about something," she whispered in my ear. "Do you have some time after class?"

I told her that I did, and she squeezed me tighter. "Perfect."

The anticipation of what my teacher would say made the class discussion on Chopin's "The Story of an Hour" seem like "The Story of a Decade." Finally, the bell rang, and I congratulated myself on surviving what felt like the longest day of school ever.

"So, how have you been doing?" she asked casually as she eyed the last few students lingering in her room.

Since I assumed her question was just to fill time until we were alone, I replied with the generic, "Fine."

"Good," was her obligatory response, which was followed by a call to the last two girls standing in the doorway. "Hey, would you ladies mind giving us a moment?" Mrs. Holloway's sweet request was met with apology and obedience, and the last student out the door gently shut it behind her.

Instantly, my teacher's demeanor changed. "First of all, I don't believe for one second that your suspension was justified, and on behalf of everyone at Camden with common sense, I apologize to you."

"Oh." I was touched by her enthusiastic support. "Thanks for saying that."

"You're welcome." She smiled sincerely. "And secondly, how is Westley doing?"

"He's...OK." I tried to answer her with conviction, but I knew I didn't sound convincing.

She didn't buy my response, but she also didn't push me further. "Well, I think you are a very strong young woman, Cosette. And I'm sorry you're going through such a difficult time right now."

Although there was no way my teacher could have known just *how* difficult a time I was going through, her words were so genuine that I pretended she knew everything and loved her all the more for it. "Thanks."

"So the reason I wanted to talk to you is about your essay...the 'incomplete' one."

"Oh." I blushed having not expected our conversation to shift to business so abruptly. "Yeah, I'm really sorry I haven't finished it yet—"

"Cosette, I'm not bringing it up because of your grade," she gently clarified. "I just want to know if you've given any thoughts to my comments about finding out what more life could be beyond only your relationship."

I stared dumbly at her. Had Micah gotten to her?

"It's really all I've been thinking about these days," I confessed.

She nodded and smiled again. "I'm glad. Make any decisions?"

I paused a moment before answering. "I think that I have."

"And the answer's still Westley, isn't it?"

I nodded.

A silence lingered between us.

"Cosette..." my teacher began carefully. "I want to share something with you that I've never told a student before."

"Oh." My breath stopped. "You can trust me, Mrs. Holloway."

"I know I can..." There was silence again. "But it doesn't mean it's easy to talk about." She lifted my left hand to eye level and gazed at my engagement ring. "I, too, got engaged in high school. And we got married two months after graduation."

"You did?" This news was surprising.

"I did. I was barely eighteen. He was a year older. We'd been together since I was a freshman." A wistfulness overtook my teacher's face.

"That's adorable." I smiled hopefully. "I didn't know that you and Pastor Brian were high school sweethearts!"

Mrs. Holloway's eyes fell. "We weren't, Cosette."

"But you just said..." My confusion was only momentary before the pieces fell together.

"His name was Kevin," she revealed. "And I was head over heels for him. But we were young and a lot more impulsive than I realized at the time. Neither one of us knew what we wanted in life beyond each other."

"What happened?" I dared to ask.

"Oh, a lot of things happened." She heaved a heavy sigh. "And eventually, Kevin decided we'd made a mistake by getting married so young. And he left me."

I was blank. "Did he go crazy or something?" My mind struggled to make sense of what would have to happen to a man to make him not want to be married to Jessica Holloway. "Was he mistakenly lobotomized? Did he develop blind amnesia? Was it a routine hypnosis gone wrong, and now he thinks he's a cat?"

"No, nothing like that." She laughed. "I think we both just expected too much from the other person, you know? We made idols out of one another, and when things got tough and we only had each other to look to for answers, we failed."

My hands recoiled into my lap. "Why are you telling me all this?"

She smiled sadly. "Because, Cosette, every day you come into my classroom, I see myself." My teacher coaxed eye contact out of me before she continued. "You are a smart, compassionate, beautiful girl with a world of possibility at her fingertips. And I want to say to you what I wish someone would have said to me when I was your age..."

I kept my eyes with hers expectantly.

"You have a lot of options. And I just think you should weigh them all carefully before making any permanent decisions."

My heart stopped.

How was this conversation happening right now?

Mrs. Holloway couldn't have known about Micah, about the garden.

She couldn't have known I was eloping.

But this conversation wasn't a coincidence.

Just like Dave the mechanic hadn't been. Or the man with his son at the coffee shop. Or Micah bursting through my door the moment Westley bore down on my chest.

Or anything else, ever.

So what was it then? A test? A gut check? A warning?

"Thanks, Mrs. Holloway." I tried to smile graciously. "I promise that I will."

CHAPTER 89

I cleared at least three inches of snow from my car before driving home, and when I looked out the front window an hour later, another three had replaced it.The blizzard that had been forecasted all week was here.

I turned on the news to check the weather just in time to watch Camden Community scroll across the bottom of the screen among the growing list of schools that had preemptively closed for Thursday. I was so happy I could have done cartwheels.

I couldn't have handled another day like today.

Bronwyn had come home from work early to beat the snow, I guessed, and had already undressed from work and was in her lounging clothes. Using it as an excuse to be near her and Ginger, I cooked a pasta dinner for my family, though I knew it would be eaten in shifts as people were hungry and not together as a formal meal.

Bronwyn sat with Ginger on her lap at the breakfast table, reading to her from a stack of books made of thick, cardboard pages. I stole as many glimpses as I could without being so obvious it would annoy Bronwyn, but it was rare for me to see my sister enjoying her maternal role the way she was in that moment, and it was something I didn't want to forget.

Not that there wouldn't be millions more of those moments in the future, I reminded myself. Bronwyn was going to be just fine. I just wanted to remember this particular one because after the wedding, I wouldn't be living here to witness them.

Those two things were now inseparable in my mind—my wedding and Bronwyn—as if one's existence depended upon the other's. I would marry Westley on Friday, and as a result, Bronwyn would get to live. I would save Bronwyn and be rewarded by marrying Westley.

The logic wasn't obvious, but I didn't dare try to poke holes in it. It was my shield, after all. The bubble I'd encased myself in to keep safe from thinking about the life I wouldn't have in the garden.

Mrs. Holloway had meant well, I knew. But even if I walked her same path, it didn't mean her fate would be mine. Westley wasn't Kevin, and I definitely wasn't Jessica Holloway. And our situations weren't exactly symmetrical. Had my teacher not married her high school sweetheart, no one would have died.

Right?

I refused to think about it anymore. My argument felt weak even though I was only trying to convince myself.

"I left something for you in your room," Bronwyn said without looking up from her book. "It's for Friday."

I appreciated that she had said "Friday" and not "wedding" in case my father was somewhere in the house, but knowing Bronwyn, I was hesitant to let that appreciation carry over to what awaited me in my room. "Oh...I thought you already gave me a gift?"

"Yeah, well, I'm feeling generous." She doused her words with sarcasm. "It's the whole 'something old, something new, something borrowed, something blue' shit. It covers three out of the four. You'll just need something new."

I was touched, but I couldn't let Bronwyn see just how much, so I turned my back to her to hide my smile. "My dress is new. I guess I'm covered then."

Ginger's babbling filled the silence.

Eventually, Bronwyn responded, "Too bad I won't get to see it."

I smiled bigger. "You already did," I confessed. "It's the one you showed me from the magazine. And you were right.

It's perfect." I could feel her looking at the back of my head. "So...thank you."

I could still feel her eyes on me for a while longer. Then, without speaking, she stood and took Ginger with her upstairs.

Her sudden departure didn't bother me. In fact, I was glad she didn't respond. What she left blank in that moment, I would fill in for her, forever giving her the benefit of the doubt that what she would have said if she could have was that she loved me in the only sad, dysfunctional way she ever knew how to love.

I ate my dinner alone in the kitchen before heading up to my bedroom. My door had been left open, and when I walked through it, my eyes were instantly drawn to a small jewelry box on my dresser.

I picked it up and lifted its lid.

Inside, there was a note attached to a ribbon:

I found this in Mom's things. It's old, it's blue, and I sure as hell better get it back.

—Bronwyn

I lifted the paper, and at the other end of the ribbon, there was a ring.

An inscription written in calligraphy on the inner band caught my eye.

W & C forever.

W. and C. Will and Corryne.

I smiled at the connection and my sister's thoughtfulness. I slipped the ring onto my right hand and then held it up to catch it in the light.

The "blue" of my sister's gift was a stone set in the center of the ring. A sapphire.

It was gorgeous.

I extended my other hand out to admire both of my rings together, the emerald and the sapphire.

Individually, they were both beautiful jewels, but as I looked back and forth from one to the other, I noted that they did not complement each other. The blue and the green, each so bold in color, were meant to be worn alone. They didn't share the spotlight well. In fact, set side by side, the two stones seemed to clash.

I decided I didn't care. Both rings were too important for me just to choose one to wear on my special day.

At least until Friday, I just had to wear them both.

CHAPTER 90

I didn't know what to pack.

I pulled out the only suitcase I owned—a carry-on I'd received as a gift from the Greene family the year we flew to Florida for spring break—and opened it onto my bed.

For situations like mine, the kind where a high school girl secretly elopes with her boyfriend, it's difficult to decide what to take along and what to leave behind, especially when there's a strong possibility that everything left back would be thrown out into the snow when my father discovered what I'd done.

In the end, I went for sentiment over practicality, assuming with Westley's inheritance windfall, I could replace things like clothing more easily than memories.

I took down all the photographs from my walls, stuck them flat in between the pages of my baby book, and placed it at the bottom of my suitcase. Then, I went through the rest of my bedroom as if preparing it for a garage sale—assessing value to my lifetime of stuff and keeping only what I couldn't stand to part with.

I was reaching into my bedside bookshelf to remove my fifth-grade copy of *Charlotte's Web* when I noticed the Bible Micah had given me. Knowing Westley didn't own one, I decided that I would make room for it and pulled both books from the shelf.

When I did this, a white envelope slid out from the pages of the Bible and fell onto my bed. I blinked at it twice before realizing what was inside it.

Westley's vows.

I'd forgotten about them. Again.

I wanted to punch myself in the face.

Instead, I picked up the envelope and tore it open.

Cosette,

I can't remember a time before I loved you, and there will never come a time when I will stop.

We've always had the love story that everyone else dreams of, and I will spend the rest of my life giving you the happily ever after you deserve.

Whatever you need, I will be. Whatever you want, I will give it to you. I promise to protect you, to comfort you, and provide for you, for now and always.

You are mine, and I am yours.

I love you.

—Westley

I stared at the words, reading and rereading them and loving the man who wrote them.

How could I ever regret choosing him?

CHAPTER 91

It was a restless night.

I was able to sleep, though not well since I couldn't guard my unconscious mind from thinking about what was forbidden.

The garden.

Ever since my last visit when I'd learned the cost of choosing to live there, I'd refused to remember it. Or at least to enjoy remembering it. But I couldn't control what I dreamed, and each time I awoke that night, lying on my bed and not in a bed of tulips, my heart sank. The dreams weren't as vivid as the one I'd had in the farmhouse. And I didn't feel like any of them were as meaningful as that one had been.

I wondered how long this would continue, how long I would grieve my paradise lost once I was no longer eligible to be a part of it.

When morning finally came, I pulled on my robe and headed down to the kitchen.

As I walked past the window, I could see that the sun was rising to a clear sky. The morning's first beams of light stretched across the deep white ocean of snow that had submerged all of Middlebury, and the ground seemed to glow in the dawn.

I would always hate snow, I knew. But there was something in its stillness, in the frozen suffocation of the earth, that I found...beautiful. There was nothing buried beneath it all, I knew. No color, no life. Yet, part of me still hoped that there could be. That maybe all the beauty of the garden was possible here too. Hidden, but still there.

"Well, Cosette!" my grandmother greeted me after I finally pulled myself from the window and into the kitchen. "I'd begun to wonder if you'd moved out it's been so long since I saw you." She hugged me with both arms, and I returned it.

"Just been busy is all, Grandma," I smiled genuinely at her.

The rest of my family was in there too. Thanks to the snowstorm, there was really nowhere else any of us could be.

I grabbed the box of cereal on the table in front of my dad and took the seat next to him.

"School's closed," he offered, his eyes fixed on his tablet screen.

"Yeah, thanks," I acknowledged.

I gave him the space to say more, but he didn't.

Bronwyn was feeding Ginger oatmeal in her highchair, and the five of us ate our breakfasts separately, yet all in the same room.

Ginger was the only one not accustomed to so many people being in a room together but saying nothing to each other.

"Coco!"

I grinned at her and crunched my cereal.

"Coco! Up!"

I looked to my niece and saw her arms reaching for me.

Bronwyn at first glared at me and then—to the shock of everyone—sighed, removed her daughter from her seat, and sat her in my lap.

Grandma and my dad eyed my sister curiously.

"What?" she barked at them. "Ginger asked for her."

My niece's face lit up, and she threw both chubby arms around my neck.

This was the last time I was with my whole family at once in that house. And it was perfect.

CHAPTER 92

Westley told me not to worry about anything, but there was still one thing that I was concerned about when it came to our wedding—or the wedding night at least.

My scars.

Back in my room after breakfast, I locked my door and examined the markings on my legs for the millionth time.

When I wasn't looking at them, I allowed myself the hope that they were fading. That my body was regenerating new flesh under the blue that had scabbed over my shins, and soon I would shed all traces of my injury.

But each time I laid eyes on them, the reality of my condition set in again. The blueness was bright. My flesh was irreparably stained, and this wasn't likely to change before my husband-to-be demanded an explanation about it.

I knew I needed an answer. So I looked for one in the only place I could think to.

On the Internet.

After image-searching several variations of "blue skin," I finally came to a page that contained pictures of something other than weird-looking comic book characters and the Blue Man Group.

I clicked on a link to a medical website and was directed to a page with the words "Hyacinthum Cicatrices" written at the top in bold, followed by a definition:

Burn-like scars categorized by their bluish hues. Considered a medical mystery, doctors have determined no causal source or common link among

*the people who develop this worldwide phenome-
non that reported cases suggest affect less than one
billionth of the population. The marks most often
appear on appendages, though recently the United
States has reported the first case of facial disfig-
uration and internal scarring attributed to this
condition.*

I gasped out loud when I scrolled down the screen.
It was Avalon.

My heart swelled when I saw her face on the screen.
Though her image was flat, her eyes reflected the same blank
sadness they had the first time we met.

I imagined where she could be now, where she had gone.
Why she hadn't told me?

I pictured her somewhere, in a setting other than
Maplecrest, wearing that same hopeless expression—all
alone.

It was more than I could bear. I reached for my phone
and quickly typed a message to her.

Please just tell me if you're OK...I miss you—CM

I returned my eyes to Avalon's, lamenting her lot in life,
but my phone buzzed a minute later and pulled me back to
reality.

It was from her.

Gabriel came back.

The amount of relief I felt at that moment was immeas-
urable.

Not only was my friend safe, but her boyfriend had come
back for her.

I clicked off of Avalon's image, assured now that the pain
on the face in that photo was no longer a reality for her.

I can't wait to hear all about it.

◆◆◆

Avalon assured me we'd catch up soon, and now that I knew she was with Gabriel, it was much easier for me to concentrate on being happy with Westley.

Which I would be, in less than a day.

I couldn't stop smiling the entire time I was showering and dressing for my last day at home. I was so excited for my new beginning.

As I blow-dried my hair, I imagined where Westley and I would live when we came back to Middlebury. I was sure we'd just rent an apartment since we'd be leaving for school in the fall, and I hoped we could find one near enough to my house that I could be around as much as possible for Bronwyn once she started her cancer treatment.

I hadn't read much into things like chemotherapy or radiation since I didn't know if my sister would need those things after she received my bone marrow. My hope was that she wouldn't need anything beyond my help, that one shot of my marrow would work like the antidote to an evil spell in a fairy tale.

From above the roar of my blow-dryer, I thought I could hear voices in my bedroom. I turned it off for a better listen.

"You're a complete freak!" Bronwyn's voice was hushed but angry. "You stay the hell away from me!"

"I'm sorry," a male voice pleaded. "I didn't know..."

Micah?

I flung open the bathroom door and found them both there, on opposite sides of my bedroom. Micah looked panicked. Bronwyn looked homicidal.

"What is going on?" I was afraid to ask the question.

"You stupid bitch!" Bronwyn spat through a clenched jaw. "You told him!"

"Told him what?" My eyes darted to Micah to explain my sister's latest wrath.

"I'm sorry," he whispered. "I just wanted to pray for her..."

My eyes grew so huge I felt they would fall out of my head.

Oh. No.

484

"You didn't…" I begged Micah to be joking, but I knew he wasn't.

"I don't want your goddamn prayers or your goddamn pity." Bronwyn glared at Micah. "If you think you can use my illness as an excuse to get into my sister's pants, then you're a bigger asshole than Westley."

"Bronwyn, I promise you that's not why I came here." He closed his eyes. "I just wanted to offer you some comfort because I knew you were hurting."

"You don't know shit about how I'm feeling!" My sister glowered before turning her venom on me. "How dare you tell him I'm sick, Cosette? It's none of his business!"

Bronwyn was hurt. She was angry. She was betrayed.

And she was right.

She had told me not to tell anyone about her cancer. And though I'd had a reason to tell Micah—a great one that she wouldn't believe—I'd still broken her trust.

"You're right," I submitted to her. "I am so, so sorry, Bronwyn."

"You think I care about 'sorry'?" she snapped. "You told him my secret—I guess now I get to tell him yours."

My heart stopped, and I shot a look at Micah. "Please, don't," I said, but I knew any attempt to stop her was futile.

"OK, I won't." She smirked. "Since you like to talk so much, I'll let you tell him."

I could tell Micah didn't want to listen to what Bronwyn was saying, but the temptation was too great.

"Tell me what, Cosette?" he asked me instead of her.

"I don't even know why she's keeping it a secret from you—it's not like you even matter to her," Bronwyn continued, ripping the bandage off as slowly and painfully as possible. "No one matters to her unless their last name is Greene."

"Cosette?" Micah repeated.

I'd been backed into a corner by Bronwyn enough times to know she didn't bluff. If I didn't confess, she would tell him. And now that I knew what it felt like to hear the truth about the garden from Sidona, I couldn't let Micah get his devastating news delivered by a third party.

"Westley and I are getting married," I muttered, glaring at my sister.

She smiled back. "Paybacks are a bitch, bitch."

My eyes shifted back to Micah, who was looking around my room at my pictureless walls. His eyes landed on the full suitcase in front of my closet.

"West turns eighteen tomorrow..." He sullenly pieced everything together. "You're eloping."

We both sighed.

"Well, it looks like my work here is done," Bronwyn said sweetly. "I'll leave you to your weird-ass love triangle."

She pushed past us both and slammed my door behind her.

Both of us waited for the other to break the silence.

"Micah, you knew this day was coming," I reminded him gently. "What does it matter if it's tomorrow or ten years from now if the answer is the same?"

"Ask yourself the same question, Cosette." Micah's words came out harsh. "Why are you rushing into this?"

He tried to avoid my eyes, but I met them anyway.

"Because this is what I want," I stated truthfully. "I want to marry him."

"I know you do, Cosette." Micah accepted my explanation, but added one of his own. "I just also think you're marrying him *now* because you don't want to be eligible anymore. Marrying my brother gets you out of having to decide."

His words hurt, and I didn't want to think about why.

"Why don't you see that me marrying your brother *is* a decision? You used to be all about free will, Micah, but you keep interfering with mine," I pointed out, frustrated. "That's the only reason you even came here today!"

"Give me some credit, Cosette." Micah was offended. "I came here to pray for your sister!"

"Which would be wonderful if that were the *only* reason, but if it had been, then you wouldn't have done it behind my

486

back!" Micah's motivation began to play out in my head like a movie, and the more I realized, the more upset I became. "You thought that if Bronwyn's health was no longer a factor, then I'd choose the garden!"

"Well?" he challenged. "Am I right?"

I looked at the ground. "I've already chosen. Please respect that."

"Fine. Have a nice life, Cosette." He went for the door. "I'll show myself out the way I came."

In the time it took me to decide to follow him, he had enough of a head start to get out the front door.

"Micah!" I called after him. "Micah, wait!"

I ran onto my front porch, but he was gone, a fresh set of footprints in the deep snow cut short, marking the spot where he transitioned home.

CHAPTER 93

I thought the plows would never come.

It had taken me almost two hours to dig a path out of my driveway for my car. Fortunately, the frustrated energy I had left over from my fight with Micah fueled most of the workout. Since I didn't know how to operate the snow blower, I had to remove it all manually with a shovel, and by the time I could back my car out of the driveway, my hands and feet were frozen.

The end of the driveway was as far as I was going to get, however, until the county trucks came to clear the roads in my subdivision. My car handled great in the snow, but there was so much of it covering the streets that I doubted even a tank could make it through.

Of course, I knew that just because the streets in my neighborhood were clear, it didn't mean that I'd have a clean path to my destination. The farmhouse was on a dirt road, and I wasn't sure anyone even bothered to clear those at all.

I had to at least try to get there though. It was the only place I could think of where I might find Micah. And I *had* to find him.

We couldn't end things like this. If marrying Westley meant saying good-bye to Micah, then I wanted a chance to do that the right way. I didn't pretend we were going to see eye to eye about my decision, but I also knew I couldn't part with him on these terms.

He'd meant well with Bronwyn, just like he'd meant well with Westley; I could see that. I wanted him to know I wasn't angry with him, and I wanted the chance to thank him for all he had done for me.

Micah had changed my life. He had saved my life. From here until forever, I would be someone new, someone I wouldn't have been if he'd never come back to Middlebury. I wanted him to know that, to know that just because I wasn't going to the garden, it didn't mean that his mission had been a failure.

I threw my shovel back into the garage and then stepped back outside to listen. In the distance, I could hear the sounds of metal scraping asphalt. The trucks were only a few streets over from mine. It wouldn't be long now.

I thawed myself out and threw on dry clothes before quietly gathering my suitcase and wedding dress to load into my car. If I was able to find Micah before I needed to leave for Maplecrest, I would come back home to have a more nostalgic good-bye to my childhood home; but if I didn't, at least I had my breakfast memory.

As I shut the door to my bedroom, I could hear the soft sounds of lullaby music coming from Ginger's room. On my way down the hall, I carefully peeked my head in and saw her asleep in her crib, curled up with her bottom in the air.

Bronwyn's voice carried up from down in the kitchen, and because I knew it was safe, I tiptoed inside.

Ginger breathed the deep, short breaths of a baby in restful sleep. I knelt beside her crib and lowered my face to her level.

"I love you, Gigi," I whispered. "I'll see you soon."

One of her hands lay at the edge of the mattress, and I kissed her fingers through the slats.

Back in the hallway, I lifted my suitcase off its rollers to carry it down the stairs just as I heard the plow truck barrel down my street. Its noise cloaked my exit from the house, and I was able to load everything into my car undetected.

A salt truck turned onto the road, and I waited for it to pass before backing out of my driveway and following it out of my subdivision.

CHAPTER 94

To my happy surprise, County Road 121 was clear.

The salt from the trucks had turned much of the frozen ground into slushy mud, but I knew that getting to tell Micah good-bye was well worth the price of a dirty car, so I sloshed my way through it.

The snow had piled higher than the farmhouse mailbox, and because its driveway had not been cleared, I almost passed it entirely. I slowed to a stop at the edge of the property and left my car on the street. I found a piece of paper and wrote, "Gone Hunting," with the current date and time and stuck it on my dashboard in case anyone stopped to check on my vehicle while I was away. I was proud I'd so quickly thought of this alibi, though I didn't know if mid-January was hunting season or if my note would actually cause me more trouble from police who would want to arrest me for breaking some sort of no-killing-animals-at-this-time-of-year law if they stumbled upon my car.

I risked it and waded my way through the snow and up to the house.

When I made it past the evergreens and the house came into view, the emotion that flooded into me caught me off guard. The day was still, and the house was buried in a thick blanket of white. The snow had minimized its neglect, and had I not known better, I might have thought it was some-one's home.

I no longer feared this place as I once did. Instead, I felt a fondness for the farmhouse and the secrets it kept for me, for the purpose that this decrepit, seemingly useless structure had served in my life. This was where I'd learned of the garden. It provided me with the vacancy I'd needed to weep on more than one occasion. And it was where I'd spent the moments after Micah's healing when I first accepted that anything, *absolutely anything*, was possible.

Even if I couldn't say good-bye to Micah here, I was still glad I came.

Before I could open the door, I had to kick away a pile of snow that had drifted in front of it, but eventually, I made it inside.

"Micah?" I called out, my voice echoing against the walls. "Micah? If you can hear me, I want to talk to you..."

I'd never confirmed how communication worked from my world to his, or if it was even possible, but I kept trying anyway.

I looked around the room at the candles, the metal mixing bowl, and the rocking chairs. The disturbed dust on the floor. Everything was as I had left it.

There was, however, one thing that was different.

On the kitchen table, I noticed an open book. At first glance, it looked like a Bible similar to the one Micah had given to me. I picked it up.

At the top of the page were the words "Song of Songs 8."

I skimmed the text long enough to read the words "kisses" and "bed" and "breasts" before I turned to the cover to make sure what I was reading was really the book I thought it was.

After confirming its title, I turned back to the marked page, equally confused and curious about this particular Bible story.

When I looked more closely at this particular page of text, I noticed the section that began with a small number six had been underlined:

Set me as a seal upon your heart,
  as a seal upon your arm,
for love is strong as death,
    jealousy is fierce as the grave.
Its flashes are flashes of fire,
    the very flame of the Lord.

"Can I please have my book back?" a voice asked.

I jumped so high I dropped the Bible.

"Micah!" I yelled, instantly forgiving him for startling me. "You're here!"

He halfway smiled. "So are you."

I bent down to pick up the Bible and handed it over to him.

"I can't believe you have complete access to the garden, and you still come here to hang out," I joked, filling what I anticipated to be an awkward silence between us.

"Sometimes the garden can feel pretty crowded," Micah stated.

"Well, then it's a good thing I'm *not* going." I elbowed him in the ribs. "Nothing worse than an overpopulated paradise."

He ignored my comment. "Cosette, I'm really sorry about today, about coming to Bronwyn. You were right; that was not the way to handle the situation—"

"And I'm sorry for not telling you about the wedding," I jumped in, relieved he'd broken the tension. "I should have told you sooner, but I was afraid you'd be mad."

"Guess I proved you right." He frowned. "But I've been thinking about it, Cosette, and I want you to know that I *do* accept your choice. It isn't the one I made for myself, but that doesn't mean it's wrong for you."

"Do you really mean that?" I waited for him to nod before allowing myself to smile. "Oh, thank you, Micah!" My heart soared. "There's so much I'm grateful to you for, and I couldn't stand it if you thought that I didn't appreciate all you've done just because I'm staying here."

"No, I know that your decision to stay here has nothing to do with me," he admitted. "And besides, it'll be good to have you keeping an eye on my brother."

I grinned. "I'm going to do my best."

Micah smiled back, but he still looked sad. "So, I thought of something I wanted to run by you."

"Yeah?"

"Yeah...I was thinking about you and Westley getting married, and I kinda figured that if circumstances were different—like maybe *I* hadn't chosen the garden—that I probably would have been invited to the wedding." He shrugged and then added, "Assuming, of course, that you two weren't eloping like this."

"Hmm," I considered this. "Yeah...I'm thinking you probably would have been the best man."

"It would have been me or Trick, for sure." He raised his eyebrows. "But for argument's sake, let's pretend I won the toss-up."

"Sure."

"Well, as hypothetical best man, and future brother-in-law to the bride, I figured it was probably only etiquette that I get you a wedding present..." Micah hesitated. "That is, if you're interested."

"I could use a new pair of shins if you've got them," I reminded him.

He laughed. "Yeah—no. But, I thought I might take you on a trip...if you have the time."

I held my breath. "To the garden?"

"I thought you might want to say your good-bye in person."

I was immediately torn. On one hand, the thought of going back there, just one last time, was the definition of an opportunity of a lifetime. I imagined the flowers, the trees, and the views, and instantaneously, chills of excitement swarmed my body.

But on the other...

I was afraid. So afraid.

I feared reawakening the hope I had let die that the garden was a part of my future. I feared reopening that wound so soon after it had closed, that the scar it would cause would be far greater than any markings on my legs.

"We don't have to stay long, Cosette," Micah offered. "Whatever you want."

Whatever I want.

I searched myself to find out what that truly was.

"OK," I agreed. "Let's go."

CHAPTER 95

"Are you sure this is OK?" I asked Micah as we stood with his arms around me. "I mean, I'm not going to get you into any trouble for taking me there when I've already decided I'm not choosing to stay, am I?"

"No, of course not," he assured me. "You're still eligible. We're not doing anything wrong."

"OK."

"So, where to?" Micah asked me. "Wanna revisit a part of the garden you've already been to or see something new?"

Something new? I was intrigued. I'd already experienced so many wondrous places. The possibility of all I hadn't seen was exhilarating.

But wait.

What if Micah showed me a part of the garden so amazing it made my choice even *more* difficult than it already had been? I didn't know what a place like that would be like, but I didn't doubt it existed. This was the garden, after all.

"Somewhere I've already been," I decided. "The tulips."

This felt like the safest choice; I'd been there with Micah, but I'd also visited them in my dream, the one where I'd glimpsed my future with Westley and our family. I could go to the flowers, I assured myself, without completely losing sight of the reason this had to be my last visit to the garden.

"I can do that." Micah grinned. "Good choice."

"Wait!" I stopped him. "You aren't going to transition me to some distant corner of the garden and make me run over mountains to get there, are you?" I narrowed my eyes. "I've got a wedding I can't miss."

"No worries," he promised.

I forced my body to stop trembling. I would stay for just a few minutes—that was it. Just long enough to remember everything one last time. Just long enough to keep it with me.

Micah began to pray, and I instinctively braced myself.

One more time. Just one more time.

The heavy cold that had settled in the farmhouse lifted, and I felt the ground beneath my feet shift and loosen.

A warm breeze blew through the air, and the world around me turned to dust and was carried away.

I inhaled until my lungs were full and held my breath.

And then, we were there. No turbulence. No pain. Just flowers.

An infinity of them.

My heart leaped inside of my chest. If beauty could be blinding, I would have lost my sight forever.

I exhaled.

"Are you all right?" Micah asked carefully. "Are you hurt?"

"No." I shook my head. "I'm absolutely perfect."

"Great. I'm glad." He beamed.

I panned the landscape; the sea of tulips nodded their heads up and down in the breeze. A breeze, I suddenly realized, that I couldn't hear rustling through the fields.

"You're managing my senses, aren't you?" I asked Micah.

"Yes," he confirmed. "Need me to dial back some more?"

"No." I shook my head and then hesitated before asking, "Is there any way you could let up a little...let me feel more?"

"Are you sure, Cosette?"

"No," I admitted. "But do it anyway."

This was my last time. I wanted to remember everything there was to remember.

The music began softly. Far away at first, but then closer. It moved through the air, alive.

Like the heat from Micah's hands when he healed me, it entered me and coursed through my body.

Instruments and voices, words I did not know but understood, spoke to me.

I listened.

It was soothing and exciting. Fast and slow. Complete and unresolved.

I joined in the song. A song I'd never heard before, but somehow, I knew it.

And so did Micah.

The flowers even seemed to be crying it out, moving and swaying with the melodies, like a million little bells ringing in perfect time, perfect harmony.

We danced to this music. Wildly, unabashedly, in celebration. In the company of a faceless musician I could not see and could not deny.

Finally, when I didn't think I could move another step, I fell down on the ground with my guide, consumed by joy.

We listened for a while more. Then anticipating that I wanted to speak, Micah quieted the music.

"Is this how you feel all the time?" I turned to look at him. "So...complete?"

"When I'm in the garden, yes." He smiled wistfully.

"How in the world do you pull yourself away from this to spend so much time with me?" I laughed.

Micah grew serious. "I want you to have it too, Cosette." He paused. "I want everyone to have what I have."

"I know what you mean, Micah," I admitted. "I really do."

It was at that moment I became aware of where we were.

The ground was harder and emptier than before. We were still among the tulips, but we'd moved beyond them into a clearing.

I quickly sat up and looked around me.

"What's the matter?" Micah joined me, concerned. "What is it?"

I looked across the opened space, to the fields where I'd dreamed Westley had disappeared with our children. With my son and my daughters who looked so much like Ginger.

Ginger, the daughter of my sister.

My sister, who was dying and needed me to save her life.

I sighed. "It's really hard to let this all go, Micah."

He nodded. "I know."

"It's like I lose and I win no matter what."

"Yeah," he admitted. "It is...but you win either way too."

"Thank you for this." I met his eyes. "Thank you so much."

"Congratulations, Mrs. Greene." He smiled. "Welcome to the family, Sis."

CHAPTER 96

I pulled into the Maplecrest parking lot just before midnight.

My drive had been uneventful. Both the roads and the skies were clear.

And so, surprisingly, was my mind.

I left Micah in the garden. He offered to come back with me, even to drive me to Fort Wayne. But I declined.

"This is how I want to remember you," I explained. "This is where I need to tell you good-bye."

He looked as though he would protest, but he didn't. "I am happy for you, Cosette. I'm happy for your choice."

I blinked back my tears. "Thank you. I'm happy for yours too."

I wrapped both of my arms around him and squeezed him as tight as I could.

And then, I let him go.

Shortly after I arrived at the hospital, I got a text from Westley.

I'm coming out. Hope you're here.

I smiled at the message.

Where else would I be?

Minutes later, Westley emerged from the hospital doors. I immediately jumped out of my car and ran into his open arms.

"Oh, Cosette!" He held me at arm's length to look at me. "I've missed you so much."

"You'll never have to miss me again, West." I beamed. "Happy birthday."

CHAPTER 97

Before we pulled out of the lot, Westley fiddled with his phone, mapping out directions for a destination he wasn't sharing with me.

"I should probably warn you, Cosi," he said mysteriously. "This is not going to be a traditional wedding."

"Really?" My interest was piqued. "How so?"

"Well, I had to be careful in planning it so that I didn't tip anyone at the hospital off to what I was doing," he explained to me, putting the car into reverse. "So that ruled out little white chapels."

"So where are we going?" The butterflies Westley always gave me were on the verge of hatching.

"You'll see," he teased. "We've got a drive. You should get some rest."

Westley turned out of the parking lot and headed to the highway, and I snuggled up under his arm.

Familiar had returned. Comfort was back.

I pressed my face into his chest and breathed him in.

And for the first time since he left, I slept easy.

◆◆◆

"Cosi," a whisper roused me. "Wake up. We're here."

I opened one eye. It didn't feel as though I'd been asleep very long. The clock on my dash confirmed the feeling.

"Where are we?" I sat up and rubbed my eyes.

"Indianapolis," Westley revealed.

I looked out the window at the illuminated parking garage. "Why?"

501

"This is where we're getting married," he announced.

"In a garage?" I was groggy.

"Of course not!" He laughed and kissed my head. "At the botanical gardens."

"What?" I was suddenly wide-awake.

"There's an indoor section open year-round. Lots of people have weddings there. It looked really beautiful online..." Westley was alarmed by my reaction. "Is that OK?"

"Yeah," I recovered from my surprise. "We never talked about it, I know, but I really like the idea of getting married in a place like that. In a garden."

"What a coincidence." He smiled sarcastically. "Guess I know you better than either of us realized."

"Guess so..."

Westley had reserved a hotel room in a tall building downtown not far from where we'd be getting married in the morning. After we dropped our bags in the entryway of our room, he picked me up off my feet and kissed me.

And I kissed him back, like I'd never kissed him before. Desperately. Achingly.

He pulled away. "Cosette, why are you crying?"

I hadn't realized I was. "I guess I'm just so happy to have you back, Westley."

"Hey..." he soothed, drying my cheeks. "You don't have to worry anymore. I'm not going anywhere. Happily ever after...it's beginning."

"I know." I nodded, swallowing back the rest of the tears I hadn't known were there.

"I love you, Cosette."

I looked into his eyes, and I knew he meant it. As much as any person could love another, Westley loved me.

"I love you too."

◆ ◆ ◆

The medication Westley was on for his disorder required him to get at least eight hours of uninterrupted sleep, and since it was after three in the morning before he took it, it was almost noon by the time he woke up.

502

But I didn't mind.

I lay beside him, my head on his chest, until his breathing told me he was asleep. Then I moved back to my side of the bed.

I watched him sleep all through the night; I watched as his black silhouette brightened with the dawn, the first rays of daylight peeking through the cracks in the window blinds.

"Have you been up long?" He squinted at me, yawning.

I just shrugged. "Most brides don't get much sleep the night before their wedding."

A smile lit up his face, mirroring the one I knew was on my own.

"Mrs. Greene." He bit his lower lip to stifle his smile, but it could not be contained.

"That's me."

◆◆◆

We wheeled our belongings through downtown across the intersections that separated us from the botanical gardens. We stopped only once, at a men's clothing store. Westley needed to find something to wear for our ceremony since I hadn't packed him anything wedding-worthy in his bags for the hospital.

The gardens were enclosed by a dome of glass walls, and when we stepped through the tall doors of the entryway, we were immediately hit with a wave of greenhouse heat.

Westley smiled at me. "Well, you've always hated the cold..."

A thin, middle-aged man greeted us in the lobby, and while he and Westley discussed the business end of our wedding, I went wandering toward the gardens.

I stepped through another set of doors, and I found myself standing within the curved walls we'd seen from the street.

There were flowers everywhere. Arranged ones, potted in ornate stone planters. Trellises and arches lined the pathways, each with blossoming ivies woven throughout. There were manicured trees, rosebushes, and everything else I imagined would be in the royal courtyard of a fairy-tale castle.

It was beautiful. It really was. But as much as I wanted this as the setting for my wedding to excite me...it didn't.

It was staged. An imitation.

But I think I knew that it couldn't have been anything less than that. No amount of improvements could have made it comparable to its archetype.

Westley came up from behind me and wrapped his arms around my waist.

"Isn't it perfect?" he whispered.

I leaned back into him. "As perfect as I could ever hope for."

CHAPTER 98

Westley helped me carry my things to a dressing room.

"Text me when you're ready," he told me. "I'm going to go meet the minister."

I told him I would and kissed him good-bye.

There was a large vanity and bright lighting in the room. I sat down on a cushioned seat and began unpacking all I would need to transform myself into a bride worthy of Westley Greene.

It took me less time that I expected to apply all the powders and colors to my face that I thought were necessary, and then I pinned my brunette waves up the way I remembered Eastlyn had done for me the previous year at prom. When I was finished, I examined my reflection in the mirror.

She looked different to me now than she had just a few short weeks before, I noted, but I didn't know how to describe what was different. And I didn't have the time to figure it out. I had to find a way to put on a wedding dress alone that last time had taken the help of two additional hands.

It was tricky, and I didn't get it right on the first attempt. But after minimal sweating and only one broken fingernail, I was in my dress.

There was a full-length mirror resting against the wall, and I studied my whole self in it.

I smiled.

I was ready.

In the highest-heeled shoes ever to be walked in, I carefully stepped toward my phone to text Westley that it was time. But before I could reach it, it began to buzz with an incoming call.

Bronwyn.

My heart began to thump. "Hello?"

"Am I interrupting the honeymoon?" my sister asked flatly.

"No. Still getting ready for the ceremony," I answered her, worried. "Is everything OK?"

There was a silence that lasted a moment too long.

"I got the lab results back."

My heart banged against my ribs. My body froze. I was suddenly terrified of hearing what she was going to say next.

She didn't wait for me to ask.

"You're a match, Cosette," she revealed.

My knees buckled, and I fell onto the cushion. "I am?" I immediately began crying.

My prayer had been answered. I could help save Bronwyn's life.

Thank you, God. Thank you, God.

"You are," she repeated. "And so is Ginger."

My heart stopped.

"What did you say?"

"My doctor must have used the word *miracle* a thousand times," she remarked. "She said the odds are almost nonexistent, but yeah—both of you are matches."

This was impossible.

My sister continued, "So, hey, go get married wherever you want to. I've got a spare donor."

I couldn't speak.

"Are you even there?" Bronwyn demanded. "Or did you put down the phone to make out with Crazy Train?"

"I-I-I'm here," I stammered.

"OK, did you hear what I said?" She didn't wait for me to respond. "Don't let me mess up your plans, Cosette. You can do what you want."

I nodded like a bobblehead.

My silence annoyed my sister. "Well, OK...I'm hanging up now."

She did.

Ginger and I were both matches. My niece could save her mother. I tried to wrap my head around all of these things, around what this meant.

Bronwyn had said it was a miracle.

But it was more than that, wasn't it? For me. It was more than that for me.

This was provision.

CHAPTER 99

There was a knock at my door.

"Cosette, are you OK?"

I had no idea how much time had passed since Bronwyn called.

My phone had been ringing. I assumed it was Westley, but I couldn't even open my eyes to check.

"Cosi!" His voice was almost frantic. "Please, are you OK?"

"Yes," I mustered the syllable.

"I'm coming in." Westley barged into the room and ran to me. "Oh my god, Cosette? What the hell happened?"

I felt catatonic. "Bronwyn called," I answered faintly. "I'm a bone-marrow match. So is Ginger."

He sighed in relief. "That's great news, right?"

"It is," I affirmed. "Just a lot to take in..."

"I'm sure," he sympathized. "And we can spend all afternoon talking about it, after the wedding." He cupped my face in his hands. "I'm not trying to be a jerk, Cosi, but there are people waiting for us to do this, so if we're still going to today, we should hurry..."

I did my best to regain myself, to pick life back up where I'd left it when Bronwyn called: my wedding.

It occurred to me then that Westley was wearing his new clothes, and I was in my gown. And we weren't yet at the altar. I frowned in disappointment. "You weren't supposed to see me in my dress yet."

"It doesn't matter." He smiled. "Every time I look at you, it's like the first time. I'll still be surprised the next time I see you, I promise." His eyes looked me up and down. "And I'm sure I'll tell you this then too, but you are absolutely the most beautiful girl in the world."

"I love you, Westley." I grinned.

He handed me a tissue and stood to leave. "I'll be waiting for you."

I nodded, and he shut the door softly behind him.

Immediately, my tears returned.

"Oh, God..." I cried. "What am I supposed to do with this?"

I said this out loud. I wanted an answer.

"I've already chosen. I've chosen Westley. But you just can't accept it! You keep changing all the circumstances..."

Silence.

"It shouldn't matter whether or not I go to the garden. I know you now—you're part of my life! But that's not enough for you!"

I was yelling.

"Can't you just be happy for me?" I buried my face in my hands. "Can't you just let me choose Westley and love me anyway?"

I sobbed and sobbed, and the room was still.

And then...it wasn't.

I felt movement beneath my feet, beneath the ground.

I looked down at the tile floor and saw the stone tile cracking. In several places, all at once.

What was happening?

Was my dressing room located right on top of a fault line?

Was the earth going to break open and swallow me up?

Was God...was God *smiting* me?

I couldn't rule it out. I had just been yelling at him. And he probably didn't come by his reputation for being angry accidentally.

"I'm sorry!" I apologized. "You don't have to be happy for me! It's OK!" Then I added, "But also, you don't have to kill me!"

The cracking continued until all the tiles crumbled to pieces in one final shattering.

And then, there was silence again.

And dust. Dust that, when it finally settled, revealed something new. Hundreds of somethings, it seemed. Growing up from the ground. Green, thick stalks poked up from where the tiles had been moments ago, sprouting leaves, blossoming.

Tulips. They were tulips.

Within seconds, the room was filled with them. White tulips, just like the ones from the garden. The ones Micah had brought to me as offerings of peace.

I caught my breath.

They were beautiful.

They were a gift.

They were for me.

God wasn't smiting me, I slowly began to realize as I stood, openmouthed, staring at this miracle before me.

He was answering my question. In the only way I'd ever been able to hear him speak.

And his answer was...

Yes.

CHAPTER 100

I took a deep breath and looked out in front of me.
I smiled.
I had no doubts.
"Are you ready?"
"I am. I really am."
"Then let us go, my dear."
She squeezed my hand in hers, and together, we ran as fast as my legs could carry me, toward my choice.

ACKNOWLEDGEMENTS

I must first give my humble thanks to The Author. Thank you to God for unconditionally loving me and giving me the choice to love you back.

Thank you to my husband, Jonathan. Without you, I couldn't have written one word. You are the co-author of this book, and my co-author in life. I love you.

Thank you to my daughters for supporting my work in all the little ways you have. Your faith in me made this possible.

Thank you to Mom, Dad, Erica, and Kris. Your fingerprints are all over this book because your fingerprints are all over me.

Thank you to Bethany for enthusiastically and adamantly demanding I tell this story.

Thank you to Karen and Roy for knowing I was a writer before I knew it myself.

Thank you to Shelley and Julia. You were my biggest cheer-leaders.

Thank you to Sue for your selfless gift. We miss you.

Thank you to my RP and HP families. You supported me, rooted for me, and loved me through this crazy dream of mine.

And to the others who pushed me, prayed for me, and joined me in this exciting adventure—thank you!

43738617R00316

Made in the USA
Lexington, KY
11 August 2015